DEAD MED

FREIDA MCFADDEN

For my anatomy lab partners. We're all lucky to still be alive.
Especially you, Megan.

AUTHOR'S NOTE

Dead Med was originally published as *Suicide Med. Dead Med* is a revised edition with about 20% changes. I hope you enjoy the revised version!

PROLOGUE

THE NIGHT BEFORE THE ANATOMY FINAL EXAM

DANIELLE

"I WISH I HAD BECOME AN ASTRONAUT INSTEAD."

I use the back of my forearm to swipe at strands of dark hair that have come loose from the tight bun at the back of my head. The attempt fails, and the escaped locks fall back into my field of vision. This is getting annoying—I wish I could use my hands to clear my hair from my face. Unfortunately, my hands are clad in two pairs of latex gloves that are covered in preserved bits of Agatha's insides.

Agatha is dead.

"Or maybe a boxer..."

I try to tune out the ramblings of my lab partner, Victor Pereira. Victor's jittery voice has been a soundtrack to every dissection I have ever done. It might have been more tolerable if Victor offered to help.

Instead, he sits perched on a stool, intently watching my handiwork. I'm tempted to rub my dirty gloves on his face.

"Anything but a doctor," Victor concludes.

You're not a doctor yet, I nearly point out, but I hold my tongue. I need to focus right now, and the last thing I want to do is get drawn into an argument.

It's close to midnight on a Sunday night, and Victor and I are the only two medical students in the first-year cadaver lab. I specifically chose this time because I knew the lab would be quiet and free from any distractions. I was right—all I can see are rows and rows of dead bodies covered in a layer of clear, thick plastic to prevent desiccation; all I can hear is the whir of the fans working above my head. This would have been the perfect studying atmosphere if Victor hadn't insisted on coming along.

"I'll miss Agatha," Victor says. "I mean, when the class is over."

During the first week of anatomy class, we named our cadaver Agatha. I hadn't wanted to name her—after all, this had once been a real person who had a real name of her own. But I felt silly voicing my objections, so I stayed quiet as the other members of my lab group tossed around name suggestions. It had eventually come down to Agatha or Medusa. I was relieved when the group settled on Agatha.

Agatha does seem like an appropriate name, somehow. "Agatha" is a frail old woman who has metal rings around her sternum and blood vessels grafted onto her heart. Of course, it's impossible to know for sure, but I can make an educated guess that Agatha died of heart problems.

I try to imagine what sort of woman would make the decision to dedicate her body to a medical school. After everything I've seen this year, that's one thing I myself would *never* do. The last thing I want is a bunch of snotty twenty-two-year-olds making fun of all my subcutaneous fat.

I hold up the musculocutaneous nerve between my forceps. The nerve is thick and yellow.

"I'm hungry," Victor announces. "Are you hungry?"

"You're joking."

When I'm in the anatomy lab, food is the last thing on my mind. The smell of formaldehyde combined with the image of lacerated flesh is enough to kill any appetite I might have had. A few times, I've seen one of my classmates popping candy in their mouth, and I'm always in awe.

"Of course I wouldn't eat in here." Victor snorts, even though it wouldn't have been the most ridiculous thing he's ever done in the anatomy lab. For example, he once wore a hoodie in the lab and then *wore it home*, despite it being stained with cadaver juice.

"I'm going to the vending machines," Victor says. "You want something?"

"No, thanks."

Take your time, I'm tempted to add.

Victor hops off the stool and sprints out of the lab. That guy never does anything at less than ninety miles per hour. The heavy metal door slams behind me, and the room is plunged into complete silence.

It's heavenly.

Our final exam in anatomy is tomorrow. It's the biggest exam we've taken so far in the short course of our medical school career, and I want to do well because I hope to land a position in a good dermatology program when I graduate. As part of our exam, we have to go around this very lab, identifying labeled structures on different cadavers. I have to know every identifiable structure back and forth if I want to do well.

It's not that Victor is a bad person or anything, but I've always considered myself a loner. I prefer solitary activities, and I hate when solitary activities turn into group activities. Studying is a solitary activity.

"Now it's just you and me, Agatha," I whisper. I add apologetically, "Although I know that's not your real name."

I dig my fingers into Agatha's forearm, attempting to separate the muscles. When I tug on the muscle I'm holding, Agatha's fingers curl into a partial fist. I shiver slightly.

And that's when I hear the sound.

It's a loud noise that comes from outside the lab. It's a crash or… No, not really a crash. It's more like…

A *bang*.

What *was* that? Even though the sound originated outside the heavy metal doors of the anatomy lab, it still resounded through the room, loud and clear. And then, while the echo of the noise is still in my ears, I hear it again a second time.

What could have made a bang that loud? The only thing I could think of is…

A gun.

But it couldn't have been a gun. Why would there be a gunshot in the hospital? Much less *two* gunshots. It doesn't make sense.

Where are you, Victor? How long does it take to pick out a bag of chips?

While I'm contemplating my next move, a noise from across the room grabs my attention. It's the heavy door to the anatomy lab swinging open, squealing on its hinges. Thank God—Victor has *finally* selected his snack and has returned. Maybe he'll be able to tell me what that unsettling noise was.

I squint through my thick lenses at the doorway, and I feel a rush of relief at the sight of the familiar face of my classmate.

"Hey!" I call out. "Did you hear that noise a minute ago?"

He doesn't answer me, which I find a bit odd. It's also odd that there's something splattered on his scrubs. His dark-brown jacket is hanging open, and his hands are shoved deep into the pockets. He walks toward me, the expression on his unshaven face completely blank. A drop of saltwater trickles down the side of his face.

"Is everything okay?" I ask him.

Again, he is silent. He just stares at me.

Now that he's closer, I get a better look at the splatter across his chest. It's dark red and still slightly damp. I'm not entirely sure what it is, but it looks almost like…

Oh God.

I take a step back. "What—"

Before I can complete my sentence, something dark obstructs my vision. It takes me several beats to realize there's a gun pointed at my face.

My knees go weak. I grab onto the edge of the table, trying to keep myself upright. I lower my eyes to Agatha's mutilated corpse, clearly unable to offer anything in the way of aid. The gun is inches from my forehead, and I can feel the heat radiating from it. There's no doubt in my head anymore about what that bang was.

He's already fired this gun tonight.

Oh God. I don't want to die like this. Not here, not now. It can't end this way. I've done some bad things in my life, but I'm pretty sure I don't deserve this…

All I can think about is how pathetic it would be to die in the anatomy lab. The janitor will probably discover me here tomorrow morning. Will he even notice that I'm a medical student and not *one of the bodies*?

"Please…" I whisper.

His eyes are as black and impassive as the barrel of the gun. When he speaks, his voice is flat and toneless: "Do exactly as I say if you don't want to die."

PART I

HEATHER

1

THE FIRST DAY

"Look to your left and look to your right."

My eyes lift at the words of our dean of students at DeWitt Medical School, Dr. Marvin Bushnell. He has a huge, Santa Claus-esque belly and sweats with the mere effort of speaking. He's been talking to us for about five minutes, and he's already got a shiny forehead and huge pit stains. But he barrels on, totally oblivious to the amount of fluid his pores are secreting.

I obligingly look to my left because it's clear everyone else in the auditorium is doing it. Two seats over is a male student with a messy brown ponytail and ratty leather jacket that smells of cigarettes and possibly some illegal substance. I can understand not dressing up in a suit and tie for your first day of medical school, but I'd think at least you'd want to *shower*.

And now for the look to the right: that one is my new roommate, Rachel Bingham. Rachel is not looking left or right. Rachel is rolling her eyes quite dramatically.

I had this fantasy in my head that my med school roommate and I would become BFFs and we'd braid each other's hair and have pillow fights, et cetera. So far, I'm ninety-nine percent sure Rachel hates me. Maybe I'm being paranoid, but it's something about the way she's looked at me since she arrived a week ago in our shared suite, her stringy brown hair falling in her face, ripped jeans held together by the grace of God, and only a single suitcase to her name. She even mocked my long-distance relationship with my boyfriend and soulmate, Landon. *Hey, you might last a few months. Maybe.*

I turn my attention back to Dr. Bushnell, who is about one passionate speech away from a serious cardiac event.

"In four years," he says to the hushed crowd, "both of these people will be physicians."

Rachel snorts audibly now. I try to flash a friendly smile in her direction, but she's having none of that. She rewards me with another eye roll, and I focus my attention back at the dean. Fine. Rachel won't be my friend. I'll find another friend in the class.

Probably.

"It's not true anyway," Rachel stage whispers in my direction.

I raise my eyebrows at her. I'm so pleased she's talking to me that I don't even care that she's speaking over the dean on our first day of medical school.

"What isn't true?" I ask.

"We won't all be doctors," she says. She tucks her dark-brown hair behind her ear so that I can get my first good look at her deep-brown eyes.

"We won't?"

Rachel laughs. "Don't you know?"

"Know what?"

Her lips curl into a slightly evil grin. My roommate may be genuinely evil. Are people really evil in real life? Or just in comic books?

"In every class," she says, "ten people flunk and need to repeat the year. Five drop out, never to return. And, of course, in the last few years, there's always one who..."

Now she pauses and draws an ominous line across her thin white neck with a well-chewed fingernail.

"One who *what*?" I prompt her.

Rachel frowns at me. "You really don't know?"

"Know *what*?"

She shakes her head. "Why do you think the school is nicknamed Dead Med?"

I did *not* know that nickname.

She can't be serious. She's just messing with me. She's just pissed off that I left too many bottles of moisturizer in our bathroom. (I have really dry skin.)

Dean Bushnell is saying something that I completely missed, which is followed by a round of applause. I need to start paying attention and quit my doomed attempts to befriend my roommate. The dean shifts away from the podium, and another man walks up to take his place. This man is far younger than the dean, maybe fortyish, but he carries an old-man cane in his right hand and walks with a pronounced limp.

"Hello," the man says, pushing his spectacles up the bridge of his nose with his forefinger. I can't help but notice he's wearing a bowtie. Who wears a bowtie in everyday life? "I'm Matt Conlon, your anatomy professor."

Right—Dr. Conlon. When I interviewed here at DeWitt, the first-years had been singing praises about this guy. "Dorky but really fun," they'd said. "He's the best thing about the first year."

Up on the stage, Dr. Conlon is now gesturing wildly as he describes how totally awesome anatomy is.

"The human body makes perfect sense," he explains. "It's the most intricately constructed machine in the world. And after you finish my class, you're going to understand how that machine works, inside and out. And you're going to realize how amazing it is."

I don't even need to look at Rachel to know that she's rolling her eyes.

"Thank you for letting me act as your guide on this incredible journey," Dr. Conlon says, and he gives a little bow.

Really, he *bows*. God, could this guy be any dorkier?

Following Dr. Conlon is a string of other professors: an elderly guy with a monotonic voice who will be teaching us biochemistry, a wild-haired female epidemiology professor, and a short, dapper man who will be jointly teaching physiology and histology. Lastly, a thin fortyish woman wearing a sharp blue dress suit steps up to the podium.

"My name is Dr. Patrice Winters," she says. "But you can call me Patrice. I've been acting as the school's wellness counselor for the last four years."

Have you ever met a person who you just disliked

instantly? For me, that's Patrice Winters. I don't know what it is about her exactly. Maybe it's the way her makeup is applied so perfectly and not even a single hair in her blond-streaked pixie cut is out of place. Maybe it's the way she talks to us like we're a bunch of children who need to be told what to do. Maybe it's her voice, which somehow grates on my very soul.

"Whatever happens to you," she says, "I'm here for you. And I'd like each of you to make an appointment with me sometime in the next month." She pauses meaningfully. "It's not optional."

Rachel leans in toward me now and whispers, "You know why we have to see her, don't you?"

I'm afraid to hear the answer to this one. "Why?"

"They don't want any more of us overdosing," she says. "The drug problem is out of control here. Every year for the last three years, there's been a student who OD'd and died."

"That's not really true." I shift in my seat. "Is it?"

"Of course it is." She says it like it's common knowledge, which makes me wonder if it is. "Last year, the girl who OD'd did it in the bathroom by the anatomy labs. You can still see the crack in the sink where her head smacked against it before she hit the floor—they never fixed it."

And then she leans back in her seat, smiling at the way my mouth is hanging open.

As I WAIT in the slow-moving cafeteria line to get lunch during our break from orientation, I mull over what Rachel told me about the drug problem at DeWitt. I never heard about it, but that doesn't mean it's not true —med school is stressful, and it wouldn't be surprising if some students turned to drugs in order to deal.

But not me. I would *never*.

I'm so deep in thought that I haven't noticed the line has moved forward but I have not. Before I have a chance to get moving, a horrible weight lands on my foot, crushing the delicate bones that Dr. Conlon has not yet had a chance to teach me about. I gasp in pain as I instinctively grab my foot.

What the hell was *that*?

That's when I notice a frightening bearlike creature looming over me. Actually, it turns out to be a human being, but he's roughly the size of a bear. The foot that he used to crush mine with is practically the size of a tennis racket. This guy is big in all directions.

"Oh my God, I'm so sorry!" the bear cries. "Are you all right?"

No, I am *not* all right. My foot is broken, you stupid bear. Well, maybe not broken. But definitely badly bruised.

Still, I manage to nod and look up at his face, which is nowhere near as scary as the rest of him. The bear has a shock of red hair that's disheveled despite being very short and freckles pouring over either end of the bridge of his nose.

"I'm really sorry," the bear says again. He looks like

he means it. "I didn't realize anyone was behind me." He hesitates. "I'm Abe."

"Heather," I say. I release my broken foot just long enough to grab his outstretched hand. Thankfully, he doesn't crush my hand in his when he shakes it. I hate it when men do that, and it's pretty clear Abe could easily demolish my hand if he got the inclination to do so.

"You're a first-year?" he asks.

Nope, I just hang out at med school orientations for kicks.

"Yep," I say.

"Neat," Abe says then appears to run out of things to say. He rubs his gigantic hands together, clears his throat, and awkwardly turns back to the lunch line to examine his food options. It's going to be either arroz con pollo or fish. And the fish is scary looking. So chicken and rice it is.

2

LANDON IS SUPPOSED TO CALL ME TONIGHT AT NINE P.M., and it's now eight minutes after nine. With each passing minute, I'm getting more and more ticked off.

I don't want to be that kind of girlfriend—the kind where he has to call at the exact time he said he would or else I get all pissy. But then again, how hard is it to call on time? Is it really so difficult to pick up the phone and call me at the time I asked him to? He knows it's my first day of school and I'm all keyed up. Why is he doing this to me?

It doesn't help that Rachel is driving me out of my mind. First, she was going on and on about how eighty percent of college relationships end during med school. I don't know where she got that ridiculous statistic, but she wouldn't shut up about it.

Then, she asked me what I wanted to specialize in when I graduated. When I told her I wanted to be a pediatrician, she looked at me with utter contempt for falling into the "traditional gender stereotypical role." Apparently, *she* wants to be a surgeon.

The other weird thing is that Rachel hasn't bought any books. Not even Dr. Conlon's book, *Anatomy: Inside Secrets*. You'd think if she wanted to be a surgeon, she'd be studying her ass off right now in anticipation of our first anatomy lab tomorrow. Or at least half-heartedly trying to read the lab manual like I'm doing.

Instead, she's sitting on her bed in a lotus position, just watching me. It's a little creepy. Our bedroom is too small for two people to share—we're always on top of one another. There's just barely room for both of our beds, our desks, one dresser, and a single bookcase. We have to share a single closet. I can't even walk into the room without tripping on something.

"Are you waiting for your boyfriend to call you?"

I look up at Rachel, who is blinking innocently. I make a face. "His name is Landon. And… he's going to call any second now."

Rachel snorts. "Just don't get too hung up on the guy. If he dumps you, you might turn to pills. And I don't want to be the one who finds you when you…"

"What?"

Rachel makes a choking sound as she clutches her neck.

I stare at her, horrified. "I'm not going to overdose on pills!"

"You never know. I mean, who walks into medical school thinking, 'Hey, I'm going to become a drug addict'?"

My mouth falls open.

"The question is," she goes on, "where are the drugs coming from?"

I shake my head. "What do you mean?"

"Three students in three years got their hands on enough pills that they accidentally died. Someone is giving them those pills."

"So… another student?"

"Maybe." She twists her body to one side then the other. "But for so many years in a row? More likely, it's one of the professors. A first-year professor, who can get to all the students early."

We got introduced to every single one of the first-year professors this week, and none of them seem like drug dealers. Especially not Dr. Conlon with his dorky bowtie. The idea is laughable.

I'm about to tell Rachel that she's full of it when my phone starts ringing with Landon's number. My ringtone is Miley Cyrus's "Party in the USA," which resulted in some choice comments from Rachel last night. But screw her. I like that song.

"Hello," I answer breathlessly.

I hear chewing on the other line. "'Lo?"

"Hey," I say, rising from my bed. Rachel is still staring at me, so I back out of our bedroom into the living room. "What's up?"

More chewing. "Not much."

"Um," I say. "Are you eating?"

"Just an apple." I hear him swallow.

"Didn't you get dinner?"

"Yeah," Landon says. "But, like, I got hungry again."

Typical Landon. He always gets hungry about an hour after dinner.

"Oh," I say. I grip the phone tighter. I wish I could give Landon a hug, feel his body against me. The person on the other line almost doesn't seem like it's him. We've barely been apart for a week, and already, this long-distance thing sucks. I didn't expect it to feel so… distant.

Landon and I first met in freshman chemistry. We were assigned to be lab partners, and I got taken in by his dimples and brown curls. Also, he was just so *smart.* I would have burned the lab down with my Bunsen burner if not for him.

For months, Landon and I were just friends. Then, one day, while we were walking together, I felt his hand slide into mine. We've been together ever since.

"I miss you," I say to him.

"I miss you too," he says.

I grip the phone tighter, pushing it against my ear. "How much do you miss me?"

He sounds baffled by the question. "What do you mean?"

"Like, on a scale of one to ten."

"Oh." He considers this for a moment. "Maybe… seven?"

"Seven!" I burst out.

"Is that too high or too low?"

I let out a huff. "I miss you a *ten.*"

"Well, it's only been a week, Heather. Can you give me a little time to work up to a ten?"

"I guess so," I say grudgingly. I suppose he's right—it *has* only been a week.

We spend the next half hour or so chatting about our respective days. I fill him in on all the weirdo students I met today. He clucks sympathetically when I tell him about how that bearlike student stepped on my foot and almost broke it. And I laugh when he tells me about how a ripe pear that he packed in his backpack exploded and got over all his new books and papers.

"I wish I'd been there to see that," I say.

"Yeah," Landon says. "I wish you'd been there too. You would've pissed your pants laughing."

I close my eyes and imagine that Landon is sitting beside me. My left hand squeezes my knee.

"I miss you so much," I say.

"I miss you too, Heather," Landon says. "I miss you a ten."

"I miss you a ten too," I say. It's all I can do to keep from covering the phone with kisses.

When I hang up, I have a good feeling in my stomach. It helps to know Landon is here for me. Landon is my first… well, no, he's more like my second… well, anyway, he's my first *love*. I love him. And he loves me. This is going to work out. I've got nothing to worry about.

3

DeWitt Med doesn't have a locker room per se. What we've got is a long hallway of lockers, not segregated in any way by gender. Meaning that I've got two choices:

1. Be a prude and run to the ladies' room to change into scrubs for lab
2. Change my clothes in front of *boys*

I stand in front of my locker, clutching my scrubs for far too long, trying to make a decision. The ladies' room is all the way at the other end of the floor, so I'll save some serious time if I change my clothes right here. And it's not very crowded, at least not yet. However, I'm still retaining a modicum of modesty, and I'm not sure if I can make myself do it. My body isn't quite as bikini-ready as I'd like it to be.

In any case, I need to decide soon. Because I look like an idiot just standing here.

I'm just about ready to start pulling my shirt over my head when a door swings open and about a dozen students filter into the hallway, most of them male.

No, *all* of them male.

And loud.

I quickly pull my shirt back down.

One of the students yanks open the locker three doors away from mine and gives me a charming smile. And oh my God, this guy is cute. I mean, seriously cute. If someone made a movie about our med school class, he'd be playing himself. His face is classically handsome, but most of all, I can't stop staring at his hazel eyes, and I have to admit, at this moment, Landon is the farthest thing from my mind.

Especially when Dreamy McCutie pulls off his shirt.

Wow, look at that chest. Sheesh.

"What's wrong?" he asks me as he fishes through his locker for his scrub top. "You forget something?"

Oh God, I need to stop staring at this guy.

"No," I mumble, still clutching my own scrubs to my chest. "I just… need to go change."

Dreamy McCutie yanks a crisp green scrub top from his locker and winks at me. "So what are you waiting for?"

I swallow, feeling like a silly little girl at a boy-band concert. I should not be swooning over random guys in my class. I have a boyfriend who I love, who I want to marry. And even if I didn't, I *still* shouldn't be swooning.

And I definitely shouldn't be changing my clothes in front of this guy.

"Excuse me," I say, and I race off in the direction of the ladies' room.

I arrive at the ladies' room about a minute later. It's a comforting sight, packed to the brim with other female students who are also too chicken to change clothes in the hallway. We prudes definitely make up the majority.

The stalls have already all been claimed, but I feel comfortable enough in the female company to get undressed by the sinks. I stand next to the sink at the far end and grab onto it to keep my balance while I pull my feet out of my pants legs. But as my fingers grip the sink, they hit a defect in the otherwise smooth white porcelain. It's a significant crack, which has not yet been repaired.

Last year, the girl who OD'd did it in the bathroom by the anatomy labs. You can see the crack in the sink where her head smacked against it before she hit the floor.

Rachel's words echo in my skull as I yank my hand away from the sink. My head is spinning as I stare at that crack in the flawless white. This is it. This is where it happened.

The girl responsible for this crevice was standing right where I was a year ago. She was changing into her scrubs in anticipation of her very first lab. Like me, she was probably a mix of excited and nervous.

She had no idea that only a short while later, this would be where she would die.

4

To say I'm anxious about this lab would be an understatement. I am terrified.

Everyone has assured me I'll be okay. That you get so involved in what you're doing, you forget it's a real dead body. It's sort of like dissecting that plastic dummy we used during our CPR course.

Anyway, that's what I keep repeating to myself over and over. But what if I faint? What if I vomit? What if I vomit then faint in a puddle of my vomit? I'll never live that down.

I stand outside the door to the lab for far too long before I work up the nerve to enter. Long enough that I'm starting to get a few funny looks. About five other students push past me before I heave a deep breath and step inside.

The lab is cold. Really cold. Little goose pimples rise up on my forearms, and I hug my chest for warmth. Also, it's bright. Bright enough that I have to squint for a few seconds until my eyes adjust.

Also, the room is filled with dead bodies.

There are a couple dozen metal tables spread throughout the room. The bodies have been covered with plastic, but several gray mounds have been exposed by the lab groups. The only good thing I can say is that the bodies have been positioned face down, so no dead eyes are staring up at me. But it's still pretty creepy.

I hug my chest tighter.

"Heather?" A soft-spoken voice comes from behind me, and a (hopefully clean) hand falls on my shoulder. "Are you okay?"

I look up. It's Abe, the nice bearlike guy I met yesterday. He's got a little furrow between his red-orange brows.

I decide to be honest with him. "I'm feeling a little… squeamish."

"Oh!" He looks appropriately concerned but not judgmental at all. "Do you think you're going to faint?"

I shake my head. "No. But… it's not outside the realm of possibility, you know?"

Abe scratches his chin, where he's got a bit of red stubble growing. "Well, you wouldn't be the first person to faint in the anatomy lab. It's not *that* big a deal."

I consider telling Abe my fear about fainting in the puddle of vomit, but I decide against it.

"It would be embarrassing," is all I say.

Abe nods in understanding. I hadn't realized when I met him earlier, but he has really nice, kind green eyes.

"How about this? If you faint, I'll catch you and whisk you out into the hall before anyone notices," he says.

"You'd *catch* me?" I'm a bit skeptical, considering Abe seems like kind of an oaf. Maybe I'm just being biased because of his size. Then again, he did manage to practically break my foot yesterday.

"Seriously, I have catlike reflexes," Abe assures me, although he's grinning. "So which table were you assigned to?"

"Thirteen," I reply.

Abe brightens. "Hey, me too."

I feel a flash of relief. Whatever else I know about this guy, he definitely will make sure I'm okay if I start to faint. Despite his intimidating size, he seems very nice.

We weave through the tables of dead bodies, finally coming to a stop in front of a table with a big laminated paper that says "13" on it. This is us, I guess, lucky 13. We're the first to arrive, and the body is still draped in thick, clear plastic.

"You okay?" Abe asks me, lifting his eyebrows. "Should I… remove the plastic?"

I nod and brace myself.

Abe yanks the plastic off the body. Too fast. Embalming fluid or other cadaver juice squirts into the air, generously peppering my forearms. I scream in absolute horror.

"Oh my God, I'm so sorry!" Abe gasps.

He's sorry, and I'm drenched in cadaver juice. I race over to the nearest sink and submerge my arms in the hottest water the sink will provide. I soap myself up practically to my shoulders, wash my arms off, then do it again. This is so disgusting.

Well, at least it didn't get in my face. Although I

wouldn't be surprised if that's Abe's encore. From now on, I'm keeping my mouth closed during the lab—the last thing I want is to taste the cadaver.

By the time I get back to the table, two more members of my five-person lab group have arrived. One is a tiny, olive-skinned girl with dark-brown hair swept back into a ponytail—she looks almost like a child standing next to gigantic Abe. And then there's the other member of the group: Dreamy McCutie, the guy who changed in front of me by the lockers. My knees buckle slightly when I see him.

"I'm really sorry," Abe says to me again when I return.

I nod at him, noting that Dreamy McCutie is snickering slightly as he pries open our dissection kit. Abe must have told them what he did to me. I'd vow revenge on him if he didn't look so upset about the whole thing.

"I'm Heather," I say to my two new lab partners. I don't bother to offer my hand, since they're both already wearing blue rubber gloves.

"Mason," says Dreamy McCutie (apparently actually named Mason). He glances up at me only briefly before going back to rifling through our dissection kit. He fishes out a scalpel and examines the blade carefully through narrowed hazel eyes.

The tiny girl gives me a little wave and speaks in a voice that's barely a whisper, "I'm Sonya."

"Nice to meet you, Sonya."

"Sasha."

"Oh, sorry. Sasha."

I can barely hear her. She's one of those people who would benefit from a volume knob.

"Mason and I are roommates," Abe explains to me. "They usually assign roommates to be lab partners to make it easier to share study materials."

"Oh." I glance at tiny Sasha. "But Sasha and I aren't roommates."

"I live alone off-campus," Sasha explains.

I get this really bad feeling in the pit of my stomach. We're still expecting a fifth person in our lab group, and Sasha doesn't have a roommate. That means that the most likely person to be our fifth lab partner is…

Oh great.

As if on cue, Rachel arrives at our table. She looks like she'd rather be anywhere but here. Her dark hair is pulled into a messy ponytail so that strands fall along her cheeks, and she's not even wearing scrubs—she's wearing a T-shirt and sweatpants. Worst of all, I'm pretty sure she's not wearing a bra.

"Hey," she says, running a hand through her loose strands of hair.

Mason manages to tear his eyes away from the dissection kit long enough to notice Rachel's breasts, and his breath catches slightly. "Hey," he says.

We go around the table with another set of mumbled introductions. To Abe's credit, he doesn't seem remotely interested in Rachel's chest.

Now that the trauma of being splattered with embalming fluid has worn off, I take a look at our cadaver. He's really big—a good two hundred fifty pounds, at least. But he's tall, fit, and carries the weight evenly. He could have been a bouncer in a bar. His face is pressed into the cold metal of the table, but I place his age around fifty. There's a tattoo on his right arm that I can't make out due to the dryness of his skin.

"He looks like a Frank to me," Mason speaks up. "What do you girls think?"

Rachel shoots daggers with her eyes. "To me, he looks like a human being who had a name of his own."

"Aw, come on," Mason says, flashing a killer smile.

"You're naming this cadaver over my dead body," Rachel says through her teeth.

"Fair enough," Mason says. He winks at me as he menacingly lifts a scalpel out of the dissection kit. Abe shakes his head at his roommate. Seriously bad taste. Fortunately, Rachel is too distracted by the cadaver to notice.

"I brought gloves," Abe volunteers, nudging my elbow with his. He points under the table, where there's a little tower of glove boxes. "Three different sizes. I heard you're supposed to double glove in order to, uh, keep out the smell."

"Don't kid yourself," Rachel says. "*Nothing* is going to keep out the smell. Tonight, we're all going to stink like formaldehyde."

My roommate—always a burst of positivity.

"So who wants to make the first incision?" Abe asks the group.

Anyone but me. I step away from the table, trying to make myself invisible.

"I'll do it," Mason volunteers with a shrug. He holds out his right hand. "Scalpel," he barks.

Before I know what I'm doing, I start fumbling with the dissection kit and remove a scalpel, which I obediently place in his right hand with a resounding *plop*.

Rachel's eyes widen, and she looks furious. "You know," she says to Mason, "Heather's not your scrub nurse."

Well, she's right. But let's face it: between the five of us, Mason is the only one who looks like a real surgeon. I can almost picture him in the operating room, slicing through the skin of a real patient's back. His hands are so steady. Mine are shaking like a leaf, and I'm not even doing anything. I'm just standing there.

"Dr. McKinley!"

My heart practically jumps out of my chest. I whirl around and come face-to-face with Dr. Conlon, our anatomy professor. He's dressed in scrubs (no bowtie), which makes him look much less dorky than he did on stage the other day. I noticed before how black his hair is, but I didn't realize how bright-blue his eyes are, even behind thick glasses, and he looks younger up close than I originally thought he was. He's still clutching that cane in his left hand.

"Dr. McKinley," he repeats. How does he already know my last name? "How are you going to learn anything from back there?"

I avoid eye contact. "I'm not a doctor."

"And how are the rest of you feeling?" Dr. Conlon asks my partners. "Are you making the first incision, Dr. Howard?"

Mason nods. "Just about."

"Dr. Kaufman…" Dr. Conlon lays his eyes on Abe.

"Can you tell me the names of the three erector spinae muscles?"

I have no idea what the answer to that question is. Does Abe know? I don't think he does, based on the way he's squirming. But Dr. Conlon doesn't make him suffer for too long.

"Going from lateral to medial, we have iliocostalis, longissimus, and spinalis," Dr. Conlon says. "The mnemonic is 'I Love Sex.' Or if you'd prefer, 'I Love School,' depending on which you like better, school or sex." He winks at us.

Okay, Dr. Conlon isn't so bad. He's kind of cool. Even though he wears bowties.

As he limps away, Rachel leans toward me and murmurs in my ear, "God, what a sexist pig. Who does he think he is?"

"Our anatomy professor?"

"It's like they forget there are women in this class too," Rachel continues to rant. "It's not as if women make up… oh, I don't know, half of all students entering medical school…"

I try to block out the sound of her voice as Mason's steady hand draws the blade of the scalpel down the length of the cadaver's back. There's a layer of thick yellow fat beneath the skin, and I brace myself for that queasy sensation, but to my surprise, it doesn't come.

I look up, and Abe is raising his eyebrows at me. I give him a thumbs-up sign.

Wow, I might actually get through this in one piece.

5

News flash: Medical school is really hard work.

I knew it would be. Obviously. But it's really, *really* hard. Harder than premed biology. Harder than organic chemistry, and I only pulled a B in that through the skin of my teeth (and a lot of help from Landon).

The weeks pass rapidly, but the days are slow. And the labs are endless. We have anatomy labs three times a week, and each session feels like I'm stuffing an encyclopedia's worth of information into my brain.

"If I have to memorize one more nerve or artery today, my head will explode," I say to Abe at least once per lab. It's become my catchphrase.

My brain just isn't that big. But Mason's is, apparently, because he knows everything before the lab even begins.

Dr. Conlon gives weekly quizzes for anatomy class so that students can assess our progress before the first big exam. They're not going super well. I failed the first two and was pathetically happy when I eked out a passing grade on the third.

Well, not a pass exactly. It was a *low* pass. To make us feel less competitive, instead of A, B, C, and D, we have honors, high pass, pass, and low pass. But they're obviously the *exact same thing*. Essentially, I got a D on the last exam, which is nothing to be proud of.

Why am I doing so badly? I'm studying nonstop. Literally. I take the lab manual *to the toilet* with me. But somehow, it's the wrong material. Or else I'm studying the right material, but it all flies out of my head seconds before the quiz.

The anatomy labs themselves don't make me feel any more confident. Dr. Conlon is always sneaking up behind me to ask a question I can't answer.

"Dr. McKinley," he says to me one day. "What is that?"

I used to sort of like it when he called me "Doctor," but with each poor quiz grade, I like it less.

I follow the path of his gloved finger, pointing deep into the cadaver's abdominal cavity. I have absolutely no idea what he's pointing to.

"The celiac artery?" I guess.

Dr. Conlon's blue eyes widen.

"The main pancreatic duct," I quickly correct myself.

His black eyebrows rise in horror.

I take one more stab in the dark: "The… gastroepiploic… vein?"

The usually patient Dr. Conlon, so befuddled by my

answers, just stumbles away, shaking his head. Apparently, I'm unteachable.

"What *is* it?" I whisper to Sasha, who is standing across from me.

Mason would have known and likely shouted out the answer, but he's at some other cadaver right now. He follows around his favorite teaching assistants in order to soak up as much information as he can. He only graces us with his presence for about half the lab, although he still manages to do most of the work.

Sasha looks down at where I'm pointing.

"It's the duodenum," she says without hesitation. She's tiny and quiet, but she knows her stuff.

"Shit," I say.

Sasha seems somewhat traumatized by my profanity, so I add, "Sorry."

She nods. "It's okay."

"Why am I so bad at this?" I whine.

Sasha shrugs. "Just study more," she says, not unkindly.

Sasha and I don't connect. I thought that after my failed friendship attempt with Rachel, I might be able to hit it off with my other lab partner. But Sasha is too quiet and seems completely uninterested in communicating with me beyond exchanging information about anatomy. Every attempt I've made to get to know her has completely flopped. I asked her if she had a boyfriend, and she just looked at me blankly.

Not only that, but Landon and I barely talk anymore. Every time I call him, he says he's busy studying, and he often seems distracted. He barely calls *me* at all. He had insisted this long-distance thing would work, but I'm starting to have my doubts. On a scale of one to ten, he probably misses me only like a three… or maybe even a two.

So in summary, I have no friends, my relationship is falling apart, and I'm failing anatomy.

It all seems so impossible. I'm being tasked to memorize encyclopedias' worth of material, and there are only so many waking hours in the day. I've always been someone who needed a lot of sleep, and by around nine in the evening, my eyelids are sagging, and nothing sticks anymore.

If only there was something that could help me stay awake longer.

6

I MAY NOT BE GREAT AT ANATOMY, BUT I HAVE BECOME A Master of Procrastination (MoP).

I was all right at procrastinating in college. I mean, I always managed to get on social media a few times during the course of any study session. But this year, I've stepped it up. It seems like every time I need to study, I end up becoming desperately curious about what all my former friends from high school are up to. And then I try to figure out what that song in my head is. And take a few online quizzes. And I text message literally everyone I know.

So instead of studying, which is what I should be doing right now, I decide this is a perfect time to look up the details of the alleged drug problem at our school. Rachel isn't around, so it's perfect timing.

The information is so easy to find, I'm slightly embarrassed that it took me this long. All I have to type in is "DeWitt Medical School" and "drug overdose."

Pops right up. How is it possible that I didn't know about this?

Drug use is apparently rampant at our school and at the nearby college. Nobody entirely knows the source, but three years ago, a student at DeWitt overdosed and died. Then it happened again each of the next two years.

The student who died last year was named Darcie Peterson, and she was a first-year student. She was failing anatomy (sound familiar?) and apparently turned to amphetamines in an effort to boost her studying efforts. She collapsed in the girls' restroom and was discovered to have died from a burst brain aneurysm thought to be related to her substance abuse.

There's a quote from Dr. Conlon that's repeated in several of the online articles: "Darcie was a wonderful student and a wonderful person. She had so much potential. This is a great tragedy."

So much potential.

A door slams, and I nearly jump out of my skin. I minimize the window on my laptop seconds before Rachel strolls into our bedroom. I can't say exactly why, but I don't want her to know I was reading about the drug problem at DeWitt. Mostly, I'm afraid she'll say something to make me feel worse about it than I already do.

Without asking if it's okay, Rachel lays out her yoga mat on the floor and starts playing some music that is probably supposed to be soothing, but it just gets on my nerves. Besides, I'm studying (kind of). Listening to classical music is supposed to make you study better, but I can't concentrate with music playing, and anyway, this isn't classical music.

"I'm trying to study," I say to her.

She's already on her hands and knees on the mat. "So study. Who's stopping you?"

I can't imagine Rachel would understand, considering I've yet to see her crack open a book. "You know," I say, "we've got our first exam coming up soon in anatomy."

"You're kidding." Rachel straightens out her legs and spine so that her body makes a triangle with the floor.

I don't get it. I'd say she must have a photographic memory so she doesn't need to study, but it's clear from the lab that Rachel has no clue what's going on. Isn't she worried about failing?

Maybe I should try yoga. Maybe if I did some meditation and stretching, I'd stop worrying about the exam too.

Or maybe some pills would do the trick. Apparently, they are pretty easy to get around here.

Oh my God, why did that thought just pop into my head? I'm really starting to lose it. I've never failed a class before in my life, and anatomy isn't going to be the end of me. I don't need pills to study.

I can do this.

7

I SHOW UP EARLY AT THE DEWITT LIBRARY THE NEXT day, equipped with my anatomy atlas and my textbook, along with a water bottle and a baggie full of chocolate bars and potato chips. Yeah, that pretzel and Coke yesterday were just the tip of the iceberg. All I eat anymore is snack food—I haven't had a real meal in days.

Abe is meeting me so we can study together—the primary social activity at DeWitt. We've decided to try to study together more regularly, although he can't meet every night since he's—amazingly—got a part-time job at a student health clinic. He texts me that he's almost here, and I try to flip through the chapter on the thorax on my own. It's hard to concentrate, though. I keep thinking about my abysmal quiz grades.

"You look deep in thought."

I snap my head up. It's not Abe, like I expected. It's Mason. He looks mildly amused at the expression on my face as he slides into the seat across from mine at the table.

"Mind if I join you?"

I could never study around Mason Howard. He's pretty much the biggest distraction I can imagine. I would have thought spending all this time with him in lab, during which time he's proven himself to be the biggest asshole on the planet, would diminish his appeal, but it hasn't. He's just that sexy.

He looks way too good right now. Every med student I've seen so far today looks like they haven't slept in weeks, but Mason seems like he's just come back from a long vacation at a spa. His clothes aren't wrinkled, and his jaw is clean-shaven. His books are lined up in a neat stack on the table, and I can't help but see one of his anatomy quizzes sticking out of the textbook. The grade at the top is one hundred. Figures.

"I put in some quality time last night with Frank. But now it's time to hit the books," Mason says.

Despite Rachel's discomfort with naming the cadaver and a long email-rant she sent out to the entire class about how disrespectful it was, Mason still calls him Frank. It doesn't bother me. And to be honest, I like how much it seems to infuriate Rachel.

"I feel like I should give up right now," I mumble.

Mason frowns. "Why? What's wrong?"

He really has no idea.

"How do you do it, Mason?" I sigh. "You know *everything*."

"Well, I want to go into plastic surgery," he says with

a shrug. "I'll never match in a plastics residency if I don't study my ass off. What do *you* want to do?"

"I *thought* I wanted to be a doctor," I say.

I meant it as a joke, but it's sort of true.

Mason winks and flashes me this smile that makes my heart skip in my chest. Ugh. I need to stop being such a girl!

"Don't look so stressed out, Heather. Don't worry. You'll be fine."

"What if I'm not?" I say. "What if I fail the exam?"

"So you'll get a job at the post office," he jokes. "And one day, you can come back with a shotgun and blow the brains out of all the other students."

I don't laugh. The whole thing is kind of in poor taste considering we're at a school nicknamed Dead Med.

"Come on," he says. "You're going to do fine on the exam. I promise."

Mason reaches across the table and puts his hand on top of mine. And my hand starts to tingle like I'm having a stroke. I hate myself for having a schoolgirl crush on Mason.

"You'll be fine, Heather," he says. "Don't worry so much."

If I were Mason, I wouldn't worry either.

A throat clears, and I look up. It's Abe. He's standing at the other end of the table, holding his anatomy atlas and looking sort of peeved.

"I thought we were studying together," he says to me.

I yank my hand away from Mason's. "We are."

Mason's lips twitch. "Don't worry, Abe," he says as he stands up. "I'm not horning in on your action."

Abe's cheeks turn scarlet. It's sort of cute how his complexion is so pale that it shows all his emotions.

"I'm not..." he stammers. "I mean, we're not..."

"I have a boyfriend, you know," I say to Mason, sticking out my chin. "At another school."

"Is that so?" Mason doesn't wipe that grin off his face. I wish Abe would slug him, especially since he looks like he'd like to.

"Get out of here, Mason," Abe says to his roommate. He doesn't lay a finger on him—it's pretty clear that Abe isn't the kind of guy who goes around slugging people.

Mason is still smirking as he relocates himself to a desk in the back of the library. I notice he's one desk away from little Sasha, and he stops to talk with her for a minute before getting to work. I've yet to have a successful conversation with Sasha, so it's surprising to see *anyone* talking to her, but especially Mason.

Abe sets down his books on the table and slides into the seat across from me.

"I thought we could start with the heart," he says.

"Fine by me."

"Or we could do the lungs, if you'd prefer?" he offers.

I don't have a great understanding of the heart, but it's probably no worse than anything else in the thorax. I'm equally confused about everything.

"Let's just do the heart."

Abe nods and pulls out a stack of index cards. He

lays them down on the table, and I see that he's drawn color-coded diagrams of the heart. I gasp.

"Wow," I say.

"What?"

"I just…" I grin at him. "I didn't realize you were such a huge nerd."

Abe looks down at his nerdy index cards then back up at me. "I'm not a nerd! I'm *organized*."

I shake my head at him. "That's exactly what a nerd would say."

He picks up a blank index card and flicks it in my direction. He obviously meant to hit me with it, but the card doesn't even make it across the table. It just kind of flies into the air then flutters slowly to the ground. Abe and I both watch it then simultaneously bust out laughing.

"Pretty pathetic, huh?" he says.

"The trick is to form it into a plane," I explain.

I grab another blank index card and form it into a little makeshift paper airplane. I aim it in Abe's direction, and it hits him directly in the forehead.

"Ouch!" Abe cries, rubbing his forehead. He grabs himself another blank card. "Okay, you're asking for it, McKinley…"

And then we spend the next thirty minutes making planes out of index cards. I am such a bad influence.

At some point, we get tired of acting like children and start studying for real. It's intimidating that Abe knows his stuff so much better than I do, but at the same time, it's motivating. Someone once told me that it's always better to study with someone who knows more than you do.

If that's the case, Abe is screwed.

It's dark out by the time we decide to call it a day. We're both carrying an armful of books as we head down in the elevator to the parking lot.

"Where'd you park?" Abe asks me.

"Second floor. You?"

"Third." Abe steps out of the elevator. "It's dark out. I'll walk you to your car."

I make a face and stand in the doorway to the elevator so the doors won't close.

"I'll be fine."

"It's safer if I walk you," Abe insists.

The elevator starts to close on me, so I step aside. Fine. If Abe wants to waste his time walking me to my car, that's his business.

"This is Connecticut, you know," I say. "Not Detroit."

Abe shrugs. "Still."

"How are you going to protect me anyway?" I challenge him. "Are you carrying a weapon?"

He rolls his eyes. "I don't need a weapon. Nobody's going to attack me."

"How come?"

"Heather, come on."

Okay, I guess Abe is a pretty big guy. Still, he's not some kind of Superman who can dodge bullets. (Can Superman dodge bullets? I'd assume so. As long as they're not made of kryptonite.)

"So what would you do if some guy attacked you?"

Abe shrugs. "I don't know. Sit on him?"

Actually, that would be pretty effective.

I have to admit, it *is* pretty dark out, and the parking lot isn't particularly well lit. It's late enough that the lot is completely silent aside from our footsteps echoing on the pavement. As I walk by a white Lincoln Continental I had thought was empty, I detect movement from within the dark car. Like someone is sitting there, waiting. But when I peer through the vehicle's tinted windows, I can't make out a face.

"Hey."

I nearly jump out of my skin at the voice coming from behind me. I reach for Abe's arm and grab onto it for dear life. But when I turn around, it's just a kid from school. A second-year, whose name is Gerald or Harold or something along those lines. He's standing behind us, his hands shoved deep into the pockets of his jeans.

"Hey," Abe says back, although he sounds as confused as I feel.

"You're Abe, right?" Gerald/Harold says.

Abe's brow scrunches up. "Uh, yeah…"

Gerald/Harold looks me up and down, frowns, then looks back at Abe. "Well, I just wanted to say hi."

"Okay." Abe gives him a little wave. "Hi then."

Gerald/Harold stands there for another few seconds, like he's got something else to say. But then he turns on his heel and scurries off in the other direction, casting glances over his shoulder at the two of us.

"What the hell?" Abe says, which is exactly what I'm thinking.

"Friend of yours?"

"Not even close."

That whole interaction was seriously strange. A shiver goes through me, and I'm suddenly very glad Abe insisted on coming with me. I was joking around with him before, but he could clearly defend me if he needed to.

"This is me," I tell him, gesturing at my scratched-up Ford.

Abe waits until I'm inside the car and have started up the engine before he turns around and heads in the opposite direction. I'm guessing he had a good study session, too, because there's a bounce in his step as he walks away.

8

Mason is staring into the chest cavity of our cadaver, a perplexed look on his irritatingly handsome face.

"That's odd," he says.

I look at where Mason's staring. He's looking at the spleen, I think. "What?"

Mason dives into the chest cavity with his gloved hands and pulls out the heart.

"Look at this heart," he says.

I look at it. I have no idea what he's talking about. "Um…"

Mason's hazel eyes meet mine. "It's *perfect.*"

"You think I did a good job on the coronary arteries?" I feel a little burst of happiness. I really thought I butchered them.

"No, that's not what I'm saying." Mason shakes his head. Damn. "I mean, look at Gladys at the next table. Her heart is the size of a cabbage. Bernie at Table Eight has black lungs. We know why practically all these people died." He pauses. "But not Frank."

"So?"

"So don't you think that's a little strange?" Mason asks.

I never thought about it before. I guess he's right, though. Frank seems healthier than most of the other cadavers in the room. He's a big guy and seems like he'd been strong as an ox. But even if there isn't an obvious cause of death, there must have been a reason. After all, he's dead.

Abe joins us at the table, getting close enough to me that I can smell the coffee on his breath, which I actually sort of like. That guy drinks more coffee than I do, and that's saying a lot, but I guess that's the only way to manage both med school and a part-time job. At this moment, he's practically levitating with caffeinated energy.

"You need to lay off the coffee, Abe," I say.

"Look who's talking." He snorts. "When I said we were dissecting out the fascia lata yesterday, you asked if I said fascia *latte*, and you almost started salivating."

"No, you're way worse," I say. "I think you're developing a tremor."

Abe holds out his left hand, and we both lean in to inspect it. He's definitely shaking a bit—more than I would have expected.

"I *need* coffee, though," he says. "It's my drug of choice." As soon as the words leave his mouth, he freezes. "I shouldn't have said that."

"It's okay—it's not like it's a secret that there's a drug

problem at the school." I drop my voice, glancing at Mason, who is too entranced by the dissection to pay attention to us. "Do you have any idea where all the pills are coming from?"

"No." His answer comes quickly. "No idea. Not my thing."

I crack a smile. "Who needs drugs when you've got extreme-caffeine coffee?"

"Exactly," he says. But he doesn't smile back.

9

Our first anatomy exam is today. I didn't sleep at all last night.

I meant to sleep. Believe me, it wasn't my intention at the beginning of the night to stay awake for twenty-four hours straight and leave myself feeling like I'm about to collapse.

I went to the library yesterday after spending several hours in the lab, going over anatomy. Abe insisted that I leave with him at midnight, and I did it only because I knew he wouldn't go until I did. But when I got back to my room, I continued studying. My room looks like an anatomy tornado hit. Every time I even contemplated closing my textbooks, it just seemed like there was too much that I didn't know. By four in the morning, it just felt pointless to try to sleep.

I'm pretty tired.

At eight a.m., I change into my green scrubs and join the large group of my classmates in front of the anatomy lab, waiting for the practical portion of the exam to begin. I can almost see the nervous energy radiating from the group. I showered this morning, but it's obvious many of my classmates didn't bother. We're a pretty scruffy crew.

You could probably fill a small lake with the amount of coffee we've had to drink this morning. Several dozen of us are clutching identical white Styrofoam cups. This is my fourth cup in the last two hours, and I'm starting to have palpitations. And there's a very real chance I might wet my pants.

"Hey, Heather." It's Phil, the boy with the messy ponytail that I'd spied on the first day. "You nervous?"

Obviously.

"I'm just really tired from staying up all night," I say.

Phil reaches into his pocket and produces a small container filled with tiny white pills.

"Want one?" he asks.

I can't even conceal my horror. Oh my God. He's offering me *drugs*. Phil is the kid in our class who's dealing! And he just offered them to me—in front of *everyone*!

"Um, are those…?"

"Mint-flavored caffeine tablets," Phil says. "Got 'em at the gift shop."

"Oh." My heart slows to a less frightening speed. "No, thanks."

"Are you sure?" Phil asks. "It's like drinking a cup of coffee, but you don't have to pee!"

I shake my head and wander off in search of Abe. Instead, I find Rachel leaning against the wall, her long dark-brown hair hanging loose around her shoulders and obscuring the lettering on her T-shirt. She's tapping her toes against the floor impatiently, and every few minutes, she lets out an irritated sigh.

Mason is standing next to Rachel, looking fresh as a daisy. He's also staring so blatantly at her chest that I can't help but say something.

"What are you looking at?" I bark at him.

Boy, I'm irritable today.

Mason lifts his eyes and looks at me in surprise. "I'm trying to read her T-shirt."

Oh. I guess that could be true.

Rachel smiles at him. "It says, 'I am the doctor my mother wanted me to marry.'"

Mason starts to laugh. He looks Rachel straight in the eyes and says, "Not yet you're not."

The doors to the anatomy lab open, and the students file in like we're on some kind of death march. The first part of the exam is the practical, where various structures on different cadavers are tagged with pins, and the students are given a sheet of paper and clipboard on which to record their findings. I have to confess, the clipboard makes me feel very professional.

I whip out my lucky pen, a black ballpoint with a rubber handgrip that I've been using since college. I used my lucky pen for every big exam in college, and on the one occasion I forgot the pen, during an exam on electricity and magnetism, I got a big fat F.

I choose my own cadaver as my starting point and uncap my lucky pen. Our cadaver's insides are nearly perfect, thanks to Mason's immaculate dissections and the fact that Frank was inexplicably healthy when he died. I clutch my clipboard to my chest, trying to stop shaking, although it's hard after all that coffee. My breaths are coming too fast, and my fingertips start to tingle. I'm hyperventilating. I need a paper bag.

"Are you okay, Heather?" Abe has materialized at my side, looking concerned.

I look him over and am relieved that his short red hair seems as disheveled as the rest of my classmates', and he has familiar dark circles under his eyes.

"I'm fine," I reply.

And I mean it. Now that Abe is standing next to me, I feel about one hundred percent better. There's something about his presence that calms me down. Don't laugh, but I sometimes feel like he's my guardian angel.

Dr. Conlon limps to the front of the room. All eyes are on him, waiting for his instructions. He smiles, his blue eyes twinkling, "Why does everyone look so nervous?"

Nobody laughs. *Just start the exam, you asshole.*

Dr. Conlon clears his throat: "As I went over with you before, you've got one minute to identify each pinned structure and one minute for each X-ray. When the time is up, I'll call out 'next station.'" He looks around the room. "And don't worry. The test really isn't that hard. Any questions?"

No hands go up.

He holds up a stopwatch in his left hand, "Okay, then, begin!"

I look down at the first structure to identify. It's my own cadaver that I've been working on for a month, so I should know the answer. The pin is secured into a blood vessel that seems to be running into the back of the heart. Or is it the front of the heart? I suddenly feel disoriented. If only I could pick it up and examine it… but no touching is allowed on the exam.

I think it's the pulmonary vein. I'm like ninety percent sure.

Maybe eighty percent sure.

I poise my lucky pen over the sheet of paper on my clipboard, printing the words "pulmonary vein," but nothing shows up on the paper. I try again, but all I can see is the indentation of the words I had tried to write.

My lucky pen is out of ink.

You have *got* to be kidding me.

The clock is ticking. I have less than twenty seconds left at this station. I shake the pen, trying to coax the last bits of ink into the point. I only need the pen to last for about fifty or so words. *You can do it, pen! Please, pen! Don't let me down…*

"Psst… Hey." Abe is nudging me. I look at him, and he's holding out a pen to me. "I always bring a spare."

Like I said, Abe's my guardian angel.

I nod gratefully at him and take the pen. I scribble down my answer just as Dr. Conlon calls out, "Next station!"

I THINK I'm going to be sick.

The second the exam is over, I run to the ladies' room near the anatomy labs and lean over a toilet. My stomach is churning, and I fully expect to see the bagel I forced down this morning regurgitated before my eyes—

but nothing comes. I lean forward, gagging. I want to throw up. It's the only way to get rid of this horrible feeling in the pit of my stomach.

I'm starting to understand why a first-year med student might start taking drugs. Because I'm desperate for anything to get rid of this horrible feeling.

Finally, I give up on my attempted vomit and collapse onto the bathroom floor, not even caring about the mysterious yellow puddle right next to me. I lean my head against the door to the stall and let out a dramatic sob. I don't care anymore who hears me. It's not like I'll be in medical school much longer after that performance.

The exam was a bona fide disaster. Dr. Conlon called the test "easy." Easy? The test could have been written in Ancient Hebrew and I probably would have scored equally well. Even my lucky pen (now in the trash, having betrayed me) couldn't have rescued me from that train wreck.

But maybe Dr. Conlon was right. Probably the test really was easy, and I'm just too dumb to cut it in med school.

More and more, I'm beginning to think that's the case.

I don't even know how long I sit on that filthy bathroom floor, wallowing in self-pity, replaying all the events that led up to my stupid, stupid decision to go to med school. I should have known when I took the MCATs and had to leave to pee four times during the exam that I didn't have the stamina for med school. The fact that I had admired the hell out of my childhood pediatrician,

Dr. Marsha Stoltz-Humberg, with her kind eyes and the smiley face sticker on her white coat, wasn't enough of a reason to put myself through this.

When I finally struggle to my feet, the first thing I do is stumble over to the bathroom mirror. I look awful. My face is blotchy, my eyes are bloodshot, and my dirty-blond hair is everywhere. I make a half-hearted attempt to clean myself up, but really, what's the point?

And then I make the mistake of looking down at the sink. At the fissure in the porcelain that still hasn't been repaired since that student broke it when she collapsed here and died. The thought makes me so sick that it takes everything I have not to run back into the toilet stall to try to throw up again.

As I stumble out of the bathroom, I call Landon's number on my cell phone. I lean against the wall outside the bathroom, waiting for him to pick up. He knew I was taking an exam today and that I was panicking about it. But the phone rings and rings then finally goes to voicemail.

I don't leave a message.

I stare down at my phone. I have never felt so alone in my entire life. Med school was such a mistake.

"Oh shit… What happened?"

I jump in surprise at the voice traveling down the hall and immediately try to hide my red, splotchy face. But then I lift my eyes and see who it is. It's just Abe. Thank God.

"I'm okay," I mumble, looking away from him.

"I was looking everywhere for you," he says a little breathlessly. He halts in front of me, and his green eyes widen slightly when he sees my face, but he doesn't comment. "You really hid yourself well. I thought I was going to have to call in a SWAT team."

I force a tiny smile. "Yeah."

Abe shifts between his feet, looking a little uncomfortable. I want to tell him that I almost definitely failed the exam, but the truth is, I don't want him to think I'm dumb. I don't want him to know I bombed an "easy" test.

"Hey," Abe says. "That test was super hard, huh?"

I almost gasp. Say what? Abe thought the test was hard too? Is he just being nice? Abe is really smart, and if he thought the exam was hard, maybe I'm not too dumb to live.

"You… you thought the test was hard?"

"Oh, definitely!" Abe says, nodding vigorously. "I don't know what Conlon was smoking when he said it was easy. That was brutal."

"Yeah, it sort of was," I say, perking up for the first time since handing in my test paper.

"Some of the pins in those bodies…" Abe shakes his head. "I mean, I had no idea. I felt like I was looking at an abstract art exhibit."

I finally smile for real. Encouraged, Abe continues, "And those multiple-choice questions on the written exam? I could have filled in the bubbles before seeing the test and gotten the same score."

I laugh. "I know exactly what you mean."

Abe rests his large hand gently on my shoulder. "Come on," he says. "I'm going to walk you to your car."

"Okay," I agree.

"And then," he adds, "we are going to drown our sorrows in pizza. And beer. I'm buying."

I dutifully follow Abe to the parking lot. A minute ago, I'd been having some incredibly dark thoughts. Thank God for Abe.

10

Dr. Conlon is taking his sweet time grading those exams. Honestly, this is sadistic. How can he make us wait so long? I'm going to get an ulcer at this rate.

After classes are over for the day, I find myself wandering in the direction of Dr. Conlon's office. I don't have anything in mind, exactly. I'm not going there to beg him to tell me my grade or anything.

His office is just around the corner from the anatomy lab, and I wonder if he can smell the formaldehyde from there. Of course, he's probably used to the smell by now. Maybe it smells good to him. He probably likes it. You'd almost have to if you have a career in anatomy.

The door to Dr. Conlon's office is closed, but I can see the light on under the door. He's inside. I can hear soft voices talking, but I can't make out any of the words. I hesitate, wondering what the hell I'm doing here. Do I really think Dr. Conlon is going to tell me my grade after saying flat out that he wouldn't do that? I'm not that charming.

The door to the office swings open suddenly, and I jump back to keep from getting smacked in the face. And the person who steps out is none other than Mason Howard. He seems equally surprised to see me.

"Heather!" His face breaks out into a grin. He always seems so cool and collected. And sexy, of course—hard to forget that one. "What are you doing here?"

"I just…" I clear my throat. "I needed to talk to Dr. Conlon."

"Oh?"

"Yeah…" I wonder what Mason's doing here. He isn't here because he thought he had failed, that's for sure. Maybe Dr. Conlon wanted to personally congratulate him for getting the highest grade in the class.

"Well, I'll see you later," Mason says with a wink.

He nudges my shoulder as he walks past. Don't tell anyone, but I sort of love it when he touches me. My crush on Mason hasn't abated in the least.

I peek into Dr. Conlon's office and see him sitting at his desk, shuffling through some papers. His cane leans against the side of his desk. I'm debating whether or not to knock when he looks up and spots me.

"Dr. McKinley!" he says, a smile on his lips.

I try my best to put on a surprised face. "Oh, I, um, I didn't realize this was your office, Dr. Conlon!"

He squints at me. "You didn't?"

"No, I didn't," I say, continuing with my lie. "It's, um, really nice. I like the, um…" God, I know nothing about decorating. "I like the wood." Okay, that sounded awful. I have to say something else. "And… I like your bowtie."

Stop talking, Heather. Right now.

"Um, thank you," Dr. Conlon says, a perplexed look on his face. He adjusts his glasses on his nose. "Is there something you wanted to talk to me about?"

I squeeze my hands together. "Well, um… I guess, since I'm here…"

"Have a seat," Dr. Conlon says, leaning back in his chair and folding his arms across his chest. I close the door to his office and sit down in the chair in front of his desk almost gingerly, as if afraid it might collapse under my weight. Which is actually possible, considering how many cookies I've consumed in the last month. "What's up?"

"I just…" I bite my lower lip. "I think I failed the exam, Dr. Conlon. I *know* I failed it."

Dr. Conlon furrows his black eyebrows. "Heather…"

"I studied so hard, I swear!" Now I'm *crying*, for God's sake. What's *wrong* with me? I've morphed into this stereotype of a hysterical medical student. I wipe my eyes with the back of my hand and notice Dr. Conlon is gawking at me. I hope he doesn't think I'm on drugs. "I just… I don't know what happened! The test was so hard… Maybe I just… I'm not as good as… Sometimes I don't know what I'm even doing here… I just feel like…"

"Heather." Dr. Conlon runs a hand through his black hair. "Stop, okay? Stop. You passed, okay?"

What?

"I… What?"

"You passed."

I don't know what to say. Honestly, I sort of want to jump across the table and plant a big sloppy wet kiss on my professor's face. But that would be unprofessional. So instead, I settle for tearfully thanking him for a solid five minutes, followed by a brief speech about how he is the kindest man I've ever met in my life, concluding with something about how he ought to win a Nobel Prize.

After I finish making a complete idiot out of myself, Dr. Conlon sighs and shakes his head.

"Christ," he says, but he's smiling. "I forgot what it was like to be a medical student."

I wipe my eyes. I really can't picture Dr. Conlon twenty years younger, starting out as a nervous young medical student. Dr. Conlon always seems so confident. He knows everything about the human body, as far as I can tell.

"I didn't know you had to go to med school to teach anatomy," I comment.

"You don't." Dr. Conlon lowers his eyes as he toys with a button on his shirt sleeve. "I dropped out of med school."

Before I can stop myself, I blurt out, "But why? You're so smart!"

Nice job. I can't believe I just said that to my professor.

But to my relief, he laughs. "Believe me, getting a doctorate in anatomy is not exactly a walk in the park."

I watch as he puts his left palm on the handle of his cane and absently fiddles with it. I asked Abe once if he knew what's wrong with Dr. Conlon, and he said he had no idea. I wonder if his disability has anything to do with why he left medical school. I wonder if he resents us for doing what he couldn't do.

Dr. Conlon gives me a stern look.

"Now, Heather," he says, "you better not tell anyone I told you that you passed. If I see a line of one hundred and fifty students outside my door, I'm going to be really angry at you."

"I won't tell," I promise.

He smiles. "Good. And you need to have more confidence in yourself. I see the way you are in the lab, and you've made huge progress."

I almost faint with joy. Finding out I passed the exam and that Dr. Conlon thinks I'm smart is an incredible high. I'm pretty sure there are no little white pills that could make me feel any better than this.

11

I SING IN MY CAR ALL THE WAY HOME FROM DR. Conlon's office. My radio is blaring some top-forty pop station, and I'm screaming out Ava Max and Dua Lipa songs at the top of my lungs. Thankfully, the windows are up, so nobody has to go deaf from my horrible voice. I love to sing, and I do it probably more than I should, considering I can't hold a tune. A few times, Landon has told me that if I didn't stop singing, he was going to stuff a gag in my mouth.

He was joking, obviously.

When I get back to the dorm, there's only one person I want to talk to, and that's Landon. Okay, things haven't been super great with him lately, but that's about to change. I'm going to make an effort to make it work from now on. Maybe next weekend, I'll drive out to see him.

Before placing the call, I bring up a photo of Landon that I've got saved in my camera roll. In the picture, he's lying on his bed, his curly brown hair tousled, grinning with those adorable dimples at the camera. It's like I've somehow almost forgotten what he looked like. I trace my fingertip over the curves of his face, trying to remember how much I care about him.

I do. I know I do. Even though he's sort of been a jerk lately.

I minimize the photo then flop onto my stomach so that I can call him and take advantage of these warm feelings. It takes seven and a half rings, and he answers just when I'm certain the voicemail will pick up. What is he always doing that he can't manage to answer the phone in the first few rings?

"Hey," Landon says.

"Hi. It's me," I say.

Thank God, he doesn't ask who "me" is. And for once, he doesn't sound distracted.

This relationship could work. It's *going to* work. Two hundred plus miles isn't so far for true love.

"Hi…" Landon says.

Actually, he sounds… oddly serious. But whatever. I'm not going to obsess for once. I prefer Serious Landon to the apathetic guy he's been lately.

"So guess what? I passed my anatomy exam!" I almost get chills when I say it.

"That's great… I knew you would."

"So… I thought maybe we could celebrate this weekend," I say, twirling a lock of hair around my fingertip. I didn't even notice until now how bitten up my fingernails are. "I could drive in Friday night…"

"I don't know if this weekend is good," Landon mumbles.

"Why not?"

There's a long pause on the other line. Too long. What's going on? "Landon?"

"I just..." He sighs loudly. "I don't know what we're doing anymore. I mean, is this enjoyable for you?"

"It's not about enjoyment," I say. "I want to be with you. We both knew the long-distance thing was going to be hard."

"But... *shouldn't* it be about enjoyment? I mean, we're twenty-two years old. Why shouldn't we be able to enjoy ourselves?"

Landon might be the love of my life. But at this moment, I hate the bastard.

"I mean, if this isn't making us happy..."

He's dumping me. He's *dumping* me! How is this possible? We have been together for *over three years*! How could he? We love each other, damn it! Unless...

"Is there someone else?"

"No... Well, not really," Landon stammers. And now I really hate him. "There are other... I mean, aren't there guys at school that *you're* interested in?"

"No!" I say in an affronted voice, although I can't help but think of Mason.

"I'm sure there are."

"Go to hell, Landon."

There's a long silence on the other line. I grip the phone in my fist, not wanting to be the one to break the silence. If I talk first, he wins. I can't let him win.

"I need to go study now," Landon finally says.

"Fine, go study." I don't wait for a reply. I hang up

the phone and hurl it across the room. It smashes against the wall, and I hear a resounding *crack.*

Well, that was a dumb thing to do.

I try to tell myself that if something as small as being apart for a month could break us up, obviously, it wasn't true love. We're just two people who dated a while in college and broke up when life got in the way.

A sudden ache in my chest nearly knocks the wind out of me. I had considered the possibility that Landon and I might break up—of course I had—but I hadn't imagined how badly it would hurt. The sick, dark feeling seems to consume all the organs I learned about so far this year—my heart, my lungs, my esophagus. Even my pancreas seems to be aching for Landon.

I would give anything to make this pain stop. If there were a pill I could take to feel better, I'd swallow it in a heartbeat.

No. *No.* I'm *not* going to go down that path.

But what can I do to feel better? There must be *something* that could dull this awful pain.

I pace across the bedroom a few times, then I grab my keys off my desk and head out the door. I get to the stairwell, but instead of going downstairs, toward the exit, I find myself going upstairs.

Abe lives upstairs—one flight up, to be exact. But I'm not looking for Abe right now. I'm looking for his roommate.

Mason.

No matter what negative things I could say about him (and there are many), that guy is very, very attractive. He has those hazel eyes and that killer grin. When he gets into the hospital as a third-year, the nurses are going to go wild for him. He'll probably sleep with half the hospital staff.

An hour with Mason will help me forget about Landon. Mason is like the perfect rebound guy—he's hot, and I don't care about him at all. And he looks like he'd be up for a little no-strings-attached action. I'm pretty sure all hot guys are at least halfway decent in bed, if only because they get a lot of experience.

I stand outside the door to Mason and Abe's dorm room, taking inventory of my appearance and working up my nerve. Okay, I don't look amazing or anything. I don't have a scrap of makeup on, but at least I'm showered and wearing clean clothes, even if my jeans and sweater aren't outright sexy.

Maybe I should go back downstairs and put on some lip gloss. Of course, if I do, I'll probably chicken out. Oh God, this is scary. How do you hit on a guy?

I knock timidly. Once.

I hear footsteps, and it's pretty obvious that those resounding thumps belong to Abe. Crap. How am I going to explain to him that I want to hook up with his roommate? Before I have a chance to think about it, the door swings open.

Abe's face lights up when he sees me. "Hey, Heather."

"Oh, hi…" I wrack my brain to think of a believable reason why I'd need to talk to Mason. I draw a blank.

Abe raises his red-orange eyebrows at me. "What's up?"

I swallow. "Is… is Mason home?"

Abe frowns. I wonder if he has any idea what I'm thinking. "No, he's probably at the library. He's always at the library."

Damn. "Oh."

Abe steps aside. "Are you okay, Heather? Do you want to come in?"

I like Abe, don't get me wrong. But I came here for a booty call, and now that it's not going to happen, I feel completely deflated. Still, Abe can lend a sympathetic ear, at least. And I'm clearly not going to get any studying done.

I've never been inside Abe's dorm room before, and let me tell you, their living room is disgusting. I mean, really disgusting. There are two empty pizza boxes and a few half-full beer bottles on their coffee table, and I can see a partially eaten crust abandoned under the table. I scan the floor for insects or rodents and can't find any, but I do spot a pair of boxer shorts hanging off the edge of their ratty, stained futon sofa. Abe is nice enough to yank it off.

"Sorry," he says, blushing. "Not mine."

I'm seriously considering asking him to put a blanket on the futon so that I don't have to sit on it directly. Of course, yesterday, I was elbow deep in Frank's intestines, so maybe I shouldn't be such a diva. I plop myself down between a brown and a yellow stain and bury my face in my palms in an overly dramatic gesture.

Abe's large hand falls on my back. He rubs my shoulder gently.

"Heather," he murmurs. "Talk to me. What's wrong?"

I just shake my head. To say it will make it real.

"Come on, Heather," he says. "It's *me*."

Finally, his kindness gets the better of me. I start sobbing, mourning three lost years of a guy I thought I was going to marry someday. I'm definitely not going to marry him now. I may even hate him.

Abe just sits with me, rubbing my back, eventually getting up to fetch me some tissues (well, toilet paper). I'm glad it's just Abe with me, because I am not attractive when I'm crying. My eyes swell up, and my nose is clogged with fresh snot. Good thing Mason isn't here to see this.

Abe scoops up the hand that isn't holding snotty tissues and squeezes it in his own. He could easily crush my hand in his, but his touch is surprisingly gentle.

"Talk to me, Heather," he says again.

"Landon broke up with me," I manage, and that sets off a whole fresh wave of tears.

If it were someone else, I'd probably fudge the details. I'd probably say that "we broke up." But what's the point of lying? Abe is my best friend here. If I can't tell him the truth, then who can I talk to?

"Wow," Abe murmurs. "I'm really sorry. That's… awful."

I nod and blow my nose noisily into a fresh tissue. There's so much snot that I have to lay my first tissue on his coffee table and get a fresh one for a second blow. I feel pretty gross. I glance up at Abe, who doesn't seem to be bothered by my snotty tissues.

"Sorry," I say anyway.

He frowns. "For what?"

I hold up the tissue. "For being disgusting and full of snot." I allow myself a tiny laugh.

But Abe doesn't laugh. "Heather, you could never be disgusting."

"Um, yeah, I think I could."

"No." The way he's looking at me makes my heart speed up suddenly. "You couldn't. Never."

I'm about to tell Abe that he's never seen me when I'm sick with a bad upper respiratory tract infection when he leans forward and presses his lips against mine.

This, I did not expect.

But it's not bad. Actually, it's quite nice. Landon always used to scratch me up with the stubble of his facial hair, but Abe's lips are incredibly soft, and even the bristles of his five-o'clock shadow are gentle against my chin. As he kisses me, he slides his hand up the back of my neck, lacing his large fingers into my hair, pulling me closer to him. And I'm letting him do it.

I can't even say how long it lasts. But when Abe pulls away from me, I'm breathless. We're both shaking, and his green eyes are wide.

"I'm so sorry," he breathes.

"You don't look sorry."

Abe rubs his face with his hands. "I wanted to do that for so long," he murmurs. "You have no idea."

He's right. I had absolutely no idea. I'm a total idiot.

This explains a lot, though.

"I'm sorry," he says again, and now he's the one who looks like he's going to cry. "I really like you, Heather. I mean, a *lot.* I just… want to be *something* to you. I don't want you to freak out. We could just be friends again if that's what you want."

"Is that what *you* want?" I ask him.

He runs a shaking hand through his red hair. "If it's what you want."

"But what do *you* want?" I press him.

He stares at me.

"You," he says, like it's the most obvious thing in the world.

I look at Abe. Honestly, I never thought of him this way. As a *man*. He may not be as handsome as Mason, but he's not bad-looking at all. He's actually pretty cute, and he has really nice green eyes and huge muscles. As long as you don't mind guys who are roughly the size of a grizzly bear.

"Okay," I say.

His eyes widen. "Okay what?"

I reach out and squeeze his knee. "Okay, you can kiss me again."

Abe's face lights up, and he grins at me like Christmas and his birthday came all at once. And then he kisses me again.

12

Dating Abe is an experience like I had never imagined.

Abe's number-one concern in life seems to be Making Heather Happy. It's almost overwhelming. Even if it was three in the morning, even if he was studying, even if there was snow and hail and a tornado outside, all I had to do was let out a small sigh and he'd race out to buy me a little present to cheer me up. (Not that I'd let him go out in a tornado or anything. I'm not *that* high maintenance.)

And the flowers… Dear God, the flowers. I don't know how Abe got the combination to my locker, but I start finding flowers waiting for me almost every day. What baffles me further is how he finds time to put them in there, considering we spend nearly every waking minute together.

I also love that he is such a gentleman. One day, when we walked into the parking lot at school, there were puddles all over the ground from an earlier rainstorm. I mentioned I was worried about getting my shoes wet, so Abe scooped me up off my feet. A few times when I was dating Landon, he picked me up to carry me to bed, and he always grunted and strained like he was carrying a baby elephant. But Abe didn't even break a sweat as he trotted across the parking lot with me in his arms to deliver me to my car with perfectly dry shoes.

Of course, the crux of every med school relationship is studying, and Abe and I are no exception. More nights than not are spent lying in Abe's bed, textbooks in our laps, my legs crossed over his. Those are the times I like best.

The second anatomy exam is much less painful than the first, and I'd be lying if I said it wasn't thanks to studying with Abe. We study pretty much every night he doesn't work at the clinic. It makes me feel a bit like a loser that it took Landon's tutoring to get me through premed courses in college, and now Abe is carrying me through anatomy.

"I think I'm holding you back," I sometimes say to Abe when I'm feeling especially guilty.

"No way," Abe insists. "I learn the material better when I go over it with you."

It could be true, although I suspect he'd help me even if it weren't. The fact that Abe has a part-time job on top of med school is unthinkable to me. How is it possible that he's balancing a *job* on top of the mountain of work we have to do for school? All I can think is that his brain must be wired differently.

That or he's got a little helper in the form of pills.

No. No way. Abe isn't on drugs. I'd know if he were, and he just… he isn't. He *wouldn't.* I'm sure of it. I'd sooner believe he's some sort of cyborg sent from the future with the singular purpose to excel in anatomy.

This time, I wait until the grades are posted rather than stalking Dr. Conlon in his office. I make Abe come with me for moral support, although he's oddly uninterested in his own grade. The grades are listed on a piece of paper by our mailboxes, although thankfully, our names aren't used. We each have a five-digit ID number to locate our grades. I scan the list until I find my ID number then let out a little involuntary squeal when I see my grade: seventy-six.

That's a pass! Not even a *low* pass! It's a bona fide pass!

I throw my arms around Abe, an action that might have knocked down a smaller man. But Abe just laughs and hugs me back. Then it turns into at least a minute of making out. When we finally separate, I cry, "I passed!"

"I figured that much," he says with a grin.

"Not even a low pass," I say proudly. Although I feel a little silly for being proud of what is essentially a C. "How did you do?"

I assumed he'd have done better than me, so I was prepared for that. What I wasn't prepared for is the confused expression on his face.

"Oh," he says. "I guess I should check."

What the hell? How could we be standing a foot away from our midterm grades, but he didn't even bother to look at his own grade?

"A ninety-one," Abe announces. He shrugs. "Pretty good, I guess."

"Pretty good?" I repeat, astonished. "Abe, that's *awesome*! That's honors."

"Yeah," he says and allows himself the tiniest of smiles. Although I can see in his eyes that he truly doesn't care.

And that is just super weird, folks.

13

ALTHOUGH I'D BEEN LOOKING FORWARD TO Thanksgiving break as a reprieve from school, it ends up leaving me more exhausted than anything. My parents were in rare form and managed to pick on me nonstop nearly the entire long weekend. For example, the second I walked into the door of my parents' house, my mother hugged me and said, "Heather, your hair smells."

I had just been driving for nearly six hours straight, and that was definitely not what I wanted or needed to hear.

Besides, I had showered just before I left. Between you and me, the smell never entirely comes out of my hair. I looked online for solutions and had tried vinegar, tomato juice, Coca-Cola, and even baking soda, but nothing quite gets out the formaldehyde. I barely even notice it anymore. And that worries me more than anything.

After we finally got off the subject of my hair, my mother gave me the third degree about my wonderful new boyfriend. Abe and I had toyed with the idea of him coming to my house for the holidays or vice versa, but we decided our parents would have a fit. But as my mother grilled me, I desperately wished Abe were standing by my side. If only to look imposing.

I leave early on Saturday morning, and it's not a moment too soon—I can't wait to see my boyfriend. When I get back to the dorms, I barely take a second to throw my bags in the room and glance at my reflection in the hall mirror. I'm wearing a tight tank top and a pair of straight-cut blue jeans, which seem good enough. I suspect Abe would be okay with it if I showed up wearing a potato sack.

I kick off my boots and slide sandals over my bare feet and hurry upstairs to Abe's apartment. Usually, we meet at my apartment because his is truly disgusting. A few weeks ago, I walked into the living room, and there was a dead roach lying right in the middle of the floor. I pointed it out, and to my surprise, Mason and Abe seemed to already know it was there.

"It's a warning to other roaches," Mason explained. "So they know what will happen to them if they come in here."

Abe just looked embarrassed and scooped up the roach with a paper towel.

Anyway, roaches or not, I'm too excited to see Abe, and I don't want to wait around downstairs. I knock on the door, and Mason answers.

So here's the weird part: Mason always seems really put together, but right now, he looks *awful*. His hair is sticking straight up, and it looks like he hasn't washed it in weeks. He's wearing a DeWitt Med T-shirt that has a big brown stain on the front of it, and it smells worse than my hair. He's got several days' worth of stubble on his face, and those gorgeous hazel eyes are bloodshot.

"Mason?" I say.

I almost ask him if he's drunk.

Or on drugs.

Mason blinks at me a few times, like he's trying to place me. I practically expect him to ask me my name. Then his eyes narrow.

"What do you want?"

I've never known anyone in my life who was on drugs. But when I look at Mason, that's my only thought: *This guy is definitely on something.* I've never been so sure of anything in my life.

But it's none of my business.

"Uh…" I squeeze my fists together. "I just came to see Abe."

Mason frowns for a minute.

"Oh." His shoulders sag. "Right. Of course. He's in the shower."

"He is?"

The bathroom door is just off to the right, and there's a puff of steam wafting out from underneath.

"Yeah," Mason says. And then he adds, sounding very much like his usual self, "But I'm sure he wouldn't mind some company."

He smiles at me then, and before I can question his appearance any further, he slips out the door to the apartment.

Mason had an intriguing idea. How hot would it be

if I get into the shower with Abe? Of course, it would be a bit of a surprise, but what guy wouldn't get turned on by something like that?

I'm going to do it!

I go down the hall, gently opening the door to the bathroom, and silently slip into the room. Once inside, I blink several times as my vision clouds with steam. The mirrors are completely fogged over so that I can't even make out my own reflection. Abe's voice echoes from behind the white shower curtain, softly humming a tune. It sounds like Journey.

I pull my shirt over my head and wiggle out of my jeans, accompanied by my panties. I then unhook my bra. Finally, I'm totally naked in the middle of the bathroom, the steam curling my hair, becoming very aroused by the idea that Abe is naked, too, just beyond the shower curtains.

And then I happen to look down.

I hadn't noticed Abe's blue scrubs lying on the floor of the bathroom when I came into the room. But I get an eyeful of them now. They look different from the way they do in the anatomy lab.

They are covered in reddish-brown stains, which are still slightly damp.

What *is* that? It looks like… well, like *blood*. But it couldn't be. If Abe had that much blood on his clothes, he'd be dead.

Or someone else would be dead.

I crouch down, trying to get a closer look at the stains. But I knock my elbow into the sink, and although I manage to stifle a cry of pain, the sound alerts Abe to my presence. He opens the shower curtain and discovers me standing there.

"What are you doing?" he cries.

"I… I…" I stammer.

"I'm in the shower!" he shouts at me. *Well, duh.* "You need to… to get out!"

"But—"

"Get out!" He really is screaming this time. I can see the veins standing out in his neck, and his right eye is twitching slightly. "Now!"

I nearly slip on a puddle of water as I fumble to put my clothes back on. I'm *so* embarrassed. As I pull my tank top over my head, I notice that the pattern of water droplets sounds different. The downpour of water is steady now—Abe isn't moving in the shower. He's just standing still, waiting for me to leave.

What the hell is going on?

I'm tempted to storm out of the room and go home, but curiosity and confusion keep me there. What were those stains on his scrubs? It would have been easier to believe it was something innocent if not for the way he reacted. I sit on his ratty futon couch, avoiding a rather large new coffee stain, and wait for Abe to finish his shower. I will never forget the tone of Abe's voice. I've never heard him sound that way. He was furious but also something else, something even more perplexing:

He sounded terrified.

A minute later, the flow of water stops, and Abe emerges from the bathroom with one towel around his waist and another clutched in his hands. His usually pale face is very red and not just from the steam of the shower. He can barely make eye contact with me.

"Give me a second to get dressed," he says. "Okay?"

While he's in the bedroom changing, I sneak into the bathroom to see if the scrubs are still there. They aren't. But since he wasn't holding them when he came out of the bathroom, that means he must have wrapped them in a towel. Again, very strange.

Abe emerges from the bedroom wearing a clean pair of jeans and a baggy green T-shirt. The second I see him, I blurt out, "What's going on, Abe?"

Abe doesn't say anything right away. He sinks onto the couch beside me. "What do you mean?"

"What were those stains on your scrubs?"

"What?"

He's stalling for time, pretending he has no idea what I'm talking about. So I tell him my suspicions, just to see his face. "It looked like blood."

His face grows several shades paler. That's not the reaction I was hoping for. I wanted him to laugh like I'd said something preposterous. *Scrubs covered with several pints of blood? How could you think something so silly?*

"I was helping Dr. Kovak with a procedure at the clinic," he explains. "It… it got a little messy."

And then I notice his hands. More specifically, I notice his fingernails. There's a dark-brown substance caked into the nails that didn't entirely come out in the shower.

"You weren't wearing gloves during the procedure?" I ask.

He stammers out some sort of explanation that

doesn't make any sense. Whatever he said, it's so clear that he's lying to me. Except *why*?

"What were you doing, Abe?" I say.

His eyes drop, avoiding mine. "Just working."

"You swear?"

His shoulders heave. "I swear."

I have given him every chance to tell me the truth about what he was doing. And he's still lying through his teeth.

14

I HARDLY SEE ABE FOR THE NEXT FEW DAYS. HE'S clearly avoiding me.

I'm too agitated to study. How can I? Every time I try to concentrate on anatomy, I start imagining what Abe could possibly be hiding from me. Why were his clothes covered in blood? Why was it caked into his nails?

When I get home from class today, I discover a huge basket of flowers that takes up half my bed. A lavender card is embedded between two lilies, and I open it up to see Abe's handwriting: *Please forgive me.*

Rachel is lying in my bed with headphones over her ears. She pulls them off and makes a face.

"I think your boyfriend is single-handedly supporting the flower industry."

I bring my nose close to the bouquet to inhale the scent. I love lilies, and Abe knows it. And the fact that he doesn't have much money to drop on flowers makes the gesture even sweeter. I almost feel guilty.

Almost.

"Seriously," Rachel says, "will you just forgive him already? Before I asphyxiate from all the pollen?"

I stare at my roommate in surprise. "You approve of my relationship with Abe? I can't believe it."

Rachel shrugs. "Well, he appears to make you happy and… I guess he's not as horrible as most guys." She shakes her head. "So what despicable thing did he do to piss you off anyway?"

I just shake my head. I wish I could tell Rachel everything. But even though we've been living together for months, I don't trust Rachel. Especially since I'm fairly sure she's hooking up with someone in the class, and she won't tell me who. She frequently disappears late into the night and returns with her hair disheveled and a secret smile on her face. I asked her about it once, and she told me she didn't have time for silly things like sex.

Anyway, this is Abe's secret, and I don't want to share it with just anybody, even if I don't know what it is.

Instead, I leave the flowers on the bed and drive back to the hospital. I've got to talk to *someone* about this. But Abe is my best friend at this school—really, my only close friend. So there's one other person who comes to mind that I can confide in.

Dr. Patrice Winters's office is directly above the anatomy labs. I saw her one time, as required, when school first started, but the session barely lasted half an hour because I didn't feel like I had much to say back then. Today, I've got a lot more to talk about.

It's a long shot that she'll be around—I fully expect to have to make an appointment—but I figure it can't hurt to drop by. Patrice is a therapist, so anything I tell her will be confidential, and that's exactly what I'm looking for right now.

I'm surprised to see the door to her office is ajar. I walk over tentatively but stop when I hear a familiar voice from inside. I recognize it instantly as belonging to Dr. Conlon.

"Thank you so much, Patrice," he's saying. "You're the best. Really."

"Anything for you, Matt," she replies.

I freeze. I may just be a med student, but I'm also a girl, and I recognize flirtation. Patrice's words are just dripping with it. Is there something going on between the two of them? I wouldn't be surprised. But if there were, wouldn't they close the door all the way?

Before I can contemplate further, the door is yanked open in front of me, and I nearly fall into the office. Dr. Conlon's blue eyes widen when he sees me. "Heather?"

I straighten up, trying to smile. Patrice looks decidedly annoyed, but her face changes when she hears Dr. Conlon say my name. Her features soften, and she holds out her hand to me.

"Heather McKinley," she says. "Please come in."

It's like she's been waiting for me. Creepy.

Dr. Conlon limps off and closes the door behind him. Patrice gestures at the sofa in front of her desk, which is light blue, and I sink into it so deeply that I'm worried I might not be able to get up. Patrice has mood lighting going on in here, although part of me wonders if that was for Dr. Conlon's benefit.

"So, Heather," Patrice says, sliding a pair of half-moon glasses up her narrow nose. "What brings you to see me?"

"It's…" I want to tell her everything, but I can't. This woman makes me uncomfortable. "It's silly."

"Nothing is silly, Heather," she assures me.

I squeeze my fists together. Okay, I need to just say it. If I don't talk to somebody about this, I'm going to burst. Even if that somebody is Patrice.

"It's about my boyfriend," I say. "He's a student here. Abe Kaufman."

Patrice nods.

"He's acting weird," I continue. "I mean, *really* weird."

Patrice nods again.

"Not like he's on drugs or anything," I add quickly. "I don't think so. I mean, definitely not. But…"

"Yes?"

I chew on my lower lip, not sure how much I can say. I don't want to get Abe in trouble, but if this session is truly confidential, I should be able to tell her everything. "I found blood all over his scrubs. Like, soaking them."

Patrice nods yet again. I wish she'd say something. I'm beginning to regret having come to her. This lady is the opposite of what I'd call "understanding." But I'm already telling her, so I may as well go through with it. And anyway, there's nothing to tell. Not yet.

"It was weird, that's all," I say. "And it was… scary."

"So he was injured?"

"No, that's the thing." I think back to that night when I burst into the bathroom while he was showering. "I'm pretty sure he wasn't injured. I saw him in just a towel, and he wasn't bleeding from anywhere. So where did all that blood come from?"

"What did he tell you?"

"He works part-time at a clinic." I crinkle my nose. "He said he was doing some *procedure*, and it got messy."

"That sounds like a reasonable explanation."

"Except why was the blood on his *hands* too?"

"On his hands?"

"In his fingernails. I *saw* it."

Patrice is quiet for a moment, as if turning over this revelation in her head. "So you believe he's lying to you."

"Yes."

"And what is it that you think he's done?"

Even though it was an obvious question to ask, it throws me off-balance. Because there is only one conclusion that can be drawn after seeing that much blood on my boyfriend's clothing.

"I don't know," I finally reply. "Abe is a good guy. I don't believe he'd… you know…"

"Perhaps it was less blood than you thought?" Patrice suggests.

"Maybe…"

Maybe she's right. Yes, it looked like a lot of blood. But I once had a simple nosebleed that completely soaked my shirt. Just because it was all over his clothes, that doesn't mean it was some person's lifeblood. Maybe it really was just a procedure he was assisting in, just like he told me.

But I can't shake the feeling that he was lying to me.

I've stopped studying at the library because I don't want to run into Abe.

Instead, I have found a little empty classroom that is fairly quiet, and I can spread out my books and attempt to get some work done. It's harder to study without Abe, but I can't be around him right now.

I've managed to get through an hour of anatomy, although I'm not sure if any of it is sticking. I've got a little time left before the final exam, and I've got two passing grades under my belt. I can make it through this exam. I don't need Abe.

Although that's not the reason I want to see him so badly right now.

I take a break from anatomy and head to the bathroom. After I relieve my bladder, I look at my reflection in the mirror while I'm washing my hands. I look exhausted. My hair is pulled back in a messy ponytail, and not the stylish kind. My face looks very pale, and I've got a blemish popping up on my chin. I splash some water on my face, and that brings a tiny bit of color into my cheeks, but it doesn't really help much.

Like I always do when I'm in here, I look down at the crack in the sink. There's no memorial for Darcie Peterson—the girl who died here last year—and this is as close as it gets. It used to freak me out, but as the term has gone on, it has reminded me to be strong. Yes, med school is hard. But there are worse things.

I could be dead.

The door to the bathroom swings open, and one of my classmates, a stringy guy named Victor, enters the small space. Except this is a ladies' room—not a coed bathroom. When he sees me standing there, he doesn't leave.

"Hey, Heather," he says.

"Uh." I glance pointedly at the row of stalls. "This is the *girls'* bathroom, you know."

"Oh!" His eyes widen like he didn't realize it, although I don't know how that's possible. "Sorry!"

And yet he still doesn't leave.

"Hey," he says. "Are you studying with Abe right now?"

The question is almost as strange as the fact that Victor doesn't seem to be making any motion to exit the ladies' room. Why is he asking me about Abe? I don't think I've seen Victor exchange two words with him. "No…"

"Do you know where he is?"

I shake my head. "I'm not sure. Back at the dorms, maybe."

"Sorry." He rubs his hands together. "I thought you two were an item."

"We are." Sort of. "But he's… He's not here."

"Okay…" Victor considers this new development. "Well, when you see him, can you tell him I'm looking for him? And it's, like, *important*."

I frown at Victor. He's wearing jeans and a T-shirt,

and I can't help but notice how painfully skinny he is. He's shifting between his sneakers, squeezing his shaky hands together. He looks more anxious than he should, considering we don't have any exams this week.

"Is everything okay?" I ask him.

"Just struggling a bit. You know." He lets out an odd-sounding laugh. "Anyway, make sure you tell Abe I'm looking for him. Please?"

I am troubled by the note of desperation in Victor's voice. "Okay," I agree.

What is going on here? He sounds the same way that Gerald/Harold guy sounded in the parking lot when he wanted to talk to Abe. Abe seemed so baffled when that happened. But now, I wonder if that was all an act.

What is my boyfriend hiding from me?

15

Our final exam is tomorrow morning.

I've still got a few hours left in the evening until I'm too tired to think straight. The exam should be in the forefront of my brain right now, but all I can think about is Abe. I can't stop wondering what he's hiding from me and why he refuses to tell me the truth. Until I get an answer, I'm not going to be able to focus.

My only choice is to confront him.

I'm going up to Abe's room, and I'm going to offer him an ultimatum: the truth or I walk. Simple as that. If Abe cares about me, he'll make the right decision.

I hope.

I felt so sure of myself when I composed my plan to confront Abe, but as I walk up the stairs, it occurs to me that I've never successfully talked anybody into anything in my life. I'm a complete pushover. That's why I always try to bring friends with me shopping, so the saleslady won't talk me into buying half the store. How am I going to be strong enough to force Abe to tell me what is obviously a really big secret?

And then there's the other side of the coin. If he does confess, maybe I won't want to hear it. What if he really did kill someone? What then?

But no. It can't be that. It *can't*.

I knock on the door to Abe and Mason's apartment and wait patiently for the sound of Abe's heavy footsteps. They don't come, nor does the sound of Mason's comparatively lighter footsteps. The inside of the dorm room is completely silent.

It hadn't even occurred to me that Abe wouldn't be home. But of course, it's the night before the big exam. Everyone is at the library.

I clench my fists in frustration. It's Abe's fault that I can't focus, and now he's not even home. What now?

On a whim, I rest my hand on the doorknob. I hadn't really expected it to be unlocked, but then the knob turns under my palm. I apply some gentle pressure, and the door swings open.

"Hello?" I call out.

There's no answer. Nobody is home. Abe and Mason both went out, leaving their dorm room unlocked.

It is, in fact, a golden opportunity.

But I can't go into Abe's room and start shuffling through his things without his permission. That would be a terrible thing to do. I wouldn't be able to forgive myself, and moreover, if he found out, he would never forgive me.

Then again, Abe is never going to tell me the truth. If I don't figure it out on my own, we are done.

Before I can stop myself, I enter the dorm room. As always, it's a bit of a mess, but nothing unusual. I step around a pair of jeans that have been abandoned on the floor and also a pair of scrubs, although these scrubs, thankfully, are not stained with blood.

And then I'm in Abe and Mason's bedroom.

I walk over to Abe's desk, pushing away the surge of guilt in my chest. I'm doing this for *us*—so that our relationship has a chance. I can't take his lies anymore, but maybe if I find out the truth on my own, it will be something I can live with.

Yeah, just keep telling yourself that, Heather.

Abe's desk is a complete pigsty. It's even worse than the rest of the apartment. There are papers stacked everywhere. And what's even stranger is that it doesn't look like the papers have anything to do with anatomy or even biochemistry. I sift through them, a sense of growing dread in the pit of my stomach.

What the hell is all this?

And then, while I'm holding a stack of papers, I spot something else lying on the desk. Something that terrifies me beyond words.

Oh no. This is so much worse than I ever could have imagined.

PART II

ABE

16

THE FIRST DAY

"Look to your left and look to your right. In four years, both of these people will be doctors."

Following the instructions of the dean of the medical school, I look to my left, coming face-to-face with a maroon-painted wall. I blink a few times then turn to my right, where there is an empty seat. And next to that empty seat is my roommate, Mason, who looks like he has completely lost respect for me now that I'm playing along with the dean.

I can't blame him.

I'm about to redirect my attention back to the dean when something catches my eye. Or should I say, someone. *Her.*

The girl I'm going to marry.

Okay, you're rolling your eyes right now. I don't blame you. I get it—I sound like a tool saying that. My friends from college would kick my ass. But when you know, you know. And right now, I *know.*

I'm not what you'd call a ladies' man. I'm not a romantic either. But right now, I can practically hear harps playing in the background. I'd do anything for her. I'd do anything to get her.

For most of the rest of the morning, I can't quit staring at her. I try not to be too obvious about it, but sheesh. I've got it bad.

And then at lunch, I manage to step on her toes with my big clumsy foot. And I find out her name is Heather. And she has a boyfriend.

But who knows? Maybe I'll get lucky.

Stranger things have happened.

I NEED A JOB.

Some of the other students here are loaded. Mason, for example. I'm not loaded. My parents both work blue-collar jobs, and I took out so much money in loans that if I start to think about it too much, I want to throw up.

That's why during my first week of classes, I start searching for a part-time job. Something with pretty flexible hours and hopefully decent pay. When I see an ad on the bulletin board outside the anatomy lab for part-time work at a medical clinic, it seems perfect.

Until I get there.

First of all, it's in a terrible part of town. If I wasn't me, I'd be scared to walk around this neighborhood. And Dr. Stanley Kovak's clinic is a dive. That's really the only word for it—well, the nicest word I can think of, anyway. His waiting room is a tiny area, barely bigger than a closet, with three folding chairs pushed up against a wall, peeling white paint, and one dim light bulb that dangles precariously from the ceiling. The entire place smells like a urinal.

But the pay? It's *really* good. Way better than McDonald's. So I stick around for the interview.

There's no receptionist to be seen, so I take a seat on one of the folding chairs, which creaks ominously under my weight. I had been "buzzed" in, so I assume that Dr. Kovak knows I'm here. There are no magazines to read in the waiting room, but it seems like the people who come to a clinic like this aren't that excited to be thumbing through a copy of *Good Housekeeping*.

After several minutes, the door to the back opens, and a man sticks his head out. "Abraham Kaufman?"

"Abe," I say, rising to my feet.

His eyes widen slightly at my size, which isn't an entirely unusual reaction.

"Come on in," the man says. "I'm Stan Kovak."

Dr. Kovak is at least half a foot shorter than me with very close-cropped gray hair on his head, fine lines on his tanned skin, and two days' worth of stubble on his chin. He's wearing rumpled blue scrubs that look like he slept in them. He herds me down a short, poorly lit hallway to a room with what appears to be a long stretcher in it. There's a sheet on the stretcher, which is covered in brown stains. Thankfully, he doesn't tell me to sit on it.

"So you're applying for the job?" he asks me.

"That's right," I say. I hand him a folder, containing references from former jobs I've held: working as a cashier at a grocery store, taking tickets at the movie theater, and working as a lifeguard for three summers.

Kovak takes the folder but simply lays it down on the counter without even flipping through it. "I desperately need help." He rubs the stubble on his chin. "It can get very busy here, and my assistant just quit. You said you're a medical student?"

"Yeah."

"What year?"

"First."

He nods in approval. "I get a lot of students from the school at the clinic. It's a long wait for the student health center, so they like to come here instead. I need help checking them in, getting vital signs, scheduling appointments. It'll be a good experience for you."

"I'm sure it will be," I say confidently, although something about this examining room makes me uneasy. What are those brown stains on the sheet? "I'd be thrilled to work here."

"Great." He folds his arms across his chest. "When can you start?"

"That's it? I got the job?"

He cracks a smile. "You're the only one to apply."

Something about this revelation sets off a red flag in the back of my head. How could I be the only one to apply for such a lucrative job? It pays more than twice as much as what I made at the supermarket. Then again, if he wants a medical student, most of the kids in the class are too busy to work on top of everything. And I was really quick to apply. What's that thing they say about not looking a gift horse in the mouth?

"I can start tomorrow," I tell him.

17

I'VE NEVER HAD A SERIOUS GIRLFRIEND BEFORE.

I've dated. But between being premed and working, on top of school, there was never time to squeeze in a relationship. You can only cancel on a girl so many times because you need to pick up an extra shift at the supermarket before she stops returning your messages.

And now I'm as busy as I've ever been. Anatomy and biochemistry and three nights a week at Dr. Kovak's clinic doesn't leave much time for a girlfriend. I need to keep my head down and focus on getting through the next four years.

Fortunately or unfortunately, Heather is ridiculously out of my league. The more I get to know her and we become friends, the more painfully obvious that is. I'm kidding myself by holding out even the tiniest hope I'll end up with her.

As we're studying the female pelvis side by side in the library, Heather crinkles her nose like she always does when she doesn't understand something (which I'm sad to say is a lot). She leans forward over our anatomy atlas, and I get a whiff of her shampoo. Peaches, like usual. I'm starting to love the smell of peaches. I bought a bunch of them for our refrigerator, just so I can sniff them.

Okay, as I'm saying it, I realize how weird that sounds.

"Why is the female pelvis so confusing?" Heather moans.

She flips the anatomy atlas upside down as if that might clarify things.

"I know, it's confusing," I agree. Although truthfully, I'm not *that* confused. I've always learned things quickly. But it seems to comfort Heather when I agree with her about the difficulty of the material.

She yawns. "Oh God, I am *so* tired right now."

I expect her to reach for her coffee and take another sip (she's an addict like I am), but instead, she does something unexpected. She drops her head onto my shoulder and shuts her eyes.

I freeze, scared to move because I don't want her to pull away, and I *really* don't want her to realize how much this is turning me on. *Don't look down, for crap's sake!* She's got to hear my heart pounding in my chest. The people at the next table can probably hear it.

Then Heather lifts her head and yawns again. "Maybe I need to take a break. I'm going to walk around a little."

"Sure," I reply, too quickly. "Do you want to grab some more coffee?"

She shakes her head.

"Actually," she says. "I was thinking I'd give Landon a call. Is that okay?"

Landon. The asshole boyfriend. I hate that guy.

"Go for it," I say, forcing a smile. "Tell Landon hi," I add, then I hate myself.

My hands clench into fists as I watch Heather fiddling with her phone as she leaves the library. I need to stop thinking about Heather. For one, she's got a boyfriend. Also, I've got enough on my plate.

"Quit staring at Heather, you perv."

The voice above my head nearly makes me jump out of my skin until Mason slides into the seat next to mine, a knowing grin spreading across his face. Mason can be annoying, but it's hard not to like the guy. He's entertaining, and he's incredibly funny, especially if you're not someone who's easily offended. Before classes revved up and I got my job, we shot pool together a few times at a local bar and had a great time, but now, we're both far too busy. I've got to admire all the hours he puts into his schoolwork—he sleeps as little as I do, even though he's not working a job on the side.

"Hey, Hulk," Mason says, that grin still plastered on his face. He's been calling me Hulk, after the Incredible Hulk from the comic books. I admit it's not an entirely unfair comparison. "So what's going on with you two?"

"I don't know what you're talking about," I lie.

"Bullshit," Mason says.

I shrug innocently.

"Yeah, okay." His grin twists into a smirk. "I can see why you don't like her. I mean, she's only a five. Maybe a six at best."

Asshole.

"Just 'fess up," he says. "Maybe I can help you."

I look at Mason with some interest. I've noticed the way the pretty girls in our class drool over him. Maybe he actually could give me some decent advice.

"Okay, fine," I say. "I'm interested in her."

"No kidding."

I fold my arms across my chest. "So what do I do? How do I get her?"

"First off," Mason says, "you need to grow a pair, Abe. Seriously, man. Have some confidence—Heather isn't that great. She's just Heather. She's not out of your league or anything."

That's debatable.

"What about the boyfriend, though?" I say.

Mason laughs. "Boyfriend? Come on—that won't last. Give it two more weeks."

And as it turns out, he's right.

Two weeks later, on the dot, Heather knocks on the door to my dorm apartment. I hadn't been expecting her, and strangely enough, when she sees me, her face falls.

"Oh," she says. "Is, um, Mason here?"

Why is she looking for Mason? She hardly talks to him, even in the lab. She seems to hate him, based on the comments she's made.

"No," I say. "He's probably at the library."

"Oh," she says again. And then her face crumples.

"Heather…" I follow her to our futon, where she collapses into deep, wracking sobs. She buries her face in her small hands, and I rub her shoulders to comfort her. Comforting Heather is not a chore. I feel sleazy, though, about using the fact that she's sad as an excuse to touch her. Then I feel like a tool for feeling sleazy.

"Landon broke up with me," she blurts out between tears.

Landon broke up with her? The asshole boyfriend is out of the picture? Holy shit, that's the best news I've heard all year. Except…

Why the hell did she come here looking for *Mason*?

Oh. *Oh*.

I get it now. She's looking for a little rebound hook-up. And the first person she thought of was Mason. *Mason*. Not me. I'm not even on her short list.

Shit, if Mason were here instead of me, they'd be in our bedroom hooking up right now. Well, maybe not. Mason wouldn't do that to me. But just the fact that it was even a remote possibility makes me furious.

Mason's the biggest asshole in the class, and Heather wanted to hook up with him. There's probably a lesson in that. If I want Heather, I should be a jerk to her. Being a nice guy is getting me nowhere.

But I'm not a jerk. I'm a nice guy who's never done a bad thing in my whole life.

Still, Mason's right about one thing. It's time to grow a pair. So I lean forward, and before I have a chance to chicken out or overthink things, I kiss her.

"Abe?" She gasps for a second before she melts against me.

And here's the shocking part… She doesn't slap me. She doesn't pull away either. Against all odds, she's kissing me back. She's surprised, but it turns out she wants me too. Not as much as I want her, but no pressure there.

Just like that, she's mine.

18

NOBODY AT SCHOOL LIKES PATRICE MUCH, BUT WE ALL have to see her. It's *required.*

Patrice is in her early forties with brown hair in a pixie cut and long legs. She's not bad looking, but I don't find her remotely attractive. Her office consists of several shelves of alternating books and dolls. (Why dolls? We're not children. I swear to God, if we do any role-playing with Raggedy Ann, I am out of here.) She has a small desk in the corner of the room, but she sits in a chair that faces a sky-blue sofa. When I sit down on the sofa, I feel myself sinking into the cushions to the point where it might take me a good minute or two to get back on my feet. Maybe that's the point.

"I want you to put yourself at ease," Patrice says. "I want this to be a safe environment for you."

I wish I were anywhere but here.

"Tell me, Abe," Patrice says. "How has school been going so far?"

"Uh, fine."

"Just fine? Not stressing you out?"

"I'm not on *drugs*, if that's what you're asking."

Patrice raises an eyebrow, but who are we kidding? That's why I'm here. I'm here because there is a rampant drug problem at the school, and they don't want anyone else overdosing this year.

But I don't do drugs. I would never. I don't even drink, for Christ's sake. Coffee is my worst vice.

Patrice crosses her long legs. "I just know how stressful medical school can be. I want you to know this is a safe space."

"Okay, got it."

"And if there's anything you need to talk about"—she leans forward, as if she's about to share a secret—"you can come to me. Anything you say will be confidential."

"Great," I say. "So… can I go now?"

Patrice frowns and scribbles something down on the little pad of paper on her lap. Then she looks like she's underlining whatever she wrote. I can only imagine what it says. I don't want to be labeled as uncooperative, but I don't have time to get my head shrunk. I don't need it either.

"Yes, Abe," she finally says, "we can conclude our session. But please keep me in mind if you have any concerns in the future."

I will never come here again.

19

THERE'S SOMETHING SKETCHY ABOUT KOVAK'S CLINIC.

No kidding, right? I knew it from the start, before I signed up to work here. But now I have started to wonder if it's even worse than what I thought.

For starters, why do so many of his patients pay in cash? I get that insurance is a pain in the ass, but medical care is expensive. And yet at least half of all his patients slip me a pile of bills on their way out.

And then there's the large number of students who come by the clinic. There's nothing specifically suspicious about that, given that we are so close to both a large college and the medical school, but a lot of them also pay in cash. Which seems pretty strange for a 20-year-old college student.

Plus, every single one of them says the same thing when they make an appointment. *I've got a cough that won't go away.* Those exact words. It's not even cold and flu season yet!

Today, I'm sitting at the tiny desk in the waiting area

when a student from my class named Victor comes in through the heavy wooden door that protects the clinic from the questionable neighborhood that surrounds us. Victor is nearly as tall as I am but skinny as a string bean and always struck me as the kind of guy who never stops moving. When he sees me, he stops short, but then a knowing smile lights his face.

"Abe," he says. "Hey."

"Hey." I look down at the intake form in front of me. "You're here for… a cough that won't go away?"

He winks at me. "You know it."

Okay…

After I send Victor into the examining room, he is in there for roughly five seconds, which I guess is long enough for Kovak to examine his throat and do whatever is apparently worth the stack of cash he hands me on the way out. Also, I didn't hear him cough once.

When Victor is gone, I lock the cash in the desk drawer, like Kovak instructed me to do. The desk has two locked drawers—one contains the cash, and the other has only been opened once. I don't have the key, but I know that there's a gun in that drawer—loaded.

There's nobody here at the moment, so I leave my desk and head to the examining room that Victor just vacated. Kovak is inside the room, washing his hands. He has good hygiene, at least. Although I know for a fact that the sheets on the stretcher haven't been washed since I've been working here.

"Dr. Kovak?" I say tentatively.

He wipes his hands on the pants of his scrubs and turns to me with a smile. "Yes, Abe?"

I don't know what to say next. There's a question running through my head, but I'm not sure how to say it. *Are you dealing drugs to students?* How can I ask that of my boss?

"Are you…" I clench my hands into fists and then release them. It would be almost ridiculously easy to pick Kovak up by his shirt collar and shake the answers out of him, but I'm not that kind of person. "What was Victor here for?"

"Just a cough," he says. And then he winks at me.

What the hell is up with all the winking?

"Right." I look behind me at the waiting room to make sure it's empty. "But he wasn't actually coughing."

Kovak keeps the smile plastered on his face as he looks up at me. "Abe," he says, "you're happy at this job, aren't you?"

"Uh, yeah…"

"And I pay you very well, right?"

That's an understatement. In addition to my salary, he will often slip me a cut of the cash that comes in every day. "Yes, sir."

He has to reach up to put a hand on my shoulder. "I want you to know how much I value your help here. I hope you'll continue to work with me. Honestly, I'm not sure what I'd do if you ever left."

His dark-brown eyes are trained on my face. Despite the fact that he's nearly a head shorter than me, a shiver of fear goes down my spine as I think about the gun in that desk drawer.

"I'll stay," I say softly.

He claps my shoulder. "That's m'boy."

DeWitt medical school has a drug problem. Everybody knows it. So many students have died that people refer to the school as Dead Med. But I never knew where the drugs came from until now.

And not just that, but somebody is feeding the students to this clinic. They are being sent here in droves. And if the rumors are true, that person is one of our professors—not just that, but a professor with access to the newest class of students.

There's only one name that comes to mind. Only one professor who works extensively with first-year medical students. Who knows which ones are struggling. Who does one-on-one tutoring because he is just *so* nice.

And that's Dr. Conlon, our anatomy professor.

20

The popcorn is popped, and I'm waiting for Heather to come over with a movie. We're watching some chick flick about a girl who hates this guy but then I guess they fall in love. No, I don't want to see it, and no, I haven't grown a vagina. But Heather seemed excited about this movie, so we're watching it, end of story.

The only problem is I can't stop thinking about that clinic.

Dr. Kovak is selling drugs to students. I'm certain of it now. And if that's the case, I can't keep working there. I can't be part of that.

Except I'm not sure he'll let me leave.

Because it's not just students he treats at the clinic. There have been some really unsavory men who have shown up to be treated—one guy had what looked like a knife wound *on his face*. Kovak isn't just going to let me leave with a smile and wave. I know way too much for that.

Plus, the man has a gun.

I don't know what to do. I'm scared to quit or blow the whistle, but I can't just let this keep going on. I've got to *do* something. I have nowhere to turn.

I try to push thoughts of Stanley Kovak out of my head as I make an effort to clean up the coffee table. I toss the half-eaten pizza slice from last night in the trash and brush crumbs off the futon. Our place is a mess—I know it. I'm a slob, and Mason's spent his whole life having maids pick up after him, so between the two of us, we're not in great shape.

Heather arrives at my door right on time. She's wearing a tank top and jeans and just looks so cute that I want to forget the dopey movie and hook up on the futon instead.

She can never know what goes on at the clinic where I work. I would *die* if she found out.

She grins at me. "Got the popcorn?"

I nod. "Yep."

Heather catches the look on my face. "Abe, what's wrong? Don't you want to see this movie?"

I force a smile. "Yeah, definitely."

She puts her hands on her hips.

"Okay, fine," I say. "I don't want to see it. But I'm willing to watch it."

Heather blinks at me. "Why?"

"Because," I say. "I want to hang out with you. Who cares what we're watching?"

Her eyes soften. "Tell you what," she says. "Let me go grab my purse, and we'll go out and see that zombie apocalypse movie that's playing in the theater."

I stare at her. "Seriously?"

"Seriously."

"You really want to see that?" It's hard for me to believe any woman would want to see that movie.

"I just want to hang out with you," Heather says, and she winks. "Besides, zombies are awesome. No?"

I'm going to marry her someday. I've never wanted anything this badly in my life, even getting into med school.

"Heather," I say. "I love…" Crap. I can't say it. "I love seeing movies with you. A lot."

Her brown eyes twinkle. "I love seeing movies with you too. A lot."

I can't screw this up. I wish I had never taken that stupid job.

21

Patrice said that if I had a problem, I could come to her and that it would be confidential. Now I've got a problem, and it better be confidential, because if she tells anyone, I might end up in handcuffs.

I make an appointment with her for immediately after anatomy lab is over—I'm not going to smell great, but she'll have to deal with it. Except just as I am leaving the lab, Dr. Conlon approaches me, gripping his cane in his left hand. Despite the fact that he walks with a cane, he is the youngest of all our professors by at least a decade, and yet there is a weariness in his eyes that makes him look older.

"Dr. Kaufman," he says.

"Uh, hi." I shift between my dirty sneakers, which I only wear for anatomy lab. The second I get out of here, I change into another pair. "What's up?"

Like the rest of us, Dr. Conlon wears scrubs to the lab. And also like the rest of us, he always manages to glove up and get dirty over the course of the four to five hours. I'm sure he is just as eager to change into clean clothes as I am, but here we are. He looks me over, staring at me like he is sizing me up. "Did you spray down the body before you covered it?"

"Uh…" I tug at the collar of my scrubs, wanting desperately to change into something that doesn't have formaldehyde and flecks of preserved intestines on it. "Yes?"

He doesn't move away from the entrance to the door —he's still blocking me. "It looked desiccated today. You need to do a better job."

"Okay. I will." When he doesn't move aside, I add, "You mean *now*?"

"Yes, Dr. Kaufman. *Now*."

This sharp tone is not what I have come to expect from Dr. Conlon. He's generally really nice in the lab. Easygoing. Everyone in the class seems to like him, even students who aren't doing as well in anatomy. Why is he suddenly being an asshole?

"I, uh… I have an appointment to get to," I explain.

"An appointment?"

"With Patrice."

He sucks in a breath when I tell him this. Despite the fact that we have all been encouraged to have regular visits with Patrice, he looks distinctly unhappy to hear that I am going to see her. Except why?

Is he worried about something I might say to her?

My gut is telling me Dr. Conlon is the one pushing students in the direction of Kovak's clinic. After all, I heard about the clinic from the sign posted on the bulletin board outside the anatomy lab. And now, right after I confronted Kovak, he's suddenly giving me a hard time. Maybe Kovak has shared my feelings about the clinic.

Maybe that's why he doesn't want me to talk to Patrice. He's afraid of what I might reveal to her.

"Fine," he finally says. "Go. Just don't forget next time."

He doesn't have to tell me twice.

Even though I'm in a rush, there is no way I am going to Patrice's office without changing first. I swap out my scrubs for the T-shirt and jeans I had been wearing before, and I stuff my tainted sneakers in my locker. By the time I make it to Patrice's office, she is waiting by the door, looking pointedly at her watch.

"Sorry," I say breathlessly. "It was... I got... held up."

She nods and steps aside to let me enter the office. I plop down on her sofa, and same as last time, the cushions collapse under my weight. A spring pops under my butt, and I sink even a little deeper.

Patrice takes her place in a chair across from me and folds one of her long legs over the other. Like last time, she's got that pad of paper on her lap, and for a moment, I wonder if I have made a mistake coming here. I don't like the idea of her writing down everything that I'm saying.

"I'm so glad you contacted me, Abe," she says. "So few students have reached out this year. But I am here to help you."

"Right." I run my fingers through my hair, clutching at the strands hard enough that it hurts. "I know."

"Is there something in particular you wanted to talk to me about?"

"Uh…" I lean forward, my head now cupped between my giant hands. "I just…"

"What's wrong? Tell me."

Is this a bad idea? Once I tell Patrice, she's going to go to the administration and tell them everything. She has to. "If I were to tell you something that was… not entirely legal, would you have to report it to the dean? Or, uh… the police?"

She arches an eyebrow. "It depends what it is. But yes, if you inform me of a crime that might put other people in danger, I am obligated to report you."

Does this qualify as a crime that puts other people in danger? Several students have already died from drug overdoses. So I'm going to say yes.

"Abe? Do you have something to tell me?"

I don't want to put my entire medical career at risk. I'm not like Mason, who has parents who can lawyer up and save him. But at the same time, I can't do *nothing*. If there's a chance that the clinic is at fault for the student overdoses, I have to say something.

Even if it puts my *life* at risk.

"I think…" I heave a deep breath. "I think I know where the drugs are coming from."

Her eyes widen. "Oh?"

"Yes." I try to shift on the sofa, and it groans ominously. "I work at a clinic that a lot of students go to. I… I think the clinic is distributing drugs to students."

"You think?"

"I'm pretty sure."

She nods, her pen poised on that notebook of hers. "Where is this clinic?"

I give her the address, all the while trying to push away a sick feeling in the pit of my stomach. I have started the wheels rolling on something that could end up destroying my life. I don't know if I made a terrible mistake, but on the other hand, what else could I do?

"I'll look into it," she says.

"What are you going to do?"

She crosses her legs, her eyes on mine. "Don't worry. I'll be discreet."

I debate if I should tell her my suspicions about Dr. Conlon. The more I think about it, the more certain I feel that he is the one pushing students in the direction of that clinic. But I've seen Patrice talking to him many times, and I am pretty sure that they are friends. Maybe even more than friends. She might not appreciate the unfounded accusations, so I decide to keep my fool mouth shut.

22

Heather wanted me to come to her parents' house for Thanksgiving, but I begged off because Kovak offered to pay me double to work on Black Friday. I need money even more badly now that I've got a girlfriend. She always offers to pay, but I *hate* letting her do that.

Yes, I'm still working at the clinic. Patrice told me that the school is investigating the clinic but hasn't come up with anything yet. That's comforting, I suppose. Maybe I've got it all wrong. Maybe the whole operation is on the up-and-up.

Yeah, right.

The clinic is especially busy—a lot of people coming in and out. A lot of patients who have a "cough that won't go away." I try not to think about it. If Patrice said they're investigating, it's out of my hands.

It's close to midnight when we finish up with the last patient of the evening. Dr. Kovak is in very good spirits, which makes sense because we pulled in a fortune in cash tonight. He unlocks the desk drawer that contains all of the money, and he grins as he flips through the thick wad. He peels off a bunch of bills and thrusts them in my direction. "Thanks for your help tonight, Abe."

He might not be thanking me if he knew that I reported him to my school. But I'm no dummy, so I take the money.

Just as I'm stuffing the bills into my wallet, there is a loud banging on the door to the clinic. A hoarse voice on the other side of the door yells, "You in there, Kovak? Let me in!"

"Shit," Kovak mutters under his breath.

I look at him, confused. "Should we let him in?"

"We definitely should not."

The banging continues, growing louder by the second. Whoever is behind the door is not going away. "Let me in! You can't cut me off that way!"

Quietly, Kovak lifts up a potted plant in the corner of the room, revealing a key hidden beneath. He brings the key back to the desk and unlocks the bottom drawer. He pulls out the gun nestled within and lays it down on the table.

My heart is ratcheting in my chest. "You don't need a gun. I'm here."

"Trust me," he says. "You won't be able to handle him on your own."

Just as he says the words, the lock on the door splinters as it bursts open. The man standing before us is almost as big as I am, reeking of sweat, with his pupils so large that his eyes look black. His face is bright red, nearly purple.

And there's a knife clutched in his right hand.

Kovak is right. I can't take this guy on my own, not with a knife in his hand. But when Kovak raises the gun and points it at him, I am desperate to keep this from happening.

"You need to walk away, Hooper," Kovak says.

But the man isn't stopping. He barrels forward, his teeth bared. It's clear that Kovak doesn't want to shoot him, though, and that hesitation costs him. In a split second, the man, Hooper—unclear if that's his first or last name—has crossed the room and twisted the gun out of Kovak's hand. The gun falls to the floor as Hooper presses the blade of the knife against Kovak's throat.

"I want everything you've got," he snarls. "All the money and all the drugs." He looks up at me with his black pupils. "Get it right now, or he dies."

"The kid doesn't know where all that stuff is," Kovak manages. "I can get it for you if you let me go."

"Stop stalling!" the man snaps at him. "I want it *now*!"

Hooper presses the knife into Kovak's neck, slicing through his skin so that a drop of blood trickles down his throat. This guy is not listening to reason. He is going to murder my boss right here and right now.

Unless I do something to stop him.

The gun that fell out of Kovak's hand is still on the

floor. Hooper is too high to even register that it's there. I have to be quick because if he figures out what I'm doing, he will kill Kovak. But if I don't grab that gun, he might kill us both.

I do it fast. I scrape the gun up off the floor and wrap my fingers around it, pointing the muzzle in Hooper's direction. All I meant to do was threaten him so he'd let go of Kovak, but the second he sees the gun in my hand, he loses his shit. He pushes Kovak to the floor and turns his attention to me.

"What the hell do you think you're doing?" he growls at me. "You don't even know how to use that thing!"

Well, he's right about that. I've never shot a gun before. But it seems pretty self-explanatory.

Either way, I'm about to find out. Because this man is coming at me. And he is not stopping.

I pull the trigger on the gun. The shot that rings out is startlingly loud, and the kickback is strong enough that I almost feel like I've been shot. But the effect is instant. Hooper stops moving, his body goes limp, and he drops to the floor like a ragdoll.

I've never shot anyone before, but I was right—it wasn't hard. On my very first try, I nailed Hooper right in the chest. He's now lying on the floor, his eyes open but his body very still, and there is a pool of blood rapidly growing beneath him.

Oh Christ.

"He… he's dead," I choke out.

"No shit," Kovak breathes.

I thought I was in trouble before, when I was simply working at a clinic where I suspected drugs were being sold. But now, things are much, much worse. I have murdered a man. I shot him, and now he's dead at my feet.

I'm finished.

My legs give out beneath me, and I fall to my knees, burying my face in my hands. What the hell am I going to do? I am royally screwed. There is no coming back from this. My life is over.

"Kaufman," Kovak snaps at me. "No time for prayers. Get back on your feet."

I manage to raise my eyes from my hands to look up at him. Unlike me, Kovak doesn't look the slightest bit shaken by the dead man on the floor of the clinic. He has squared his jaw, and he's ready to get to business.

He's acting like this has happened to him before.

"Abe," he says in a voice that is gentler than before but still firm. "You need to pull yourself together—*now*. If somebody discovers a dead body in this clinic, we are both in a world of trouble."

He's right.

"But…" I shake my head. "What do we do?"

"First of all," he says, "get off the floor."

Obediently, I scramble to my feet. There's blood all over my scrub pants and my hands. There's blood everywhere.

"Good," Kovak says. "Now we need to get rid of the body."

"*What?*"

"Look," he says impatiently, "this guy was a lowlife

—nothing but trouble. That's why I cut him off. Nobody will ever miss him. And the ones who do will be glad he's gone. But if the police find him here, both of us are screwed. So we need to get him out of here. We need to make sure nothing connects us to his murder."

I stumble backward, my bloodstained hands in the air. "I'm not helping you get rid of a dead body."

"Fine. Do you want to call the police and spend the next ten to fifteen years in jail?"

"It was self-defense! He was coming at me!"

Kovak smirks. "And what do you think is going to happen when they dig deeper and find out what goes on at this clinic?"

"I… that has nothing to do with me."

"Yeah? Well, good luck trying to prove that with the court-appointed attorney."

He's right. I look so guilty right now. I'm the one who shot the guy, and I was working at a clinic that sells drugs to students. Not just that, but I told Patrice about it, so it's obvious that I knew what was going on. There is no way I will get out of this with my reputation unscathed.

I can kiss being a doctor goodbye. I can kiss *Heather* goodbye.

"I can't do this without you," Kovak says quietly. "I can't even lift him without your help."

That much is clear. This guy would be hard for me to handle on my own, and Kovak is a lot smaller than I am. It's going to take two of us to get rid of him.

Am I actually considering this? Am I contemplating *disposing of a dead body*?

"What..." I swallow a lump in my throat. "What do we do with him?"

A slow smile spreads across Kovak's face. "Don't worry. I've handled situations like this before. I know just the place."

23

We spend the rest of the night getting rid of the dead body.

By morning, Hooper is at the bottom of the lake about two hours away from here. We have cleaned all the blood off the floor of the waiting room, although if the police showed up, I'm sure they would be able to find traces of it. Probably big globs of it if they look hard enough. But Kovak says that when they do find Hooper's body, it's unlikely they will ever connect him with the clinic.

I just have to hope that he's right.

The sun has already risen in the sky by the time I get home from the worst night of my life. My scrubs are covered in Hooper's dried blood, and there is still some blood caked on my hands, but thankfully, I've got a coat to cover the worst of it. Mason is home, but he's a heavy sleeper.

The first thing I do when I get back to our dorm room is head straight for the shower. I strip off my bloody scrubs and abandon them on the floor of the bathroom. I don't know what exactly I'm going to do with them. I should probably burn them, except I'm not sure how. Anyway, I'll worry about it later.

I step into the shower and turn the heat up as high as it will go. As it turns out, it goes up pretty high. But I welcome the steaming hot water streaming down on my sore body. The scalding pain takes my mind off of what I just did.

I killed a man. I threw his body into a lake.

I will never be the same.

Okay, I can't let this drive me out of my mind. I'll get rid of the scrubs, and eventually, this will all be a distant memory. Things are going great with Heather, and I'm going to keep it that way. I'm going to marry her and spend the rest of my life making her happy. She doesn't have to ever know the terrible thing I did tonight.

I'm lathering my short red hair with shampoo when a sudden noise in the bathroom startles me. At first, I think it must be Mason, but then I realize that it's Heather. Naked Heather. In the bathroom. With *me*.

And my bloody scrubs are on the floor.

I rip back the curtain to discover her standing in the middle of the bathroom, her eyes widening at the sight of the pile of bloody scrubs. "What are you doing?" I cry.

The shock on her face breaks my heart. "I…"

"I'm in the shower!" I shout at her, as if that fact weren't painfully obvious. "You need to… to get out!"

I am screwing things up really badly. I have been

desperate to go to the next level with Heather, and under any other circumstances, I would be celebrating. But I'm too scared to think straight. I need her to leave —*now*. Before she looks down at the floor.

I finish showering as quickly as I possibly can. Of course, the dirty scrubs are still on the floor, and I don't know what to do with them. I roll them into a ball, wrap them in a towel, wrap a second towel around my waist, and then I come out of the bathroom.

When I enter the common area, Heather is sitting quietly on the couch. That seems like a good thing—she didn't storm out in a fury—but I can tell she's shaken. I also know that there's no way she's going to let me get away with this. Heather may be a pushover, but this is a big deal. I just kicked her out of the bathroom. Naked.

"Give me a second to get dressed," I tell her. "Okay?"

She nods wordlessly. But her gaze is focused on the towel I'm clutching in my hands.

I throw on a clean pair of jeans and a T-shirt. I don't know what to do with the scrubs, so I just stuff them under my mattress. I need a more permanent solution, but this will have to do for now. When I finally emerge from my bedroom, Heather is sitting on the sofa, hugging her arms to her chest. Her face is very white.

"What's going on, Abe?" she asks.

I sink onto the couch next to her. I need to gauge exactly what she saw and what she's thinking. Maybe she didn't see the bloodstains and all she's upset about is that I yelled at her. "What do you mean?"

Heather had been staring down at her lap, and she lifts her eyes. "What were those stains on your scrubs?"

Shit.

"What?" I say, stalling for time.

"It looked like blood."

What else looks like bloodstains? Nothing comes to mind, so I tell her a partial truth: "I was helping Dr. Kovak with a procedure at the clinic. It got a little messy."

Does she believe me? That wasn't just a few squirts of blood. Those scrubs had been saturated. And now, she is looking at something, and I'm not sure what it is until I follow her gaze.

She's looking at my fingernails. They still have blood caked into them.

"You weren't wearing gloves during the procedure?" she asks me.

I rub my neck with the back of my hand. "I changed them at one point. I guess…"

This is not an adequate explanation by any means, and I can tell from Heather's face that I'm not fooling anyone. But what the hell am I supposed to tell her? I can't tell her the truth, that's for sure. I wish I were a better liar.

She looks me straight in the eyes. "What were you doing last night, Abe?"

Great question.

"Just working," I say in a hoarse voice.

"You swear?"

Why is she forcing me to lie to her? Why can't she just freaking let this go? "I swear."

But she knows I'm not being honest. I'm not sure if things will ever be the same between us. I have screwed things up—maybe forever—with the first woman I've ever loved.

And that's not even the worst part. I still need to figure out what the hell to do with those scrubs.

24

I BUY A BOTTLE OF BARBECUE SAUCE AND EMPTY IT ONTO my bloody scrubs.

It's roughly the same color as the dried blood, and the smell overwhelms all other odors. Then I stuff the scrubs into a plastic bag and then put that plastic bag inside another plastic bag, put the whole thing deep into the trash bag, surrounded by old pizza and a Chinese food feast that Mason and I shared a few days ago. Then I grab the trash bag and bring it down to the dumpster myself. I'm not entirely sure when they empty the dumpster, but I think it's Monday or Tuesday.

I should be safe as long as nobody discovers the body before then.

On Sunday, I stop at a florist and purchase a bouquet of lilies, Heather's favorite, even though I spent a good minute eyeing the red roses. Roses are more romantic, but I go with my gut and get the lilies.

When I get back to the dorm, I race up the flight of stairs to Heather's room. I grip the lilies in my right hand as I knock on the door. Sweat is rapidly accumulating under my armpits. I don't know what I'll say when I see Heather. I don't want to make things worse, especially since I can't exactly tell her the truth.

I'm slightly relieved when Rachel answers the door, looking irritated as usual.

"Is… is Heather home?" I ask.

Rachel folds her arms across her chest. "She doesn't want to see you."

I hang my head. "Well, can you give her these flowers?" I ask in a small voice.

Rachel's eyes soften slightly. "Look, I… I don't know what happened between the two of you, but you really upset her."

"I know," I murmur. "I didn't mean to…"

"*You* never do," she says. I guess that "you" refers to all men.

Tell her that I love her, I want to say. But that's not the sort of thing that should come from a third party. I need to tell her myself.

25

I'M DONE WITH MY JOB AT KOVAK'S CLINIC.

I had been scheduled to work a few days after Thanksgiving weekend, but I didn't show up, and I ignored his calls. I can't imagine ever going back there. The thought makes me sick.

Instead, I head to the library at school to get some studying in. I've been keeping my head above water, but without a part-time job, maybe I could do even better. Maybe I could be at the top of the class, like Mason. I've earned enough money from my time with Kovak that I could take a few months off.

Heather and I usually study together, but she has been avoiding me since she caught me with those bloody scrubs. I figure I'll give her a few more days, and maybe she'll forget all about it.

Yeah, right.

Mason is usually at the library, so I search for him instead. I go through every single aisle of the library looking for him. I finally find my lab partner, Sasha, in the last aisle.

I've seen Sasha and Mason hook up. I'm not supposed to know about it, and Mason has been surprisingly close-lipped about the whole thing, but I once caught them coming out of the anatomy locker room together, and you could just tell. It's funny, because those two are the last couple I would've expected to start hooking up. I would have thought Sasha would know better.

"Have you seen Mason?" I ask her.

She's so small that I have to bend my neck nearly at a right angle to look her in the eyes.

A crease forms between Sasha's brows. "No, I haven't." She bites her lip. "Have you?"

I shake my head. Obviously not.

"If you see him," Sasha says, "could you tell him that I… I'd like to see him?"

It's no surprise that Mason is treating her like crap. She is way too nice for him.

"I'll tell him," I promise her, even though lecturing Mason on his love life is pretty low on my priority list.

Just as I'm settling down at an empty table to study by myself, my phone start ringing. The number for Kovak's clinic pops up on the phone, and I send it to voicemail. But then he calls again.

I should pick up. The responsible thing to do is to tell him that I'm quitting. That he will never see me again. I'll tell him that, and then I will block his number.

"Abe," he says on the other end of the line. "Weren't you scheduled to work tonight? We're pretty busy here."

"I was," I admit. "But the truth is, this job isn't really working out for me anymore, you know? So this is my notice."

"Huh." He's quiet for a moment. "Notice doesn't really work that way. Usually, you give somebody notice, and then you work for a little while longer, so they have a chance to find somebody new."

He's not wrong. But I would think given the circumstances, the rules don't really apply.

I grit my teeth. "Fine. How long do you need?"

"How about you work until I say you can stop."

A cold sensation slithers down my spine. "But…"

"Abe," he says, "you know I've got a camera set up in the waiting room of the clinic, right?"

My mouth falls open. I never saw a camera in the waiting room, but it makes sense he'd have one. He doesn't say the words, but the implication of what the camera picked up is clear.

I'm screwed.

"What do you want?" I manage.

"Hey, look, we're in this *together*, Abe," he says in an irritatingly casual voice. "I just need you to understand that. If you give me your loyalty, then we're good."

"Fine," I growl at him. "You have my loyalty."

"Fantastic. I'll see you in fifteen minutes."

I bury my face in my hands. I made a terrible mistake—I should have gotten away from there while I still could. Before, the worst that could have happened was being slapped with a drug charge. Now I've killed someone—I could go to prison for the rest of my life.

I'm trapped.

And what about Patrice? I told her what I suspected about the clinic, and she's "looking into it." What if she discovers what I've done?

This is a problem. *She* is a problem.

I'll figure out a way to deal with it later, though. For now, I've got to get to work.

When I get down to the hospital parking lot, I end up running into Mason. He's all alone, not dressed nearly warm enough for the weather. Even *I'm* wearing a coat, and I *never* get cold. But he doesn't seem like he even notices that it's twenty degrees out.

I walk toward him, even though he's in the opposite direction of my car. He's pacing back and forth rapidly, and as I get closer, I hear him mumbling to himself. He almost looks like he's on drugs, although I've never seen him at the clinic. I can't make out exactly what he's saying, but I get these chills that have nothing to do with the cold. I get this feeling that maybe I shouldn't bother Mason right now.

After all, I've got enough problems of my own.

26

I CAN'T FOCUS.

In lab today, it's just me and Rachel. She's been showing up a lot lately, and it seems like it's paying off. She knows her stuff. And for some reason, she's being nice to me today. She's trying to give me a pep talk about Heather.

"You know, Heather's a sucker for flowers," she says. "And chocolate. If you buy her enough of those, I'm sure she'll forgive you for everything." She adds, "And I'll put in a good word for you too."

"Thanks, Rachel."

Rachel smiles at me and leans over the body of our cadaver (Mason has nicknamed him Frank) to dissect the right arm. Rachel's T-shirt has become stretched out in the course of the lab, and I catch a quick glimpse of her breasts through the V-neck while she leans forward. I'm not the kind of guy who stares at women's chests, though—I swear. I don't know what the hell is wrong with me lately.

I didn't think I was that blatant about it, but somehow, Rachel seems to notice. She straightens up and glares at me.

"Hey," she snaps at me. "Eyes are up here, mister."

"Sorry," I stammer.

I'm mortified that she caught me looking. Is she going to tell anyone? That would be just what I need right now.

"Is there a problem here?"

Dr. Conlon has approached our table. His black eyebrows are raised at me. There's something distinctly threatening in the way that Dr. Conlon is looking at me.

I was never able to prove that Dr. Conlon is the one sending students to Kovak's clinic, but I still have a gut feeling it's him. He might act like Mr. Professor of the Year, but he's clearly got a dark side.

Dr. Conlon is hiding something. I would bet my life on it.

"No problem," I say, swallowing hard. "I'm just… not feeling that good."

"Do you need to leave?" Dr. Conlon asks me. His brows are furrowed in concern now.

"Yeah, I think I better…"

I need to talk to Patrice.

I CHANGE out of my scrubs first because I can't go anywhere when I'm reeking of cadaver juice. But my very next stop is Patrice's office.

I don't have an appointment, but the light is on

under her door, so I take a chance and knock. A second later, she pulls open the door. When she sees me standing there, a pleased smile lights her face.

"Abe," she says. "Please come in."

She steps back to let me enter her office and shuts the door behind us, but when she gestures at the man-eating sofa, I can't manage to sit down. She clearly doesn't like me hovering over her, but I don't care.

"Listen," I say, "did you investigate that clinic I told you about?"

Patrice lifts one of her penciled-in eyebrows. "Are you talking about the clinic where you work?"

There's a slight edge to her voice. Does she have any clue what happened at the clinic the other night? Does she know what my involvement is? Or maybe I'm just imagining it.

"Yes," I say. It's not like it's any secret.

She sits silently for a moment as panic floods my chest. She doesn't answer me for long enough that I'm tempted to sit down on the sofa just because I don't know if my legs can hold me anymore. But then she flashes me another smile.

"We investigated the clinic," she says, "and I can say that I don't think there are any issues. Seems like a regular medical clinic that has been treating a lot of students. No issues there."

I stare at her, not sure whether to feel relieved or stunned. The school investigated the clinic and found nothing? How is that possible? Kovak must be better at covering his tracks than I thought.

It's good news, though, isn't it? It means I don't have to worry.

It means Patrice isn't a threat.

"And what about Dr. Conlon?" I ask. "I think he might be behind the drug distribution."

Our anatomy professor is hiding something. I would bet my life on it. He *must* be the one sending students to that clinic.

I expected Patrice to react with shock at the accusation, but she somehow takes it in stride—like she was expecting it. Which makes me think I'm not so off base.

"I share your concerns about him," she says in a low voice. "He's been acting… well, I can't get into it. But I can't prove anything right now. I promise, though, I'll keep an eye on him."

Validation. Patrice thinks that Dr. Conlon is just as suspicious as I do.

"Thank you," I say.

"No, thank you for your concerns." She frowns. "The substance-abuse issue at the school has been a terrible thing, and I'll do anything to get to the bottom of it."

Is it terrible to say that I hope she doesn't?

27

I'M SLEEPING LIKE SHIT LATELY.

My grades haven't suffered yet, but I'm walking around with permanent purple circles under each eye. I don't know what's worse—the fact that I killed a man or the fact that I am being blackmailed over it.

Or maybe the fact that Heather hasn't spoken to me since we hooked up, and it doesn't seem like she ever will again. I even stopped going to anatomy lab because whenever she's there, she gives me this look that makes me sick to my stomach. I'm probably going to fail the final.

Right now, I am sitting on my bed, throwing a tennis ball against the wall. I keep doing it, over and over, *thunk thunk thunk*, trying to keep disturbing thoughts out of my head. It seems to work for a little while, but then I throw it just a little too hard and the ball takes a chunk of the plaster out of the wall. That kind of freaks me out. A couple of nights ago, I punched a hole in the wall in my sleep. I guess we're not getting our deposit back on this room.

My cell phone rings, and I jump to pick it up without even looking at who's calling. When I hear my mother's voice on the other line, I sort of wish I had checked. I'm not in the mood to talk to her right now.

"Abe," she says like I'm the same person I was when I left for med school. "I haven't heard from you in a while."

"Yeah," I say.

"How are you doing, sweetie?" she asks. "How's Heather?"

Oh, right. I haven't told her that Heather and I broke up. I certainly don't feel like telling her now. "She's fine."

"Are you eating enough?" she asks me.

"Yes," I mumble. I could probably afford not to eat for a year and be fine.

"Do you need me to bring you a warmer jacket?"

"No. I'm good."

"Do you need… money?" she asks me, as if she has money to spare. As if I would ever take her money when my parents need it to pay the bills.

"I don't need money."

"Okay." She can sense something is wrong, but she's not the sort of person who pushes me to share my feelings. "I just want you to know that I am so proud of you, Abe."

Oh Christ, this is the last thing I need. "Thanks."

"I mean it," she insists. "Your dad and I didn't even go to college. And now look at you. You graduated college with honors, and now you're going to be a *doctor*."

Sure, if I don't end up in prison for murder. "Uh-huh..."

She's trying to help, but this is not what I want to hear right now. I'd rather she tell me that she's proud of me no matter what. Or that she will love me no matter what I have done.

Because I've done some pretty bad things.

"I gotta go, Mom," I say.

"Are you sure you're all right, honey?"

"Yes."

"Promise?"

What's one more lie? "I promise."

28

I GET TO THE CLINIC EARLY TODAY.

I keep strategizing for how to get out of this job. Yes, it pays well. But I can't even walk through the waiting room without feeling sick about what I did to that man. I keep imagining blood covering the floor, the way it was that night.

If I could get that video Kovak has of me shooting Hooper…

When I get into the waiting room of the clinic, it's empty and the door to the examining room is closed. At first, I think that Kovak hasn't arrived yet, but then I notice the light on under the door, and as I get closer, I can hear voices. Somebody is in the examining room with him.

It's a woman.

I creep closer to the door, trying to be as quiet as I can be, which is hard when you're a big oaf like me. When I get a few inches away from the door, I can just barely make out the conversation.

"This is what I'm paying you for, isn't it?" Kovak is saying.

The woman has a soft voice, which is hard to hear from behind the door. She says something that I can't quite catch, but I hear the end of it: "It's taken care of."

"So you say," he retorts.

"I promise," the woman says. "I reassured him. He won't give you any trouble."

Kovak grumbles something that I can't make out.

"Have I ever steered you wrong in all this time?" the woman says.

I can't hear Kovak's response, but then he says, "Look, you have to go. He'll be here any minute."

They must be talking about me. Except why?

I realize a split second too late that they are coming out of the examining room. I stumble backward, but when Kovak emerges from the room, it's painfully obvious that I must have been trying to listen in. But my momentary embarrassment is overshadowed when I see the woman who walks out of the room.

It's Patrice.

I stare at her for a moment, my mouth hanging open. What is Patrice doing here? And why was she talking to Kovak about me?

Her composure falters for a moment, but she recovers quickly, flashing me that same smile she gave me in her office the other day. "Abe! So good to see you!"

"What are you doing here?" I ask her.

"Well, you asked me to poke around, didn't you?"

Her eyelashes flutter innocently. "I just had a nice chat with Dr. Kovak here. It seems like a lovely clinic."

Except she told me she already investigated. And even that aside, I *heard* that conversation. *This is what I'm paying you for, isn't it?* That's what Kovak said to her.

Holy shit.

Patrice is the contact at the school who is sending students to the clinic.

It suddenly makes perfect and horrible sense. She is the one who has intimate conversations with every single student—it's mandatory, after all—where they admit whether or not they have been struggling. She knows exactly who is most vulnerable. How easy would it be for her to slip them Dr. Kovak's name and tell them to make an appointment?

It's entirely possible Dr. Conlon is also involved, but it's clear that Patrice is Kovak's primary contact. And all this time, she has been reassuring me that she was checking out the clinic and that everything was fine.

"We should make another appointment," she tells me. "Soon."

"Sure," I mutter. "Great."

She tries to rest a hand on my arm, but I shrug her off roughly. I don't want her to touch me.

Kovak offers me the same phony smile that Patrice has pinned on her face. "Patrice and I have had an excellent discussion about the clinic, and I've answered all her questions. I don't think she has any concerns anymore, do you, Patrice?"

"None at all," she pipes up.

"In that case," Kovak says, "I'll let you go on your way, Patrice. Abe and I have a clinic to attend."

I want to throw something.

I watch Patrice walk out of the clinic, my hands balled into fists. I am about five seconds away from punching a hole in the wall. How could she have lied to me that way? How could she have pretended she was on my side?

Kovak catches the look on my face and raises his eyebrows. "Easy there, Abe. Don't do something idiotic."

"It's a little too late for that."

He chuckles, and now I'm about five seconds away from punching a hole in his *face*. "You know what, Abe? You've been doing such a great job here lately. I don't think I'm paying you enough. I think you deserve a raise."

And then he quotes an hourly rate that is twice what I am getting right now.

"I don't want it," I hear myself saying, even though God knows, I could use the money. "I just want to stop working here. Please."

He opens his mouth as if to answer, but then there's a knock on the door to the waiting room. Our first patient is here.

"Come on," he says. "We have work to do."

29

It's two in the morning, and a sound in my bedroom jars me out of my restless slumber. I sit bolt upright in bed and discover Mason in the middle of our room. He's standing over me, his phone in his right hand. I squint into the darkness and rub my eyes.

"For Christ's sake, it's two in the morning, Mason," I say. "Why are you awake?"

"Can't sleep," he mumbles.

"Okay…"

"I need help."

I shake my head, not understanding. "What?"

He runs both hands through his hair, which is already sticking straight up. "I need you to give me something to help me sleep."

Oh, great. This is the last thing I need. "Why are you asking me?"

"Because you're a drug dealer."

"*What?*"

Mason doesn't blink. "You work for Kovak. I heard what goes on at that clinic."

Shit. *Shit.* I struggle into a sitting position at the edge of the bed, realizing that neither of us is getting to sleep anytime soon. "Nothing goes on at that clinic. I'm not a drug dealer, okay?"

He starts pacing the room. "Abe, you've got to give me something. I haven't slept in a week."

"Maybe you should cut back on the coffee?"

He stops pacing and stands there again in the center of the room, taking shaky breaths. "Seriously, Abe. Just one or two pills to knock me out. I'm begging you."

I grit my teeth. "I told you, I'm not a drug dealer!"

"Bullshit!" He practically spits the words at me. "Everyone knows what you're doing. Just give me a couple of pills, you piece of shit!"

"What the hell is wrong with you?" I rise to my feet, stunned by his accusations. "I'm not a drug dealer. You need to apologize to me *right now.*"

Mason isn't a small guy by any means. He's somewhat built, although I suspect he's gotten softer in the last few months. But it doesn't matter. I'm still a lot bigger than he is. You can't underestimate the damage that a large mass can do.

Mason is quiet for a minute, and I wait. I'm almost hoping he'll stick to his guns. I almost want him to say it one more time because I feel like I'm ready to explode. My right hand balls into a fist, ready to break his nose the second he says the word "no." I can almost taste it.

But then Mason raises his eyes and says, "Sorry."

He turns on his heel and scurries out the door, plunging our bedroom back into silence.

I flop back down in my bed and squeeze my eyes shut. It was hard enough to get to sleep, but now it's impossible. I can't stop thinking about that man I killed. All the blood.

And what the police might do when they find out.

I can't sleep. I've got to get out of here.

THE SUN IS DOWN, and I'm the only person in the anatomy lab. I rip the plastic covering off of the dead body. Frank. That is what Mason started calling him, and the rest of us followed his lead. Frank is partially but not entirely dissected. His abdomen and pelvis as well as his face have been mostly ripped apart, but his arms and legs are intact, for the most part. Except for the left arm, which Rachel dissected the other day.

I pull a scalpel from the dissection kit. I look down at the tattoo on Frank's arm: *To serve and protect.* Frank had probably been a cop. His job had been to protect the public.

I dig the scalpel into the center of the tattoo, slicing clear through the skin.

I haven't been to the anatomy lab in a while because I've been avoiding Heather. At first, I try my best to stick to the instructions on the lab manual, but in the end, I'm taking out my anger and frustration on the dead body in front of me. I can't punch Dr. Kovak in the nose, but at least I can slice this dead body to shit. Three hours later, I've done a truly terrible dissection of Frank's remaining arms, both his legs. It looks like a mess. He looks more like a serial killer got at him than a skilled medical student.

But what does it matter? What does it matter if I learn the muscles and nerves of the arms and legs? I'll be lucky if I make it through the year.

I continue working until I'm too tired to go on. I put back the dissection kit and cover up Frank's body. I pull off my gloves then go straight to the bathroom and sit in a stall, staring at the wall for the better part of an hour.

30

OUR FINAL EXAM IN ANATOMY IS TOMORROW.

Like half of our class, I am in the library, trying to study. I wish I could study with Heather, but she's still mad at me, and she's studying somewhere else. At home, I guess.

I still can't believe I screwed that up so badly. If only she hadn't walked in on me in the shower.

Anyway, I've got my anatomy textbook, my anatomy atlas, and pages of crumpled notes. I've got five different colors of highlighters. Even if my life has turned to shit, at least I can pass my anatomy final.

I brought a metal water bottle with me that was a present from my mother when I started medical school. I guess she thought I'd be drinking a lot of water, although it's mainly been coffee. I'm already too jittery, though, and I'd like to try to get some sleep tonight, so I'm off caffeine for now.

I grab my water bottle and leave the library to fill it up at the drinking fountain outside. As the water level rises in the container, I remember learning in chemistry class about how water is the only molecule where the solid form has a lower density than the liquid form. That's why ice floats on water. I always found that fascinating.

Maybe I should've been a chemist. Then all this crap wouldn't be happening to me.

"Hey, Abe."

I swivel my head at the voice from behind me. It's one of my classmates—Victor. He's wearing a pair of blue scrubs, like he's been in the lab studying or maybe planning to go. (I hope it's the latter since I hate to think he hasn't changed since being elbow deep in a cadaver.) He is shifting between his feet and tugging at his scrub shirt.

"Hey," I say.

I don't know Victor very well, but I saw him at Kovak's clinic that day with a "cough that won't go away," and the memory makes me cringe.

"Hey, listen," Victor says, "I'm kind of screwed for this exam tomorrow."

"I know what you mean."

"No, that's not..." Victor picks at the cuticle of his fingernail, and I wince. I hate it when people do that. "I can't focus, and I have *so* much to study before the exam tomorrow morning."

"Right... okay..."

"So," he says.

"So."

Victor groans. "Please, Abe. I'm never going to pass the anatomy final without some help. And I need a good grade on this one, or else I'm screwed. Conlon's gonna fail me—he's not messing around. I'm desperate. You gotta hook me up."

Hook him up? Is *that* what this is about? He wants me to sell him *drugs* in the middle of the hospital? I shake my head in disgust. "Sorry, you've got the wrong guy."

"Oh, come on," he grunts. "I know you work at Kovak's clinic. *Everyone* knows. Give me a break."

Everyone knows. Everyone in the school thinks I'm a freaking drug dealer. That's my situation right now.

Suddenly, the test tomorrow doesn't seem nearly as important as my reputation.

"Listen to me, asshole," I hiss at Victor. "I am *not* a drug dealer. You need to pull yourself together and get some help. But you're not getting anything from me. Not one damn pill."

"But—"

I take a step toward Victor, and he flinches. I'm not much taller than him, but I'm a lot bigger. I could destroy him if I wanted, and he knows it. I am done messing around. "Not one damn pill," I repeat in a firm voice. "You understand?"

Victor looks like he's going to protest again but thinks better of it. He nods and then scurries away. I watch him disappear down the hallway.

That's when I make an important decision. I am done with Kovak and all his bullshit. *Done*. And he needs to understand that.

So I leave all my books behind in the library, get in my car, and drive to Kovak's clinic.

31

Kovak is working tonight.

Of course he is. It's the night before the biggest exam of the year. Why would he give up the opportunity to make a few bucks off some desperate medical students like Victor?

But the clinic is quiet when I come in. He's got somebody in the examining room with him, but the waiting room is empty. It's perfect.

I check under that potted plant, and sure enough, the key to his desk drawer is still there. I remove it and fit it into the bottom drawer. The drawer slides open, revealing the gun that is still inside. I pick it up, feeling comforted by its weight. I don't know for sure that it's loaded, but I'm willing to bet that it is. I drop it into my coat pocket.

And then I wait.

After about five minutes, Kovak emerges from the examining room with his patient. The patient looks like a student, although even younger looking than the ones in my class. Maybe he's from the college. I push away a surge of disgust.

Kovak looks surprised by my presence. Surprised, but not particularly concerned, especially since I had the wherewithal to change into a pair of scrubs. "I didn't think you were working tonight, Abe," he says as the student dashes out the door to the waiting room, leaving us alone.

"I wasn't."

"Ah," Kovak says, although he looks confused. Still not that concerned.

Then I pull the gun out of my pocket and point it at him.

Now he looks concerned.

"Abe," he gasps. "What are you doing?"

"Hands up in the air."

Kovak obliges, lifting both hands in the air.

"I want the video footage that you have of me," I say. "I want it deleted, and then I'm never coming back here again."

"Abe…" He starts to lower his hands. "Come on. Threatening me with a *gun*? This isn't you."

"Hands up," I say so sharply that his hands shoot way up in the air. "I swear to God, I will kill you if you don't give me that video. I've already done it once before."

He must see in my eyes that I am serious. I am not messing around. I am a good person, damn it, but I will kill this asshole if he makes me.

"Fine… fine," he stammers. "I'll get it for you."

I follow him into the examining room, where he digs

around in the back of the cabinet. I keep the gun pointed at him the whole time. It's amazing how easy it would be to pull the trigger and just end it all. I don't want to kill anyone tonight, but it almost seems like it would be a service to the world to do it. After all, he's responsible for so many bad things.

Finally, Kovak retrieves a flash drive from the cabinet. I hold out my hand, and he drops the flash drive into my palm.

"This is your only copy?"

He nods. "You think I want a bunch of copies of that lying around?"

I close my fingers around the flash drive. "If I find out there are any other copies, I will come back here and kill you."

He frowns. "I just don't see you doing that, Abe. You're too nice."

"Fine," I say. "Then I'll just beat the shit out of you." I pause meaningfully. "It wouldn't even be hard."

He presses his lips together, but he doesn't contradict me. He knows I'm right.

I stuff the flash drive into my coat pocket and hurry out of the office. I'll destroy the drive as soon as I get home. But before I get home, I have one more stop to make.

Patrice sent an email to the entire class, informing us that she would be hanging around her office the day before the exam, just in case one of us is in crisis. If I go back to the school, she will be in her office. And since most of the students will be focusing on studying, she will likely be all alone.

I reach into my pocket and feel the handle of the gun that is still nestled inside. I have a feeling that when there's a gun pointed at her face, I might finally get the truth out of Patrice.

I'm looking forward to it.

PART III

RACHEL

32

THE FIRST DAY

"LOOK TO YOUR LEFT AND LOOK TO YOUR RIGHT."

I roll my eyes as I look to my left. Just as I thought—Heather is doing it. Heather McKinley: my new roommate. Ugh.

Heather wants to be my best friend. She keeps suggesting we go out for drinks and asking me questions about my life. But the truth is, I can't stand her. She's nice, I suppose. But she's so painfully annoying.

First off, she brought *so* much stuff with her, you'd think she was moving into a mansion. Like five suitcases. And what's the deal with all that lotion? I've never seen so much lotion in my entire life, except maybe in the lotion aisle of a drugstore. And all her shampoos smell like fruit, which means Heather always smells like fruit. Usually peaches. I *hate* peaches.

Plus all she wants to talk about is her stupid boyfriend, Landon. He is just *so* wonderful, by the way. Did you know his favorite food is fried chicken and his favorite band is the Glass Animals? I know it. And the worst thing is that now, I can't unknow it, as much as I wish I could.

Oh, and did I mention she sings? Oh yes. She's constantly singing or humming a song by Beyoncé or Christina. And she's really, really off-key. I want to stuff tissues in my ears.

I'm using like a fifth of our shared closet, yet Heather had the nerve to look uncomfortable when I hung a few posters on the wall. She started mumbling something about how we were forbidden to use thumbtacks in the dorms. By the time I shoved the last thumbtack into the wall, she'd started to get it through her thick blond skull that the two of us will never be friends.

I can see it all laid out for Heather. She'll marry some guy in the next four years, if not her current loser boyfriend, then some other loser in our class. She'll work as a physician for a few years and then probably quit to become a stay-at-home mom after popping out a few rugrats. Heather is not exactly a high-powered career woman.

Before I left for DeWitt, my mom said to me, "Rachel, please try to make some friends this time." Or something patronizing like that. She sent me to a shrink in high school because I had no friends. Which wasn't my fault at all—trust me. Is it my fault that most people get on my nerves? And anyway, you don't go to med school to make friends. You go to *become a doctor*.

I just wish I were better at studying.

The truth is, there's a lot in anatomy that doesn't interest me all that much. Well, most of it, to be perfectly honest. There are just too many nerves, too many arteries… way too much to memorize.

So I fail a few quizzes. Big deal.

Dr. Conlon thinks it's a big deal, though. After I fail three quizzes in a row, he starts paying a lot of attention to me in the lab. He seems concerned.

"You realize you just cut through the phrenic nerve," he observes as he watches me.

Mason, who is working on the other side of the cadaver, says, "Rachel cuts through everything. She thinks it's all fascia."

Speaking of people I hate. I nearly reach out and strangle Mason for making me look bad in front of Dr. Conlon. He's the most obnoxious person I've ever met. I sent out an email to the class about how disrespectful it is to name your cadaver and asked him if he'd seen it. He told me he had, and it was "hilarious."

Dr. Conlon ignores Mason's comment and limps closer to me, squinting at my T-shirt through his spectacles.

"'I am the doctor my mother wanted me to marry'," he reads off the shirt. He smiles. "I like that."

"Yeah," I mumble.

Dr. Conlon's eyes meet mine, "It's pretty amazing that women now make up the majority of med school classes these days. It wasn't that way thirty years ago."

"Yeah," I say. "Too bad most women do peds, primary care, and ob-gyn."

"What field are you interested in, Dr. Bingham?" he asks.

"Surgery," I reply without hesitation.

I look up sharply as Mason snorts from the other side of the table. I hate Mason. And the worst thing is, he'll live out his whole life being that same arrogant asshole and never learn any humility. It's just not fair.

Dr. Conlon waits for me after lab is over that day. He's changed out of his scrubs and is back in his slacks with a dress shirt. And a bowtie. That bowtie just slays me. Who the hell wears a bowtie?

"Rachel," he says as he takes me aside, concern in his blue eyes, "I just want you to know that if you need it, there's help available for you. There are a lot of second-year or graduate students I can recommend who will be happy to spend extra time with you in the lab."

We haven't even had our first big exam yet, and already, I've set myself aside as someone who needs remedial help.

"And of course," Dr. Conlon continues, "I'm always available for questions."

I'll bet. Dr. Conlon is the biggest dork on the face of the planet and clearly does not have a rip-roaring social life. Every time I pass by his office, no matter what the hour, the light is on under his door. No wife, no girlfriend, no kids. He probably hasn't had a date in years. Maybe it's been so long, he's given up hope that it's going to ever happen again.

It is just so unbelievably perfect.

33

WHEN I WAS A JUNIOR IN HIGH SCHOOL, I FOUND MYSELF in danger of failing trigonometry.

Trigonometry is hard. The entire concept of sines and cosines just didn't make a lot of sense to me. My parents hired a tutor, some eighty-year-old walking skeleton of a woman, but each session just confused me further. What can I say—I suck at math. I kept getting my exams back full of red pen marks, and I started to worry about how I was going to get into a decent college with an F in trig.

Harvey Pritchett was my trigonometry teacher. Mr. Pritchett was a short, balding, unattractive, middle-aged man who waddled instead of walking. He was married, probably to a short, unattractive, middle-aged woman. He left a sticky note on my second midterm exam (with my spectacular grade of thirty-eight out of one hundred), saying, "See me after class."

When I saw the note, I cried. I was not exactly a picture of confidence back then. I had zero friends, sucked at sports, and wasn't really into extracurricular activities. I dressed in frumpy sweaters and baggy jeans and grew my hair out to hide the zits on my face. I had tiny little mosquito bites for breasts, and I was so skinny that you could make out every single one of my ribs and pelvic bones. I was the kind of girl that the popular girls would point at and laugh.

Anyway, trig was the last class of the day, so after the other students filed out of the room, I trudged up to the front of the classroom to face Mr. Pritchett. I was terrified. I hugged my textbook to my chest, my dark hair nearly obscuring my eyes.

Mr. Pritchett sat atop his desk in a gesture that I guessed was supposed to seem casual and friendly. Perspiration stained his armpits and formed a little line on his brow.

"Rachel, I've noticed you're struggling in the class," he said.

"I guess so," I said quietly, hanging my head.

"Is there anything in particular that you're having trouble with?" Mr. Pritchett asked.

Yeah, everything.

"I don't know."

"I'd like to try to help you, Rachel," he said, "but I feel like you're not trying yourself. I hate to tell you this, but if you don't bring up your grades significantly, I… I'm going to have to fail you."

I had never failed a class before in my life. As much as I tried to stop them, a minute later, I had tears streaming down my face. Mr. Pritchett, looking very uncomfortable, patted my shoulder in a lame "there,

there" gesture. It wasn't enough. I collapsed against his desk, sobbing into my hands. His arms slid around my shoulders and then…

Later on, Mr. Pritchett tried to say that I initiated the kiss. But that's total bullshit. After all, I was just a shy, innocent young girl. In any case, Mr. Pritchett couldn't argue that I added some excitement to his gray little life. After all, how many other short, balding, middle-aged teachers got to make it on their desk with nubile sixteen-year-old girls?

Before Mr. Pritchett, I had never even kissed a boy before. I had a few very mild crushes on boys, but nothing to write home about. There were times when I thought I might be a lesbian, although I realized I didn't have much interest in girls either. But my relationship with Mr. Pritchett was never about love—I never had an ounce of feelings for him, aside from perhaps pity and disgust. Physically, he was repugnant. He had a beer belly, he was sweaty *everywhere*, and he was covered in a thick layer of graying hair. When he was inside me, there were a few moments when I was so disgusted, I thought I might vomit.

But I did what I had to do. I couldn't fail trig. My next exam came back with an A circled on the top, even though most of the answers were still wrong.

I wish I could say that was the last time I slept with a teacher for a grade, but it wasn't. Once I did it and got away with it, it was hard to stop. You'd think most professors would be protective of their reputations and their marriages, but it's scary how easy it is to seduce them.

Some of them know my game right from the start—that's the easiest. But some of them think that I really like them, that I honestly have *feelings* for them. One or two pathetic losers even cried when I threatened to turn them in. But eventually, every single one of them gave me what I wanted.

And so will Dr. Matthew Conlon, even though he doesn't know it yet.

34

I FAILED MY FIRST ANATOMY EXAM. UNLESS SOME miracle occurred, there's no way that I passed.

Heather is also certain that she failed. She is moping around our apartment, half in tears.

"I studied *so* hard," she keeps saying. "I must just be an idiot."

Heather definitely isn't the brightest penny in the fountain. Frankly, she'd probably benefit from offering a few professors some action on the side. But no, she'd never do it. She's not that type of girl.

"Maybe you should go take a shower?" I suggest because I can't stand it another minute. And I know Heather loves showering. She takes at least two or three of them every day.

"Yeah…" she mumbles. And then, thankfully, she disappears into the bathroom.

Of course, the second the shower turns on in the bathroom, someone knocks on the door. I try to ignore it, figuring it can't be anyone for me, but the knocker is too persistent. Finally, I trudge over to the door and throw it open. It's Abe—big surprise.

"Oh, hey, Rachel," he says. "Is Heather home?"

Abe has the biggest crush in the world on Heather. Everyone knows it except her. He follows her around school like an extremely large puppy dog, saving her every time she needs it (which is all the freaking time). Abe seems like a nice enough guy, but the way he acts around Heather seriously gets on my nerves.

"She's in the shower," I tell him.

"Oh," Abe says.

He doesn't move. Am I supposed to invite him inside? I really don't want to. Why can't they go to Abe's room to study instead of hanging out here all the time? (I suspect the answer to that question is that Abe and Mason's apartment is a pigsty.)

"Listen," I say to Abe. "You know that Heather has a boyfriend, right?"

His cheeks color. "Yeah, I know that."

And then I add, for good measure, "And even if she didn't, you wouldn't have a chance."

Abe stares at me like I just punched him in the face. He lowers his eyes and mumbles, "Yeah, I know. Of course. I mean, I'd never think that…" He clears his throat. "Um, I'm going to go. You can… maybe just tell Heather I stopped by."

"Sure thing," I say, and I slam the door in his face.

Was that a bitchy thing to do? Maybe it was. But seriously, somebody needed to tell that guy the truth. I did him a favor.

I go back to the bedroom and get on my computer. I

check my email, and there's a message waiting for me from Dr. Conlon: "Please come see me after class tomorrow."

Ah, the "come see me" note. Always the start of something interesting.

35

I SHOW UP AT HIS OFFICE AROUND SIX THIRTY P.M., WHEN most of my classmates are either home or crowded into the library. Dr. Conlon should have been home having dinner with his family, but since he lives alone, he's still in his office. I knock on his door.

"Come in," he calls out. "It's open."

I open the door to his office and make a point of shutting it behind me. Dr. Conlon is working on his computer, but he turns to face me as I walk in. From the few lines around his eyes and the slight graying of his black hair at his temples, I'd place him in his late thirties. But there's something very youthful about those blue eyes, even when they're hidden behind his spectacles. The truth is, despite everything, he's a pretty good-looking guy.

None of the professors I've slept with before have been even remotely attractive. That's purposeful. I figure if the guy is a heartthrob, there's no way he'll fall for my act—he won't be desperate enough to risk his whole career for a little action from a student. But Dr. Conlon is an exception. It's painfully clear he's not a ladies' man—the bowtie says it all.

"Rachel," he begins. He folds his hands together. I've noticed the way his right hand doesn't move normally, and this action only calls attention to that fact—I can't help but wonder what's wrong with the guy. "Will you have a seat, please?"

I wore a red skirt just for the occasion. There's something provocative about the color red—men don't refuse a woman in a red skirt. I slide into the chair in front of his desk and cross my right leg over my left. Even though I'm very thin, I have shapely legs.

"Rachel, you probably know I want to talk to you about the exam," Dr. Conlon says.

I nod.

"Your grade is…" He bites his lip. "Rachel, I'm very concerned that you're not studying enough. Anatomy involves a lot of memorization, and you… well… you missed a lot of basic information. I went through your exam very carefully, and I'm worried that you're just not making an effort."

I lower my eyes. "I just don't have a great memory. I swear I'm trying my best."

Well, sort of. The truth is, I hardly studied at all. When I saw Dr. Conlon give his passionate "anatomy is fun" speech at the beginning of the year, he may as well have painted a big L on his forehead. I have nothing to worry about.

"It can be a very difficult transition from college to medical school," he acknowledges. "I know that. Is there anything going on in your life that's keeping you from studying enough?"

My eyes fill with fake tears. I rest my elbows on his desk and bury my face in my hands. Did I mention I can now cry on command? It comes in handy at times like these.

"Rachel…" he says gently. His hand is now on my shoulder. Rubbing.

Oh, Dr. Conlon, you don't know it, but you're about to get very lucky. We both are.

"Rachel, you can talk to me…" he says. "Tell me what's wrong."

Wow, he's saying all the right things. It's like he's reading from a script. Nice job, Dr. Conlon. This is going to be so damn easy.

"It's just that"—I sniffle—"I feel like I'm all alone out here. I miss my family, and I… I have no one…"

"Listen to me, Rachel," he says. "Everyone feels that way when they first start med school. Everyone. But I swear to you, you're not alone."

He puts his hand on top of mine. His palm is rough and calloused, probably from always holding that cane. I turn my own hand slightly so that I can grasp his fingers.

"Thank you," I say in a small voice. "Thank you for being so nice to me. You're the only one who's tried to help me in this place."

They should give me an Oscar, truly.

He's leaning forward like I am, so that our faces are only inches apart. I wonder if he'll kiss me first or if I'll be the one who has to make the first move. When I first met Dr. Conlon, I made a bet with myself that I would have to kiss him first.

"Rachel." He is so close to me that I can feel his hot breath. "Have you ever…"

I raise my eyebrows at him.

"Have you ever considered seeing a therapist to talk about your problems?"

Have I *what*?

My face burns. "*No*."

"Patrice is wonderful," he says. "I really think she can help you."

I nearly pound my fists against the desk in frustration. Is Dr. Conlon seriously this dense? Any other man would be ripping my blouse off by now. And *nothing* kills the mood like talking about a shrink.

Christ, what a loser.

I sigh in frustration and lean back in my seat.

"Forget it. I'll be okay," I say. I have to regroup. Maybe we can arrange a second meeting. And I can show up wearing, I don't know, lingerie.

Dr. Conlon frowns at me. "Are you sure?"

I nod. "Very sure."

"Let me write Patrice's number down for you anyway," he says.

He pulls a pen out of the penholder on his desk (who has a *penholder*?) but accidentally knocks the holder onto the floor, spilling pens all over the place. I sigh again and get up to help him clean the mess. God, what a clueless klutz. Just my luck.

I bend down on my knees, picking up what appears

to be an endless supply of pens. Why the hell does he have so many pens? Dr. Conlon is bent over in his chair, picking up pens with his left hand as I crouch next to him on the floor.

When I have half a dozen pens in my hand, he grasps my wrist. “It’s okay, Rachel. I can handle it.”

I look up at his bright-blue eyes. That’s when I notice it: his gaze flitting down my neckline to my very visible breasts. It’s just a second—he was super quick—but I saw it. And he *knew* that I saw it. His face turns a bit red—this is my chance. I put my fingers behind his neck and pull his head toward mine.

I knew I’d be the one making the first move.

“Rachel?” There’s surprise and confusion on his face.

I press my lips onto his. At first, he seems frozen and absolutely stunned, but then his arms draw me closer to him.

God, men are so easy to predict.

Not to be conceited or anything, but I’m a really good kisser. I have to be. Most professors aren’t good kissers. Most of them suck at it. Usually, they give me too much tongue—of course, when you don’t like a guy, any amount of tongue is too much tongue. And usually too much saliva. When you kiss a girl, you don’t want her to feel like you’re spitting in her mouth, trust me.

Okay, I’ll be honest: Dr. Conlon isn’t a bad kisser. He’s actually… kind of good at it. That part surprises me. And I don’t get surprised too often.

But good kisser or not, I can tell it’s been a while for him. I can’t say why exactly. Maybe it’s his eagerness. I can tell how badly he wants me by the way he touches me.

I unbutton my blouse, slide off my skirt, as he watches with his jaw hanging open. As I begin to unbutton his shirt, he looks up at me and grins crookedly. "I never thought my day would end up like this."

I return his smile. "Are you glad?"

"You have no idea…"

And then I get my second surprise: Dr. Conlon has a nice chest. Maybe I should have given him the benefit of the doubt, considering he's at least ten years younger than the youngest professor I've been with. Still, I didn't expect muscles. And no beer belly, that's for sure. I run my hands over his pecs, and I'm practically shaking.

Get a grip, Rachel!

"What?" he asks, looking concerned. "Anything wrong?"

"No. Not at all."

This is ridiculous. I can't start *liking* this guy. If that happens, then he's the one in control. And that would be a huge mistake. So I close my eyes and think of the one thing that never fails to disgust me: Mr. Pritchett. Pritchett's disgusting, hairy body. His sagging jowls. His sweaty skin.

But somehow, it isn't working. Dr. Conlon keeps kissing me, and as his mouth works its way down my neck, I can't think about Mr. Pritchett anymore. I can only focus on him and what's about to happen and how good it feels…

When it's over, Dr. Conlon slumps down in his chair. He shakes his head and rubs his face.

"Wow, Rachel. Jesus Christ…"

I'm still straddling him, and I need to get up, but I can't quite move. It has *never* been like that before. Never. I've never lost control that way before.

I don't get it. Dr. Conlon is a clueless dork who hobbles around with a cane. How is it possible that he was so *good* at that? Maybe he's younger than the others, but that shouldn't matter. The guy has no social life, no dates, nothing. This makes no sense.

"I should probably go, Dr. Conlon," I mumble.

He grins at me. "You can call me Matt. At least, in here you can."

Okay, this isn't a disaster. Yes, we just had some incredible sex. My *first* incredible sex. But he doesn't know that. He's just excited he got to score with a twenty-two-year-old. Plus, I can tell from the way he's looking at me that he's smitten.

Nothing has changed. The game is still on.

I usually don't drop the bombshell on them until the second time. Some of them seem to see it coming, although fewer of them than I would have guessed. I was surprised how many of those bald old men thought that I was genuinely interested in them. For a lot of them, it was a huge blow to their egos. And I usually took pleasure in delivering it. They were mostly a bunch of assholes.

Dr. Conlon isn't an asshole. He's a nice guy, and he cares about his students.

Oh well. I can't afford to fail anatomy. This is just the way it has to be.

36

I'm in such a good mood the next day that it doesn't even bother me when Heather is loudly singing Taylor Swift in the shower. Anyway, it's a relief to know that everything worked out with Dr. Conlon just the way I planned. Okay, not *entirely* the way I planned, but close enough.

When I arrive at the lecture the next morning, I notice that Dr. Conlon seems to be in a pretty good mood too. He's joking around with the class more than usual, and even though he's generally an animated teacher, I'm impressed by the enthusiasm he's managed to whip up for the muscles of mastication. He really needed to get laid.

Truthfully, Dr. Conlon is a good teacher. Actually, he's a *great* teacher. He's patient and good at explaining tricky concepts, but most importantly, he so obviously loves teaching. This job is his life. And that's why this is so perfect. As much as it will hurt his pride, when he figures out what I'm after, he'll cave immediately. He won't do anything to jeopardize his career.

After the lecture is over, I give the professor a five-minute head start to get to his office before heading over there myself. I'm pleased to see the way his eyes light up when I enter the room. I could probably get the keys to his car and all his credit card numbers if I wanted.

"Rachel." He beams at me. "I was hoping you'd come by…"

I close the door behind me and lock it. A smile stretches across my lips. "How are you doing, Dr. Conlon?"

"Matt," he corrects me.

In about five minutes, he's going to hate my guts.

I cross the room to his desk. He pushes his chair back from the desk to allow me room to sit down on his lap. I settle down on his legs and wrap my arms around his neck. I bring my face close to his.

"Are you busy?" I ask him.

He shakes his head, "Nah, just some paperwork."

This is the moment to drop the bombshell. But I see the way he's looking at me and… somehow I just choke. I don't know what's wrong with me. It's not like Matt Conlon is the first professor to become smitten with me.

"What?" He's looking at me, dark eyebrows raised. "Is something wrong?"

"Nothing," I say, forcing a smile.

He starts to kiss my neck, and my body melts against him. His fingers slide into my hair, and it feels so nice. Maybe I don't have to tell him right now. Maybe we can go one more time…

Oh my God, what's *wrong* with me?

I have to do this now. Right now.

I pull away from him resolutely, trying to ignore the confusion on his face as I take a deep breath.

"Actually, there is something that's sort of been on my mind…"

He frowns in concern. "What?"

"I just… I feel like I can't stop thinking about my grade on that exam," I sigh. "It's really… distracting me."

At this point, at least half of the professors would immediately say something along the lines of: *Don't you worry yourself about that grade. We'll fix that right now.* It saves both of us face if they volunteer to change my grade without having to be threatened.

But Conlon isn't going for it. Damn. He has too much integrity. He's not going to change my grade. He's going to need to be persuaded.

This is going to get ugly.

"I'm sure you'll do better on the next exam." His face brightens. "I'd be happy to tutor you myself, Rachel. I do that all the time for students who are having trouble. It's important to me that you do well."

"Yes, but…" I run my hand over the inside of his thigh. "It's going to be hard to pass with such a low grade on the first exam."

"Rachel, honey." He wraps his fingers around my wrist, stopping them from moving north. "I appreciate what you're doing, but don't you have some studying to do?"

Our eyes meet. And that's when I realize it:

He knows.

He knows exactly what I want. And he's not planning to make this easy for me.

Too bad he has no idea who he's dealing with.

"Matt," I say thoughtfully, "how do you think the dean feels about professors who have sex with their students?"

I watch him carefully for his reaction, expecting his face to drain of color. But it doesn't. He looks completely calm and collected.

"They probably don't like it too much," Dr. Conlon says with a shrug. "I've heard of professors getting fired for that."

"Really?" I say in mock surprise.

He nods. "Yeah, sure. And some of them end up wrecking their marriages too. I heard about a professor recently from another university whose wife left him after he slept with one of his students." He smiles at me. "Actually, I believe he taught at *your* former university. Maybe you knew him? Dr. Michael Hirsch?"

Oh no. No, no, no…

He can't know about that. It's not possible.

Mike Hirsch was a middle-aged guy who was just as unattractive and balding as Mr. Pritchett had been, and he also happened to teach my biology class in college. He'd believed I really liked him and had thrown a fit when I suggested he alter my grades. I'd been forced to place an unfortunate phone call to his wife. The call to the wife always came first because a call to the university would have been much more of a scandal. Of course, as soon as I called his wife, Mike realized I meant business.

But how the hell does Dr. Conlon know about that? Nobody knows. Except, of course, for Mike Hirsch, Mrs. Hirsch, and me.

"He's pretty pissed off at that student who wrecked his marriage," Dr. Conlon continues. "Would you believe he was angry enough to call some of the professors here to personally warn us about that student? As if any of us would be dumb enough to get taken in by something like that."

Oh, Christ.

I climb off Dr. Conlon's lap and back away, staring at him. He's not smiling anymore, that's for sure.

"Personally," he says, "I wouldn't worry anyway. I'm not married, and I'm the only disabled member on the entire faculty and have been for quite a while. I can pretty much get away with whatever I want. I mean, it's not like they're going to think that *I* seduced my student, right?"

"You knew all along," I breathe, shaking my head.

"Well, it was nice of Dr. Hirsch to give me that heads-up," he says. "But when you came in here yesterday wearing that short skirt... Come on, do you think I'm stupid, Rachel?"

I can't believe this. Of all the professors I've been with, I can't believe *Dr. Conlon* is the one who finally caught on to me. The entire time we were having sex yesterday, when he was acting so grateful and amazed, he knew exactly what I was up to. It was all an act. I'm furious.

"Congratulations," I say. "You figured me out."

I storm off in the direction of the door, but before I get there, I hear his voice.

"Hold on, Rachel. Where do you think you're going?"

I turn and see him playing with the handle of his cane.

"What?" I say irritably.

"You're still failing anatomy," he reminds me. "What do you expect to do about that?"

I hate him. I really truly hate him.

"I don't know," I say. "Pop a bunch of pills till I stop breathing so none of this matters?"

Dr. Conlon's face darkens. He doesn't seem to appreciate my joke, probably because there were several students who really did that. But honestly, I'm not entirely sure I'm joking.

"I'm holding special tutoring sessions," he says. "For the students who did abysmally on the exam. I'll email you the times—I suggest you show up."

"I guess I don't have much of a choice now, do I?" I snap at him.

"Nope." He pushes his glasses up the bridge of his nose. "Good luck, Rachel."

Yeah, I'm going to need it.

37

Remedial anatomy is the most humiliating experience of all time.

It's me, Victor Pereira, and Marissa Dunne. We are apparently the dumbest three people in the whole class. Dr. Conlon instructed us to arrive at the anatomy lab at four p.m., so here we are, standing in front of a dead body, waiting for him to show up.

I don't care for Victor or Marissa. Marissa is a real girly girl. She has these long, long eyelashes and wears so much mascara on them that I'm a little worried her eyelashes might smack me in the face. She's also wearing high heels in the lab, which is just ridiculous. Victor, on the other hand, always seems like a ball of jittery energy and talks so fast that he trips over his words.

I really wish I weren't here.

"I didn't know you were failing anatomy, Rachel," Victor says when I walk in.

"Yeah," I mumble, not wanting to get into a conversation with him.

"I know," Marissa agrees. "I totally thought you were really smart."

Where the hell is Dr. Conlon?

He shows up a few minutes later, dressed in blue scrubs, clutching his cane in his left hand. I can't help but notice that his blue scrubs make his eyes look *so* blue. I shift slightly in my sneakers—I need to stop thinking about him being attractive. Especially since I hate him.

"All right then." He gently tugs the plastic off the body in front of us. "Let's get started, okay?"

Victor and Marissa nod eagerly. I just stand there and glare at him.

Dr. Conlon starts wrestling a glove onto his left hand while he says, "For starters, can you guys tell me the five major branches of the facial nerve?"

Crickets chirp.

"You don't have to know all five of them," he adds. "Just one. Can you tell me one branch?"

"Ophthalmic?" Victor guesses.

Dr. Conlon pauses in his attempt to pull on the glove.

"Uh, well, no. The eye movement is controlled by three other cranial nerves. Do you know which ones those are?"

More crickets.

"Cranial nerves three, four, and six," he says as we stare at him blankly. Well, he's got his work cut out for him. Good luck, Dr. Conlon.

"I knew that," Marissa says.

"Oh, okay," Dr. Conlon says, not sounding like he believes her. "Anyway, the branches of the facial nerve are the temporal, zygomatic, buccal, mandibular, and cervical. There's a mnemonic: To Zanzibar By Motor Car."

At least this time, the mnemonic doesn't involve sex.

Victor crinkles his nose. "Where's *Zanzibar*?"

"I think it's in Australia," Marissa says.

"Actually, it's in Africa," Dr. Conlon says patiently.

"Who's heard of *Zanzibar*?" Marissa says. "Zurich would be better. That's in Switzerland. I went to Zurich in college with my boyfriend."

"Um, fine," Dr. Conlon says. "You're welcome to use 'To Zurich By Motor Car.'"

"And what's a *motor* car, anyway?" Victor adds. "Isn't that just the same as a *car*?"

Okay, I can't take another minute of this.

"God, Victor, who the hell cares?" I snap. "This is the dumbest conversation I've ever heard in my entire life!"

All three of them stare at me. Long enough that my cheeks start to burn.

"Sorry," I finally say.

I sneak a look at Dr. Conlon, and I could swear there's a tiny smile playing on his lips.

"All right," he says. "Let's get back to work."

YES, this session is humiliating. But at the same time, wow, I learn a lot about anatomy. As much as I hate Dr. Conlon right now, I have to admire how patiently he explains everything to us. Victor and Marissa have plenty more ridiculous questions in the queue, but he fields each of them expertly and doesn't even make them feel like they said something dumb.

When the hour is up, Dr. Conlon dismisses Victor and Marissa.

"Why don't you clean up here, Rachel," he says.

"Why me?" I shoot back at him as the other students hightail it out the heavy lab door.

He regards me for a minute. "We'll take turns."

"Wonderful," I say.

He pulls the glove off his left hand. "I'm glad you came today, Rachel."

"I didn't have a choice, did I?"

"You always have a choice," he says. "It's just that this time, you made the right choice."

I guess he's implying that I made the wrong choice when I slept with him. Then again, I didn't hear any complaints at the time. He's the one who banged his student, so I wish he'd drop the holier-than-thou attitude.

"Don't worry," I say. "I have no intention of making that particular bad choice *ever again*."

Dr. Conlon nods, and maybe it's my imagination, but his cheeks seem to flush slightly red. It's kind of satisfying to see him lose his composure, if only for a split second.

38

The sessions with Dr. Conlon are going well. Even Marissa and Victor are asking fewer dumb questions, and I know what I'm doing in the anatomy lab for a change. And Dr. Conlon notices the difference, which I have to admit sort of makes me happy.

"Dr. Bingham," he says to me in the lab. "What's the terminal branch of the external carotid artery?"

Mason is poised to shout out the answer the second I falter, but I'm not going to give him that chance.

"The superficial temporal artery," I answer, much to Mason's surprise.

Dr. Conlon beams at me. "Excellent."

It's weird how he acts like nothing ever happened between us. Like we didn't have mind-blowing sex in his office, right down the hall. Like he's just my anatomy professor and he's just proud of me for studying hard and getting the right answers—nothing more.

Dr. Conlon gave us an extra-credit assignment to offer a little more leeway to help us pass the class. I complete the assignment a day before his deadline and head to his office after class to hand it in. I guess I'm being a bit of a suck-up, but I want to show him that I'm trying. The fact that he cares so much makes me want to do well in the class.

When I get to his office, the door is open. Voices are coming from inside, and I recognize Dr. Patrice Winters, the class psychologist. She's always sending out these irritating, touchy-feely emails, telling us to reach out to her anytime. I'm sure she doesn't want another of us to overdose.

"Thanks so much, Patrice," Dr. Conlon is saying. "These look delicious. Peanut butter is my favorite."

"Is it?" Patrice replies. "Well, please let me know if you like them."

I watch them for a moment, and suddenly, my heart starts to pound. Oh my God, the two of them are hooking up! How did I not realize that before? It's so painfully obvious.

And for some reason, I feel a sharp jab of jealousy.

"Is there anything else you like?" Patrice asks him. "For the next time I get motivated to bake?"

That's when Dr. Conlon lifts his eyes and sees me standing in his doorway. A smile instantly lights his face. "Rachel! Come on in."

Patrice, hovering in front of Dr. Conlon's desk, looks like she wants to murder me. There's a plate of home-baked cookies on his desk, presumably contributed by Patrice.

"Hello, Rachel." She glances down at her watch. "I better go, Matt. I'll talk to you later."

Patrice stomps out of the office, slamming the door rather dramatically behind her. Dr. Conlon hardly seems to notice. Men are so dumb about stuff like that.

"Are you dropping off the extra credit?" he asks me.

I'm clutching the papers in my hand. But instead of handing them over and getting the hell out, I say to him, "Are you hooking up with Patrice?"

Dr. Conlon's blue eyes widen. He looks so flustered that it's sort of adorable.

"Rachel," he stammers. "That's… that's not an appropriate question."

"So you are then?" I press him.

"No!" he says sharply. "I'm not." He adds, "Really."

The rush of relief upon discovering that Dr. Conlon isn't hooking up with Patrice surprises me. I look down at my hand, which is still clutching my extra-credit assignment. The papers are getting all crumpled in my fist. I hold it out to him. "Here."

As he takes the papers from me, his fingers brush against mine. And I can tell from his face that he notices too.

39

About half the tutoring sessions with Dr. Conlon take place in the lab and about half are in his office. Today, we're having an evening session in his office, even though it's Friday night. If I had a social life, I'd be pretty irritated. But luckily, I don't. And neither does Dr. Conlon.

When I arrive, all three chairs in front of Dr. Conlon's desk are empty. I raise my eyebrows at him, and he says, "Victor and Marissa both couldn't make it."

"Oh?"

He nods. "Victor was sick, and Marissa was… uh, I don't remember what excuse she made up."

I smirk at him. "Yeah, Friday night is not ideal for most people."

"Clearly," he acknowledges. He smiles at me. "Thanks for showing up."

"No problem," I say. "I have no life either." Dr.

Conlon raises his eyebrows, and I feel suddenly embarrassed. "Sorry, I didn't mean to say you had no life."

"No," he says. "That's pretty accurate."

I force a smile. "Maybe you should ask out Patrice."

I don't know why I said that. I don't want him to ask out Patrice. I hate Patrice. She doesn't deserve someone like him. I'm relieved when he just shakes his head.

"Can I ask you something?" I say.

"Something about anatomy?" he asks hopefully.

I shake my head.

"Maybe you better not then," he says. He adds, "Not that I can stop you."

He's right.

"I have to know. Were there other students that you've… you know…"

His eyes widen. "No! God, no! I'd never…" He stops midsentence, realizing what he was about to say. "What I mean is… that thing between you and me, that's not… in character for me. I'm not that type of person."

He looks so embarrassed that I have no choice but to believe him.

"Okay," I say. "So why did you do it?"

He drops his face into his hands and rubs his temples.

"I'm only human, Rachel." He sighs. "I meant to turn you away, but then… I just…" He raises his eyes. "When you came into my office, all I could think was that I… I really wanted to be with you. And I knew I could. I'm sure that sounds bad, but…"

His ears are bright red. I want to get up and hug him, but that probably wouldn't be appropriate.

"Maybe we should get started," he says.

Today's lesson is about the circle of Willis, but I'm having a lot of trouble focusing. It's just me and Dr. Conlon in the office, and I pull my chair up alongside him so I don't have to read upside down, so the whole thing just feels so *intimate*. And he smells nice. Maybe it's his aftershave. I wonder how he gets the stench of formaldehyde off him.

"You're really getting the hang of this," he says.

"Well, it's my only option for passing, isn't it?" I say. I mean it as a joke, but my voice comes out a little choked.

Dr. Conlon offers me a lopsided smile. "Yeah, I wouldn't want to have to put you through *that other thing* again, huh?"

I squeeze my hands into fists, which are somehow really sweaty. "Well, it wasn't…" I swallow hard. "It wasn't *so* bad."

Dr. Conlon chuckles darkly. "A rave review."

I look down at my hands.

"Actually," I say. "It was pretty good. *Really* good."

There. I said it.

When I dare to look up again, Dr. Conlon is just staring at me. He gets my meaning loud and clear.

"I'm not going to change your grade, you know," he says. "I don't do that."

"I know."

We stare at each other for a full minute. Then he slowly leans forward and starts kissing me. It's just as good as I remembered it—his tongue moving gently against mine, his facial stubble grazing my cheek, his fingers sliding along the edge of my jaw, past my ear, into my hair. I don't want him to stop, but he does stop. He wears a troubled expression on his face.

"This isn't a good idea," he says, his eyes intently on mine.

"Probably not," I agree.

And then he kisses me again.

40

Dr. Conlon (who I am now apparently calling Matt) sets down some ground rules for our little relationship. We don't want to get caught, so we decide that we should maintain a purely academic relationship on hospital grounds. And we definitely can't meet in public or at my dorm, so that pretty much just leaves Matt's house.

"What did you do in the past?" he asks me. "You know, with the other professors that you, um..."

"It never really got this far," I admit. "It was usually a one- or two-time thing."

"Oh yeah?" Matt asks, and he looks pleased.

I decide not to share the fact that all those other men were completely repulsive to me.

So I end up driving to Matt's house, which is about ten miles from campus—far enough that the risk of some student or staff member driving by his house and seeing my car there is small. Matt's place is a modest one-story ranch house with two steps to get to the front door. It looks like the kind of place a guy would live all alone.

It's mildly disturbing how much Matt's house is a shrine to the study of anatomy. He has two skeletons—one full-sized named Jill and the other about three feet tall named Jack. He has a model of the human heart and lungs. He keeps it on the dining room table. I'm not even kidding.

"You know, your houseguests are going to think you're a necrophiliac," I comment as I finger the plastic heart. I can't imagine how he eats with that thing in front of him.

"Why?" Matt asks, genuinely puzzled. Because doesn't everyone keep life-sized models of human organs on their dining table? Sheesh.

He has several bookcases, and while not every book is related to anatomy, they're all medical texts without exception. I bend down to scan the shelves for something related to another interest or hobby, but nothing isn't related to his work. The most surprising book he owns is a chemistry text.

Matt doesn't use his cane around the house. Instead, he grabs onto the furniture as he walks to support himself. As we make our way through his living room, he keeps one hand on the couch then holds the doorframe as we enter his bedroom.

Thankfully, his bedroom is decorated a little less morbidly. It's a typical guy bedroom, all browns, blacks, and grays. It looks like he got his bedroom set from Ikea. As I look around, I can't help but wonder if he's got a whole drawer full of bowties somewhere. Before I can stop myself, I'm opening his dresser drawers, searching for bowties.

I don't even realize I'm being extremely rude until I notice Matt is staring at me.

"What are you *doing*?" he asks

"Um, I was just looking to see where you keep your bowties."

To my relief, Matt laughs. He opens a drawer in the desk by his bed, and there they are: at least a dozen little bowties in all different colors.

"Pre-tied!" I gasp. "You're kidding me! What are you—five years old?"

He shrugs. "Yeah, well, you ever try tying a bowtie with one hand?"

I look down at his right hand. I want to ask about it, why he can't use it, but I sense we're not quite there yet.

"Why bowties, anyway?" I ask instead.

Matt grins. "I don't know. I like them."

And then when he kisses me and gently pulls me into bed with him, we forget all about bowties.

Matt and I are very, very careful not to interact at the hospital. A few times, when nobody else was around in the lab, he winked at me. But even that felt like a big risk. Nobody can know our secret. If they did, we'd both be in so much trouble.

And worse, it would be over between us.

I have to admit, I'm infatuated with Matt. It's honestly a little hard to even concentrate on lectures because I get so excited just by the sight of him. I didn't even know that was possible. I wonder if he feels the same way about me, but I can't imagine he does. He's much older and, dork or not, I'm sure he's had many girlfriends before. This can't be nearly as special to him.

"How old are you?" I ask him one day as he's leading me through his house to his bedroom.

He winks at me. "Older than you."

"No, seriously," I say. When he doesn't answer, I add, "I'm twenty-two."

"I was right," he says. "I'm definitely older than you are."

I follow him to his bed, where he sits as he always does—very ungracefully. I'm not about to let this go, though.

"Why won't you tell me?"

Matt doesn't answer right away. He pulls off his right shoe then removes the thick plastic ankle brace he wears that goes nearly up to his knee.

"Because I'm really, really old," he finally says.

"If you're not going to tell me, I'm going to guess."

"Do your worst."

I squint at him, pretending to size him up. I'd already guessed he's in his late thirties, but I decide to tease him a little. "Fifty-two?"

Matt's eyes widen. It's priceless.

"You don't really think I'm fifty-two…" he says, looking somewhat worried.

"Well," I say thoughtfully. "My dad is fifty-three, and I figure you're younger than him, so…"

Matt just shakes his head.

"Older?" I say. "Fifty-four then?"

"Oh, that's it," he grumbles.

He picks up a pillow from the bed and smacks me in the shoulder with it. I laugh at him, and then he tackles me onto the bed. As I let out a squeal, it occurs to me that this is a noise I don't think I've ever made before in my entire life.

After a few minutes of making out, Matt says to me, "I'm thirty-eight."

"Ancient," I say with a grin.

"I'm sixteen years older than you," he says. "When you were born, I was a junior in high school. I'm sleeping with a girl who was a toddler when I started college."

"I was a very sexy toddler," I say.

"Undoubtedly," he says. "But it still makes me feel like a creep."

"Don't stress about it," I say. "I could never relate to people my own age. That's why I don't have any friends in the class."

"Yeah, I've noticed," Matt says.

It never occurred to me that Matt realized I have no friends. I wonder how long he'd been paying attention to me. Or maybe it's just that obvious that I'm a total loser. But I don't want to have a conversation with him about my lack of friends.

"Anyway." I clear my throat. "I'm okay with you being an old man. Just as long as you can still keep it up."

"Hell yeah," he says, and over the next hour, he very much proves it to me.

41

The weirdest thing about me and Matt (and there's some stiff competition) is that pretty much all we ever talk about is anatomy. I'm not even kidding. We can be intimate and have amazing sex, but then when it's over and he's holding me in bed, he starts talking about study strategies for the upcoming exams.

Sometimes I wonder if he's afraid of discovering that we have absolutely nothing in common.

After about two weeks of nothing but sex and anatomy lessons, I decide I've had enough. As we're lying in bed together under the covers, my body cuddled against his, I say, "I'm going to make you dinner tonight."

"You shouldn't," he says. "There's a quiz tomorrow. I can order in some food, and I'll help you study. You need to become more familiar with swallowing."

At first, I think he's making a joke. But he isn't. He actually means that I need to learn more about the cranial nerves involved with swallowing, not… well, you know.

"Hmm…" is all I say.

I'm hoping that will be a cue to let it go, but apparently not.

"What cranial nerves are involved in the oral phase of swallowing?" Matt presses me.

I sigh and pull away from him, propping myself up on one elbow.

"Matt, this is not what I want to think about right now."

He smiles sheepishly, "Sorry. I just want you to do well. I mean, this is *my* class. I ought to be able to help you a little bit."

"Well, you *refused* to help me," I point out. "You have your morals and all…"

I try to sound teasing, but I can't help but be irritated by his continued refusal to alter my grade.

"I just don't think you need to go through your life this way," he says. "You're an extremely bright girl, Rachel. You just need to focus a little bit."

Oh no, another infamous Matt Conlon Pep Talk. Yes, he is amazing in bed, but sometimes he acts like he's my *father*. I'm beginning to seriously worry that if we start talking, I'll realize he's more like my parents than he is like me.

"You don't know what it's like," I say. "Medical school is very intimidating."

"I don't know what it's like?" He snorts. "Watch it. You're talking to a med school dropout, baby."

I stare at him. Is he serious? I think he is. "You went to med school?"

"Yeah." At first, it looks like he's going to tell me more, but then his eyes cloud over. "So, um, you want to get dinner?"

Geez, it's impossible to get this guy to open up. "Why did you drop out of med school?" I ask him.

He's quiet for a second. He's not wearing his glasses, and it makes him look so much more vulnerable somehow. Younger.

"You really want to know?"

"I asked, didn't I?"

He ducks his head down and uses his left hand to part his black hair with his fingers. And that's when I see it: a thick scar running practically through the entire length of his skull. It's an old scar, long since healed up.

"What happened?" I breathe.

"I got shot in the head," he says. "That's what happened."

I stare at him. "Seriously? Oh my God."

"It was my roommate first year," Matt explains. He rests his head on the pillow and stares up at the ceiling, his eyes glassy. "Kurt. Kurt Morton. I'll never forget that name for as long as I live."

"Your roommate shot you?" I gasp.

I'm seeing Heather in a new light. She may be annoying, but at least she's not homicidal. (Yet.)

"I was more surprised than you are, believe me," Matt says. "We weren't exactly friends, and I didn't even realize he was flunking out. One night, I woke up at like two in the morning, and he was just standing there in the middle of the room, holding a gun. He started babbling about how he couldn't cut it in med school and how he resented me." He shakes his head. "I didn't even think he was serious until he pointed that gun at me. At my head. And then..."

Matt gets quiet for a minute, just staring at the ceiling. I somehow sense I ought to keep my mouth shut, so I just stroke his chest with my fingers.

"He killed himself after he shot me," Matt says. "That's the first thing I remember them telling me after it happened, like two weeks later. Also, they told me I was lucky to be alive. But when you can't move half your body, you don't feel lucky."

"My God," I say. "That's... unbelievable. So you decided not to go back to med school after that?"

He's quiet again. Long enough that I figure out myself that it probably wasn't entirely his own decision not to go back. That maybe getting shot in the head affected his ability to perform to the rigorous standards of medical school. After all, the bullet did a lot more than just graze him.

"Matt..." I murmur into his neck.

"It's okay." He tries to smile but fails. "It all worked out in the end. I'd probably be a surgeon now if I never got shot. Probably working one hundred hours a week, divorced with some kids I'd never see. I'm happier this way."

He's lying, though. Matt is a lot of things—he's really smart, he's a great teacher, he's adorable, and he's fantastic in bed. But I'm pretty sure he's not happy.

42

Our second midterm comes way, way too fast.

I'm at an advantage, what with all the private tutoring with the anatomy professor. But I'm still nervous as all hell. If I screw up, I screw up. Matt has made it painfully clear that he won't change my grade.

"You wouldn't really want me to, would you?" he says to me.

"No, of course not," I lie.

I would. Come on, of course I would.

Matt wants to live in some sort of fantasyland where I've changed all my corrupt ways, and now I'd never cheat in a million years. But that's just not true. If he offered me an A, I'd take it. I wouldn't even have to think twice.

The night before the exam, I head over to Matt's house for a study session. When I arrive, he's got all the textbooks—including the book he himself wrote—laid out on the coffee table. I settle down next to him on the couch, and immediately he tenses up again.

"Hey," he says.

"What?"

"You're on my right side."

I frown. "Huh?"

"Maybe you never noticed," he mumbles. "But I always sit with you on my left side." He adds sheepishly, "I don't move my right arm as well, as I'm sure you can tell. And I can't see as well on my right side. It just… it makes me uncomfortable."

I had no clue. He must have been positioning himself with me on his left very surreptitiously. Anyway, I get up and move to his left side, but he still looks tense.

"Matt," I say, rubbing his arm. "Talk to me. What's wrong?"

He looks at me for a minute then drops his eyes. "Honestly? Sometimes I have no idea why you want to be with me."

I can't believe he'd say that to me. I mean, *he's* the brilliant professor. I'm *nothing*. Okay, yes, I'm young. But so what? I'm just a loser who has no friends and cheated my way through college.

I start to tell him that, but before I can summon the words to tell him exactly what he means to me, he snatches one of the books off the table and says, "Never mind. We better get to work."

Okay then.

Eventually, the study session migrates to the bed. We have this bowl of grapes, and if I get three right answers in a row, he feeds me a grape. I don't even like grapes that much, but it's really hot when he feeds it to me. I like how he holds it just out of reach of my mouth, waiting for that final right answer.

"You earned this," he says with mock seriousness as he pops the last grape in the bowl into my mouth.

I swallow the grape then stick my tongue out at him. He laughs and kisses me.

"Seriously," he says. "You're going to do great tomorrow. I know it."

"I hope you're right." I rub my eyes and yawn. "Oh my God, I'm so tired. What time is it?"

"It's one in the morning," Matt notes, looking surprised. "Wow. I didn't realize it was so late."

"Damn," I say. "I better head home."

I drag myself out of bed, still rubbing my eyes. Matt has a concerned look on his face.

"Maybe you should spend the night here," he suggests. "I don't want you to fall asleep at the wheel."

"I'll be fine," I assure him.

I've started to pull on my jeans when Matt's arms wrap around my waist.

"Please stay, Rachel."

Okay, so I stay. It's not that big a deal. We take separate cars the next morning, so it's not like anyone is going to find out. And it's so nice to spend the night snuggled against Matt's warm body.

Maybe it's my imagination, but the crowd outside the anatomy lab looks even more nervous than last time.

I have a clipboard and paper to write down my

answers to the practical, and I camp out outside the lab like the rest of my classmates. Just like I'm any regular student who isn't sleeping with the professor. And just like everyone else, I'm anxious. Hell, I'm scared shitless.

Because this time, I tried. If I tried that hard and still fail, well…

"Here we are again," Heather says, nudging me on the shoulder. "Nervous?"

I try to pass off a casual shrug. "It's just an exam."

"What's with Mason?" Heather asks.

I look off in the corner, where Mason Howard is all by himself, his back pressed against the wall, staring off into the distance. Most of the class has been pulling off all-night study sessions lately, but Mason looks truly awful. His face is unshaven, his clothes are rumpled, and he has this strange, haunted look in his eyes.

Oh my God, is Mason on *drugs*? He never seemed like the type to me, but the problem is rampant at our school. And he certainly *looks* drugged.

"Hey," Heather says, "do you want to hear the latest gossip? Apparently, Sasha and Mason are hooking up. How weird is that?"

Very weird. I can't imagine Mason hooking up with sweet, quiet little Sasha, but then again, I'm probably pretty low on the list of candidates to be hooking up with the professor. There are much, much hotter girls in the class than me.

"By the way," Heather says, a small smile playing across her lips, "where were *you* last night, young lady?"

My mouth goes dry.

"I… I spent the night at school, studying."

"Whatever you say…"

Eventually, the students are herded into the lab. I can't remember the last time I've been this scared about a test. If I fail, that's it—I fail. But the worst part is that if I fail, Matt will be so incredibly disappointed. He seems to believe I have it in me to be some kind of anatomy genius, and I don't want to let him down. I don't want him to realize the truth: I'm not all that smart.

I position myself in front of one of the cadavers and try my best to steady my hand holding the pen. I can't believe how badly I'm shaking. I look over at Matt, who is at the front of the room. Our eyes meet, and he mouths to me, "You'll be fine."

And it really does make me feel better. It's nice that he believes in me, even if he may be completely wrong.

"All right, folks," Matt addresses the class, "you know the drill by now. Good luck to everyone, and you may begin."

43

Matt cooks me a celebratory dinner that night, even though it's not clear that there's anything to celebrate. He planned the dinner like a week ago, saying he was that certain I'd do well.

As for me, I'm not nearly that confident. That midterm was *hard.* I can't stop analyzing every question in my head and wondering if I got the right answer.

When Matt answers the door for me, I'm practically ready to faint. I try to gauge how I did by the look on his face, but it's hard to tell. "Did you grade my test yet?" I finally ask.

"Rach, this dinner is supposed to help you *forget* about the exam," Matt says. "The important thing isn't your grade. It's that you learned the information."

I just stare at him.

He sighs. "You got honors."

I'm so happy, I might cry. I throw my arms around him, which sends him slightly off-balance since he's not holding his cane, but he manages to grab onto the wall and right himself. And then we kiss in the hallway. For like five straight minutes.

"I *told* you that you'd do well," he says when we come up for air. "Now how about dinner, huh?"

I follow him to the living room, where he's got an elaborate meal of pasta with herbed chicken. There's an open bottle of pinot noir (my favorite) and two wineglasses next to it. And of course, there's a single candle lighting the table.

"Did you seriously cook this yourself?" I ask him. "This is incredible."

The plate looks like something a professional chef would have put together. And Matt's only got one working hand.

Matt nods. "I used to love to cook, but I don't have much opportunity to do it anymore. Doesn't seem worth it when it's just me, but I wanted to do something special for you. To celebrate your achievement."

Before we sit down to eat, I excuse myself to use the bathroom. To be honest, I just need a few moments to collect myself.

I'm very familiar with Matt's bathroom now. It's much larger than the one I share with Heather, and I love the way it smells faintly of his aftershave. He's got a grab bar set up by the toilet and the sink, but other than that, it's a pretty ordinary bathroom. I've been in here dozens of times, and there's only one difference today:

The medicine cabinet is open.

Well, not open exactly. More like *slightly ajar*. But the

point is, it's not closed, and it's clear there are medications inside it. And in all honesty, I've never been great at respecting other people's privacy. That's how I know Heather uses acne medication.

So I tap the door open all the way.

Immediately, I'm sorry I did it. Mostly because there are a *lot* of pills in here. Like, way more than I'd guess the average thirty-eight-year-old would be taking. It frightens me to see all those pills. Why is he taking so many medications? What's wrong with him?

Okay, fine, he did get shot in the head. Still, that was years ago. He seems mostly okay now.

I pick up one of the bottles: Vicodin. That's a painkiller, but I've never heard Matt say that he had significant pain before. But clearly, he does—why else would he have this medication? Where is he having pain? Why didn't he tell me about this?

Then I pick up a second bottle. This one is for oxycodone—another narcotic painkiller.

Both bottles have his name on them, prescribed by an actual doctor. But why does he have two medications that are both for pain? And what are all the rest of these bottles? Are they *all* pain meds?

What is he doing with all these narcotics? Is it possible that he's… selling them to students? Is *Matt* the source of the drug problem at DeWitt?

No. No way. Matt would never do that.

I've been in here long enough that Matt must be wondering what's taking me so long, but I can't resist looking at a third bottle. And this one makes my heart sink: it's Zoloft. I know what that is from my high school days when my parents sent me to a therapist. Zoloft is a medication for depression.

I shut the door to the medicine cabinet. I should never have snooped on him in the first place. Well, it's his fault for leaving the door open.

I spend another thirty seconds studying my reflection in the mirror on the cabinet door. I'm not pretty, in case you were wondering. My dark hair is way too stringy, and I'm always pale like a ghost, no matter how much time I spend in the sun (which, admittedly, isn't much). I don't wear makeup, but it probably wouldn't help. I'm just not pretty, end of story.

But Matt seems to think I am.

I wash my hands off with his foaming hand soap and return to the dining area. I can see Matt sitting at the table, patiently waiting for me. I watch him as he pours wine into the two glasses and places mine in front of my plate. He adjusts the candle in the center of the table, trying to get it centered perfectly, but then he swears and yanks his hand away.

"Are you okay?" I ask him, racing over to the table.

Matt looks up at me, still cradling his hand. "Really hot wax," he admits sheepishly.

"That's what you get for trying to be too romantic," I scold him.

"Yeah, I'm an idiot," he says.

I run to the kitchen and get a paper towel, which I run under cool water for a minute then fold into quarters.

"Let's see," I say.

"Nah, I'm fine," he says.

He's trying to be macho—it's adorable.

I have to coax him until he shows me the burn on his hand. It's his right hand—the bad one. There's an angry red area on the back of his hand where the wax got him, and I kneel beside him as I gently press the washcloth onto his skin.

"How's that?" I ask him.

"Nice," he sighs.

The fingers of his right hand feel very stiff, even more so than usual. I try to slip my hand inside his, but it's difficult to pry his fingers apart.

Matt notices what I'm doing and says apologetically, "The muscles are probably spasming from the burn. Plus I'm overdue for Botox shots."

"Botox?" I stare at Matt's face. He has a few lines around his eyes, but he doesn't seem like the cosmetic procedure type.

He grins crookedly. "Not for my face. It loosens up the muscles in my hand. I get shots to my finger flexors." Then he adds, "Can you name the muscles that control finger flexion?"

I stare at him.

"Sorry," he says quickly. "I shouldn't have… this is your night to relax…"

I turn the paper towel over on his hand and say, "Flexor digitorum profundus and flexor digitorum superficialis."

"That's right," he says, and he grins so wide that I'm

really glad that I read ahead this afternoon. "Come here," he says, holding out his arms to me.

An hour later, the specially prepared meal has gone cold, and the treacherous candle has burned down to nothing. But I don't care.

I'm in love.

44

I'M CAREFUL ABOUT WHEN I GO TO MATT'S OFFICE. HE said to me that I should only visit him at most once a week—any more than that is too big a risk.

But it's hard not to visit him at school. I keep thinking about him all day, and it's tempting to stop by, knowing that he's sitting in his office, probably doing nothing.

A few days after Thanksgiving break, I find myself outside the door to his office. I see the light is on underneath the door, and I can hear voices coming from inside. I get a surge of jealousy until I realize both voices are male. I glance around and see the hallway is empty, so I press my ear up against the door.

"I don't know what I'm doing wrong!" It's the voice of Victor, my classmate from remedial anatomy. He sounds even more agitated than usual.

"Your score is better than last time," Matt is saying. "I think you just need to dedicate more time to studying."

Okay, I get it. I know exactly what happened. Despite the extra tutoring, Victor has failed the second anatomy exam.

"I just can't do it, Dr. Conlon. I can't!"

"Let me give you the names of a few upperclassmen that do tutoring," he says. "I'm sure the extra sessions will get you a passing final grade, Victor. I know you can do it."

I'm pressing my ear so hard against the door that I nearly topple over when Victor yanks open the door. He flashes me a seething look, which makes me take a step back.

"Yes, Rachel?" Matt says, raising his eyebrows.

I look from Matt to Victor, my cheeks burning.

"Um, Dr. Conlon, I need to… um… talk to you about the exam…" I stammer.

Victor looks over his shoulder at Dr. Conlon then back at me with a sneer. He probably assumes I failed too. "Good luck," he mutters. "He was a total asshole about the whole thing."

I close the door behind me. Sometimes Matt scolds me when I risk visiting him, but today, he limps over to me right away. He leans in close like he's going to kiss me, but instead he murmurs in my ear, "Did he seem high to you?"

It's the last thing I expect him to say. "Uh, how would I know?"

"His pupils looked huge to me, like he's on amphetamines." He rubs his left temple with his fingers. "Or maybe I'm just imagining it."

"Victor is always sort of that way."

"Is he?"

He looks relieved by this answer. I don't know how I ever could have thought he was responsible for distributing drugs to the students. I can't imagine a less likely candidate.

But he's right about one thing:

Victor looked high as a kite.

WHEN I GET out of Matt's office, I am weak at the knees. I always thought that was a dumb expression used in romance novels, but I literally feel like I can't stand up, that my legs won't support me. I don't know how he always does this to me. All he has to do is touch me, and my whole body tingles. Another romance cliché, but it's true.

I'm shutting the door to his office when I turn and see another person headed toward me. For a fleeting second, I pray that it's a janitor or someone along those lines. No such luck.

I immediately recognize the face of my classmate, Danielle Stern. There are worse people who could have seen me, but this still is not good. Obviously. And I'm certain she knows that I came out of his office.

I play it off, trying to act casual about the whole thing. After all, I haven't done anything wrong. All I've done is come out of my professor's office. Is there a *law* against that?

Danielle isn't a friend or anything, so I acknowledge her with a quick nod, and she does the same to me.

Except why is she staring at me? Maybe I'm being paranoid, but Danielle's eyes are directed right at my chest like laser beams.

I look to where Danielle is staring. And that's when I notice, to my horror, that my shirt is buttoned all wrong. Wrong enough that it seems very unlikely that I could've been walking around like that all day.

Christ, why did I have to wear a shirt with buttons? Why didn't I wear a T-shirt like I do most days?

Well, at least my fly is still zipped.

Danielle shakes her head at me in disgust as she walks past me. I want to run after her and try to explain, but I have a feeling I'd just make things worse. I'm not exactly good at talking to people. I don't know what she's thinking, and I don't want to put ideas in her head.

I look back at the door, wondering if I should tell Matt what just happened. Then I decide against it. He's got enough to worry about as it is.

45

Whenever Matt calls me at home, I'm worried about Heather overhearing. If she's in the room with me, I press my cell phone tightly against my ear so that there's no chance of my professor's voice being heard and recognized. Maybe I'm being paranoid, but I'm pretty sure you can't be too cautious when you're screwing the professor.

"Hey, Rach," Matt says. "Do you feel like coming over and doing some studying?"

Half the time, when he says that, he means sex. The other half of the time, he means studying. I can never tell by his voice which is which.

"Sure," I agree.

I close my anatomy text, get up off my bed, and pull my coat off the chair in front of my desk. Heather raises her light-brown eyebrows.

"Where are you headed?" she asks.

"Nowhere," I mutter.

"Who was that on the phone?"

"Nobody…" I clear my throat. "Just going out to study."

"Then why aren't you bringing any books?"

A rush of blood comes into my cheeks. "Um, I'm going to, uh…"

"Oh, come on, Rachel!" Heather gushes, nearly bouncing on her mattress. "Tell me who it is! Please? Is it Leo Chang? Chris Johnson?"

Yeah, right, like I'm going to tell Heather anything when she's acting like a complete child. It's bad enough that Danielle might know. Anyway, it's not like she's been honest with *me*.

"Tell me why you broke up with Abe."

That stops Heather in her tracks, and her lips twist into a pout. "Fine, go have fun with your prince."

I take the now-familiar drive to Matt's house, weaving through the back roads. As I make the final turn on the wooded path, I notice that I've started humming a song from the radio. Oh, great. Matt's turning me into *Heather*.

I pull into the driveway and park behind Matt's car—a large white Lincoln Continental. Considering he's the youngest professor I've ever slept with, I find it amusing that he drives a car that looks like it's owned by an eighty-year-old. In a lot of ways, Matt acts very much like an old man. It's something I always tease him about.

Matt yanks the door open almost before I even have a chance to knock. I can't help but suppress a smile.

"Happy to see me?" I ask, closing the door behind me as I enter the house.

"You have no idea," he says. And before I can even get my coat off, he pushes me against a wall and starts kissing me.

About two hours later, we're both exhausted, and as we lie in bed, holding hands, I make the executive decision that we should order pizza. Matt nods soberly.

"Yes, I think we're definitely too tired to cook," he says. He grabs for his cell phone. "Toppings?"

"Hawaiian, what else?" I say.

"That's my girl," Matt says with a grin.

He's the only other person I know who loves ham and pineapple on a pizza as much as I do. We're definitely soulmates.

We lie in bed a bit longer, then Matt decides he's too sweaty and wants to take a shower. I've suggested showering with him in the past, but he's rejected my idea, saying he's too worried about slipping and breaking his neck. (See? He really is an old man.) So I lie in bed, playing games on my phone until the doorbell rings.

I knock on the door to the bathroom and stick my head in. "Pizza's here. I'll go get it."

Matt sticks his head out from behind the curtain. His black hair is plastered to his scalp, and he has water in his eyelashes. He looks so sexy.

"My wallet's on the kitchen counter," he says.

I roll my eyes. "I can afford a small pizza."

"I want to pay," he insists.

"You don't have to pay."

"Rachel," he says. "If there aren't twenty dollars missing from my wallet when I get out of the shower, I'm going to fail you in anatomy."

I stick my tongue out at him and slam the bathroom door closed. I throw on one of Matt's T-shirts, figuring it's big enough to conceal most of me, and that way, I don't have to get dressed. Then I take the money from my own wallet (I don't believe his threats) and throw open the door for the pizza guy.

Except it's not the pizza guy.

It's Patrice.

Oh shit.

She's clutching a Tupperware container, and her face goes completely white when she sees me standing there. She nearly drops the Tupperware but manages to hold onto it at the last second. But she's clearly speechless. She just stares at me, her mouth hanging open.

I try to think of an excuse—some reason why I might be here. I mean, it's not totally ridiculous that a student might be at a professor's house. Maybe we're having an extra tutoring session.

Except I'm having a little more trouble thinking up an explanation for why I'd be wearing his shirt.

Well, maybe I came over here for a tutoring session. Then, while in the middle of the session, I spilled some red fruit punch on my clothes. And of course, Matt offered to wash and dry them for me, and in the meantime, he gave me his shirt to wear.

Yes, I can see how it looks, Patrice, but this is completely innocent.

Of course, we're still just staring at each other when Matt limps into the living room. His hair is still damp from the shower, and he's dressed in a T-shirt and boxer shorts. This is getting harder and harder to fit into my little makeshift excuse.

"You got the pizza, Rach?" Matt asks me. It takes him like another half second to realize who's standing at the door. His eyes go wide, and he looks like he might fall on his face. He grabs onto the couch to support himself and says, "Oh shit."

"Matt," Patrice manages. She glares at me and pushes her way into the house. "What's going on here?"

Well, I think that's pretty obvious at this point.

"You said you were *sick*." Patrice shakes the Tupperware in his face. "I brought you some soup."

"Oh," he says weakly. "Thanks."

"I can't believe you, Matt!" she murmurs loudly. "How could you *do* this? Especially with *her*!"

Especially with me? What does *that* mean?

"Rachel," Matt says in a pained voice. "I think… maybe you better go."

I get a sick feeling in my stomach. I go back to Matt's bedroom, where I put my clothes back on. I can hear her scolding him in the living room, although I can only make out some of the words.

"… you of all people, Matt, I really can't believe… so stupid and irresponsible… could lose your job… *obviously* she's playing you… not like she's so pretty you couldn't possibly resist…"

I hate Patrice so much.

I come back out into the living room, where Matt is now sitting on the couch with a glazed look on his face. Patrice is just glaring at me. I don't even say goodbye as I hurry out the front door. As I'm on the way to my car, the pizza delivery truck pulls up.

46

I CRY THE WHOLE WAY HOME.

The more I think about it, the more I'm certain that Patrice is in love with Matt. She came over with soup for him when she thought he was sick, for God's sake. And that's why she was so angry with me. Not because she thought Matt was compromising his morals or jeopardizing his job or anything. But because *she* wanted him.

Patrice is going to blow the whistle on us. The whole school is going to find out about me and Matt. He's going to lose his job. And I'm going to get kicked out of school.

But wait, maybe not. If she's in love with him, she wouldn't do that to him. Maybe she'll protect our secret. But if she does, it will be on the condition that he ends things with me immediately.

I just can't bear the thought of that.

When I get home, I park in front of the dorm, but I don't go inside. I don't want Heather to see me like this.

Instead, I rest my head on the steering wheel and sob loudly. Stupid Patrice. I can't believe that just happened.

I'm wiping snot from my nose with the back of my sleeve when my phone buzzes. I reach for it, and my heart leaps when I see Matt's number. "Hello?"

"Hey," he says quietly. He doesn't sound happy.

I swallow, trying not to let on that I've been crying. "Is Patrice still there?"

"No, she's gone," he says.

"Okay," I say carefully. "So, um… is she going to… tell on us?"

He's quiet for a moment. "No," he finally says. "She isn't. She just believes very strongly that we should end things. And… she made some good points. Really good points."

I can only guess what Patrice must have said based on the little I overheard from the bedroom. Apparently, I'm a treacherous vixen who's playing him for a grade.

"How about you?" I squeak. "Do you think we should end things?"

Matt sighs. "Rachel, come on. Look, I'm wild about you, but we could both get in so much trouble. Is it really worth it?"

He's wild about me. I squeeze my eyes shut. "Yes," I say. "It's worth it."

There's a long pause on the other line. Finally, he sighs. "This has got to be the dumbest thing I've ever done."

I bite my lip. "Does that mean I can come back over?"

"Well, I can't eat this whole damn pizza by myself, can I?"

At that moment, I almost say it. *I love you, Matt.* The words are on the tip of my tongue, but I can't quite push them out.

47

MATT WARNS ME THAT WE HAVE TO BE EXTRA CAREFUL now that Patrice knows about us, and maybe I shouldn't come over so often, but soon after, he seems to throw caution back to the wind. After a few weeks, I've practically moved in with him. I'm at his house more and more, and he doesn't seem to mind one bit.

My routine is that after anatomy lab, I go back to my apartment to shower then go straight to Matt's house. He told me that I don't need to bother with the shower —he barely notices the smell of formaldehyde anymore.

"I've eaten my lunch in that lab," he admits to me. "What really bothers me is the damn body mist you guys always spray on yourselves to cover up the smell."

But as much as I hate to admit it to Heather, I don't feel comfortable not showering after lab, especially if there's going to be sexy time.

Okay, here's my confession: I don't love anatomy lab.

My grades are better, and I sort of know what I'm doing in the lab these days. But the truth is, I don't enjoy it. I still dread anatomy labs and feel relieved when each one has ended.

Somehow, I don't think I'm going to make a great surgeon. Maybe I need to rethink that career choice.

Matt, on the other hand, would have made an incredible surgeon. Not only does he have an encyclopedic knowledge of the human body, he truly loves anatomy and learning about the way the human body works. Even though he's a great professor, it's a loss to the world of surgery that he decided to give up on finishing medical school.

"You never regret not becoming a surgeon?" I ask him one day while lying in bed.

He shrugs. "There are a lot of things a person can do with their life. It's only natural to sometimes wonder what it would have been like if I had chosen another path. But I'm happy with what I do, and that's what matters." He squints at me. "And how about you? Do you ever regret giving up your life to go to medical school?"

I make a face. "I'm not giving up my life."

"Don't be naïve," he says. "Medicine has already become your life, and you've only just started. Just wait till you've got a pager attached to your belt and you're spending Christmas Eve in the emergency room."

"Sounds like fun," I say with a smile. *Not.*

"I can see you becoming a great doctor," he says earnestly. "But you have to know why you're here. Why you *want* to be a doctor. The real reason."

The reason I went to med school is almost too

embarrassing to admit. Then again, I trust Matt. I want to be honest with him.

"I didn't want to be like my mother," I say. "She just stayed at home with the kids and never had a career of her own." I sigh. "So you figured me out. I'm just like all those other girls who don't want to end up like their mothers. I guess I figured a surgeon is about as far away from a homemaker as you can get."

Matt laughs. "Rach, trust me: you are in no way like any other girl. None that I've ever met before, anyway."

I rest my head against Matt's shoulder. It's so nice to lie here with him. All those times with those other professors—it feels like some sort of nightmare. Whatever happens between us, I'll never, ever do that again. Now that I know what it's like to be with someone I really like, I can't go back. It's pretty amazing.

"You're quiet all of a sudden," he comments.

"I'm just… happy," I say.

And for the first time in my life, I realize it's true. I didn't even realize how miserable and alone I felt before Matt came into my life. I press my face into his shoulder, and I murmur, "I love you."

I look up at Matt's face and see a change come over him. He looks down at me, and for the first time, he also looks truly happy.

"I love you too, Rachel," he says.

And then something happens that ruins everything.

48

It's about two weeks before the final exam in anatomy. We're working on the arms, although I've noticed that more and more students are cutting lab in order to study. I can never do that, though. Matt would kill me.

Today, I'm the only one in my lab group of five who showed up. I work my ass off, separating the forearm muscles all by myself. Well, not all by myself—Matt comes by a bunch of times to assist me. Hopefully, nobody notices he spends practically half the lab period at our table.

When the lab ends, I'm dead tired. My back is killing me from leaning over the cadaver—I even managed to inexplicably work up a sweat. I head straight for my locker, hoping to change clothes quickly, go home, and take a long, hot shower, followed by a visit to Matt's house. But the note stuffed under the door of the locker makes me forget all about my plans.

I know all about you and Dr. Conlon. Put the answers to the final exam under the door of Locker 282 or else everyone will find out the truth.

The note, of course, is unsigned. I crumple it up and stuff it in my pocket, suddenly paranoid that someone else is watching me. There are only a few people in the hallway, and none of them seem to be paying attention to me.

Who would write a letter like this? God, it could be anyone. Our class is full of really competitive people, and in all honesty, a lot of people in the class don't like me very much. I don't think I could even come up with a short list of suspects.

I glance down the hallway. The way the lockers are numbered, Locker 282 is all the way down the hall on the right. I slam my own locker door closed and walk in the direction of the locker. It's one of the top lockers, right in the middle of the row. There's a combination lock holding the door closed. I peer through the vent in the door, trying to see what's inside. Of course, all I can see is blackness.

Whoever wrote that letter means business. If someone reports me to the dean, Matt and I will *both* be in a lot of trouble. And how, exactly, am I supposed to explain my honors grade on the second exam after failing the first?

Shit. What the hell am I going to do?

49

The next morning, I show up in the office of Matt's secretary, Anita. Anita is a grandmotherly woman who Matt says has been with him since he started.

"I don't know what I'd do without her," he says sometimes.

She dotes on him like he's her son (or grandson). Anita is a favorite among the med students, too, mainly because she always keeps a big bowl of candy on her desk, and we're all hungry. And she smiles a lot.

Anita never has a smile on her face for me though. I'd venture to say she hates me.

When I show up in her office, she practically sneers at me. I'm sure Matt didn't confide in her about the two of us, but she ran into me a couple of times leaving his office, and she suspects something. And clearly, she doesn't approve.

"Hi, Anita," I say, trying to appear as friendly and peppy as possible. I thought about bringing her chocolates but decided it would seem like I'm trying too hard.

"Hello, Rachel," Anita replies, barely looking up from her computer.

"Um, I'm wondering if you can tell me something," I begin, tugging at my T-shirt nervously. "Do you know who is assigned Locker 282?"

Anita still doesn't look up. "No."

"Is there any way to find out?"

"Locker assignments are confidential," Anita snaps at me.

"They are?" I never heard that and wonder if it's true. "Um, do you know when Matt will be here?"

Anita is staring at me. I have no idea why until I realize what I just said. Shit.

"I mean," I say, blushing bright red, "do you know when *Dr. Conlon* will be here?"

Anita narrows her eyes. "No, I don't."

"Okay, thanks..."

I've lost all interest in finding out about Locker 282 and just want to get the hell out of there. But Anita isn't going to let me get off that easily.

"Miss Bingham," Anita says in a tight voice, "I've worked with Matthew Conlon for many years, and he's a very good professor and a good man. And someday, he'll find a woman who loves him. I think it's downright despicable that you're taking advantage of the fact that he's very lonely right now."

A burst of anger rises inside of me. "You have no idea what you're talking about."

Anita shakes her head. "I never thought I'd see the day when a twenty-two-year-old snot-nosed med student would tell me that I have no idea what I'm talking about. I knew I was right about you, and I've told Matthew as much."

Oh, great. Anita is talking trash about me to Matt. But it won't do much good to fight with Anita. Anita hates me, Patrice hates me. Everyone thinks I'm the worst person in the world for getting involved with Matt. And maybe they're all right.

"I'm sorry I bothered you," I say quietly. "I wish you could understand."

A tiny flash of doubt falls over Anita's face, but it passes quickly. I'm a medical student, and I'm dating my anatomy professor. Nobody is going to understand if this gets out.

50

I CAN'T TELL MATT ABOUT THE LETTER.

I'd like to, but I sense it's a mistake. Matt won't negotiate. Despite his resolve not to let anyone fail and the fact that he's sleeping with a student, he's irritatingly ethical. He's not going to hand someone an answer key just because they threatened him. He has way too much integrity for his own good. He'd rather lose his job than negotiate.

I'm not quite so hardcore.

Cheating doesn't bother me. Obviously. Okay, I know it's wrong, but it's not on the order of murder or torture. I don't like being blackmailed, but it's hard to throw stones. I blackmailed plenty of professors, and if I could have taken advantage of another student, I'm sure I would have. The opportunity just never came up.

Don't laugh, but I do some detective work to figure out who Locker 282 belongs to. I start inconspicuously wandering around in the corner where the locker is located, although I realize I'm at a disadvantage, considering the blackmailer knows who I am.

Naturally, my first thought was that it might be Danielle Stern, considering I'm pretty sure she suspected something was going on between Matt and me when she saw me leave his office with my buttons mismatched. I watched her around the lockers, and I was almost positive that I saw her slamming the door to Locker 282.

The next day, I fall into step with Danielle while we're heading to our lockers before lab. Danielle glances up at me and doesn't seem particularly thrilled by my company, but she doesn't shove me out of the way at least. Danielle is very studious—she always has her nose in a book and always has the answer when she's called on in class. She's fairly attractive but never dates. She wants to be a dermatologist, which is one of the most competitive specialties, so she has to be on the ball. I wonder what she'd do to land a spot in a choice dermatology program.

"Hi, Danielle," I say brightly. "Going to the lab?"

Danielle shifts her backpack to her other shoulder and peers at me with curiosity. Or is it suspicion? Danielle and I have exchanged only a handful of words this year, and we haven't spoken since the time she saw me coming out of Matt's office.

"Yes," Danielle says. "Of course."

"Right," I say after an awkward pause. "Me too."

If this med school thing doesn't work out, I don't think detective work is in the cards for me.

"Great," Danielle replies tonelessly.

It's pretty clear Danielle doesn't like me. Does that make her a suspect? More likely, it just makes her like everyone else.

When Danielle turns the corner to get to her locker, she looks irritated that I'm still following her.

"Isn't your locker on the other end of the hallway?" she asks.

"Uh…" I curse myself for not preparing for this obvious question. "I switched lockers."

"Why would you do that?" Danielle asks. She drops her backpack on the floor and looks at me curiously.

Just open your locker already!

"Too many boys changing down there," I say finally.

Danielle gives me a funny look, and I know why. Several of the girls in the class have been whispering about how I stripped down to change in the middle of the hallway when I hadn't been wearing a bra. What can I say—I was in a hurry. I often don't wear a bra because my boobs are tiny, and the only time they elicit the slightest bit of attention is when I'm braless. Anyway, I'm sorry I did it. No wonder all the girls hate me.

Danielle turns toward the lockers, and I hold my breath. For a second, it seems like she's going for 282, but then her fingers descend onto the padlock for 284.

So Danielle isn't the blackmailer. Or maybe she is, but when she saw me tagging along with her, she decided to open a different locker. Maybe she claimed two lockers right next to each other to mislead me. Whoever sent me that letter would take precautions to keep from getting caught. Danielle isn't an idiot, that's for sure.

In any case, I'm no closer to figuring out the identity of the blackmailer.

I also don't know how to comply with the blackmailer's request. I have no idea where a copy of the exam answer key might be or how to get a hold of it. I always simply demanded that my grade be changed—I never went through the fine art of cheating. For all I know, Dr. Conlon hasn't even written the exam yet.

But if I don't get a copy of that exam, my medical career is going to be over.

51

The next day, I come to the lab to find that the arms and legs of my cadaver have been desecrated.

My legs nearly buckle when I see it. I dissected one arm in the previous lab, but the remaining three limbs have been all but ripped apart. It's all I can do to keep from throwing up.

The only other person from my group who showed up to lab today is Sasha, who looks equally horrified.

"What kind of sick person would do something like this?" sweet little Sasha says. She's nearly in tears.

I feel guilty. It's my fault that someone has done this to our cadaver. The blackmailer is sending me a message. And it's working. I'm dealing with a sick person who has no morals.

I make some half-hearted attempt to hide the whole thing from Matt. But Sasha is having none of that. The second Matt gets to our table, little Sasha speaks up: "Dr. Conlon, somebody did something terrible!"

As Matt surveys the damage, I catch the look of

growing horror on his face. "Jesus Christ, what the hell happened here?"

I have to look away. If he sees my face, he'll know something is up.

Matt, on his part, is furious. He gets up in front of the class and makes a long, angry speech about competitive behavior. He has no clue.

He's still fuming later that day when I come by his office.

"It's disgusting," he says as I sit down on his lap. "And to think, the person who did that is going to become a *doctor* someday. Disgusting."

"Well, all med students are competitive," I remind him. "That's how we got here in the first place."

"There's a difference between being competitive and *that*," he says, shaking his head. "There are lines that can be crossed."

Matt's in major denial. He believes cheating is very wrong, yet he's sleeping with the Queen of the Cheaters. He knows everything I did, but he must not really think about it. If he did, he'd be disgusted by me.

"It's different with you, Rachel," he says, as if reading my mind.

"Why?" I ask.

"Well," he says, "you understand now that what you did is wrong."

Yes, he is definitely in denial.

"Maybe it's just different because you *want* it to be different," I suggest.

Matt looks up at me. I'm always amazed by how

blue his eyes are. It always manages to catch me off-guard.

"Maybe you're right." He pulls me closer to him on his lap and kisses me on the lips. "Man, why couldn't I have fallen for a girl who's less corrupt?"

I kiss him back. "I love you," I say softly.

Our eyes meet, and the smile fades from his face. *Say it, Matt. Tell me that you love me. Remind me why this is all worth it.*

"I love you too," he says, and I nearly sigh with relief. He raises his eyebrows. "Is everything okay?"

"Uh-huh," I manage.

Just peachy. Can I have a copy of the final exam, by the way?

"Good." He leans in and kisses my nose. "I'm going to go to the bathroom. I'll be right back."

Matt grabs his cane and hobbles out of the office. I probably shouldn't hang around in here because it's a risk, but he shuts the door, so I figure I'm safe.

I sit down in Matt's chair, which is still warm from his body. I absently play with one of his paperweights. The inscription on the marble weight reads "Dr. Matthew Conlon, Professor of the Year."

Damn it. I don't want to screw up his life by getting him fired. But what can I do?

That's when my eyes fall on the computer.

The screensaver isn't on, and the desktop is in plain view. I see a folder on the desktop that is called "Anatomy." I click on it, knowing that at Matt's speed of walking, I have a good few minutes before he returns. I hadn't expected to find anything but certainly not a folder called "Exams." It seems almost too easy, like it has to be some sort of trick. But then again, Matt didn't expect anyone to be nosing around his private computer.

I click on the icon, and it opens up a directory containing several folders. I click on the folder with the current year and find a file labeled "Final." When I click on it, I can see that I'm staring at the final exam for my class.

My heart begins to pound. This might be my only opportunity to obtain a copy of the exam and satisfy my blackmailer's request. I take a deep breath and press the button to print the exam.

I eye the door to the office as the printer slowly, *slowly* lays down ink on the papers.

"Hurry up!" I whisper to the printer, which has got to be the slowest printer in the history of the world.

Images of muscles and nerves appear on the blank papers, and it's all I can do to keep from ripping the papers out of the machine.

Just as the last page is finishing, I hear Matt's key fitting into the lock. I quickly close the documents on his desktop and yank the pages out of the printer, seconds before the door swings open. I fold the sheets in half and stuff them into the pocket of the jacket I had thrown on his chair.

When Matt enters the room, it seems like he immediately knows what I did. His eyes are boring guilt into my chest. He trusted me. Then again, I did this for him. It wasn't a betrayal—not really.

"Are you okay, Rachel?" he asks, his brow furrowed in concern.

I nod weakly, "Yeah, I, uh… It's been a hard day, I guess. I think I'm going to head home."

"Of course," he says softly. "Lie down. Get some rest."

If he ever finds out what I did, that will be the end. But he's not going to find out.

52

Heather isn't home when I get back, but I still can't bring myself to take out the exam in our bedroom. Instead, I lock myself inside the bathroom. It's the only place I'm safe.

I pull the exam out of my jacket pocket. I have to admit, it's sort of exhilarating to have it in my possession. Anyone in the class would have killed for a look at this. And I have it! I'm holding it in my hands right now!

I start flipping through the pages of the exam. Okay, I stole it for the blackmailer, but there's no reason I can't look at it myself. I mean, yes, I earned that honors on the last exam, and that's all well and good. But how can I turn down a *guaranteed* honors grade? I'd be a fool *not* to look. It's not like it matters in the long run that I learn this stupid anatomy.

I'm on the second page of the exam when I feel an ache in my chest. A lump forms in my throat, and suddenly, the diagrams of nerves and muscles swim before my eyes.

I can't do this.

For the record, I still don't think cheating is wrong. Well, okay, maybe I do a little bit. But what feels worse is betraying Matt. He trusts me. He believes I'm earning the grades I'm receiving. It's important to him that I learn anatomy. If he knew I looked at this exam, it would *kill* him.

Moreover, he believes I've changed. He believes I'm a good person, and I know it sounds dumb, but that makes me want to be a good person.

I'm not going to cheat ever again. I'm done.

And even though Matt is sixteen years older than me and my professor, maybe this can work out. Maybe there's a chance this can be more than just a fling. We'll have to keep things quiet for a while—at least until I finish my preclinical years—but I don't mind the secrecy. It's worth it. And then maybe someday, I can bring him home to meet my parents, and they'll know for sure that I'm not a lesbian.

But first, I have to protect myself. And if that means giving in to the blackmailer, then so be it.

53

I SEAL THE EXAM IN AN ENVELOPE AND BRING IT TO school with me the next day. Before classes are due to start, I hurry over to the locker hallway and go down to Locker 282. I look around and make sure that the hallway is completely deserted. I compress the envelope as much as possible and then slide it carefully under the locker door. It barely fits.

I can't believe I just did that.

Matt wouldn't approve. I know that for sure. But my intentions are good. Nobody can know about the two of us until anatomy is long over. Truthfully, I don't care as much about the fact that I'd get kicked out of school—I just don't want him to get fired.

There are guest lecturers teaching anatomy that morning, so I decide to skip them and go straight to his office. He's usually working there in the morning. He sometimes scolds me for missing lectures, but he has to admit that none of the other professors are nearly as good teachers as he is.

The light is on under his office door, and I knock gently.

"Come in," he calls.

I gingerly open the door. He's working at his computer, his blue eyes pinned on the screen. I love the way he looks when he's hard at work.

"Hi," I say.

He turns away from the monitor and looks at me.

"Hi," he says. There's something guarded in his tone.

"I just came by to see you," I say. I'm trying to sound sexy, even though I feel a bit foolish, especially with the way he's looking at me.

"Uh-huh," he says.

My stomach sinks. Something changed. Does he know? But how can he?

"Sorry I skipped class," I say.

"It doesn't really matter, does it?" He raises his eyebrows at me. I'm quiet as he reaches into his desk drawer and pulls out a sheet of paper. He holds it out to me. "You left something in my printer yesterday, Rachel."

I take it from him, my hands trembling. It's the last page of the final exam.

Oh no.

I don't know what to say. As I stare down at the page, the whole world around me fades to black. I sink into the chair in front of his desk so I don't fall to the floor. I can't even lift my head to look at him.

"I'm sorry," I mumble.

"Don't be," he says. "I'm the stupid one. Your old

professor even warned me about you and I didn't listen. *Everyone* warned me about you."

"It's not like that," I try to say, but I know my words sound lame.

"Then what's it like, Rachel?"

When I raise my eyes to meet his, I expect to see anger, but all I see is hurt. I wish he'd be angry at me. I want him to start yelling and cursing. That would be easier to deal with—I'm used to anger. One professor threw his stapler at me, and I needed stitches on my forehead.

"I'm sorry," I say again.

"Please stop saying that," he says. "I feel dumb enough as it is. I can't believe I fell for your bullshit act."

"It wasn't an act," I say.

"Please." He holds up his hand. "Enough with the lies. Let's just say we both lied, okay? You lied about being interested in me. I lied when I pretended I wasn't the lonely, pathetic loser you knew I was all along."

"You're not a pathetic loser."

"Let's not kid ourselves anymore, okay?" he says. "We both know what I am. I'm a disabled anatomy geek who hasn't had a date—much less a second date—in years. You know the last time I'd been with a woman before you? I don't even want to think about it."

I don't know what to say. My mouth feels dry.

I want to try to explain to him what happened. I could tell him about the blackmailer, about how I did it to save his career so that we could still be together. I really want to tell him. But I hear the words in my head, and it all sounds like a big lie. He'll never believe me in a million years.

Matt closes his eyes. "You got me, Rachel, I have to admit it. I really believed that..." He shakes his head and opens his eyes again. "Look, I'll let you keep the honors on the last midterm, and let's just forget this ever happened, okay? I'll change the final exam questions, and we'll call it even. It's... it's a valuable lesson for me, I guess."

I want to cry. I don't care about the grade. That's not what matters to me anymore.

"Matt," I say, speaking through a sizable lump in my throat. "You have to believe me. I never faked anything with you. I swear."

He glances down at the exam paper still in my hand. "Yeah, okay."

"I know how it looks," I admit. "But you also know how hard I studied for that last midterm. I mean, we studied together. You were quizzing me—I couldn't have faked that. And I wasn't faking my feelings for you either. I... I love you."

Matt looks at me like I just slapped him in the face.

"Please just get out," he says, his voice breaking on the words.

What else can I do? I get out. And as I am shutting the door, Matt drops his face into his hands, and my heart breaks in two.

54

I CRY. A LOT.

I feel like a hypocrite for all the times I mocked Heather for crying over Abe. I get it now. This is the worst pain ever. I miss him so much. And knowing how much he hates me just makes it a thousand times worse.

I keep reliving the whole thing over and over. I imagine the crushed look in Matt's eyes when he handed me that exam paper. Maybe I made a big mistake—maybe I should have gone to Matt right away when I got that note.

Of course, the main thing I keep thinking is:

If only I had noticed that last damn piece of paper in the printer.

It's silly to think about "if only" though. It's over with Matt. He hates me, and he'll never forgive me. The best thing to do is just to move on.

I don't go to class or lab, mostly out of respect for Matt. He's required to go, so the least I can do is be the one to back out gracefully. I keep to the library when I have to go to school. I try studying for the final, hoping that a stellar performance might convince him that I hadn't been trying to con him.

Unfortunately, it's pretty hard to concentrate. Plus I lost the best tutor I've ever had.

On the night before the final exam, I find myself in the library, studying late. There aren't many students around, but I recognize Sasha, my quiet little lab partner. I like Sasha. She doesn't talk much, she seems nice, and she's not terribly annoying. I wonder if Sasha might consider being my friend—I could use a friend these days.

"I'm glad I'm not the only one here on a Saturday night," I comment to Sasha as I slide into the seat across from her.

"It's never empty here on Saturday night," Sasha replies with a kind smile. "Do you usually study at home?"

"Sort of," I say, thinking of all the late-night "study sessions" at Matt's house.

I guess I must look pale, or maybe my eyes are bloodshot from all the crying, because Sasha is giving me a funny look.

"Are you okay, Rachel?" Sasha asks.

Sasha is reaching out to me—maybe I should confide in her. I eye Sasha, a tiny little pixie of a girl with olive skin and a plain face. Sasha looks much younger than twenty-two, more like a high school girl, and I can't imagine she could know much about love or sex.

Then again, didn't Heather say that Sasha is

hooking up with Mason Howard? Sasha must know *something* if she's getting it on with a guy like Mason.

"It's just this guy I've been seeing," I finally say. I appreciate how Sasha doesn't immediately start grilling me to find out his name, like Heather would have. "We sort of… we broke up recently. I really messed things up."

Sasha frowns. "I'm sorry. Did all the studying get in the way?"

"No, not really," I nearly laugh at how opposite Sasha's question is from reality. "I just… did something dumb. He wouldn't even let me explain."

"So you're having a fight?"

"No, it's over," I assure her. "I did something pretty unforgivable."

"You cheated on him," Sasha says, nodding with understanding.

"No, it's not that…"

And that's when I realize something:

I didn't do anything wrong.

Okay, technically, I did. I stole an exam. But I did it for honorable reasons. The worst thing I've done is that I wasn't honest with Matt about why I did what I did. He deserves to know the truth before he decides to dump me. Honestly, I owe it to him.

"Sasha," I say. "I have to run out for a few minutes. Can you watch my stuff?"

Sasha looks confused but nods in agreement. I leave behind all my belongings, and I run out of the library. I hurry up the stairs, past the anatomy labs, over to Matt's office. It's dumb because of course, he'll never be here. But I have to try.

Just as I get to Matt's office, the door opens, and the prongs of his cane peek out. I race over then pause, doubled over, trying to catch my breath.

"Matt," I gasp.

He looks up at me. There's no affection in his blue eyes.

"What is it, Rachel? I've been stuck here all night rewriting the exam."

Well, at least he seems more angry than hurt right now.

"Can I talk to you for a minute?" I ask.

"There's nothing to say," he mutters.

"Please."

Finally, he nods, although his expression is still wary. He backs up to give me room to enter. He gestures toward the seat, and I sit down while he plops down in his own chair. He crosses his arms and glares across the desk at me.

I had been working on a brave little speech as I ran over here. Something about how I gave in to the blackmailer to save his career and only did it because I care about him so much, and if he couldn't understand that, then maybe we *weren't* meant to be together. But he keeps looking at me with that hurt and angry expression, and the second I open my mouth to speak, everything I planned to say suddenly flies out of my head.

And then I'm crying. Huge, ugly tears are gushing down my cheeks. My shoulders shake with wracking sobs. I don't think I've ever cried so hard in my whole life. I wipe my eyes, trying to keep up with the rapid flow of tears, but I can't.

"Rachel," I hear him saying, "Rachel, please stop crying…"

"I… I can't!" I sob. "I miss you." I sniffle and hiccup. "I know you don't believe me, but I only stole that exam because someone was going to tell on us."

He frowns. "What are you talking about?"

"I got a note." I wish I'd brought the note. Oh well. "It said that if I didn't put the exam in Locker 282, everyone would find out about the two of us. I couldn't let that happen."

"Yeah, sure…"

"It's true!"

He's quiet for a minute. The only sounds in the room are the whir of the heater and my persistent sobs. I'm not sure I'll ever be able to stop. They'll put me in the *Guinness Book of World Records* for crying.

Finally, he sighs loudly. "I don't know what to believe anymore…"

I look up at him and wipe my eyes. "It's true," I insist again, trying to keep my voice from shaking. "I swear it's true. I swear on my life."

Finally, Matt stands up and hobbles around the desk. He touches my shoulder gently, and I look up at him. I feel really unattractive with my swollen eyes and runny nose.

"Look, Rachel," he says, "I do believe you, but… it doesn't matter. We're wrong for each other. For starters, I'm your professor, and I'm also a lot older than you. Maybe we had some fun together, but that's it."

"It was a lot more than that for me," I whisper.

Matt pulls a tissue from a box on his desk and gently wipes my cheeks. The gesture is so tender that I start to cry harder.

"Yeah," he says, "it was more than that for me too."

It probably can't ever "work out" with Matt, but I don't care anymore. I just want to be with him right now —that's all that matters. I stand up and fall into his arms, and he clings to me like he's missed me as much as I missed him. When we kiss, I realize I can't bear to ever be apart from him again.

"Matt," I murmur, "I do love you. I really do."

"I love you too, Rach," he says, and I remember how much it hurt when I thought I'd never hear those words ever again.

That's when we hear a knock at the door.

"Shit," Matt mutters. He looks at the door, willing the person to go away. No such luck—there's a second, more urgent knock. "Shit," he says again. Then louder, "Who's there?"

The student behind the door calls out his name, and my stomach clenches. What the hell is *he* doing here in the middle of the night on a Saturday?

"I'll get rid of him," Matt promises. He runs his hand through his short black hair to comb it out slightly. "Although it probably wouldn't look too good for you to be seen here, huh?" He glances around his office, "Do you think you can make yourself out of sight for a few minutes?"

I scan the room.

"The desk," I say. I approach Matt's large mahogany

desk and lower myself onto my knees. My body fits perfectly into the nook underneath the desk, and I'm completely undetectable. Well, as long as nobody's looking for me.

The floor of Matt's office is cold and hard, tiled with off-white squares. Many of the other offices have carpeting, but Matt told me he's worried about snagging his foot. The bones of my hips dig uncomfortably into the floor as Matt opens the door. I shift, hoping Matt will get rid of the intruder quickly.

The door slams closed, and Matt slides into his chair, being careful not to ram into me in my hiding place. I strain to listen, but the desk is somehow filtering out the sounds. I can only make out hushed voices.

"Is that the excuse you're using?" my classmate says.

I perk up my ears, trying to hear what's going on, when a fist slams into the thick wood of the desk above me. I nearly jump out of my skin, and I hug my knees to my chest. What the hell is happening up there?

I tug on Matt's pants, but he doesn't acknowledge me. I have no idea what to do. I want to come out, but that would look really suspicious. It's bad enough I'm in Matt's office late on a Saturday night, but I don't think I could explain why I'd be hiding under the desk. I can't. If I come out, we're so busted.

"Tell me how you killed him!"

I can just barely make out the words, but that's what it sounds like. Except that makes no sense. Matt didn't kill anyone—that I know for a fact. I must have heard him wrong.

That's when I hear the most terrifying sound I've ever heard in my life: a soft click.

I don't know what it is, but I've never heard anything quite like it. And suddenly, I know with absolute certainty that there's something terrible going on in this room.

55

Something terrible is happening in this room. I might be hiding under the desk, but I'm sure of it.

I feel in my pocket for my phone, figuring I can text 911. But then I realize I left my phone back in the library. It's lying inside my backpack right now, useless.

I've got to come out. Whatever is going on, I've got to stop it.

Except then Matt's left hand snakes down underneath the desk. He's making some kind of sign at me. He's pointing emphatically at the ground. He wants me to stay hidden.

Okay, one more minute. One more minute and I'm coming out.

Just when I can't stand it another second, I hear Matt's sorrowful voice, loud and clear.

"I'm really sorry," he says.

Sorry? Sorry for what?

And then I hear the explosion, and Matt's legs jolt with the impact.

I have to clamp my hand over my mouth to keep from screaming. Even though I've never heard a gun go off before except for in television or the movies, I know instinctively what it is. The intruder had a gun. And for some reason, he has fired it.

And now it's very quiet in the room. It's so quiet that I can hear my own heart thudding in my chest. And another sound: whimpering. If Matt got shot, wouldn't he yell? Curse? *Something?* I tug on Matt's pants leg, but he ignores me again. I wait for him to gesture at me again, but he doesn't. And then I see his left hand, hanging limply off the side of the chair.

Oh no. Oh God…

I want to come out, but something stops me. I remember how fervently Matt had pointed at the ground, signaling to me that I needed to stay hidden. He did that for a reason. I need to stay down here—my life may depend on it.

So I wait.

After what seems like an eternity, I hear the door to the office open and the footsteps of someone walking out then shutting the door behind him. Matt and I are alone again, or so it seems. I wait hopefully to hear Matt's voice, for him to tell me that everything is okay and it's safe to come out. But it's getting pretty damn obvious that isn't going to happen.

And then I hear a second gunshot, coming from outside the office. Oh God.

I hug my knees, not sure what to do. If only I had brought my phone, I could call for help, but without it, I can only wait. I force myself to count to one hundred, then I crawl out from underneath the desk. My knees ache from being bent in that position for so long. I grab the top of the desk to steady myself as I rise to my feet, but my fingers slide right off the surface. The desk is wet. I look at my fingers and see the dark-red substance on them.

That's when I see Matt slumped forward in his chair, right in front of me. For half a second, I'm able to kid myself that he's just unconscious. But when I see the blood coming from the back of his head, I know that isn't the case. I cover my mouth, smearing blood across my lips, trying to keep from passing out.

I'm still nearly four years away from being a doctor, but it doesn't take any advanced degree to know that Matt Conlon is dead.

I bend down in front of his body and lay my head down on his lap. I cry for the millionth time this week, this time knowing that he won't be able to comfort me. I reach for his limp hand and hold it in mine. How can it end this way? It isn't fair…

As I sob into his slacks, I hear Matt's voice speaking. But the voice is coming from within my head: *What are you doing, Rachel? I tried to save you! Get the hell out of here!*

He's right. I've got to get out of here. Before *he* comes back. He already fired two bullets, and I'm willing to bet that gun has plenty more.

I rise to my feet, wiping my eyes with the back of my hand. I take one last look at Matt. His head is leaning forward as if he is resting, and his arms are hanging off the sides of his chair. His blue eyes are cracked open, staring into nothing. There are only slight flecks of blood on the front of his shirt—the wall behind him has taken most of the brunt. I mouth the words "I love you" then open the door to his office and get the hell out of there.

PART IV

MASON

56

THE FIRST DAY

"Look to your left and look to your right."

Christ, this is stupid.

I'm not into the whole "motivational speech" crap. Dean Bushnell is trying to get us all psyched up. I get it. But this is just dumb.

Besides, he's wrong. Not everyone in this room is going to be a doctor. Some of them are going to drop out. Some will flunk out (probably that girl two seats over with the bullring through her nose). And if the last few years are any indication, a bunch of them are going to turn to drugs to get through the year. And one of them might take *too* many of those pills and stop breathing.

Not me, though.

I'm going to graduate in four years with the highest honors, and I'm going to land myself the best residency in the whole damn country. Wait and see.

I look over at my roommate, Abe. I've been calling him the Incredible Hulk as a joke. No kidding, slap a little green paint on the guy, and he'd be a dead ringer. Minus the temper, though. Abe is too mild-mannered to be in med school. He's a good roommate, though—he's a slob like me.

Abe's really taking in the dean's inspiring words. His jaw is hanging open, awed by the whole experience. He's going to be one of those touchy-feely doctors—you can just tell. When he rotates in the hospital, everyone will write on his evals that he has a great bedside manner.

Nobody's going to say I've got a great bedside manner. I'll be shocked if a few of the residents I work with don't write down that I'm a huge asshole. But who cares? They're going to love me on my surgery rotation, and that's all that matters. That's what I was born to do.

My father is a cardiothoracic surgeon. Dr. Walter Howard is the head of cardiothoracic surgery at Yale and one of the most respected surgeons in the country. I used to want to do what he was doing, but he told me don't bother. Angioplasty is killing his field. When I graduated college, Dad took me aside and said, "Plastics, son. That's where the money is."

It's plastic surgery or bust.

When I was six years old, my mom brought me to this really fancy dinner to honor my dad.

My dad is tall—*really* tall. Practically a giant, or that's what it felt like anyway. Back then, he had this black beard that scared the shit out of me for some reason. When he gave his speech, I listened as hard as I could because I thought his black eyes would maybe shoot laser beams at me if I didn't.

"Mommy," I whispered. "What's it mean that Daddy is a pioneer?"

In school, they said pioneers settled Middle America. I was pretty sure my dad hadn't done that. But it seemed possible.

"It means he's done surgeries that nobody's ever done before," my mother whispered back. She added, "He's a great man."

Then everyone in the room stood up and wouldn't stop applauding for my dad for at least five minutes.

When I visited my grandparents on my father's side, they wouldn't shut up about my father. They would drag out a box that was as old and dusty as they were, filled with perfect test papers and report cards with rows of straight As. They saved *everything*.

"Did Dad ever get less than an A in school?" I asked as I wiped the dust off a thirty-year-old transcript and sneezed loudly.

"I think Walter got a B in gym once," my grandmother recalled. "But everyone got a B in gym that semester." She added, "That gym teacher was a little soft in the head."

Sometimes, my mother would bore me with the story of how she met my father. I always tuned her out, but over the years, the details sank in. Elise Howard, née Elise Mason, was a year out of college and working at an art gallery, although her studio apartment was largely funded by—guess who—her rich parents. My dad was an attending surgeon then, almost a decade older than my mom, and he approached her at a gallery function and asked for her number. They started dating, and he proposed only a few months later.

"Sometimes, you just know," Mom would sigh.

Bullshit. The truth was—and I'm going to be blunt here—my mother was really hot. I saw the photos. My dad always used to go around saying she was the prettiest woman in the room. All my friends in high school used to call her a MILF.

My dad, on the other hand, isn't what you'd call a handsome guy. But he's as intimidating as all hell. He cocked his finger at my mom, and she came running.

I got straight As in high school. Even in *gym*. Yeah, I worked my ass off. I had plenty of friends and even occasional girlfriends, and I ran track and played soccer, but most of my time was spent studying.

And then I bombed the SATs. Or that's what it felt like when I saw my father's face. I didn't get a perfect 1600—I was ten points short.

"It's an all-right score," my father said with a shrug.

The word "asshole" was on the tip of my tongue, but I couldn't say it. *I* was the one who had messed up. My dad got a perfect score on *his* SATs.

I hung my head and mumbled, "Sorry, sir."

I was valedictorian of my high school class—the best out of a whole class of snooty rich kids at a private school with a disgustingly high tuition. My speech was about the path to success, and I expected to do better than any other person who was graduating that year. My dad liked the speech—or at least, he was nodding a lot. I believed in my words. I was going to be a huge success someday.

I got a perfect score on the MCATs to get into med school, by the way.

Ever since I decided to attend DeWitt Med, people have been asking me: Why not Yale? DeWitt is a good school, but Yale is Ivy, and I had connections there (not that I'd have needed them to gain admission). There's no comparison. People acted like I'd lost my mind.

Even my father was pissed off that I picked DeWitt over Yale.

But I had a really good reason for not going to Yale. At Yale, everyone would have assumed that I got in because my dad is a big cheese there, not on my own merit. And on every rotation, everyone would be comparing me with the great Dr. Howard. I'd never have a chance to get out from under his shadow.

DeWitt is perfect for me. When I look around at my classmates, I know that I can stand out here. I can be in the honor society and impress the hell out of all the professors. I won't be one of a huge crowd of over-achievers at Yale or one of the other Ivies. Plastic surgery is one of the most competitive residencies to get into, and being number one in my class is a great way to get there. If I succeed, if I become a plastic surgeon, maybe someday, I'll have a house that is bigger than my father's and a wife who's hotter than my mom. Maybe someday, they'll have a dinner honoring the great Dr. Mason Howard.

57

I STUDIED ANATOMY ALL SUMMER. I WANTED TO BE WAY ahead of the class even before school started. I had my father bring me home some suture material so that I could practice tying knots because I heard sometimes they let you practice in the anatomy lab, and I wanted to be the best from the onset. I couldn't wait to get my hands on a scalpel and start cutting.

My lab partners were no big surprise. On the first day of orientation, Abe nudged me after lunch and said, "You want to be partners for anatomy?"

"Sure," I said.

"Also," he said. "I was thinking maybe we could request to Dr. Conlon that Heather McKinley could join our group…"

I had no clue who he was talking about. He nodded his head in the direction of a pretty blond girl in the corner of the lecture hall. Well, she would have been pretty if she had less junk in the trunk. Abe didn't mind, though—I took one look at his face, and I got it.

"Sounds good," I said.

Poor guy—I had already heard Heather yakking about her boyfriend.

In the lab, Heather is a complete disaster. I mean, really bad. She's trying hard, but she just doesn't get it. And I have much better things to do than waste my time explaining every little thing to her five times. Good thing Abe has endless patience with her. With his hand-holding, maybe she has a snowball's chance in hell of passing.

I prefer Rachel, Heather's roommate. Rachel doesn't have a clue either, but she doesn't care. Plus she has fantastic tits, and she never, ever wears a bra. I think about her a *lot* when I'm alone in my room, if you catch my drift. The best part is that she despises me. It's really fun to try to get a rise out of her. The easiest trick is calling the cadaver Frank. Rachel hates that.

"Can't you respect that he is a real human being?" Rachel snaps at me. "He's not some inanimate object that you can just give a name to."

"He seems pretty inanimate to me," I say with a shrug and poke him in the arm.

Her brown eyes flash. "It blows me away that you're going to be responsible for other people's lives."

Rachel doesn't know what the hell she's talking about. You can't make it in medicine if you don't learn to distance yourself from the patient.

My fifth lab partner is Sasha. She's at least a head shorter than me and was practically mute at first, but it soon becomes obvious that Sasha knows her stuff when it comes to anatomy. The first words we exchanged were when Sasha was looking at the tattoo on Frank's arm. She had stretched out the skin taut in an attempt to read the words. The dye had faded somehow in the embalming process, and the words were barely legible.

"To protect and serve," Sasha read.

"What the hell does that mean?" I asked.

"It's the police force motto," she said.

I was sort of blown away. What was a cop doing in an anatomy lab? It just seems… strange. But whatever.

58

My life is studying. Okay, not entirely. I eat sometimes (while studying). I take a piss (sometimes while studying). I sleep a little. But mostly, I study.

I go to the hospital library every night and read through my textbooks until my eyelids are like lead. Then I head home, where I study some more. It's hard. But my grades make it worth it.

Sasha is often at the library as late as I am. At first, she sat at the far left corner of the library while I was on the far right. But then I moved to the left corner because it was closer to the anatomy textbooks in the library. I'm guessing that's why she chose that corner too.

The medical student lounge has free coffee, and usually, Sasha would go downstairs to get a cup every night at around eleven o'clock. Eventually, she started bringing me a cup too. Black—cream and sugar are for losers. I'd die without coffee.

"Don't you ever go home?" I ask her one Friday night in the library.

"Don't you?" she retorts.

I wink at her. "I think it's pretty obvious that I don't."

Sasha smiles. "I just want to be a good doctor."

She's holding the anatomy textbook in her hands. Her hands are so damn tiny, it's almost weird. The book is so heavy that I can see her fingers shaking. If Abe were here, he'd offer to carry the book for her, but that's not my style. Still, the truth is, I'm pretty into Sasha. She's not hot in an obvious way, but I dig that about her. She's been replacing Rachel in my fantasies lately. Some guys get intimidated, but I've always thought smart girls were extremely sexy.

"Why do you want to be a doctor anyway?" I ask.

Sasha raises an eyebrow. "Is your next question about how I'd change the health care system in America?"

I laugh. "No, I'm serious. I don't want your bullshit med school interview answer. I mean, everyone's got a reason for being here, right?"

"What's your reason?" Sasha asks.

"Money, power, and respect," I reply without hesitation. "Not necessarily in that order. Although at the interview, I think I said something along the lines of 'wanting to help people' or some crap like that." I smirk. "Okay, your turn."

"My father had Parkinson's disease," Sasha says. "He got it young and died a year before I started medical school."

I frown. "I'm sorry."

"His care was completely mismanaged," Sasha goes on. "It took him a long time to even get diagnosed, and then it seemed like we were being shuffled from one rude doctor to another. I want to become the one doctor who could have helped him."

I take a long sip of my coffee. "Christ, Sasha… That's a terrible story."

She's tearing up now. Shit, I hate it when girls cry. I never know what the hell to do.

So I kiss her.

Five minutes later, we're ripping each other's clothes off in the deserted medical student locker room. It's been a *long* time for me. I can't get enough of Sasha's bare skin and her tiny, sexy body shoved against me. She smells like flowers and coffee. For some reason, the smell of coffee is turning me on—go figure.

"Condom?" Sasha whispers between kisses.

"Yeah, hang on…" I mutter. I grab my abandoned jeans and retrieve my wallet from the back pocket. Ever since high school, I always carry an emergency condom. I'm careful to replace the condom after I use it, which has sadly been a rare occasion lately.

The sex is quick, but (in my humble opinion) pretty damn good. With everything I put into my studying lately, I don't have the stamina for a marathon. And especially not on the cold, hard floor of the locker room. When it's over, I toss the condom in the garbage. If anyone sees it there, they're going to be pretty amused.

Then we get dressed in silence. I watch Sasha doing up the buttons on her blouse with her tiny little fingers while I grin like an idiot. I can't help myself—that was so awesome.

But this is just sex to her. Nothing more. Just a release for two people who have done nothing but study for a full month.

59

I'M SITTING ON MY BED STUDYING (WHAT ELSE?) WHEN Abe stomps into our shared bedroom. The first thing he does is accidentally knock over the stack of books next to the bed, and the texts go flying all over the floor. Typical.

"Hulk smash," I say.

Abe doesn't crack a smile like he usually does when I make that joke. He sighs loudly and flops down on his bed. Then he stares up at the ceiling like a hormonal teenager. "It's hopeless," he mutters.

"Heather?" I ask.

He nods. "I can't take it anymore. Seriously."

I don't get it. "What's so great about her anyway?"

Abe rolls onto his side and frowns at me. "What's so great about Sasha?"

Shit, I didn't know he knew about me and Sasha. He's more observant than I gave him credit for.

"That's nothing," I say, which is the truth. Sasha would never let it be any more than that.

He sighs and rolls back the other way. "She's great, that's all. And her boyfriend is a total asshole who doesn't appreciate her."

I hate to see my roommate suffering this way.

"Okay," I say. "You know what you do?"

Abe sits up, all eager for my advice. I get the sense he doesn't have a whole lot of experience with girls.

"You kiss her," I say.

His eyes widen. "I can't do that, Mason!"

"Why not?"

"It's a violation of her space," he says.

Oh, Christ.

"Abe," I say. "You have to be aggressive. Nice guys finish last. Don't be a nice guy."

"Maybe," he says thoughtfully, "I can be a slightly less nice guy who finishes a little better than last."

"Just kiss her, dude!"

Abe shakes his head. "She'd probably just slap me."

That's actually a distinct possibility.

"It's worth the risk," I say.

Abe looks dubious.

"Abe," I say. "You have been her friend *way* too long. If you don't make a move fast, soon, you're going to be painting each other's toenails and putting her hair in curlers."

He looks like he's considering what I'm saying, but I doubt he'll do it. For a big guy, Abe is a huge wuss.

A WEEK before our first anatomy exam, my classmate Brogan Scott approaches me in the hospital after the class we just took together.

I've been avoiding Brogan like the plague lately. I get the sense she's interested in me, and that's just not what I want on any level. Yeah, Brogan is hot as holy hell, but so what? She just doesn't do it for me. Plus, I'm willing to bet she's super high maintenance.

"Mason," Brogan says in a singsong voice. She puts her hand on my arm for good measure. "Where have you been hiding yourself?"

I smile tightly. "What's up, Brogan?"

"We're having a party the night of the anatomy exam at my house," Brogan says. She's renting a house with a couple of other girls in the class, none of whom are girls I'd like to spend an evening with. "You *must* come."

I suppress a groan. Alcohol + Party + Brogan = Big Mistake. And even if I manage to avoid Brogan, I can't imagine the party being that much fun if her annoying, stuck-up friends are there. Then I get an idea for something that might make the party tolerable.

"Listen," I say. "Can I bring Sasha?"

"Who?" Brogan asks.

"Sasha Zaleski. My lab partner."

Brogan makes a face. "I'd rather not, Mason. I don't want more girls there. The ratios are already way off."

Is she joking? Is this junior high school, where she's counting girls and boys in the room?

"Then forget it," I say.

Brogan pouts at me. I bet that works on most guys,

but not this guy. I just have no interest in her. If I can't hang out with Sasha, then I don't want to go to the party.

"There just isn't *room*," Brogan insists.

Yeah, I'm sure she can't squeeze tiny Sasha into her huge house. She sighs loudly and crosses her arms.

"Listen, Mason, if you change your mind, you're welcome to come. But just you."

I'm pretty sure I won't be changing my mind.

60

All the studying pays off. The day before the anatomy exam grades are announced to be posted, Dr. Conlon calls me into his office. I can't imagine what my anatomy professor wants to tell me, but it can't be bad news—I kicked ass on the anatomy exam.

Dr. Conlon is pulling a book out of one of his shelves when I come in. He tosses the book onto his desk then grabs his cane and limps back to his seat. His cane nearly snags his desk in the process, and he plops down into his chair.

Dr. Conlon is a loser. I hate to say it, but yeah. He just is. The cane and the limp aren't even half of it.

I mean, the man wears bowties. Enough said.

"Sit down, Dr. Howard," Dr. Conlon says to me, a stern look on his face.

I don't like it that he calls us all "doctor." It's patronizing, especially since a fair number of my classmates will never become doctors. But I'm not going to say anything. Anyway, I sit down in front of his desk.

"May I ask you a question?" Dr. Conlon says.

I nod, intrigued.

Dr. Conlon doesn't just ask me one question but lets loose with a rapid fire of difficult anatomy questions. He asks about the gut anastomoses, the innervation of the muscles in the pelvic floor, and a bunch of stuff that's ridiculously obscure. He doesn't even tell me if I'm right or not. By the end, I have to admit, I'm struggling to keep my composure. These questions are *hard*.

Finally, after the fifteenth question in a row, I interrupt him: "Listen, what's this about?"

Dr. Conlon reaches into his desk and pulls out some stapled papers that I recognize as my exam. He tosses it down on the table.

"I've never seen anyone get a perfect score on the practical exam before," he says. "I had to make sure you weren't cheating."

"And?"

"You know your shit, Howard. I'm impressed."

I smile.

"What field are you interested in?" he asks me.

"Plastics," I reply without hesitation.

Dr. Conlon nods. "I have a good friend at UCSF in the plastics department. If you keep this up, I'd be happy to write him a letter on your behalf. Or even give him a call."

I feign surprise. But of course, I knew about Conlon's connections to plastics at UCSF. It's one of the best programs in the country—makes me curse the fact that I'm not a California native. One of the reasons I'm here at DeWitt is because of Dr. Conlon and what he can do for me. I'll rotate over there and impress the hell out of them, of course, but a letter would be gold.

"Thank you, sir," I say.

Dr. Conlon smiles. "Keep up the good work."

Everything is falling into place.

61

It's two a.m. on a Thursday night. And I'm at the library.

I got here a little late because I had to finally do my laundry. Buying new underwear was getting old. There was so much laundry, I had to use every available washer to get it done. I really hate doing laundry. The second I get married, I am done doing laundry.

Sasha is sitting across the table from me. She's going through some flashcards she made for biochem. I watch her biting her lip as she tucks her short dark hair behind her tiny ear. That girl is dedicated, all right—it's so sexy.

Sasha must have sensed me looking at her because she glances up expectantly. I'm going to brag here: we've had sex maybe a couple of dozen times now. We do it either in the locker room or the med student lounge. The lounge is more comfortable because it's got a couch, but the risk of getting caught is higher, so we usually just go to the locker room.

We've got a whole system going—if we're up for it,

we tap a yellow highlighter on the table five times. I've initiated more than she has, but she's done her fair share of highlighter tapping. It's gotten so that every time someone taps their pen in class, I start to get excited.

The sex is usually fast. It's a little embarrassing, to be honest, but Sasha hasn't called me on it yet. Anyway, it's good—really, really good. The truth is, I think about Sasha a lot. All the damn time. Right now, I'm trying to focus on the cranial nerves, but I keep looking up at her instead. I wonder if she's up for a study break.

Sasha cranes her neck to look at the textbook I'm reading, which is Dr. Conlon's book. She crinkles her nose.

"You highlight a lot," she comments.

"Yeah. So?"

"You highlighted every sentence on that page," she points out.

I glance down at the page in front of me.

"Not every sentence," I protest.

"There is literally one sentence that you didn't highlight," she says.

Okay, fine. She's right.

"Highlighting helps me focus," I say.

I have five different colors of highlighters, which I use for different levels of importance of the information on the page. Yellow is the critical stuff.

Sasha closes her textbook and yawns. I sneak a glance at her own highlighter, hoping for a few taps signaling she's in the mood. But no luck. Damn. I guess I'm going to have to go at it alone when I get home.

"Leaving?" I ask her.

She rubs her eyes. "Maybe I'll put in another hour with Frank."

That's one other thing I like about Sasha. She isn't scared to be in the anatomy lab alone at midnight.

"Hey, Mason," she says. "You ever get curious about Frank?"

"Yeah, sure," I admit.

In the last two months, I have probably spent more time with Frank than any other person in my life. It seems strange that I know nothing about the man, other than that he might have been a cop. Not even his real name.

"I wonder how he died," Sasha says thoughtfully. "Almost everyone else knows how their cadaver died, but I just can't figure it out with Frank. He's got a great heart, perfect lungs, perfect kidneys, no liver cirrhosis…"

That's been bothering me too. Frank is in mint condition. I'm no pathologist (and never will be… ugh), but usually, there are at least some signs that an organ is failing. Hearts often become enlarged when they're struggling, lungs turn black, livers grow firm. But Frank has none of those problems. His death is a complete mystery.

I wonder if we'll ever find out how he died.

WHEN I GET HOME that night, I find Abe sitting on the futon, clicking through the late-night television channels.

Abe's eyes are bloodshot, and he looks awful. He barely glances at me as I walk in.

"Hey, Hulk," I greet him. "Where's Heather?"

I've gotten used to the sight of them snuggled up on our futon. It almost doesn't make me want to vomit anymore.

"Heather is going to leave me," Abe says in a flat voice.

So much for sleep. I drop my books on the floor and push aside some dirty white tube socks to sit down next to Abe. We're both slobs. "What happened?"

"I should never have been with her in the first place," Abe mutters. "I mean, she's way out of my league…"

Abe either has the worst self-esteem ever or else he's looking at Heather through a pair of eternal beer goggles. She's not *that* hot, seriously. And Abe's a really good guy. He's easygoing, smart, affable, and even sometimes makes an effort to clean our bathroom, especially when Heather is around. He gets good grades, too, even though he's splitting his time, working at some student health clinic two nights a week. And I don't think he's awful looking or anything, not that I can judge that kind of thing. I've got to make him see there are other possibilities.

"Cheer up," I say. "In less than two years, we'll be working in the hospital, and you'll have more cute nurses flirting with you than you'll know what to do with."

Abe is barely listening. He stares ahead at the television, his eyes unfocused.

"I'm going to keep her," he says. "No matter what I have to do, I'm not going to let her get away."

"Okay..." There's a disturbing desperation in Abe's voice. *No matter what I have to do.* What the hell does that mean? "Look, you should get some sleep."

"Can't," Abe mutters, changing the channel absently. On the nature channel, a lion is ripping apart a young zebra. Okay then.

If there is one thing I'm *not*, it's a future psychiatrist. Abe's problems are his own. Whatever misguided shit Abe intends to do on Heather's behalf, that's his business. I have too much of my own work to do.

62

Dr. Conlon's morning lecture is on the extraocular muscles. The muscles that allow the eye to move are controlled by three pairs of cranial nerves: the oculomotor nerve, the trochlear nerve, and the abducens. The mechanism is pretty complicated, and weakness of any one of these nerves causes the affected eye to deviate in a way that would cause vision to double.

I have to admit that Dr. Conlon is a damn good lecturer. The eye is a very complicated organ, and there are a lot of dumb people in my class. But by the end of the lecture, everyone seems to get it.

When we're in the lab an hour later, even Rachel seems well versed in the extraocular nerves. She recites them to Dr. Conlon proudly as her nipples poke through her T-shirt. And he seems excited she got it right. Or excited by her nipples. Either way.

"And where's the rest of your group?" he asks.

It's just me, Rachel, and Sasha today. Abe and

Heather aren't around—they're probably somewhere making out or something.

"I have no idea," I say to Dr. Conlon, and then I add, "Guess they have something better to do."

Dr. Conlon just shakes his head.

"By the way," I say. There's something that's been on my mind, and I've got to ask him about it. "I was just wondering… Do you know what happened to our cadaver? Like, how he died?"

Dr. Conlon raises his black eyebrows. "Excuse me?"

"Well, he just seems so healthy…" I laugh, but somehow it comes out a little strangled. "I mean, aside from being dead."

I'd always thought of Dr. Conlon as being good-natured, but his blue eyes suddenly grow dark behind his spectacles.

"That's confidential, Mason," he snaps at me.

I just stare at him. It was an innocent question, and his response was… well, pretty surprising.

"Sorry," I stammer.

Without another word, Dr. Conlon grips the handle of his cane and limps away from our table. He seemed so furious all of a sudden. What the hell was that all about?

Almost like he's hiding something, isn't it?

I shake my head, wondering where that thought came from. I'm overworked and not sleeping nearly enough. But I can't shake the feeling that something is very wrong with this whole situation.

63

"How much weight have you lost, Mason?"

I'm flipping through the pages of my anatomy textbook as I sit on the bed in my room. My mother called me and immediately started grilling me on whether I'm taking care of myself. She's right—I'm not eating enough, and what I eat is crap. But what can I do? I'm sure as hell not going to start cooking myself healthy meals every night. It's cafeteria food or else ramen noodles. Or if I'm feeling motivated, I'll crack open a box of macaroni and cheese—the kind where the cheese comes in a fine powder.

"I'm fine, Mom," I say.

"Come home this weekend," she says. "Have a home-cooked meal."

I don't point out that any "home-cooked meal" is in fact cooked by the housekeeper. For years, my father and I have been complimenting my mother on Georgette's food. My mother would routinely burn toast.

"I guess so," I say.

Thanksgiving break isn't for a few more weeks, and some real food would be amazing. I could probably spare a couple of hours of studying for that.

"You can bring your girlfriend if you'd like," she adds in a sly voice. "We'd love to meet her, darling."

My mother has always taken too big an interest in my personal life. She misses my college girlfriend, Sienna. My mother would have married Sienna herself if she could have.

"I don't have a girlfriend, Mom," I try to tell her.

"You?" she snorts. "Of course you do."

I don't know what to say to that.

After giving it some thought, I decide to invite Sasha to come. She's not my girlfriend, but I can't imagine asking anyone else. But I'm really into her these days, and it wouldn't be painful to spend a whole night together.

I ask Sasha during anatomy lab when it's just the two of us.

"Your *parents'* house?" Sasha asks, genuinely surprised.

Christ, it's not like I gave her an *engagement ring*. I carefully play it down.

"I just want a friend with me to help get me through the evening," I explain. "Come on, aren't you a little bit curious?"

"A little bit," Sasha admits with a smile. "What should I wear?"

I pick Sasha up at five o'clock on Saturday night, and my parents are a forty-five-minute drive away. I told her to dress casual, and she looks… perfect. She's wearing a knee-length skirt—could be shorter, but probably better it's not since I'm bringing her to meet my parents. I like that I can see a tiny bit of cleavage poking out of her neckline. And when she leans forward, I catch a glimpse of a lacy black bra strap. So damn hot.

"Wow," I say.

Sasha's olive skin colors slightly, which is even sexier. "What?"

"You look… really nice."

I can't stop looking at her. I mean, I always think she's attractive, but *damn*.

And that's when I decide: tonight, after we leave my parents' house, I'm going to ask Sasha out on a real date. No-strings-attached sex is fun, but it's not enough anymore. I probably sound like a tool saying this, but I want Sasha to be my girlfriend. I'm going to talk her into it somehow. I can be very persuasive.

"I love your car," Sasha says as she climbs into the passenger's seat. She sweeps her dark hair off her olive shoulders as she looks down at the gears. "You drive a stick?"

"Yep."

"I'm impressed. Sticks are cool."

She thinks I'm cool. Score one for Howard.

At first, I tune in to the radio, but we end up talking so much that I just turn it off. Mostly, we talk about school and our classmates. Sasha knows all the gossip, which makes me feel really out of the loop. I've been studying too much, I guess.

Then again, there's no such thing as too much studying, right?

We get to my parents' house just before six. I still have my keys to the front door, but I figure the polite thing to do is ring the bell. My mother would never forgive me if I busted into the house with company, not giving any warning.

My mother responds to the bell herself. She gets this huge smile on her face when she sees us, although she doesn't hug me. We're not a family that does lots of hugs, which is fine by me. My mom looks about ten years younger than the last time I saw her—all those lines on her forehead are gone. Botox, I'm almost positive. Not that I'd ask.

"Hello, darling," Mom coos. Then she turns to Sasha. "And this must be Sasha."

Sasha nods. "That's right," she says, fiddling with her shirt collar.

As we walk inside, I can smell dinner. It smells amazing. So much better than the cafeteria crap. I glance over at Sasha, who looks pale.

"What's wrong?" I whisper.

"This place is *huge*," she whispers back. "When I lived at home, I shared a bedroom with my two sisters."

I always thought of my parents' house as just home, but now that Sasha pointed it out, I guess she's right. The foyer opens up into an impressive living room, with three leather couches and the latest model in large-screen television sets. In the far corner of the room is a fireplace that is now burning bright-orange flames. A wide, carpeted staircase leads up to the second of three stories that make up the house.

I can see a little crease form between Sasha's brows,

and instinctively, I fling my arm around her shoulders. She stares up at me with her mouth hanging open—I've never done anything like that before. But she doesn't push me away, so I count that as a win.

"Sasha," my mother gushes, "I absolutely *must* give you a tour of the house."

"Um... okay..." Sasha says.

"Mason," my mother says, "would you be a dear and take your and Sasha's coats into the den?"

As my mother drags away my date, I wander in the direction of the den. As expected, my father is sitting in a reclining chair, reading *The New England Journal of Medicine*. Dad's black hair is now threaded with gray, as is his beard, but his dark eyes still scare the shit out of me. I instinctively straighten my posture as I carefully arrange the coats on an empty sofa.

My father looks up at the sound and peers at me over the rim of his reading glasses.

"Mason," he says in a deep, rumbling voice several octaves lower than mine. "I'm glad you were able to make it."

I nod.

"How is school going?" he asks. "At the top of your class, I assume."

I nod again. "Yes, sir."

"Of course," my father says. "You're my son, aren't you?"

My father stands up, and I straighten my spine further, but I'm still not as tall as he is. He's six foot one, and I'm an inch shy of six feet. It kills me that I didn't even hit six feet. And when I stare at people, they don't cower in fear. They just smile at me and maybe ask me if I want to go on a date with their granddaughter.

I'm nothing like my dad. And that disappoints the hell out of him.

"Well, I'm going to get washed up for dinner," my father says as he brushes off his pants. "I'll see you at the dinner table, Mason."

"Yes, sir," I say, letting out a breath as my father leaves the room.

I lag behind in the den. This one room feels like a castle compared to my dorm back at school. It's nice to be able to walk across the room without bumping into furniture or tripping over Abe's dirty laundry.

I cross the room and find myself at my father's desk. It's a large mahogany piece that cost a small fortune—I'm no stranger to expensive furniture, but I actually gasped when I saw the price tag on it when it was delivered last year. I sit down at the desk, wondering when I'll have enough money to afford a den of my own that looks like this. I still have four years of medical school ahead of me, then a long, low-paying residency. My parents lend me a lot of money, but they wouldn't be willing to bankroll me if I wanted to buy a house, and I'd never ask.

I try to open the desk drawer, but it's locked. Typical of my father. I feel around under the drawer and immediately touch the outline of the key that is taped to the bottom of the drawer. My father is still using the same hiding places.

Open the drawer.

I hear the command loud and clear, as if someone is

speaking to me, right in my ear. A deep male voice that I can't identify. I look around the room, but nobody is there.

Huh. That's weird.

Open the drawer, Mason.

"Hello?" I say aloud. Someone definitely said something that time. I *heard* it. I glance over and see that the door to the room is closed. I'm alone.

The television? Could it be the television? I walk over to the set and examine it for a second—it's not turned on. The stereo is off too. And besides, they said *my name*.

Where the hell did that voice come from?

I return to the desk and examine the drawer. When I was younger, it used to be a game to unlock my father's desk drawers without him knowing about it. There was never anything interesting in the drawers back then. Usually, I just found some boring bills, and once, I found a copy of their mortgage, with numbers so high that it made me dizzy. I'm a little old now to be digging around in my father's desk drawer. Still, I find myself pushing the key into the lock.

I don't know what I had expected to find. But I hadn't expected to find a .357 Magnum.

I pick up the gun, and a handful of bullets roll to the front of the drawer. I know how to shoot. My dad firmly believes in the right to bear arms and had taken me to a range for shooting practice when I was younger. We even went hunting a couple of times, but we didn't kill anything, probably because I was so loud that I scared all the animals away. This gun feels lighter than the ones

I had held before, easily concealable in one's pocket. But still really powerful.

Take the gun.

The sound of the command startles me, and I nearly drop the gun on the floor. I blink my eyes, desperately looking around the room.

"Who's there?" I snap.

The room is empty.

I take a deep breath and study the gun in my hand. My father keeps it around for protection, but the house is already alarmed up the wazoo. There's no way anyone is getting into this fortress, and even if someone did, isn't there some statistic that showed that you're more likely to accidentally shoot a family member than a burglar? Or something like that.

I'm certain now that nobody else is in the room. But this voice is real. I heard it loud and clear. And it seems to somehow know something I don't.

"Why do I need it?" I say aloud.

No answer.

Well, what did I expect? To have a conversation about firearms with some invisible person?

Still, I can't shake the feeling that I'm going to need this gun.

I take a deep breath then scoop out the bullets and lock the desk drawer. I place the gun and the bullets in the pocket of my coat that's lying on the sofa. Then I leave the room to join my family for dinner.

64

"THIS LOOKS DELICIOUS, MOM," I SAY AS I DIG INTO the lemon-pepper chicken that is courtesy of Georgette.

"Delicious, Elise," my father echoes.

I look over at Sasha, waiting for her to offer a compliment, but she just frowns. Finally, she says, "The cook did a great job."

I almost smack myself in the head. How could she have said that?

"Do you cook much, Sasha?" my mother asks her.

Sasha is toying with her food, shifting her mashed potatoes into a little pile. "I used to. For my father. But now I live alone. I mostly eat TV dinners."

As Sasha finally takes a bite of her mashed potatoes, I want to yell at her, *Elbows off the table!* I don't know why I care so much. When I'm at school, I eat with my elbows on the table about one hundred percent of the time, and Abe eats with his *feet* on the table most of the time. But right now, I'm seeing Sasha through my parents' eyes. And they're not impressed.

I don't know what I was thinking, considering asking Sasha on a real date. Yes, she's smart and hot and… well, a lot of things. But she doesn't fit into my life here. I can't have a girlfriend like Sasha. I have to project the right image, and Sasha honestly just isn't that special. At least, not in a way that anyone but me can appreciate.

On top of that, she isn't even American. She's Russian or Slavic or something like that. She may have been born here, but it's pretty clear from her name that her ancestors didn't come over on the Mayflower like mine did. If my mother heard her last name, she'd probably have a stroke.

It's fine that I've been hooking up with Sasha, but how could I have invited her home with me? It's embarrassing.

By the end of the meal, Sasha is barely speaking at all, just staring down at her plate, absently moving her food around with her fork. In fact, nobody is talking very much. I can't wait to get the hell out of here.

"Your girlfriend seems… nice," my mother says to me at the end of the evening.

"She's not my girlfriend, Mom," I say, and relief floods my mother's features.

The drive home is tense. I barely look at Sasha and instead keep my eyes pinned on the road ahead of me, watching the headlights of oncoming cars flashing by. Why did I bring her tonight? What a dumb mistake. She's not my girlfriend—she's not even my friend. I should have let our relationship stay what it was instead of trying to turn it into something it could never be.

"I didn't realize you were so rich," Sasha says, breaking the silence.

"I'm not rich," I say.

"Oh sure."

"My dad's a surgeon. What can I say?"

"Have you ever worked a day in your life?"

What a bitchy thing to say. Who is she to judge me?

"Flipping burgers? No." My grip on the steering wheel tightens. "But I've worked hard in school. It's not like I paid off my teachers to get good grades."

Sasha doesn't say anything for a long time. Finally, after several minutes, she speaks while looking out the window.

"You better never screw up, Mason," she says. "They'll eat you alive."

For some reason, I think of the Magnum still in my pocket.

65

A FEW DAYS AFTER THE DINNER AT MY PARENTS' HOUSE, I take my father's credit card and make a trip to a large local bookstore to raid the shelves for anatomy texts. The bookstore has a full floor dedicated to medicine, and there is no shortage of overpriced textbooks and review books. Our second midterm is in a few weeks, and there's no time to mess around.

I pick out half a dozen books and lug them to the checkout counter. The act of carrying the texts to the counter is enough to make me gasp for breath. Wow, pathetic. When was the last time I've been to a gym? Oh well, no time for that now. I'll get in shape again after residency is over.

The girl ahead of me in the checkout line reminds me a lot of Sienna from college. She's tall—long blond hair loose down her back, great tits, great ass. This is the sort of girl my parents would have wanted me to bring home—someone who wouldn't embarrass me.

I hadn't even realized I was staring at her until she catches me. My face gets hot, and I quickly look back down at my stack of books.

"Got anything to read?" the girl asks me teasingly, gesturing at the two-foot stack.

She's interested. Go for it, Howard!

I flash her a smile dripping with charm. "I've got an anatomy exam coming up."

She glances down at the titles of the books. "You're in med school?"

"My first year," I confirm.

"I'm Erin," she says.

"I'm Mason."

"So what kind of doctor are you going to be?" Erin asks me.

"A surgeon."

Erin seems properly impressed by this. She then reveals she's a junior at DeWitt College, and she's majoring in art history. My mother would love this girl. They could have a blast discussing Monet or some crap like that.

I'm trying to decide if I should ask her out when she reaches out and touches my arm. "So when are you going to ask me for my number… Doctor?"

"Um," I say. Wow. I'm not used to girls being *quite* so forward—I think I'm going to like being a med student. "Can I have your number, Erin?"

Erin scribbles her digits on a blank page in one of the textbooks I'm buying, and I think to myself how perfect she is. She's beautiful, tall, reasonably articulate, and I bet anything she's really easy. This is the kind of girl any guy would be thrilled to have a date with.

So why can't I stop thinking about Sasha? What is *wrong* with me?

66

My life is still mostly studying. I got the highest grade in the class on the first exam, and I want to make a similarly strong showing on the second one. My only regret is that I can't break my own record. I go to the library every day after class and stay there until I can barely keep my eyes open.

Sasha continues to keep me company in my corner of the library. We still talk, and she still brings me coffee when she goes to get herself a cup, but we haven't had sex since the dinner with my parents.

"Black, no sugar," she says as she places the cup in front of me.

"Thanks, Sasha," I say. "You're the best."

"Am I?"

I always have to bite my tongue to keep from asking her if she wants to go to the locker room with me. I figure if I ask, she'll say no. I blew that aspect of our relationship, and I can't admit to her how desperately I miss it. I made a huge mistake that night at my parents' house. But I'm glad that I at least have her company during the lonely nights in the library.

A few days before the test is scheduled, I'm sitting in the back of the library, studying the muscles of mastication when I hear a voice from over my shoulder: "Holy shit… anatomy. Whenever I think my life is the worst it could possibly be, I remember that class, and I feel a little better."

A tall guy with a shaved head is standing over me, wearing green scrubs and a long white coat. The ID badge hanging from his lapel proclaims him to be "Resident, Department of General Surgery." He has his arms crossed and is shaking his head in amusement.

"You a first-year?" he asks me.

"That's right." I look the guy up and down. "You a resident?"

"Bingo." He holds out his hand. "The name's Norm. I'm a surgery resident."

That will be me someday. Except somewhere better than here. I take Norm's hand. "I'm Mason."

"So is Conlon still torturing you guys?" Norm asks, dragging a chair over so he can sit down.

"He's not so bad."

"He got nicer." Norm rubs his bald head thoughtfully. "You don't know what he was like in his first year teaching."

"No kidding?"

"Oh, yeah. Frankly, I think it's his fault this school has a drug problem."

I raise my eyebrows. "What do you mean?"

"I don't know... It didn't seem like it was so bad before he started working here." Norm shrugs. "But practically as soon as he started, it felt like there were drugs circulating everywhere."

"Are you saying you think he's... selling them?"

Norm seems surprised by my question. "Oh, I didn't mean that. But now that you mention it..."

"What?"

He grins. "I don't know. I heard the salary they pay professors at DeWitt is crap. I wouldn't be surprised if he decided to make a few extra bucks on the side. And hey, wouldn't that be perfect? He creates a class that's super stressful, then everyone has to buy speed from him to get through it!"

It would be kind of perfect. DeWitt has a major drug problem, and there's a lot of whispering about how a professor must be one of the sources.

Norm notices the look on my face and says, "Hey, I'm just kidding. I don't think Dr. Conlon would do that. He's too much of a square."

Is he really? Or is that all just an act? "Yeah..."

Dr. Conlon projects the stereotypical image of a dorky professor. But I've always wondered how much of it is genuine. And he's always walking around with that cane, but I haven't figured out why he needs it. It's not clear from looking at him, and he's never shared it with anyone in the class. Maybe that's all an act too.

"Plus, it would be a huge risk," Norm says. "If he sold drugs to a bunch of kids and they ended up *dying* because of it, can you imagine how much trouble he'd be in? He'd probably go to prison."

That's true. If Dr. Conlon really is selling drugs to students, he would need to be very careful. If the police found out, he'd be in deep trouble.

"Hey, man, you okay?" Norm is frowning. "Sorry, did I freak you out?"

"I'm fine," I say quickly. "I think I need to get more sleep."

"I hear that," Norm says, grinning. "Anyway, it's been nice meeting you. Maybe I'll see you in your third-year surgery clerkship. It's loads of fun."

I barely manage a distracted goodbye.

I close my anatomy text and rub my fingers into my temples. I have always believed I've got good intuition, and my intuition is screaming out that there's something fishy going on with Dr. Matthew Conlon. I have to focus on my upcoming exam, but all I can think of is all those kids who died of overdoses in the classes before me.

If he sold drugs to a bunch of kids and they ended up dying because of it, can you imagine how much trouble he'd be in?

The look in Dr. Conlon's eyes when I started questioning him about Frank's cause of death was chilling. I asked an innocent question, and he jumped down my throat. Seems suspicious if you ask me. For some reason, there's a dead cop in our anatomy lab, and I have no idea why.

I stand up so fast that my chair falls over behind me. My heart is pounding in my chest. I look around the library and see that it is almost empty now—even Sasha has gone home for the night. It's so empty that nobody even noticed when my chair fell to the floor. I wipe my brow with the back of my hand, and it comes away wet with sweat.

An anatomy professor has got to have some connections to the local morgue, right? Maybe there are strings he can pull to get a body to come to him rather than risking an autopsy. And once a body gets ripped apart in the anatomy lab, there's no chance of finding out the real cause of death.

Unless there's a med student in the class who gets too curious.

But Conlon would never allow that to happen.

I back away from the table, my hands trembling. My breaths are coming quickly—too quickly. I'm hyperventilating. I recently learned that during hyperventilation, the lungs blow off too much carbon dioxide. As the amount of carbon dioxide in the bloodstream goes down, the blood vessels going to the brain constrict, cutting off the brain's oxygen supply.

I've got to calm down.

This is ridiculous. My anatomy professor isn't a drug dealer or a murderer. He's just a nice, dorky guy who wears bowties to class every day. He's not murdering students and hiding bodies in the cadaver lab. Stuff like that doesn't happen in real life.

And that's when I hear that deep voice again:

Think about it. What sorts of things can kill a man but won't show up on a routine anatomy lab dissection? Seems like Conlon would know.

"Shut up!" I whisper.

The sound of my own voice startles me, but it seems

to put a stop to my racing thoughts. My thumping heart slows down, and I suddenly feel completely exhausted. Maybe four hours of sleep every night isn't enough. I have to start taking better care of myself before I blow everything I've worked so hard for.

67

I HAD HOPED THAT A NIGHT OF SLEEP WOULD CLEAR MY mind, but the next day, I wake up feeling just as uneasy as the night before. I wish Abe were around, because I want to talk this out with someone—try to get someone else's perspective. But it seems like I haven't seen Abe around the apartment in days. Where the hell is he anyway?

When I get to school, I check my watch and see that I still have twenty minutes before my first class. When I arrive early, I usually make a stop in the cafeteria for some much-needed breakfast and a strong cup of coffee. However, this morning, I make a beeline for Dr. Conlon's secretary's office, which is right next to his.

Dr. Conlon's secretary, Anita, looks like a grandma. She's short and chubby with poofy white hair and is always offering us "sweets." I've talked to her a handful of times, and she's always real nice to me.

"Hello, Mason!" Anita says when I walk through her open door.

I flash my most charming smile. Old women always love me. "Hi, Anita. How are you?"

"Mason, Mason…" Anita leans forward across her desk. "You don't have a girlfriend, do you? Oh, I'm sure a handsome young man like you is already attached…"

"Actually, I don't," I say.

"Oh?" She raises an eyebrow. "Well, I don't know if you'd be interested, but my niece is a very sweet girl. She's about your age. You'd really like her."

I hate it when older women try to set me up with their daughters, nieces, and granddaughters. But I force a smile. "Sure, give me her number."

Anita's face lights up, and she pulls out a sticky note to write out the number of some girl named Margo.

"You'll love her, Mason," Anita gushes. "She's such a cute girl. And so funny! And smart too… Oh, but you boys don't like smart girls, do you? Don't worry. I'm sure she's not smarter than you are. After all, you're a—"

"Anita," I interrupt, unable to tolerate another second of hearing about this girl I'll never call. "I was wondering if you could look up some information on our cadaver."

Anita looks confused. "Oh? What information?"

"I was just curious if you have the cause of death listed," I say. My stomach fills with butterflies as I wait for her response.

"Well, we should," Anita says thoughtfully. "I mean, we have to know that so that there's no chance of the person having a communicable disease."

"So, um…" I bite my lip. "Could you look it up for me?"

Anita is about to respond when Dr. Conlon limps into the office. He looks surprised to see me standing there. I swear silently to myself.

"Hi, Mason," Dr. Conlon says with a friendly smile. "What are you doing here? Anything I can help you with?"

I look down at my hands and see they're trembling. I'm about to reply when Anita speaks up. "Mason is just trying to find out some information about his cadaver."

The smile vanishes instantly from Conlon's face. His eyes darken the same way they did before. He looks like he wants to reach out and strangle me.

"Mason," he says quietly. "Didn't I tell you before that all cadaver information is confidential?"

"Well, I was trying to—"

"Don't you have a biochemistry test tomorrow?" Dr. Conlon raises an eyebrow.

"Uh, yes."

Dr. Conlon looks over at Anita. "Any information on the cadavers in the lab is strictly confidential. Nobody is to receive that information." He looks back up at me. "Is that clear?"

My stomach feels like lead.

"Yes," I say. "It's clear."

Dr. Conlon is still staring at me in a way that is pretty terrifying. He knows I'm onto him—I can see it in his eyes. I've turned myself into a threat, and now he has to deal with me.

But I won't go down without a fight.

68

I've been watching Dr. Conlon very carefully recently.

Right now, Abe and Heather are hunched over Frank's split-open skull, reviewing the cranial nerves, while Sasha reads from the lab manual. I'm at the other end of the cadaver, flipping through the anatomy atlas, but my mind is somewhere else. Our second midterm in anatomy is in a few days, but I already know the material cold. That's not my biggest worry anymore.

Dr. Conlon is dressed in blue scrubs, and he makes his usual rounds from cadaver to cadaver, gripping his cane in his left hand. His cane is cumbersome—made of dull metal and ending in four prongs arranged in a square formation. The fact that he relies on that cane makes him seem really impaired, and I have to wonder if that's the idea. If he visited a store to find a cane that would enhance his story that he can't walk very well and isn't capable of harming a fly, that's probably the cane he'd end up with.

See, I'm about ninety-five percent sure at this point that Dr. Conlon isn't disabled at all.

For starters, if you watch him walk, it's clear he's faking—he alternates which leg he limps on. Sometimes, it's his right, sometimes, his left. I'm pretty sure of that. And the pretense that his right hand isn't functional is equally bullshit. In his short-sleeved scrub top, it's clear that all the muscles in his right arm are intact. I admit, he holds his hand in a way that makes it look impaired, but if I bend my wrist as far as it will go and curl up my fingers, it doesn't look so different from his hand.

Of course, I can't prove anything. I followed Conlon out to his car a few times, hoping to catch him in the act—like, tossing his cane aside and walking without it. I had my phone ready to snap photos the second he did it. But he's really dedicated to the illusion of appearing disabled or else he sensed someone was watching, and he never abandoned that cane. He's even got handicapped plates on his car—not that those are hard to get. My father says half his cardiac patients have them.

"Dr. Conlon!" Sasha flags down our professor as he "limps" by our table.

Dr. Conlon stops and smiles at Sasha. Lately, everything about Dr. Conlon seems ominous to me, even his smile. "Yes, Dr. Zaleski?"

Sasha launches into a question about the circle of Willis, and my stomach clenches as I notice how close Dr. Conlon is standing to her. He needs to back up at least a foot, seriously. Sasha seems pleased by the attention, but she doesn't get it. Dr. Conlon's attention is *not* something she wants. And Sasha is so small and sweet and vulnerable—and she wants so desperately to do well in anatomy. If Dr. Conlon offered her some drugs with the promise of a higher score on the next exam, would she be able to refuse?

If he touches a hair on Sasha's head, I swear to God, I will kill him.

69

I didn't even realize I drifted to sleep until the ringing of my phone jogs me awake. I'm sitting up in bed, my laptop resting on my legs, still in the clothes I had been wearing last night. I recall a dream I had been having about Frank, although I can't remember the details. I fumble for the phone and hold it to my ear.

"Hello?" I mumble.

"Mason? It's Erin. Where are you?"

Erin… shit! I completely forgot we were supposed to get together for an early lunch today at a coffee shop that's a five-minute drive from my dorm. I look at my watch and realize I'm fifteen minutes late.

"I'm sorry, I…" I try to come up with an excuse, and my mind goes blank. "I'll be there in five minutes, okay?"

Erin reluctantly agrees, and I shove my feet into my shoes. No time to change clothes. I pull on a light jacket as I hurry out the door, since the weather has started to get pretty nippy lately. I can't believe I managed to stand up my first real date since starting med school. Lately, I'm finding it increasingly difficult to focus.

When I pull up to the coffee shop, I spot Erin through the window, sitting in a booth and glancing down at her watch as she pouts. This is not a girl who is used to being stood up. I again search my brain for a plausible excuse for not showing up. I can't think of one. And I can't exactly tell her I forgot all about her.

I yank the door open and nearly trip over a chair hurrying over to her table.

"Hi, Erin," I say breathlessly. "Sorry I'm late…"

She looks up at me, obviously ready to give me a piece of her mind, but her jaw falls open slightly when she sees me. I didn't look in a mirror before leaving the apartment, and now I'm sorry—I probably look like a mess. I self-consciously run a hand through my hair in a half-hearted effort to comb it out.

I slide into the seat across from her.

"I'm really sorry," I say again.

"You know, some guys will put on clean clothes for a girl," Erin says. "And shave."

I touch the stubble on my chin and try to recall the last time I took a razor to my face.

"Sorry," I say again.

Although I'm beginning to realize I'm not all that sorry. I couldn't care less about Erin. She's pretty, yeah. But so what? There are thousands of pretty girls out there.

And anyway, she's got nothing on Sasha. I still can't believe I blew that.

I wouldn't have been surprised if Erin had gotten up

and walked out on me. But instead, she leans forward and crosses her arms.

"So how was your big exam?"

I struggle to come up with an answer to her question. The anatomy exam was two days ago, and I'm only slightly distressed by the fact that I barely remember it. It doesn't seem important anymore. My life is *in danger*. Doesn't she get that?

No, I guess she doesn't.

As Erin babbles about something or other, my mind wanders. I can't help but think that Frank is the key to all of this. Frank was a cop, and I bet he knew something. He must have been investigating the drug sales, and he figured out what's going on. That's why Conlon had him killed. And Conlon is willing to get rid of anyone who's on the verge of figuring out his secret. And now, that includes me.

"Who's Frank?" Erin asks.

I stare at her. "What?"

"You just said something about 'the case Frank was investigating,'" she says.

I hadn't realized I had spoken out loud. Wow, that's a little scary.

"What are you talking about?" she asks.

"Believe me, you don't want to know."

Erin is giving me a strange look. "Are you okay?"

Okay? No, I'm not okay! My anatomy professor is a drug dealer and a murderer, and I'm probably next on his hit list.

She squints at me. "You look like you're on *drugs*."

"On drugs?" I repeat. "You have no idea how far off you are."

But the weird thing is that as she says it, I start to wonder. My thoughts have been racing lately in a way that they never have before. And Conlon clearly has access to an arsenal of substances. What if he's been slipping me something? I'm not sure how he'd do it, but I've eaten plenty of meals in the hospital cafeteria. I'm sure he could pay someone off to get access to my food.

"If you're going to talk nonsense, I'm leaving," she says. She punctuates her statement by standing up.

I look up at her as she stands there for a moment, her arms folded across her chest. I could stop her. I could maybe say something charming, and she might agree to stay and have lunch.

But instead, I just let her leave.

70

It's three in the morning.

I stumble to the bathroom, intending to just splash some water on my face. But when I see my reflection in the mirror, I'm a little shocked by how bloodshot my eyes are. I guess it shouldn't be such a surprise, though—my vision has gotten blurry in the last hour.

I stumble back to my bed and stare at the screen of my laptop. I've been scouring the internet obituaries for anyone who seems like they could have been Frank. So far, it's not going that well. A lot of people have died lately, believe it or not. But I can't give up.

My eyes drift shut. I want to sleep so badly, but every time my head hits the pillow, my heart begins to pound, and my thoughts race. I don't know what the hell is wrong with me. Maybe Conlon really is slipping me something.

Before I know it, the sun is peeking out from under the horizon. I notice that a new email has appeared in my inbox. It's from Dr. Conlon:

Mason – please come see me in my office this afternoon at two.

Maybe he's ready to confess.

Or maybe he wants to feel me out—see how much I know. Maybe he's going to threaten me. Or maybe he's trying to figure out the best way to kill me.

Still, it's worth the risk. I want to know what he wants.

I visit Dr. Conlon's office that afternoon. The door is slightly ajar, and I walk inside without knocking. At first, I feel nervous about the idea of being alone with this sociopath, but then, I realize we're not alone at all. Patrice Winters, the shrink, is sitting in a chair in front of Dr. Conlon's desk. She turns when I enter the room and close the door behind me.

Why the hell is Patrice here? Is she in on it too?

"Mason…" Dr. Conlon looks me up and down. Maybe sizing me up.

"What?" I say.

"How have you been doing, Mason?" Dr. Conlon says. His voice is gentle, and there's a crease between his black eyebrows.

This sensitive professor shit is all an act. Probably for Patrice's benefit. I'm hoping she's a neutral.

"I feel great," I say.

"Is everything all right at home?" Patrice pipes up. "With your family? Mom and Dad?"

"Yes, of course," I reply tightly.

Patrice's thin eyebrows rise. "Girl problems?"

I shake my head no. "I'm fine. Really. I don't know what this is all about."

Dr. Conlon and Patrice exchange looks. Finally, Conlon says, "Mason, you failed the last exam. You know that, right?"

The room gets really quiet. Did I know that? I don't know anymore. Something is wrong. Something is really, really wrong.

How could I have failed an exam? I'm the best student in the whole damn class! I got a perfect score on the first practical. I knew the material backward and forward. There's no way I could have failed.

Of course, Conlon was the one who graded the exam. So if he says I failed, who's going to doubt him? He's showing me that he's not messing around, that he has the ability to wreck my life. Except I'm not messing around either.

I stand up. "I have to go."

Patrice stands up too. "Mason, don't go. We need to talk."

"What's there to talk about?" I say through my teeth. "Dr. Conlon messed with my exam and failed me on purpose."

It's almost enjoyable to see the way Conlon's blue eyes widen and his jaw falls open.

"Mason," he manages. "I would never…"

"Mason," Patrice says, "this is a really serious accusation."

I shrug.

"Mason…" Dr. Conlon struggles to his feet. Or at least, he *pretends* to struggle to his feet. I'm more convinced than ever that his disability is all an act. "Please sit down. Let's talk about this."

"What's there to talk about?" I practically spit at him. "You're trying to destroy me, aren't you?"

Dr. Conlon just shakes his head. "Mason, I would never mess with your exam. This is outrageous. How could you ever think that I'd—"

"Matt," Patrice interrupts him. "Let me handle this, okay?"

She touches his arm when she says it, and suddenly, I get it. The two of them are an item. They're in this together. And now, they're ganging up on me. It all makes perfect sense.

"I know what you're doing," I say. "And it's not going to work."

With those words, I spin on my heels and leave Dr. Conlon's office. I can hear him calling my name and then Patrice's voice telling him to let me go.

71

On Thanksgiving, Abe stays at the dorms because he's working at that student health clinic again on Black Friday. His family isn't loaded like mine, so he's always trying to pick up extra shifts—presumably to support his very expensive relationship with Heather. He's not home yet when I go to bed for the night on Thanksgiving Day, but when I wake up suddenly at three in the morning (which has been happening more and more lately), he's lying in his own bed, snoring softly.

I feel confident that Abe is safe from Dr. Conlon. He earns decent but not spectacular grades and hasn't done a whole lot to call attention to himself. Moreover, he's huge, so even a completely able-bodied and athletic Dr. Conlon probably wouldn't be able to overpower him. No, Dr. Conlon would never target Abe in a million years.

Abe shifts in his sleep, mumbling a few words I can't make out. I watch his broad chest rise and fall with each breath. I've known Abe for several months now, and one thing I know for sure is that he's a good guy. A *really* good guy. He's kind, he's honest, and he'd never do anything unethical. He's exactly the sort of person I need on my side.

That's when I make up my mind: in the morning, I'm going to tell him everything. He'll keep my secret safe, and then, if something happens to me, he'll be able to go to the authorities. I can trust Abe—I'm sure of it.

THE NEXT MORNING, when I wake up, Abe has already left for the clinic. My heart sinks when I notice that his bed is empty. I had wanted to talk to him before he left. Now, I'll have to wait until tonight, and he often gets home very late from the clinic.

Just as I'm stumbling into the common room to see what there is to eat in our mini fridge, there's a knock on the door. I can't even begin to imagine who would be coming to visit us on the morning after Thanksgiving. I'm certainly not expecting anyone.

I throw open the door, and a classmate of mine named Victor is standing in front of me. He's a tall, skinny guy who always looks like he's had a bit too much coffee to drink. He raises a hand in greeting.

"Hey, Mason," he says.

"Hey."

He shoves his hands into the pockets of his hoodie sweatshirt. "Uh, is Abe around?"

I didn't know Victor and Abe were friends. I don't

even know if I've ever seen the two of them talking to each other. "No…"

"Aw, seriously?" His face falls. "Well, will he be back soon?"

"Probably not. He's working at the student clinic."

Victor's eyes light up. "Oh, it's open today?"

"Uh, yeah…"

"Awesome, awesome." He nods to himself. "I'll get it there, then."

With those words, he disappears down the hallway, a new skip in his step.

What the hell was that about? Why was Victor so desperate to find Abe? And what does he think he's going to get at the clinic that he's so excited about?

Oh. Oh shit.

I don't know how I didn't see it sooner. The student health clinic is a perfect place for med students to get drugs illegally. And Conlon even has it advertised prominently on the bulletin board outside the anatomy lab. *That's* how he must be spreading drugs to the students at DeWitt.

And Abe works there.

I can't believe I almost confided in him. I don't know exactly how much he is aware of or if he is just part of the totem pole of distribution, but it's clear Abe can't be trusted. Which means there's nobody out there that I can trust.

I can only trust myself.

72

Forty hours. That's about how long it's been since I've last slept.

I would pay any amount of money just to get an hour of solid sleep. Not that I have any money, but I'd find a way. Hell, I'd take twenty minutes of sleep. But every time I close my eyes, my thoughts race. Dr. Conlon. My exam. Frank…

I wish I could turn it off somehow.

I check my watch—it's close to midnight. Abe is lying in his bed, his breaths whistling between his lips. Even though he's asleep, he's not sleeping soundly—he tosses and turns and occasionally cries out. Once, he punched the wall in his sleep, hard enough to crack the plaster. It makes me nervous to be in the room with him.

Abe. What is his deal?

I thought Conlon might have been drugging me via the cafeteria food, but I recognize that's a wild idea. But Abe and I have shared a lot of meals together. He has had *numerous* opportunities to slip me something to cloud my brain.

I notice that I've been absently scratching at my arms. I pull up my left sleeve, and there's a rash running up the length of my forearm, covered in deep scratch marks from where I've been rubbing at it. The scratch marks are so bad that a few of them are oozing blood.

I lift my other sleeve—there's a similar rash on my right forearm. What the hell? Why am I breaking out in weird rashes?

I pull up my pants legs and lift my shirt, but I don't see anything similar there. It's just on my arms. And it almost looks like a rash from being allergic to something. What have I been touching that would make me break out in a rash like this?

Shit. It must be Frank.

A shiver goes through my body. What has Frank's corpse been contaminated with? What are we being exposed to?

Finally, I struggle to my feet, grab my car keys, and head out the door. I've got to get a look at Frank, away from prying eyes. I stumble down the stairs and manage to make it to my car.

I'm driving like shit, which is no big surprise, considering how tired I am. I keep weaving in and out of my lane—I probably seem drunk. My only saving grace is that there are no other cars on the road and no cops lying in wait. If there were, I'd probably land myself in jail.

I reach the hospital lot and park crookedly across

two spaces. I hurry into the building, the sound of my sneakers slamming into the pavement, echoing in the silent hallways. I continue running until I find myself outside the anatomy lab. I stare down at the combination lock on the lab door. I punch in the code shakily—I have to do it three times before I get it right.

The frigid air of the anatomy lab hits me like a slap in the face. My eyelids had been sagging before, but now they're wide open. I look around the room, at the rows of dead bodies under thick plastic. The only sound is the whir of the air conditioner—it's almost comforting.

I'm breathing hard as I walk over to Table 13. Frank. Like every other cadaver in the room, Frank is covered in plastic. I pull the plastic off the body, not bothering to cover my hands in gloves.

Frank's dead, and I suspect foul play. It's obvious he hasn't been shot and isn't the victim of trauma. So that leads me to believe he's been poisoned. Poisoned with something toxic enough to make me break out in a rash all over my arms. I just need to prove it.

Most of Frank's blood is congealed, but it's still there. If I can get a sample of his blood, I can send it off to a lab to be analyzed. I'm hoping there's some way they can check for poisons or other things that might be responsible for his death. And after I can prove Frank was murdered, I can go to the police and implicate Conlon.

I stare down at the cadaver. We dissected Frank's face weeks ago. It's barely even recognizable as a face anymore, pulled apart by scalpels and forceps. I wish I'd gotten a good look at him before we did this. It makes it almost impossible to recognize him from photos in the obituaries.

I look down at Frank's arm, where the tattoo had been only a few days earlier. *To Serve and Protect.* I remember I came to the end of the last lab to see Rachel dissecting the other arm, but the arm with the tattoo was still intact. But somehow, the tattoo is now ripped apart.

I examine the arm further, and my skin begins to crawl. This arm hasn't just been dissected—it's been *destroyed.* The muscles are ripped apart, the skin is sliced into pieces… and when I look down at Frank's legs, they're in the same condition.

Frank's arms and legs are all ripped to shreds.

Whoever did this dissection wasn't interested in learning. They were trying to destroy evidence—the very evidence I'd been looking for. And they were extremely thorough.

I'm not imagining this—it's real. This is concrete evidence that something is going on. Someone has mutilated Frank's body in order to protect himself.

"You're close, Mason," a gruff voice speaks up. "Don't give up."

I jump, startled. It's the same voice I've been hearing all along but louder and clearer. I look around the room, trying to figure out where the voice came from. But there's no one else in the room. It's just me. Just me and Frank. Frank.

The dead body is talking to me.

Oh Christ. Oh shit.

Without bothering to cover Frank up again, I run out of the anatomy lab. Even the sound of the door to the lab slamming closed behind me offers no comfort. I need to talk to someone, someone who I know for sure is real. But who the hell can I talk to when it's close to midnight? What other soul would still be awake at this hour?

Sasha. She always studies at the library until it closes at midnight.

I head in the direction of the library. I notice that the student working at the desk gives me a funny look when I first come in, but I flash my student ID, and she nods at me. I hurry to the far corner of the library, where Sasha always studies. When I get there, she is packing up her books, ready to head home for the night.

"Sasha," I say breathlessly as I reach her side.

She looks up at me, and the horror on her face is a reflection of my appearance.

"Oh my God, Mason," she murmurs. "What happened?"

"Sasha, please," I whisper. I fall to my knees in front of her, holding both her hands in mine. "I think… I think I might be losing it…"

"It's the stress," Sasha acknowledges. "I feel the same way sometimes."

"No, it's more than that…" I lower my head. Tears rise in my eyes. I haven't cried since I was six years old when my cat died. And even then, I tried to hide it because I didn't want my father to think I was weak. "There's something wrong with me. I know it."

"Every medical student turns into a hypochondriac," Sasha says in a soothing voice. "You've just gotta take it easy. Anyway, people who are going crazy usually have no idea they're going crazy. So I think you're safe."

"Is that a rule?"

Sasha smiles and touches my cheek. "You just need to get some sleep, Mason."

I close my eyes and shake my head to clear it. Maybe she's right. Anyone would be hearing things if they had so little sleep. I look up at her dark-brown hair and remember how I'd been surprised, the first time I touched it, by how soft it was. I haven't touched Sasha's hair in a long time. I wonder how I let myself screw things up with her. If only I hadn't brought her home with me that night… maybe we'd be something more than friends right now.

"Sasha, do you… do you want to go to the locker rooms with me?" I ask half-heartedly.

She shakes her head. "You *know* we have our final exam coming up. I need to head home and get some rest."

"What if I promise to shower first?" I say, flashing my most charming smile.

Sasha laughs and kisses the top of my head. "Go get some sleep, Mason."

And just like that, I feel better. I feel like maybe I could go home and get some sleep that night. I leave Sasha and walk back out to my car, my eyelids growing heavier by the second. For the first time in days, my heart is beating at a normal pace. Sasha is right. I'm just putting too much stress on myself.

Or maybe…

I unlock the door to my car, trying to push away the thoughts intruding on my brain. I have to get home. I have to get to sleep. I have to study.

Or maybe she's in on it too.

73

I DIDN'T EVEN REALIZE I HAD DOZED OFF UNTIL THE phone starts ringing. I open my eyes and take in the darkness of the room. Was it dark when I first went to sleep? I can't even remember anymore.

I only sleep in snatches of a couple of hours. If I could get a full eight hours of sleep, I'd feel like myself again. I even begged Abe for some pills to help me out, but he pretended he didn't know what I was talking about, like he wasn't a drug dealer. Everyone is lying to me.

I glance over at the computer, trying to remember what it is I had been reading when I drifted off. The phone is still ringing, and the sound is like nails on a chalkboard. I gingerly take the phone off the hook and hold it close to my ear, listening.

"Mason?"

It's my mother's voice. I try to answer, but my throat feels really dry, and no sound comes out of my mouth.

"Mason?"

"Hello," I finally manage.

"Oh, thank God," she says. "Are you all right? I haven't heard from you in weeks!"

"Yes," I say.

"How is school? How are your classes?"

"Fine."

"Sweetheart, you sound really tired," she says. "I know your dad puts a lot of pressure on you, but you need to take care of yourself. Are you sleeping enough?"

"Yes."

"Will you be coming home for Christmas?"

"I don't know."

"But, Mason—"

"I have to go."

I'm twenty-two years old and an adult now. She knows she can't intrude on my life if I don't let her.

"Okay, honey," she says. "But... let me know if you need anything. Anything at all."

"I will."

The truth is that I can't remember the last time I've been to class or to the lab. It somehow all faded into the background. I'm trying to save my reputation. My reputation and my life. And put a murderer behind bars, where he belongs.

But nothing I do seems to bring me closer to that goal. As it is now, I have nothing. No evidence of wrongdoing. Conlon's just going to get away with this.

Unless...

The idea, once in my head, suddenly seems so obvious. I check the date and time on my computer. The date registers as familiar, and it takes me a second to connect to the fact that our anatomy final exam is tomorrow. That means it's a Sunday—Sunday night. If I go to the hospital, there will be students in the library but no classes going on. I'll have the place to myself… all the time in the world to bust into Dr. Conlon's office and search for dirt on him.

I throw on a pair of scrubs over my boxer shorts. I haven't changed shirts in over a week, at least, but it's not like I need to look presentable. I shove my bare feet into my sneakers and pull on my dark-brown jacket. I grab my car keys off my dresser, and as I drop them into my pocket, I feel the cold metal against my fingers. My father's Magnum.

I hesitate, my fingers still on the gun. Something deep inside me is telling me to take the gun out of my pocket and leave it in my room. There isn't going to be anyone at the hospital this late. And if there is… well, maybe it's better if I don't have a gun.

And then, I hear that horrible voice again in my ear.

Take the gun, Mason.

I slowly remove my hand from my pocket, leaving the gun inside.

Not so fast. You still have to load it.

74

I DRIVE TO THE HOSPITAL AT A STEADY PACE, KEEPING MY eyes pinned on the road. I'm completely focused on the task at hand, like a secret agent infiltrating enemy headquarters. I keep my lights off, though. I'm not sure, but it seems like there is a good chance someone might be following me. Well, it's not impossible.

I flash my identification at the security guard by the entrance from the parking garage. The guard barely looks at me. That's good… better if nobody can identify me later. If I find evidence to incriminate Dr. Conlon, everyone will understand—but if I don't, well, this might look really bad. And I'm certain that Dr. Conlon will do everything in his power to destroy me when he discovers I busted into his office.

The building is empty, and the sound of my sneakers hitting the tiled floor sounds like claps of thunder. I try to walk quietly, but urgency gets the better of me. My heart is racing. Hell, I can *hear* my heart thumping in my chest.

I pass by the anatomy lab, where the lights are on and there's movement inside the room. Two students from my class are in there. Leave it to med students to be spending their Sunday night in a lab with a bunch of dead bodies. I'm irritated because it means that I'll have to make an effort to be quiet.

When I reach Dr. Conlon's office, however, I'm shocked. There's a light on under the door. It's almost midnight on a Sunday night—how could Conlon still be in his office? Now what the hell am I supposed to do?

Of course, maybe this is a good thing. Maybe I can persuade Conlon to tell me the truth.

I shove my hands deep into my jacket pockets and feel the reassuring cold metal of my father's Magnum. It's true—nobody says no to a gun in their face. At least, certainly not an anatomy professor.

I take a deep breath and knock on the door.

There's loud shuffling on the other side of the door. I hear Dr. Conlon's voice: "Who's there?"

"It's Mason Howard."

More shuffling. This is far longer than he ought to be taking to unlock the door. What the hell is going on in there anyway? Is he hiding evidence? I wait, my hands still in my pockets. Finally, the lock turns, and Dr. Conlon is standing before me. The professor's black hair is tousled, and his glasses are somewhat askew.

"Mason… what are you doing here?"

I slip through the opening in the door. Dr. Conlon gasps slightly when he sees me in the light.

"I could ask the same question of you," I reply.

Dr. Conlon rubs his eyes and limps around the side

of his desk, where he collapses into his seat. "I had some work to catch up on."

"Oh, really?" I say. "Is that the excuse you're using?"

Dr. Conlon's face darkens. "I don't know what you're talking about."

"Don't you?"

"What did you come here for?" Dr. Conlon demands. "To blackmail me? Is that what this is about?"

"No, I came here for the truth!" I punctuate my statement by slamming my fist onto the desk. The professor jumps in his chair and stares up at me.

"Look, Mason…" Dr. Conlon is getting nervous now—it's painfully obvious. *Good.* "If you need help, I'll help you. There are still a few days left before the exam. Whatever the problem is…"

"I want answers," I say. My fist closes around the handle of the gun.

"I can't tell you the answers," Dr. Conlon says, shaking his head.

"Maybe I can convince you then," I say.

I pull my father's Magnum from my pocket and point it at Dr. Conlon's face.

All of the color drains from the professor's face. He stares at the gun in disbelief, his fingers gripping the edge of the table so hard that his knuckles turn white.

He looks up at me. "Mason, don't do this. It's not worth it."

"Tell me the truth then," I say, shaking the gun. "Tell me how Frank died."

Dr. Conlon's dark brows knit together. "Frank?"

"The body lying on Table 13!" I nearly scream the words. "Tell me how you killed him."

"Oh, Christ," Dr. Conlon mutters, shaking his head. "Listen to me, Mason. I didn't kill anyone. I have no idea what you're talking about. You need to calm down."

"Don't try to trick me!" I snap. I press the muzzle of the Magnum into Dr. Conlon's forehead. "Who has the gun, huh?"

"You do," Dr. Conlon says through his teeth.

"Tell me how you killed him," I say.

Dr. Conlon slowly raises his hands into the air. "Mason, I swear to you. I have no idea what you're talking about."

He's lying. He's so obviously lying.

"I swear to you," Dr. Conlon repeats. His light-blue eyes are calm.

"There isn't time for this bullshit," I say. "I need to know the truth!"

"I swear to you, Mason," he says again.

I cock the gun. I want to see Conlon squirm, but he's not doing it. He's just slumped down in his seat, staring down the chamber of the Magnum with resignation in his eyes.

Enough of this bullshit. Time to show him I'm serious.

"I'm going to give you one more chance," I say, the gun now pointed directly at my professor's forehead. "Tell me how you killed Frank."

I pray that Conlon will come clean with me. Because I don't have a choice anymore.

Dr. Conlon shakes his head. He speaks the next sentence slowly and clearly: "I'm really sorry."

He's sorry. It's as good as a confession as far as I'm concerned.

So I squeeze the trigger, just like my father taught me to do when I was a kid.

The force of the gun firing travels up the length of my arm and knocks me back slightly. I haven't fired a gun in a long time, and I'd forgotten to compensate for the backward momentum. When I lower the pistol, I feel a sharp ache in my shoulder.

Dr. Conlon's head is slumped forward. There are little pieces of skull and brain splattered all over the wall behind him. It looks so… real. Unlike the cadaver, which never looked quite like a real human being. I let the gun slip from my fingers and fall onto the floor. I stare at my anatomy professor's dead body as the bile rises up my throat.

"Oh God, oh God, oh God…" I whisper the words over and over again as I fall to my knees on the floor.

He deserved this. You did what you had to do.

"Shut up!" I scream. I bury my face in my hands and rock back and forth. I've done something too horrible for words.

There's no taking back what I've just done. My hand rests on the gun on the floor. I pick it up and place it back in my jacket pocket. I struggle to my feet and leave Dr. Conlon's office for the last time.

But as I'm shutting the door to the office, I realize I'm not alone in the hallway. Dr. Patrice Winters is coming around the corner, wearing a dress suit that seems so bizarre since it's practically midnight. She is absolutely the last person I want to see right now.

Her symmetric features are filled with alarm as she hurries toward me. "Mason," she says, "what was that sound?"

Then her gaze drops to the gun in my hand. She freezes in her tracks as her lips form a little surprised "O." She has put two and two together, and now her fate is sealed.

Patrice opens her mouth as if to say something, but I don't want to hear it. I raise the gun, and for the second time tonight, I pull the trigger.

It's easier the second time.

Much like Dr. Conlon, Patrice drops instantly. I shot Dr. Conlon in the head, but I hit her square in the chest, possibly right through her heart, judging by the amount of blood pooling beneath her body. She dies almost instantly, right before my eyes.

The Magnum holds six rounds, and I've used two, which means I have four more bullets left in the chamber. And I'm not leaving here until every single potential witness is dead.

PART V

SASHA

75

THE FIRST DAY

"LOOK TO YOUR LEFT AND LOOK TO YOUR RIGHT."

It's a ridiculous exercise, but I do it anyway. I've been waiting for an excuse to check out my classmates, and now I've got one. I look around and scope out the competition.

I'm underwhelmed.

Everyone talks about how talented and brilliant med students are. Nobody in this room looks particularly talented or brilliant, though. For the most part, they look like a bunch of kids. Most of them are dressed in jeans and T-shirts with dumb slogans on them. One girl has the word "sweet" written entirely in glitter across her chest. I'm sure she's going to be a stellar physician.

People ask me all the time if I'm still in high school, but I'm actually twenty-six years old—older than most of my classmates. In college, I worked as a waitress to help pay my tuition and then took on a second job as a nanny (for a spoiled three-year-old brat) when Dad got sick and needed help paying bills. Do you think it's easy to be premed while working two part-time jobs? It isn't. I ended up having to take a bunch of postbacc classes just to finish my premed requirements.

I also took care of my father. He was diagnosed with Parkinson's disease when I was in high school and declined pretty fast. Lots of people live for decades with Parkinson's, but my father wasn't so lucky. By the time I was in college, he had to give up his job, and I moved back home to help my mother take care of him. It all fell on my shoulders.

Dad hated how much I had to give up for him. I'm his youngest daughter, and he came to this country from Russia in his twenties and worked hard his whole life at minimum-wage jobs so I could have every opportunity available to me. He kept saying to me, "Sasha, don't worry about me. Go become a doctor. I'll be fine."

But he wasn't fine. Soon after I graduated from college, he started having difficulty swallowing. Shortly after, he developed pneumonia and was admitted to the local hospital. He never came out.

For a long time after he died, I was angry. At pretty much everyone. I was angry at the doctors that took far too long to diagnose him, even though in retrospect, his tremors were a dead giveaway. I was angry at the hospital that gave him the wrong antibiotics for his aspiration pneumonia and then talked my mother into withdrawing care while he lay in the ICU.

And my mother—I don't even want to get into how angry I was at *her*.

But I got over it. My father wanted me to be a great doctor. That was his dream for me. And wherever he is right now, I want him to see me achieve my dream and graduate from medical school. And not *just* graduate. I intend to be at the very top of my class.

And honestly, as I look around at my classmates, that goal doesn't seem too unreasonable.

Anatomy is the central class of the first year. If you ace anatomy, you ace the year.

One of the key components to acing anatomy is Dr. Conlon's book, *Anatomy: Inside Secrets*. That's what all the upperclassmen told me. So early on the morning of orientation, I travel to the hospital bookstore to buy myself a copy.

A lot of people had the same idea as me. There's an entire shelf dedicated to Dr. Conlon's book, and now, about half of those copies have been sold. I pick up a fresh copy of the book, flipping through diagrams of the human body, mnemonics, and something called "Conlon's Law of Finger Flexion," whatever that is.

Our professor is a bit of a dork, what with the bowtie and all.

There are at least a dozen copies left on the shelf, and I'm suddenly seized by the urge to buy them all so that nobody else can have them. The bookstore would order more copies, but at least this way, I'd have a head start for the first lab.

Of course, I don't do it. Mostly because this book isn't cheap, and I can't afford twelve copies. I can barely afford the books I need.

Instead, I pull out the stack of paperback texts and load them into my arms. Conlon's book isn't that thick, but the stack is fairly heavy. I glance around to make sure nobody's watching then relocate the stack to a little nook behind a life-sized skeleton. For good measure, I toss a DeWitt Med sweatshirt on top of them.

I check once more to make sure nobody saw me before I get in line to purchase my copy of *Anatomy: Inside Secrets*. As I hand over my credit card, another student I vaguely recognize enters the store. He sees my purchase and smiles.

"I'm about to buy the same thing," he comments.

"Oh, sorry," I say regretfully. "I just bought the last copy."

76

It's not too hard to shine in the anatomy lab when put side by side with my lab partners. For the most part, they're all disasters. Heather McKinley—a total airhead. It baffles me that she's here when it took me *years* to finish my requirements to earn a spot in the class. Abe Kaufman seems intelligent enough but also appears more focused on Heather than he is on studying. Rachel Bingham talks big, but I can tell that she's struggling to master the material. And then there's Mason Howard.

I hate Mason instantly.

He's way too good-looking, for starters. Guys who look like that annoy me because they think they're God's gift to the world. If I ever get married, I'm going to marry someone butt-ugly who knows what it's like to be shit on by the world. Also, Mason is super charming. I can just see the girls in our class eating it up. It's *so* annoying. Heather ogles him all through the lab.

He acts like he's some sort of anatomy genius, but I know the truth: he studies his ass off. He doesn't mess around—he takes med school very, very seriously. He's the only person who stays at the library as late as I do.

But you know what pisses me off about Mason?

Even if I study night and day nonstop, even if every grade I get tops Mason's, he'll always have the edge over me. No matter what. Because Mason has one quality that I don't possess: charisma.

A little charisma goes a long way. And Mason has a *lot* of charisma.

"He already looks like a surgeon," Heather says to me as we stand on the far end of the cadaver table, Mason cutting as we flip through the lab manual. Heather is practically swooning.

"Don't you have a boyfriend?" I say.

"Yes." Heather blushes. "What are you saying?"

"Nothing," I murmur.

Heather clears her throat and flips the page in the manual. "How about you? Are you seeing anyone?"

I dated a boy named Alex before med school started. It wasn't very serious. He was the son of a woman my mother knew from work, and he was short. I'm short, so I always get set up with short guys, even though I'm not that attracted to them. Anyway, it wasn't a big loss to break up with him when school started. I couldn't have any distractions.

"Not really," I say.

Heather's eyes light up. "Really? Because you know, Abe is available..."

Seriously? Is Heather so dense that she doesn't realize that Abe is head over heels in love with her? He's about as interested in me as he would be in a candy wrapper on the street. Which seems to be the reaction most guys have to me.

"I'm not interested," I say, trying to turn the conversation back to the celiac plexus.

"You know," Heather says, "your hair will look so spectacular in a French twist. You have such a graceful neck. I learned how to do it last summer…"

I grit my teeth. "I'm not *interested.*"

This time, Heather seems to get it and backs down. Except then she starts humming a pop song, which is this annoying habit she has. Always singing. Sometimes I want to strangle her. I don't even get why she's here—she's easily the dumbest person in the class. The other day, we were looking at another cadaver, and she said to me, "I think this person had a hysterectomy—I don't see a uterus." I had to inform her it was a male cadaver—Mason overheard the exchange, and he couldn't stop laughing.

Anyway, my love life is none of her business. Someday I'll date again. There's just no room in my life for that right now.

77

The scores for the first anatomy quiz are posted a few days before the hard copies are returned to us. A large crowd of students is milling about the white piece of paper hung up near the lockers containing the scores posted by each student's five-digit school ID number. I see Heather backing away from the group, looking rather pale.

I'll bet she failed.

I edge my way closer to the scores, taking an elbow to the forehead in the process. That's the problem with being so small—I can't shove my way past my classmates effectively enough. But I can duck down past them until I have a clear view of the list of scores.

My ID number is 44545. I scan the list, my heart thumping so loudly in my chest that I'm sure all my classmates can hear it. When I see the number, I follow the straight black line leading to my grade: Ninety-eight.

Ninety-eight! I got an almost perfect score!

Before rejoicing, however, I decide to check the list

to see if anyone has beaten me. I don't see any ninety-nines, but there is, in fact, a single grade of one hundred posted under the ID number 20205.

I take out an index card and carefully print the number 20205. Next time, I will beat 20205. I want to be first in the class. You don't get into a top residency by being second. Right now, I'm thinking about emergency medicine, maybe at Columbia. Columbia was where my father got diagnosed, and he always said I belonged there. But that's not going to happen if I'm second.

When the second quiz rolls around, I lose a single point for mislabeling the "main pancreatic duct" as the "pancreatic duct." I'm very pleased with my grade until I scan the list and am horrified to find, once again, a second perfect score.

Belonging, once again, to 20205.

Who is 20205? I practically become obsessed. This one person somehow managed to beat me twice in a row with two perfect scores. It could be dumb luck. Maybe 20205 will mess up the next exam. But even so, it's obvious this person is very sharp. I have to take them seriously.

I make a list of possible candidates who might be 20205. I select people who frequently speak up in class and give intelligent answers. I also notice who stays late studying in the library. Of course, I don't know my classmates very well yet, and the truth is, it could be anyone. After all, I'm sure nobody would guess that I have the second-highest average in the class. Maybe 20205 is lying low.

Besides, there's more to succeeding in med school

than just grades. Take Mason, for example. Whenever Dr. Conlon comes to our table and asks a question, he always booms out the answer with confidence. And Dr. Conlon beams at him and says, "Exactly right, Dr. Howard!" Even though I knew the right answer too.

Dr. Conlon never, ever compliments me like that. When I do manage to answer before Mason cuts me off, Dr. Conlon simply smiles and nods at me. I don't think he even knows my name. And he knows *everyone's* names.

I need to be more like Mason Howard. Somehow.

Mason studies in the library like I do, so I decide to quietly observe him. I have to respect the fact that he seems to study a great deal. At least he recognizes that his looks and charisma can only get him so far without some knowledge to back it up.

I'm watching him when a classmate of ours, Brogan Scott, stops by his desk to interrupt his studying.

"Hi, Mason," she whispers. "I baked some cookies yesterday. Do you want to try a few?"

"Uh, sure," he says, smiling up at her as he reaches for one of the chocolate chip cookies.

"What do you think?" Brogan asks as he takes a bite.

"Delicious," he says.

Brogan chats with Mason as he finishes the cookie, which is incredibly irritating. This is supposed to be a *quiet* area of the library—that means no talking. As soon as Brogan leaves, I head over to the desk where Mason is sitting, intending to remind him of that fact.

"Mason," I say to him, and he looks up. He has, I have to admit, astonishingly pretty hazel eyes. I wish I had eyelashes like those—mine are practically invisible.

"There's no talking allowed in this area of the library."

Mason raises his eyebrows then he grins. "Oh, Brogan wasn't talking. She was just babbling." He makes a "blah blah blah" motion with his hand to show how she was going on and on.

"Still," I say. "She was making *noise*."

"That's for sure," he agrees. "And honestly? The cookies weren't all that good."

Mason is still smiling at me, and it's getting a little hard to stay angry at him. But I'm really trying.

"How do you stand it?" I ask him.

"Stand what?"

"Girls like Brogan."

He shrugs.

"You probably like it," I acknowledge. "I mean, who wouldn't want an attractive girl baking cookies for him?"

He shrugs again. "She's not my type, actually."

Not his type? What did *that* mean? As irritating as Brogan is, she's objectively very attractive. Who doesn't like strawberry-blond hair and legs that are like six feet long? Her legs are longer than my entire body.

Mason reaches into his backpack and pulls out a small package of Oreo cookies. He holds them out to me.

"Would *you* like a cookie, Sasha?"

"Home-baked?" I ask.

"I had them cooking in the vending machine all day," he says with a grin.

I smile despite myself. Damn Mason for being so charming. I want to continue to hate him, but it's surprisingly difficult. I stand up to take a cookie from him, and a piece of paper sticking out from the pile of study materials in front of him catches my eye. It's a copy of our last anatomy quiz, with a grade of one hundred circled at the top.

That's how I discover Mason is 20205.

And that's when things go horribly wrong.

78

I HATE VISITING MY MOTHER THESE DAYS.

It takes me about two hours to make the drive from DeWitt, Connecticut, to Brooklyn—two hours I can't spare—but I still go. I do it more out of a sense of obligation than anything else. Dad would want me to check up on her, to see how she's doing. She's not so young anymore, after all. So that's why I do it.

But I'll never stop being angry at her for the way Dad died.

Fine, he was on life support after that bout of pneumonia that spread into his bloodstream. Yes, he had a chronic, degenerative disease. But I still can't help but feel his life got cut short. If she'd just waited a little longer, he might have pulled through. She didn't even *ask* me if I was okay with it. She just decided to take him off the ventilator, and that was it. Dad wouldn't have wanted to die.

As far as I'm concerned, she killed him.

When I visit my mother about a month into the

semester, I notice the apartment hasn't changed much since my father died. Mom preserved it in roughly the state it's been in since I was in high school. The furniture is scuffed and secondhand and just hanging together by a thread. The walls are desperately in need of a paint job, but we can't afford it, and I don't have time to do it myself. The refrigerator is still making that loud whirring noise.

I immediately start cleaning the tiny apartment. Ever since Dad died, Mom has let housekeeping fall to the wayside, and my sisters are too busy with their own families to help her out. I do three loads of laundry in the basement, wash the dishes by hand (we've never been able to afford a dishwasher), and vacuum the carpet.

"You don't have to do all this, Sasha," Mom says as she watches me fold her clothes.

She speaks to me in Russian, even though my parents were pretty strict about always speaking English around the house when I was growing up. It's like since Dad died, she just gave up on everything, even English.

"It's fine," I mumble.

She watches me for another minute in silence. My mother and I have never had much to say to one another. I was always more of a daddy's girl.

"Are there any nice boys in your class?" Mom finally asks as I sort through the socks.

"No," I say curtly.

Why am I not surprised this is my mother's first question? I'm twenty-six years old and practically an old maid in her eyes. She came to this country from Russia when she was just a girl, and I gather that back there, they get married pretty young.

"None?" Mom raises an eyebrow. "Now how could that be, Sasha? Isn't the class mostly boys?"

I don't bother to point out that these days, medical school classes are at least half female. My mother would never believe it.

Finally, my mother says what she's been waiting to say since the moment I walked in: "Sasha, why don't you come back home?"

"Daddy wouldn't want me to quit," I say through my teeth.

"Daddy didn't know everything," Mom says quietly. "I think you'd be happier at home. Maybe that nice family will hire you back to watch their kids until you find a husband."

I look down at the sock ball in my hand. I want to hurl it at my mother.

"I don't want to have this conversation again, Mom," I say. "Now, if you'll excuse me, I have to use the bathroom…"

I don't need the bathroom. Really, I just need to get away from my mother. Instead of going to the bathroom, I brush past the small bedroom I used to share with my two sisters and end up in my parents' bedroom. Just like the rest of the house, it hasn't changed a bit since my father's death, but something is comforting about this fact. I open the closet and see rows of my father's shirts, all neatly pressed. I can still vaguely smell his aftershave.

"I'm trying my best, Papa," I whisper as I run my hand along the sleeve of my father's old blue shirt.

Then I really do go to the bathroom, which has also remained untouched since my father's death. His razor and shaving lotion are still on the sink counter, and a large lump forms in my throat that makes it difficult to swallow. I guess my mother misses him too. Maybe it comforts her to see Dad's stuff still around the bathroom and in the closets.

I open the medicine cabinet and see the pill bottles that contain all my father's medications. Before his death, he was taking several kinds of pills that attempted to increase the amount of dopamine in his brain and decrease the symptoms of the disease. The medications decreased his symptoms somewhat, but the dopamine had an undesired side effect: hallucinations.

I remember how my father was haunted by voices he started hearing in his head and visions of things that weren't there. It tortured him to the point that he chose to live with the symptoms of Parkinson's disease rather than continue the medications. He preferred shaking hands, poor balance, and shuffling feet to the voices in his head.

I pick up a large bottle of a medication called carbidopa-levodopa. Levodopa is converted by the body into dopamine. But that dopamine also caused the worst of my father's hallucinations—he couldn't tolerate these pills for more than a few weeks. I shake the bottle and discover that it's still almost full.

There's only a seedling of an idea in my head as I shove the bottle into my pocket.

79

I hate Mason, but I sort of like having him around in the library on the late nights. Sometimes it's just the two of us, and it's comforting to look up and see him sitting there. Sometimes I just watch him working—his brow furrowed in deep concentration as he stares at the diagrams of muscles and bones. When he catches me looking at him, he always smiles at me. He's somehow become the closest thing I've got to a friend at this school.

A few days after my visit to my mother's apartment, I approach Mason late in the evening while he's studying.

"I'm going to get some coffee." My voice cracks strangely on the words, and I clear my throat. "You want a cup?"

Mason blinks in surprise. "Uh… yeah, sure. Thanks, Sasha."

"Black?" I ask.

"Sounds perfect."

He smiles at me, and I get a little lost in those hazel eyes. Sheesh, he is *really* good-looking. But I have no interest in a guy like that. Not a chance. He's a jerk and a phony and absolutely not my type.

I head to the coffee machine down in the med student lounge and fill up two cups of black coffee. It's close to midnight, and the floor is deserted, but I still cautiously glance over my shoulder to make sure I don't have company. When I feel certain I'm alone, I pull my father's bottle of pills out of my pocket.

I open the bottle and remove a single capsule. I break it open and let the contents dissolve into one of the cups of coffee. I wait until the powder is completely invisible before I start back toward the library.

The irony of the whole thing isn't lost on me. DeWitt has a drug problem—too many students are popping pills to get through their classes. But Mason is straight as an arrow and would never take drugs. And yet here I am, drugging him.

Calling it a drug is melodramatic though—it's a *medication*. It's not going to hurt him—maybe just distract him enough that he won't be able to spend every waking hour studying. Or more likely, it won't affect him at all.

I hand Mason the cup of coffee, careful to give him the cup with the dopamine pill mixed in.

"Wow, thanks, Sasha," he says. "I really appreciate it."

I smile. "My pleasure."

80

Mason and I are dissecting the large intestines, and he's pretty focused, but I notice that every once in a while, he looks up and stares at Rachel's breasts. It's incredibly irritating. No matter how good a student Mason is, men only have one thing on their minds.

I've been slipping Mason the dopamine pills nearly every day for a couple of weeks now. As far as I can tell, it isn't affecting him at all. In some ways, I'm glad—I'm sort of scared of something terrible happening to him. What I'm doing could get me kicked out of med school in the blink of an eye.

Dr. Conlon limps over to our table, "How are things going?"

I have a few questions, but before I can ask them, Mason replies, "Very smoothly."

"Good to hear it," Dr. Conlon says. He leans over our cadaver and glances inside at the dissection we've been working on. "Very nice job, Dr. Howard."

Of course, Mason gets all the credit.

I watch Dr. Conlon's blue eyes flit up for a second to where Rachel is standing. Oh my God, is *Dr. Conlon* staring at Rachel's breasts too? Are you kidding me? I'm so angry, I nearly throw the scalpel to the ground and storm off in a tantrum. Rachel loves to go on and on about how men are all sexist pigs, but the least she could do is wear a bra so that her nipples aren't poking out through the fabric of her shirt. Rachel is a hypocritical phony, just like everyone else.

As I continue my dissection, Mason is staring down at the cadaver's upper arm. There's a tattoo on the arm that reads, "To serve and protect." He had probably been a cop. I wonder if he died in the line of duty, although I guess that if he had, there probably would have been an autopsy. More likely, he had a coronary from stress or too much fast food.

"Hey, Sasha." Mason nudges me. "What do you think this tattoo means?"

"It means he was probably a cop," I say.

Mason's eyes widen, and he looks impressed. He talks about it all through the rest of the lab, how cool it is we're dissecting the body of such an important person. He's talking faster and louder than I've ever heard him speak before, and I can't help but wonder if it's a side effect of the medication.

Nah, probably not.

It's a Friday night, and everyone is beginning to feel the crunch from our upcoming anatomy exam. I'm in the library as usual, as is Mason Howard. I brought him a cup of coffee laced with the usual hallucinogenic that seems to have no effect whatsoever. I'm beginning to wonder why I even bother.

"Do you mind if I join you?" he asks, nodding toward my table as I hand him the cup of coffee.

"Uh… sure," I agree. I feel a flash of fear as I wonder if he discovered what I've been doing. Why else would he want to talk to me?

He shakes his head at me. "Don't you ever go home?"

Wow, what a hypocrite.

"Do you?" I ask belligerently.

Mason blinks a few times, taken aback by my response, and that's when I realize it: holy crap, he's flirting with me.

Mason Howard is flirting with me.

It seems so impossible. I mean, I'm not ugly or anything, but Mason is… well, Mason. He's in a different league. Well, at least the girls who throw themselves at him on a regular basis seem to be in a different league. Those girls are gorgeous. Why would he pay any attention to *me* when he could have *them*?

"So tell me, Sasha," he says, "why do you want to be a doctor?"

For a second, I'm completely taken in by his smile. Even though I officially hate him, I find myself blurting out the whole sad story about my father and how much it changed me. And he actually looks like he cares. I'm sure he's faking it, though.

"I'm so sorry, Sasha," he says as he places his hand on mine.

And that's when I recognize he wants to kiss me. And even though I hate myself for it, I want to kiss him back. I shouldn't, though. It would be a mistake. I have to stay completely focused on—

Oh hell, now he's kissing me.

And it's a very nice kiss too. Very passionate and lustful. Much more so than with too-short Alex. I love the way his tongue gently moves against mine as his fingers lace into my short brown hair, pulling me closer to him. We kiss in the empty library for several minutes.

When he pulls away, Mason whispers in my ear, "You want to get out of here?"

God, I really do.

We end up in the med student locker room. It's not a supercomfortable place to have sex—we're stuck doing it on the floor. But we both want each other so bad, it doesn't matter. Mason's fingers are shaking so much as he unbuttons my shirt that he accidentally dislodges a button—he nearly rips my blouse open. I guess it's been a while for him. Me too.

When it's over, we collapse against the cold locker room floor, still half naked. This is going to sound dumb, but I sort of feel like I want a cigarette. I look over at Mason, who is still breathing hard and has a line of sweat beads along his hairline.

He grins at me. "That was really great."

After a moment of hesitation, he kisses me on the cheek.

It *was* really great. But he's already got an inflated ego, so I just say, "It's a nice study break."

He doesn't seem disturbed that I haven't showered him with praise.

"Maybe we could take another study break in the future," he suggests, looking at me in a way that makes me think he'd like to take another study break *right now*. I can't imagine why he desires me so much, but it's clear he does.

I've never been with a guy like Mason before. Every man I ever dated has been humble, meek, and plain—the diametric opposite of Mason. He's not my type at all. But I can't deny that I am incredibly attracted to him.

Even though I still hate him, of course.

81

I STOP DROPPING THE DOPAMINE CAPSULES IN MASON'S coffee after that. Considering he's sort of my… well, he's not my *boyfriend*, but he's definitely something to me. Anyway, I just can't do it anymore. As much as it pains me to see his amazing score on the first big anatomy exam, he earned the grade.

Also, there's a very tiny chance I'm starting to fall for him. Just a tiny bit.

Don't tell anyone. My sisters would never let me hear the end of it. I was never a girl who was taken in by a handsome face. But Mason's not just handsome, he's *really* handsome. Okay, that sounds bad. But I can't help myself. I'm really into him. I even find it endearing that he's not amazingly skilled at sex for a twenty-two-year-old, probably due to lack of experience. It just shows he hasn't spent his life chasing everything in a skirt. He tries, though—he really does.

He's not a bad guy either. He never buys me flowers, but he always holds the door for me when we go to anatomy lab together, he's never too busy to spend a few minutes chatting with me at the library, and he's *always* up for a little fun in the locker room. We're never going to have a bona fide "relationship," but there are worse people to be hooking up with.

Of course, then Mason has to go and ruin things.

After Mason has some meeting with Dr. Conlon, he *will not shut up* about the anatomy practical. He keeps telling me, "I'm the first person to ever get a perfect score on the practical. Can you believe that?"

Yes, I believe it. Now stop talking about it!

"Dr. Conlon practically offered me a TA job for next year," he goes on.

And that's the part that *really* pisses me off. I've been hoping to be an anatomy teaching assistant next year. That would look great on my transcript. If Dr. Conlon is making a short list of possibilities, I want to be in the running. So at the next opportunity, I decide to pay a visit to Dr. Conlon's office.

I show up at the end of the day, at around six o'clock. It was a half-hearted attempt, and I didn't expect Dr. Conlon to still be there, but there he is, working hard at his computer, and he doesn't look like he's leaving anytime soon. I feel a little bit sorry for my professor—I don't think he's married or has a family, and his work is probably all he has. But he seems to love what he does, at least—a lot of people can't say the same.

Dr. Conlon flashes me a wide grin when he notices me at the door. "Hi. Can I help you?"

"Can I talk to you a minute?" I ask.

"Of course! Come in, uh…" Dr. Conlon frowns, and it takes me a second to realize he's fumbling to think of my name. It's a huge slap in the face—Dr. Conlon knows *everyone's* name. He certainly wouldn't be struggling to come up with Mason's name.

"Sasha," I finally say after giving him another second to try to come up with the name on his own.

"Right, Sasha," he says in an apologetic tone. "Sasha Zaleski. Sorry, Sasha… I got a poor night's sleep last night. Now, how can I help you?"

"I just…" I squeeze my hands together. "I wanted to let you know that I'm interested in being an anatomy TA next year."

"Oh…" Dr. Conlon looks taken aback. "Well, I applaud your enthusiasm, but I'm not thinking about that quite yet. It's still very early in the year."

Right. Except that he already practically offered it to Mason. Well, I shouldn't be too surprised.

I nod in resignation. "Thank you anyway."

"I'm very sorry, uh…"

My face burns. "*Sasha*."

I'm fuming mad when I leave Dr. Conlon's office. I'm just as smart as Mason, and my grades are comparable to his, but for some reason, *he's* the one who gets all the recognition, while Dr. Conlon can't even remember my *name*. It's so unfair. Mason gets every advantage in the world handed to him on a silver plate, and I get nothing.

The next day, I start putting dopamine capsules in Mason's coffee again. Except this time, I put in two instead of one.

82

I DECIDED I WANTED TO BE A DOCTOR WHEN I WAS SEVEN years old.

Dad was teaching me how to ride a bike. All my friends already knew, and I felt left behind. I was using my sister Nadia's bike, which had previously been my other sister Alina's bike until she outgrew it. The bike was white and once had pink stripes on it, but now, it was gray, with most of the pink worn away. Everything I owned had previously been owned by two other people and had that same grayish tinge.

Dad was doing that thing with me where he'd start me going on the bike then let go when I wasn't paying attention. I kept making him promise he wouldn't let go, but he'd do it anyway. In retrospect, I realize it was for my own good. But at the time, it was making me very nervous.

Each time I discovered he was no longer holding onto the bike, I'd panic and lose control and ultimately fall. One of those times, I fell right on a broken bottle.

My bare leg was all cut up and bleeding, and Dad rushed me to the nearest emergency room.

I was fascinated when the doctor in the ER fished the pieces of broken glass from my leg and sewed up a particularly deep gash, from which I still have the scar. I didn't even cry. And what fascinated me even more was how much my father seemed to respect the doctor, almost to the point of being awed by him.

As soon as the doctor had left the room, I said to my father: "I want to be a doctor when I grow up."

Dad was completely floored. He came to this country as an immigrant, mostly working blue-collar jobs, and he always wanted something better for his kids. Especially me. He wanted me to reap all the benefits that this country had to offer.

I can still picture my dad rushing into the hallway of the ER and yelling to whoever would listen, "My daughter is going to be a doctor!" He told two doctors, three nurses, an orderly, and the guy selling hot dogs outside the hospital before we made it home.

My father may not have made it to my med school graduation, but he's watching over me. And I want to make him proud.

Okay, I admit it: I'm still sneaking off to the locker rooms with Mason.

What can I say? I'm lonely, and Mason is really hot. Why should I deprive myself? It's just casual sex. It's not like we're in a relationship.

Or at least, that's what I think.

"What are you doing this weekend?" Mason asks me as we button and tuck in our respective clothing.

"Studying," I say with a smile. "Why?"

"My parents wanted me to come over for dinner this weekend," he says, "and I thought maybe… you'd like to come with me…"

"To your *parents'* house?"

Whoa, that is intense. I don't want to meet his parents. We haven't even been on a *date* yet.

"Well, my mom wanted me to bring my girlfriend and…" He looks away, his face turning an endearing shade of red. "I mean, we'd just be going as friends, though. Just so you could help me get through the night. I mean…"

Ah, he's cute when he's embarrassed. He doesn't really think of me as his girlfriend, but this is another sign that this is a little bit more than casual sex for him. Maybe this all means more to him than it does to me. I can't help but feel flattered. And guilty.

"Come on, aren't you curious?" Mason says.

Okay, he's right. I *am* curious. What are the parents of a guy like Mason Howard like? So against my better judgment, I agree to go.

I'd die if Mason knew this, but I spend hours agonizing over what to wear for the dinner. I literally try on every outfit in my closet, which, sadly, doesn't take very long. At school, I always wear jeans. I want Mason to look at me tonight and think, *Wow*.

Unfortunately, I don't think there are any clothes in existence that will make him think that.

I finally settle on a fitted rose-colored blouse and lavender skirt that shows off a little bit of leg but isn't too slutty. I dust off my one container of eyeshadow and apply a subtle layer of makeup. I look in the mirror after I'm done and decide that I look at least respectable. Mason isn't going to wolf-howl at me or anything, but I'm hoping I at least don't look like someone he'll be embarrassed to be seen with.

Mason, on the other hand, looks amazing when he picks me up at my apartment. I mostly see him in T-shirts and jeans, so the khaki slacks and dress shirt are a stark change. He's got on a dark-green tie that makes his hazel eyes look greener. He's so handsome in his outfit that my knees get a little weak. But the best part is how his eyes light up when he sees me.

"Wow," he says. "You look… really nice, Sasha."

I look away, not wanting him to see how pleased I am. "Well, let's go."

The ride to the Howards' house takes about half an hour, and it's filled with easy conversation. We've talked so many times and had plenty of sex, but this is the first time I've felt any kind of spark between us. It's almost like we're on a real date. About halfway through the drive, Mason removes his hand from the gear shift while at a red light and takes my hand for a minute. It's such a sweet gesture that a tingle goes through my entire body.

But as soon as I see Mason's house, my excitement vanishes.

I knew Mason was wealthy, but I wasn't prepared for the enormous mansion that stands before me. It's three stories high and stretches out for the length of a city block. There's a gate to gain entrance, and I half expect to see a moat with a dragon guarding the front door. I can't help but think of the tiny apartment where I grew up, the three of us girls squeezed into one bedroom. As I step onto the walkway, I trip over my heels.

Mason gently places a hand on my back. "Are you okay, Sasha?"

"Fine," I manage, thinking that once the shock of seeing the house wears off, it will get better.

Except it just gets worse.

We're greeted at the door by Mason's mother, although I had been half expecting a butler. Mrs. Howard is beautiful. I mean, she is really, really beautiful. She has the same chestnut-colored hair as Mason, wide hazel eyes, and a slender but shapely figure. She looks much too young to be the mother of a twenty-two-year-old medical student.

"And this must be Sasha," Mrs. Howard coos as we step inside.

Even though she's beautiful, I can see in her eyes that Mason's mother is no dummy. And that she's extremely protective of her son.

"That's right," I say, wishing I could run away. I might have bolted for the door, except at that moment, Mason puts his arm around my shoulders. The gesture shocks me but also eases my anxiety. I look up at Mason, and he smiles and winks at me.

Mrs. Howard insists on giving me a tour of the house while Mason goes to put our coats away. As I follow the older woman upstairs, I feel ill. I wish Mason were with us—I feel lost in this enormous house. I'm worried that if I get separated from Mrs. Howard, they'll find me days later, trapped in a closet somewhere.

Mrs. Howard leads me down a long corridor, lushly carpeted and dimly lit. I point out a room filled with bookcases and antique furniture, which she says is "the library." They have a library. I'm hooking up with a guy who lived in a house that has a *library*. Then we pass two guest rooms and, finally, Mason's old bedroom.

I like Mason's bedroom best out of every room on the tour. It's by far the least pretentious room in the house. It looks like any teenager's room, with a single bed, a computer, stereo equipment, and music posters on the walls. My eyes rest on one shelf of his bookcase, which is packed with trophies. Naturally. But it isn't the trophies that catch my attention—it's the framed photo in the middle of the shelf, featuring Mason with his arm around a stunning blond girl.

"That's Sienna, Mason's girlfriend from college, during their trip to Switzerland," Mrs. Howard says.

"Oh," I say.

I wonder why Mason has a photo of his ex-girlfriend featured so prominently on his shelf but then remember he hasn't been in this room in months. Quite possibly, his mother put the photo there. I could tell from her voice that she thinks very highly of this Sienna girl.

"Sienna went to Paris to study art for a year," Mrs. Howard says. Because obviously, I want to know all about Mason's ex-girlfriend. "What did you do after college, Sasha?"

The question catches me off guard. Like I've said, I look young for twenty-six. Most people think I'm straight out of college or usually even younger. How did Mrs. Howard figure it out?

"I worked as a nanny and took classes," I say a little defensively.

"And where are you from, dear?" she asks me.

"Brooklyn," I reply, lifting my chin to look her straight in the eyes.

She narrows her eyes at me. "I mean, originally, where are you from? Where were your parents born?"

"Russia," I admit. I am guessing that Mrs. Howard and her parents and their parents were all born in this country.

"Interesting," Mrs. Howard murmurs. She raises her eyebrow. "How long have you and Mason been seeing each other?"

Seeing each other. She grimaces as she asks the question as if she's just said a dirty word.

"Not that long," I mutter.

"Mason and Sienna were together for two years," Mrs. Howard says.

Is that so?

"Oh?" I say politely.

Please tell me more about Sienna, will you?

"You should probably know," Mrs. Howard continues, looking straight into my eyes, "that before Sienna left for Paris, Mason gave her a ring."

My jaw drops open. I try to hide my reaction because I hate to give Mrs. Howard the satisfaction, but she can tell I'm upset. And the thing is, I don't even know why. I'm not Mason's girlfriend. I don't want to be his girlfriend. What do I care that he gave some other girl a ring?

Except maybe I do care after all.

Damn it.

After the "tour" of the house is over, I find Mason sitting at the dining room table. He's staring down at the place mat, a glazed look in his eyes. For a moment, I remember all those dopamine capsules I've been slipping him and wonder if they could be having any effect. Probably not. He's probably just tired from lack of sleep.

I slide into the seat beside him. "Hey."

He startles, even though I'm sure he must have heard me come into the room. For a moment, he looks at me like he has no idea who I am. Then he shakes his head as if to clear it and offers me an uneven smile.

"Hi," he says.

"I saw your old room," I say.

"Yeah?" Mason grins. "God, I haven't been in there in… a while, I guess. Hey, did you see if my Green Day poster is still on the wall?"

"Um, I don't remember," I say, "but I did see the picture of Sienna."

Why did I say that? Oh well, too late to take it back now.

"Who?"

Okay, he doesn't know who she is. That's a good sign.

"That girl in the picture from Switzerland," I remind him.

"Oh, her." He rolls his eyes. "Christ, is that photo still on the shelf? I think my mother is in love with her."

"Your mother says you gave her a ring..." I study his face, watching his reaction.

"Sienna and I broke up before college ended." He lifts a shoulder. "I never gave her a ring."

"Oh."

But before I have a chance to be relieved, he narrows his eyes. "But so what if I did? What's the difference to you?"

Mason has never spoken to me that way before, and it feels like a slap in the face. Maybe I'm not his girlfriend, but he's always at least treated me with respect. This is the first time he has ever made me feel like he's just using me for sex.

And when I look into his eyes, I realize even that part of our relationship is over for good.

83

I HAVE A REALLY GOOD FEELING AFTER THE SECOND anatomy exam. During the anatomy practical, I felt confident of my answers for nearly all of the pins, and the written part of the exam was like a walk in the park. I aced it.

Of course, no matter how well I do, it seems like Mason is just always a little bit better than me. When the scores are posted, I fully expect to see his number at the top of the list, just like always.

The scores are posted outside the anatomy lab, and I go to check them right before going to the lab. There's a small crowd of students looking at their scores, and I slide past them to get a closer view of the list. I look up and find my score on the exam: Ninety-four.

Ninety-four. Okay, it could be better. I'm slightly disappointed. But it's still a good grade—an honors-level grade.

But this is the moment of truth: Did anyone do better than me?

I scan the list of scores and find that nobody got a perfect hundred percent. One person got a ninety-five, and one got an impressive ninety-seven. But the good news is that neither of those people is Mason Howard, based on the ID number. Which means that for once, I beat Mason.

Victory! Ha, maybe I'll go rub it in his face.

Just out of curiosity, I scan the list, searching for Mason's number. I'm perplexed when at first, I can't find his score. Then I see it, at the very bottom of the list: thirty-seven.

Mason failed the exam.

It must be some kind of mistake. There's no way Mason could have failed. He's the best student in the class. He's the only person to ever get a perfect score on the practical. People like that don't fail exams. That can't be right.

Of course, I've noticed that Mason hasn't been studying in the library anymore. But I just figured he was avoiding me after that awkward dinner. I did see him on the day of the exam, hunched in a corner, his hair wild, a week's worth of stubble on his chin. He looked awful, especially for Mason, but I just assumed it was because of the marathon studying.

It can't be because of the dopamine I was giving him, can it?

No. No way. It was just a few pills. Dad used to take like five of those a day, and at worst, I only gave Mason two a day. And besides, I haven't given him any pills in weeks. No, it's got to be something else. Maybe some personal issues he's having.

I try to put Mason out of my mind as I go into the lab. Weirdly enough, the smell of formaldehyde doesn't even bother me anymore. I almost enjoy it because it reminds me of how much I've learned in this short period of time. With every passing day, my dream of becoming a doctor is drawing closer and closer. My father would be so proud of me.

Rachel is already standing by the cadaver, dissecting near his left shoulder. I lean over the body to see what she's doing, because in all honesty, she usually messes everything up. But instead, I see the perfectly dissected nerves running through the shoulder.

"Nice job on the brachial plexus," I comment.

Rachel smiles. "Thanks," she says, "although I can't totally take credit. Matt was helping me with it earlier."

Matt? Who's Matt?

There's nobody in the class named Matt. And there aren't any teaching assistants named Matt. Who is this mysterious Matt who's been helping Rachel suddenly turn into an anatomy genius?

Wait a minute…

Oh my God…

She's talking about *Dr. Conlon*.

Rachel is calling our professor by his first name. She's somehow gotten to be on a first-name basis with the guy. I close my eyes for a moment and recall a couple of months ago when I caught Dr. Conlon staring at Rachel's chest.

Holy shit, they're sleeping together.

Dr. Conlon limps over to us at that moment. When he sees Rachel, he gets this big dopey grin on his face.

"How is everything going, Doctors?"

"I'm just about finished," Rachel says.

Dr. Conlon leans over the cadaver slightly to get a better view of Rachel's dissection. He nods in approval, "Very nice job. *Very* nice."

Damn. No wonder Rachel never needs to study.

Dr. Conlon's eyes rest on me. For a moment, I hold out a desperate hope that he's going to quiz me or offer me assistance or praise or criticism or at least *remember my name*, but instead, he asks, "Have you seen Mason recently?"

Of course he's asking about Mason.

"No," I say.

"Hmm," Dr. Conlon murmurs.

There's concern in his eyes, and I recall Mason's failing score on the last exam. He cares more about Mason than me when he's acing the exam, and now when he's failing too. I can't win.

Unfortunately, even with Mason out of the way, I still don't have the highest score on the last exam. And of course, now, Rachel's got the edge for obvious reasons. It seems like no matter how hard I try, people keep beating me out. It's so unfair. There's no way to be number one.

Unless…

I look up at Rachel, who's talking to Dr. Conlon. He's practically undressing her with his eyes as she talks. It's so wrong that Rachel is taking advantage of the fact that Dr. Conlon is obviously lonely and probably can't get a girl to sleep with him otherwise. She's manipulating him in order to ace a class that she rightfully deserves to fail.

Why should Rachel be the only one to benefit from her little scheme?

84

I STAND OUTSIDE RACHEL'S LOCKER, MY HANDS SHAKING. Last night, I spent over an hour composing a letter to Rachel. I wrote several drafts and ended up crumpling most of them up. It took me several tries until the handwriting seemed sufficiently unrecognizable. But then I got paranoid about fingerprints, so I did the whole thing over again while wearing rubber gloves from the lab. I finally settled on the following:

> *I know all about you and Dr. Conlon. Put the answers to the final exam under the door of Locker 282 or else everyone will find out the truth.*

Locker 282 is one of the empty lockers at the end of the hallway. I put a lock on it and figure I can collect the papers late at night when nobody is around. Rachel will probably try to keep an eye on the locker, but she can't watch it all the time. It's a perfect plan.

I may be crossing a line by doing this. Believe me,

I've never cheated before. I've considered it once or twice but never ended up going through with it. But it feels like the only way to level the playing field. I mean, Rachel gets an edge through sleeping with Dr. Conlon, and Mason gets an edge because he's good-looking and charismatic—it's just not fair.

And yes, I know that's sort of bullshit.

I look around the hallway before removing the note from my pocket. I take a deep breath and slide the piece of paper under the crack at the bottom of Rachel's locker. As soon as the white sheet disappears, regret washes over me. I almost wish I could somehow retrieve it. But it's gone. I did it.

And actually, I don't feel *that* bad about it.

I back away from the locker, hurrying down the hallway. I don't want anyone to see me. I'm heading in the direction of the library when I practically slam into a very pale-looking Mason stumbling out of the men's room. He collapses against the wall like his legs can no longer support him.

"Mason?"

I bend down next to him. He doesn't look up at me at first—he just stares at the floor with that glazed look in his eyes. He's still unshaven and looks like he hasn't even showered in days. He looks *horrible*, more like some vagrant from the street than the confident guy I started hooking up with a few months ago.

Shit. I didn't do this to him, did I?

It seems so unlikely. I tossed those pills in a dumpster ages ago. Yes, I *have* heard of certain drugs triggering a psychotic break in vulnerable people, but… that can't be what happened to him, could it?

No. No way. It must be the stress. Or maybe he's started taking some of the illegal drugs that are being passed around. Yes, that could definitely be it.

"Mason?" I repeat.

Finally, he looks up at me. I gasp at how bloodshot his eyes are.

"What?" he says. His voice cracks slightly when he speaks.

"Are you okay?" I ask.

The question seems almost ridiculous. He is so obviously not okay.

"No, I'm not *okay*." Spittle flies out of his mouth as he speaks. "I'm going to be *murdered*. Just like Frank."

There's something very frightening in his eyes, something very unfamiliar. I remember how, at the beginning of the year, he smiled at me across the table in the library, and I got lost in his eyes. I remember the passion with which he had ripped my blouse open and pressed his lips onto mine. He seems like an entirely different person now.

Mason needs help. That's obvious. I could talk to the dean or maybe tell Patrice. Or even Dr. Conlon, who is already concerned. But I'm scared. What if they find out that someone has been drugging him? How long will it take Mason to put it together after he remembers all those cups of coffee I brought him? He's a smart guy, after all. And I was so careless.

And really, isn't this what I always wanted? To get

Mason out of the picture? He's been my greatest competition in the class, and now, he's no longer a threat. And who's to say it's because of the dopamine pills? It probably isn't. I'm sure it's just that the stress has finally gotten to him. But if I 'fessed up what had really happened, I'm sure I'd get blamed. And maybe kicked out of medical school.

No, nobody can find out about this.

After all, what's the worst that can happen?

85

When I arrive at the anatomy lab the next day, Rachel is staring down at the cadaver with a horrified expression on her face.

We've been working on the arms and legs—earlier in the week, Rachel completed a perfect dissection of the left arm, undoubtedly with the aid of her lover, Dr. Matthew Conlon. I remember how Mason used to ogle Rachel too—what is so damned attractive about Rachel? Why are men falling for her left and right? Of course, it probably didn't take much to lure in a pathetic loser like Dr. Conlon.

I approach Rachel, who seems nearly frozen.

"What's wrong?" I ask.

That's when I see for myself what Rachel is staring at.

Somebody has massacred our cadaver. The arms and legs have literally been shredded. Someone has taken a scalpel and done a truly horrible dissection that is bordering on brutality.

"Oh my God," I breathe.

My first thought is: Mason.

Mason must have done it. God knows why, but I saw something terrible in his eyes yesterday. And if he's capable of doing this, what else is he capable of?

I have to tell someone. I have to get Mason help. I have to—

"What happened here?" Dr. Conlon limps over to us. There is a concerned crease between his dark eyebrows.

Rachel whispers in my ear, "Sasha, don't…"

I don't know what that means, though.

"Someone destroyed our cadaver!" I speak up. The tears welling up in my eyes are real.

Dr. Conlon's mouth falls open as he inspects the damage. Rachel is strangely silent. I wonder if she's told Conlon about the blackmail letter. He seemed a little too cheerful in class this morning to know about it.

But he doesn't seem cheerful anymore. Dr. Conlon's face grows very dark.

"I can't believe a student in my class would do such a sick thing," he says. He looks up at me. "Do you have any idea who did this?"

I need to confess. I need to tell him all about Mason. That he's sick and needs help—before it's too late. I don't need to admit to my part in it.

But I can't say it. My jaw feels glued shut. And before I can stop myself, I slowly shake my head no.

Here's the sad truth:

I want Mason to fail.

Nobody deserves to get through life as easily as he

does. Nobody deserves to live in that giant house with two doting parents, to be handsome and brilliant, to get absolutely everything he wants in life. I want Mason to sink deeper and deeper into the hole.

So deep that he can never crawl out.

86

I TRY TO PUSH THE GUILT OUT OF MY HEAD AS I LOSE myself in studying.

The library is open until midnight, and I intend to stay there until closing time. For some reason, it's comforting to stare at diagrams of arteries, nerves, and muscles. I try to blank out everything except anatomy.

But it's hard to focus. I keep thinking about that letter I stuffed into Rachel's locker. Is Rachel going to get me a copy of the exam? And if she does, will I look at it? I've never cheated before. This crosses a line.

And of course, if Rachel doesn't get me the exam, should I make good on my threat and blow the whistle on their little sex romp? An offense like that is enough to get Dr. Conlon fired and Rachel kicked out of school. I don't have much sympathy for Rachel, but I'd feel sorry for Dr. Conlon. He's a really good teacher who cares a lot about his students. I can tell his job means everything to him. It's not his fault that Rachel is playing him for a grade.

But really, what I can't stop thinking about is Mason. As I look at the diagrams of the arms and legs, I can't help but think about what he did to our cadaver. The dopamine capsules are long out of his system, though—the matter is out of my hands. Mason has friends, a roommate, and his family to look out for him. It shouldn't all fall on my shoulders.

But then sometimes I think back to the way he used to kiss me. The way he'd smile at me. The way we ripped each other's clothes off like the ship was going down. Mason isn't just my classmate. At one time, I actually really liked him.

I look down at my watch—it's a quarter to midnight. I've barely been able to focus at all in the last few hours, and the library will be closed soon. I may as well get packed up to leave.

"Sasha!"

I practically jump out of my skin at the sound of my name. I look up and gasp when I behold the person who used to be Mason Howard standing before me. He looks *awful.* His clothing is wrinkled and stained, his hair is disheveled, he has a week's growth of a beard on his face, and there are dark circles under his eyes.

He seems out of breath. He kneels down in front of me and takes my hand in his like he's about to propose. There's a terrible, haunted look in his bloodshot hazel eyes.

"Sasha…" he whispers.

I try not to let on how shocked I am by his appearance. I force a smile. "Hey, Mason."

"Sasha, I think…" He takes a deep breath. "I think

there's something wrong with me. I… I think I'm losing it…" As he speaks the words, his eyes fill up with tears.

I've never seen Mason cry. I've only seen a man cry once in my entire life: when my father watched me graduate from college.

"Please help me," he whispers.

He buries his face in his hands, his trembling fingers reaching into his brown hair and compulsively pulling at the strands.

Why should I help him? Nobody ever helped me.

He looks back up at me, the desperation plain on his face. He's having his first lucid moment in a long time, and he's realizing what is happening to him. It's almost heartbreaking.

Almost.

"Calm down," I say, trying to put conviction into my words. "You're fine. Everyone gets nervous before a big exam."

Mason is shaking his head, mouthing the word "no."

"Come on," I say. "Think about it: people who are crazy don't know they're crazy, right? You're just being a typical med student hypochondriac."

I watch his face, waiting to see if he'll buy it.

"Maybe…" he says slowly.

"You just need to get some sleep," I say in my most gentle voice. Hey, maybe I've got a career in psychiatry. As if.

Mason's shoulders sag.

"Yeah, maybe you're right." He sighs and looks back up at me. For a moment, he's his old self as he offers me a half-hearted grin, "Hey, do you want to go to the locker rooms...?"

Even with everything going on, I'm tempted. Even with his disheveled appearance, Mason is still very attractive. But I can't. Not after everything I've done to him. Just looking at him makes me hate myself.

87

Usually, when I start studying, I'm like a machine. I keep going until I've gotten through everything I intended to learn at the beginning of the session and then some.

But today, once again, I can't concentrate.

I keep thinking about Mason. As much as I hate to admit it, I'm worried about him. Really worried. I don't know what's going on in his head. And it scares me. The last time I saw him, there was something terrifying in his eyes. Every time I try to concentrate on my work, I see those bloodshot hazel eyes.

Finally, I give up on studying and decide to head over to Mason's suite. I've never actually been there before because we've been keeping our relationship casual and a bit hush-hush, but it doesn't seem to matter anymore since it's pretty much over. And I'm a little bit curious to see where he lives.

I drive over to the dorm where the vast majority of students are residing. I briefly considered living in the dorm because it was so cheap, but at my age, I couldn't stomach it. I needed my own apartment and my privacy —I couldn't imagine having to abide by some dorm rules and have a roommate sharing my bedroom.

Mason's apartment is on the third floor of the dorm. I find his apartment, and after only a brief hesitation, I knock on the door. By the heavy footsteps, I can tell that Abe is the one coming to answer the door. He looks slightly breathless as he pulls the door open, and I feel a twinge of sympathy as his face falls when he sees it's only me. I suspect he was hoping for Heather.

"Oh, hey, Sasha," he says. "Mason isn't here right now."

He knows about me and Mason. He's cleverer than I've given him credit for. I wonder who else in the class knows. Probably everyone.

"Do you know where he is?" I ask.

Abe glances at his watch.

"He's usually back by now," he says. "Do you want to wait?"

I look down at my own watch. It's about eleven at night. Where *is* he? I feel too antsy to go home, so I say, "Okay, I'll wait."

Abe steps back to let me in. I venture into the apartment, which is a total guys' apartment. There's food and laundry strewn everywhere, and the futon looks almost too dirty to sit on. I push aside some books and papers and make a small square of space to rest my behind. Abe at least has the decency to blush.

"Sorry the place is such a mess," he says as he plops down next to me.

"It's okay," I say. "My sisters were kind of slobs, so I'm used to it."

My stilted conversation with Abe makes me realize how little I know him. Or really, anyone in my class besides Mason. Abe is my lab partner, and we've had probably hundreds of verbal exchanges, but every single one of them has involved anatomy. Or at the very least, biochemistry.

"Are you feeling ready for the exam?" Abe asks me.

Back to familiar territory. I nod. "Sort of."

He laughs. "If anyone is ready, it's you."

"What is that supposed to mean?"

He shrugs. "You know it all, Sasha. Everyone knows that you're the top student in the class."

He's *got* to be messing with me. "No way."

"Way," he says. "I mean, Heather always says..." He stops mid-sentence, his words trailing off. He looks really sad again.

"Abe?"

He doesn't answer. His green eyes seem very far away.

"Do you," I venture carefully, "want to talk about Heather?"

It's not like me to make an offer like that. I'm feeling so guilty lately. Maybe talking to Abe would be penance for some of the things I've done wrong. Or at least it would be a start.

"No," he says. "I really don't."

Well, if he doesn't want to talk about it, it's not like I've got time to kill.

88

I'M WORKING ON DISSECTING THE RIGHT FOOT OF THE cadaver, one of the few parts that hasn't been shredded to bits by a scalpel courtesy of Mason. I'm carefully separating the muscle bodies of the extensor digitorum longus. The rest of Frank's limbs are too badly mangled to be tagged for the anatomy practical, but I'm hoping they might tag something in his right foot. I feel pride when Dr. Conlon finds one of my dissections to be worthy of an exam question.

"What are you working on, Dr. Zaleski?"

I look up, and my eyes meet Dr. Conlon's. Up close, he has the brightest blue eyes I've ever seen in my life, even hidden behind his glasses. I'm glad he remembered my name for a change.

"Just separating the extensor muscles of the foot."

Dr. Conlon makes his way around the table to get a closer look at my dissection. I watch a smile grow across his face.

"*Excellent* job," he comments. "Of course, what less could I expect from the best student in the class?"

I avert my eyes—I'm not used to compliments. It's even more surprising to hear from him than it was to hear it from Abe yesterday.

"I'm not… I mean, I don't have the highest grades or…"

"Nobody else in the class has had such a consistently superb performance on all the exams and quizzes," he says. He looks at Frank's foot again. "As well as superior skills on the dissections. Don't think I haven't noticed."

I don't know what to say. All this time, I thought Dr. Conlon barely knew who I was.

"Um… thank you…"

He smiles again. "And if you want that teaching assistant job for next year, it's yours."

My heart soars. "Are you serious?"

"Absolutely," he says. "I hope you're interested. I'd be disappointed if you said no."

"I'm interested!" I almost yell. I clear my throat, suddenly embarrassed. "I mean, of course I'd like to do it."

He folds his arms across his scrub top, "You know, after teaching this class so long, I can tell exactly what kind of doctor each student will become, just from watching them in the lab."

"Really?"

He nods. "This class brings out a lot of qualities in people, both good and bad."

I stare up at Dr. Conlon's face, trying to read his

expression. Does he know it was me who left that letter in Rachel's locker? Is this all his way of toying with me?

No. There's no way.

"So what kind of doctor am I going to be?" I ask him.

Dr. Conlon hesitates for a long time then finally smiles again. "Well, I don't want to give away the surprise. You'll know soon enough."

What the hell does that mean?

"By the way." He clears his throat. "Have you… Have you seen Rachel around?"

I shake my head, not meeting his eyes.

He coughs and lowers his eyes.

"The two of you have spent a lot of time in the lab together," he observes. "Would you say that she… has a good grasp of the material?"

Now, why would he ask that? I can tell by the tone of my professor's voice how smitten he is with Rachel. Doesn't he realize that she's getting good grades only because of him? Is it possible that Rachel is using him to cheat without his knowledge?

Poor Dr. Conlon.

"Honestly?" I ask.

"Yes, honestly. Does she know the material or not?"

"She doesn't."

Dr. Conlon's shoulders sag. "Okay, thanks, Sasha."

89

My mother calls me on the Friday evening before our final exam. I'm on my way out to the library, and I get irritated when her name pops up on my phone, but I answer anyway. I realize that I've only been home to visit her twice since the year started, but I don't feel guilty. Honestly, she's lucky that I visit her at all.

"How are you doing, Sasha?" Mom asks me. "Do you have time to visit this weekend?"

"My final exam in anatomy is on Monday," I explain, the irritation seeping through my voice.

"Oh." She sounds like she doesn't quite buy this as a legitimate excuse. "How about for Christmas? Can you spend the week here?"

"Maybe a few days," I say vaguely.

"I hope you do," Mom says quietly. "It's very lonely here."

I feel my blood pressure creeping up. "Well, that's your fault, isn't it? If Dad were still alive, you wouldn't feel so lonely."

There's a long pause on the other line. Finally, Mom says, "I know. I wish he were still here too."

I nearly throw my phone at the wall.

"What are you talking about?" I cry. "If you hadn't taken him off the ventilator, he'd still be here! It's *your fault* he's dead!"

"Sasha!" Mom gasps.

I shut my eyes and feel the tears rising to the surface. I can't believe I just said that to my mother. But I'm not sorry. I meant every word of it. I've been itching to say it since the day he died.

"It's true," I manage.

"Sasha," Mom says in a quiet, sad voice. "I didn't take your father off the ventilator. The doctors just followed his wishes. He signed an advance directive saying he didn't want to be kept on life support."

What is she talking about? This is total bullshit.

"No way," I say. "Dad would never have done that. Never."

"He did it for *you*, Sasha," Mom says. "He realized that as long as he was alive and sick, you'd never be able to live out your dream. He didn't want you to waste your life taking care of him."

No. She's lying. I don't believe her. My father loved life—he'd never agree to something like that.

"He was so proud of you," Mom says. "You being happy and becoming a doctor was all that mattered to him."

"And if not for you," I say through the lump in my throat, "he'd be able to watch me graduate from medical school."

And then I hang up on her, my hands shaking. I just can't see how what she's saying could be true. Dad knew that if he wanted me to go to medical school, I would have gone. He didn't have to be *dead*. I mean, yes, I did want to stay at home and take care of him in those last few years. But I wasn't going to do that forever.

I had every intention of leaving him to go to med school. I really did.

90

FOR A SUNDAY NIGHT, THE LIBRARY IS SURPRISINGLY crowded. When I look around, several of my classmates are feverishly outlining textbooks and studying drawings of muscles, arteries, and nerves, trying to put in a last-ditch effort to prepare for our final exam tomorrow. It makes me nostalgic for the days when it was just me and Mason.

I feel confident I'll at least earn an honors grade in the class. I know the anatomy atlas backward and forward, and I put in countless hours in the lab this week, memorizing all the structures. But is it enough to get the top grade in the class? I don't know.

I haven't checked Locker 282 yet. I have no idea if the exam is in there or not. I walk by the locker every day, debating if I should risk checking it. But I can't bring myself to do it.

I haven't seen Mason since that night in the library. Maybe he decided to pick another location to study, one less distracting. There are students scattered all over the hospital studying this weekend. Despite how awful he looked the other day, I can't believe he isn't putting everything he's got into this exam.

Believe it or not, I almost went and talked to Patrice about him. I stood in front of her office for about five straight minutes, my hand poised to knock on the door. But in the end, I couldn't do it. I want to get the highest score in the class on this exam—and if Mason rehabilitates himself, that might not happen.

Of course, the only surefire way to get the highest score lies in the contents of Locker 282.

I'm debating whether to get up and check the locker when a familiar voice makes me stop short.

"Sasha?"

My breath catches in my throat. It's Rachel Bingham. Great.

"Um… hey, Rachel…"

"I'm glad I'm not the only one here late at night," Rachel says, sliding uninvited into the seat next to mine. The comment is a little patronizing—it's not like Rachel needs to be here late studying when she's sleeping with the professor.

"It's never empty here at night," I say irritably.

Rachel sighs loudly and looks off into the distance. I feel like she expects me to say something, so I finally ask, "Are you okay, Rachel?"

"It's just this guy I've been seeing," Rachel says.

This guy? You mean *our professor*, don't you? God, I hate her.

"We sort of… broke up recently," she sighs. "I really messed things up."

I frown. Rachel and Dr. Conlon aren't sleeping together anymore? Does that mean she hasn't been able to get the answers to the final?

"I… I'm sorry. Did all the studying get in the way?"

"No, not really."

Rachel doesn't look like she wants to say anything more, but I need to know what happened. I need to know if those exam answers are waiting for me.

I have to feel her out. "So you're having a fight?"

"No, it's over," Rachel assures me. "I did something… unforgivable."

"You cheated on him?"

That seems unlikely. Rachel doesn't seem interested enough in men to have sex if it wasn't for a grade. From the comments I've heard her make, she seems to despise men.

"No, it's not that…" Rachel bites her lip.

She looks away, and that's when I realize that there are *tears* filling her eyes. Oh my God, is she *crying*? I'm confused. Is she crying over her grade? She can't possibly have been *in love* with Dr. Conlon, could she? No way.

This is the weirdest conversation ever.

Rachel stands up rather abruptly, nearly knocking over her chair. She looks almost manic.

"Uh, I've got to go for a minute," she says. "Watch my stuff?"

I nod, perplexed. I don't bother to mention that nothing ever gets stolen out of the library. I left my purse here all the time when I snuck off to the locker room with Mason.

After Rachel disappears, I try my best to go back to studying, but it's difficult. All I can think about is what Rachel was talking about. If she and Dr. Conlon are over, will the exam still be in that locker?

I've got to know.

I stand up. I glance around, and nobody seems to be particularly paying attention to me. Now is the time, before Rachel gets back.

I hurry across the floor, in the direction of the anatomy lab. My heart is pounding, and my palms are sweaty. For all I know, Rachel is lying in wait in the locker room, and she's going to bust me the second I open that locker. But that's a chance I've got to take.

A few minutes later, I'm standing in front of Locker 282. My combination lock is hanging from the door, and for a moment, the combination flies right out of my head. But then it comes back to me: 28-16-8. I start turning the dial.

Before I pop the lock open, I check the hallway one last time. Empty.

The door to the locker swings open, and there it is: the final exam. My heart beats wildly as I pick it up and flip through over a dozen pages of anatomy diagrams and multiple-choice questions. I can't believe I'm holding *the final exam*. I can't believe my plan worked. I'm going to get the highest score in the class on the final.

But as I stare into the empty locker, somehow, a distant memory fills my head—my father bouncing around the ER, telling everyone who would listen: "My daughter wants to be a doctor!"

Sasha, you make me so proud…

I look back down at the final exam, and I suddenly feel ill. All I wanted was to make my father proud of me. If my mother is to be believed, he gave up his own life so that I could have my dream.

And all I know is that if my father could see what I'm doing right now, he would not be proud. He would be ashamed of me.

Before I can change my mind, I start ripping the final exam into shreds. I tear up every single page into about a dozen pieces and hurl them into the nearest trash bin. It doesn't even register that I'm crying until the final shreds of paper have been deposited into the garbage.

Please, Papa, forgive me…

I'm just glad he isn't alive to see me like this.

91

AFTER SEVERAL MINUTES OF SOBBING IN THE LOCKER room, I manage to collect myself. Being in the locker room late at night makes me miss Mason almost desperately. If I told him about my dad, he'd understand. He'd understand everything. He isn't nearly as much of a jerk as I always made him out to be.

I wander around the floor, just trying to clear my head, half-heartedly looking for Mason. I use the bathroom by the anatomy labs, and I can't help but notice that huge crack in the sink that's been there all year. I don't understand why nobody fixes it. I wonder what kind of blunt impact must have created that fissure.

Eventually, I find myself at the vending machines. During school hours, the vending machines usually have a line in front of them, but now, they're completely deserted. I stare at the different candies and cookies suspended in the machine, but I don't have much appetite. I remember how Mason offered me vending-machine Oreo cookies the first time we talked in the library. That feels like a million years ago now.

I decide on some peanut butter cups, and as I'm getting ready to drop my change in the machine, I hear footsteps coming from behind me. For a moment, I get my hopes up that maybe it's Mason, but when I turn around, Rachel is hurrying toward me. Rachel's lipstick is smeared, and it isn't hard to guess what she's just been doing.

So much for the big breakup.

I'm not going to judge her, though. All right, I'm going to *try* not to judge her. Or at least, I'll try to try.

Any contempt I have for Rachel fades, though, when I realize that the red on Rachel's face isn't lipstick—it's blood. Fresh blood, not the old clotted kind that we find in the cadaver. And it's all over her shirt as well.

"Oh my God," I gasp.

Rachel is crying. She's wiping her eyes with the back of her hand, spreading more blood onto her face. Holy crap, where did all that blood come from?

"Sasha," Rachel says in a low voice, "something terrible has happened."

Yeah, no kidding.

"What happened?" I ask, sounding a lot calmer than I feel.

"Mason Howard…" Rachel's eyes well up with a new batch of tears. "He… he *shot* Dr. Conlon!"

Oh God…

"Dr. Conlon and I were…" She lowers her eyes. "We were… you know, sort of seeing each other. I know it's wrong, but… it just sort of happened. And… and I was in his office when Mason came in and…"

Rachel collapses against the wall, sobbing hysterically. And that's when I get a second jolt of shock. She wasn't just sleeping with him—she actually *liked* him.

"Is he… dead?" I ask.

Rachel nods slowly.

Oh no.

"We need to get help," I say.

Nobody can ever know what I've done.

PART VI

DR. CONLON

92

THE NIGHT BEFORE THE ANATOMY FINAL EXAM

IT'S STRANGE WHAT YOU THINK ABOUT WHEN SOMEONE IS pointing a gun at your face.

It's happened to me twice now. While two is a relatively small number, it still seems way above average. Most people have never had a gun pointed at their face even once. And it's not like I'm some sort of drug dealer or gangster—I'm an anatomy professor. It's not clear why this should keep happening to me.

The first time someone pointed a gun at me was the far more surprising of the two. I suppose once you realize such a thing is possible, it loses its shock value a bit. No offense intended to Mason—it's still very scary to have him pointing his gun at my face. Especially since I'm pretty sure he intends to kill me.

I was twenty-two years old the first time. In retrospect, that seems incredibly young. So young that it's surprising I was even allowed to go out and live on my own and pay bills and make important life decisions. I was an idiot at twenty-two. Well, no more of an idiot than the average twenty-two-year-old, but you lack good judgment at that age. The frontal lobe isn't fully myelinated yet.

And yes, I do realize the irony of my saying such a thing in light of the fact that I'm currently having sex with a twenty-two-year-old girl. I'm a hypocrite. I'm not going to make excuses for myself.

Anyway, back to Kurt Morton and the gun he so rudely pointed at my head. I was sleeping when Kurt's mumbling woke me up. And there he was: sitting on his bed across from mine in the darkness, playing with that damn revolver.

"It's all over, Matt," he mumbled. "I'm fucked."

"Shut up and go back to sleep," I said brilliantly.

That was a dumb thing to say, right? But I was incredibly tired, and also, I was too young to realize how bad this situation was. I thought I was immortal. If I had it to do over again, I would have said something different. Maybe along the lines of, "Please, *please* don't shoot me in the head, Kurt."

"I'm flunking out," he said, his voice cracking. "Did you know that?"

I shook my head. "Wow, man, that sucks."

Again, not the most brilliant thing I could have said. I've had a lot of time to go over this in my head and highlight my mistakes. Could I have stopped him? We'll never know.

"What do you care?" Kurt shot back. "Mister *honors student*."

Yes, I was an honors student. I wanted to be a

surgeon back then. But we all know what happened to that particular dream.

And that was when Kurt went from playing with the gun to *pointing* it at me. I aged about twenty years in that moment. I stared down the barrel of the revolver, thinking to myself, "Holy shit, he's going to kill me."

The next thing I remember, it was about two weeks later. Someone was asking me my name, if I knew where I was, what the date was, and my birthday. Also, they told me I'd been shot in the head and that Kurt was dead.

They called me "lucky" a lot. Kurt was aiming his gun right at my face, but his hands were shaking, and he instead hit me on the left side of my skull. If he'd had steadier hands, I might have ended up like Ann, a girl on the rehab unit who was two years younger than me. Her boyfriend shot her through the eye, and the bullet's trajectory veered downward and severed her spinal cord. Aside from being blind in one eye and having a deformed face, Ann was paralyzed from the neck down, dependent on a ventilator to breathe for the rest of her life. It could have happened to me. Or more likely, I could have died.

Although once you get shot in the head, you lose the right to ever call yourself lucky.

What I lost was half my skull. It was smashed to smithereens by the bullet, so they just took it off. If you pressed your finger against the left side of my scalp (and believe me, I attempted this a few times during moments of boredom and/or itchiness), there was nothing but brain underneath the skin. I had to wear a helmet when

I walked in case I fell. Well, not *in case* I fell. I couldn't move half my body, so falling was fairly inevitable.

My right arm and leg got stronger, though, although never even close to full strength. Good enough, though, that I could walk (more or less) and dress myself and bathe myself if you gave me half the day to do it. They gave me a new skull too. For a brief time, I deluded myself that I might return to medical school. This was probably quite hilarious to the people around me.

It was my neuropsychologist who set me straight. Dr. Watson. He spent hours doing tests of my memory and reasoning and problem-solving. When it was over, he laid out the results for me in his office. He used a lot of big words, but the message was painfully clear: I'd never be able to go back.

Naturally, I argued with him.

"I read that I could arrange to get extra time on exams," I said. "All I'd need would be your documentation."

"Sounds great, Matt," Dr. Watson said in a voice that made it obvious that my idea was not, in fact, great. "But what will you do when you're doing surgery on a patient or performing a procedure? How will you arrange for extra time in that situation?"

We went back and forth for the better part of an hour. I don't know why I bothered—he was right. I couldn't go back. I'd never be a physician.

93

I WON'T BORE YOU WITH THE DETAILS OF HOW I managed to get a doctorate in anatomy, through a combination of taking advantage of every allowance given to people with disabilities as well as just studying my ass off. When you go from having a near-photographic memory to not being able to remember what you had for breakfast that morning, it's a tough transition. My memory improved, though, thankfully.

But you don't want to hear about that. I'm sure what you'd really like to know is how it came to pass that I started having sex with my twenty-two-year-old student.

About a week before the school year was set to begin, I got the call from Dr. Michael Hirsch. I was in my office, going over the syllabus for the upcoming year. I was debating in my mind what to get for dinner that night (who am I kidding—it was going to be a TV dinner) when the phone rang.

"Is this Dr. Conlon?" a deep voice wanted to know.

"Yes…" I said.

"Matthew Conlon?" he persisted. "The anatomy professor?"

As if another Dr. Conlon would be answering my phone.

"Yes," I confirmed.

"My name is Mike Hirsch," the man said. "*Dr.* Hirsch. I believe you have a former student of mine in your upcoming class. Rachel Bingham?"

I faced my computer and clicked on the class roster for the upcoming year, which contained each student's name, a photo, and their undergraduate university and major. I searched under B and found a plain-looking brunette named Rachel Bingham who had majored in evolutionary biology.

"Yes, that's right," I said.

"Dr. Conlon," Hirsch said. "The reason I'm calling is to give you a heads-up. Rachel is… someone to look out for."

I raised my eyebrows at the innocuous-appearing photo of Rachel Bingham.

"Does she cheat?"

"Rachel destroyed my marriage," Hirsch said, his voice filled with anger. "And if you let her, she'll wreck your life."

The whole thing sounded ludicrous. I laughed it off at the time. But then, a week later, I saw Rachel in person, and I got it—I understood how this girl was capable of wrecking a man's marriage. She had a certain seductively dangerous quality to her—it was incredibly alluring.

Still, I had every intention of turning her down. Truly, I did.

Then… well, I don't know what happened. I was giving her Patrice's number, and she was getting ready to leave my office, but then I made the dire mistake of peering down her shirt, and I got to thinking about how long it had been since I'd been with a woman. Three years—three *years*. So I thought to myself that I'd do it just this one time. Just once, and then I'd set her straight that it would never happen again.

Then, somehow, I fell in love with her.

You might be wondering why I fell for her, which is the same thing Patrice asked me. I've never been the shallow type, so I can assure you I didn't fall for her perfect twenty-two-year-old body. If I'm being honest, I'd have to say that I genuinely don't know how it happened.

I suppose it mostly had something to do with the way she made me feel about myself. Who doesn't want to feel desired by a beautiful young girl?

All I know is that I've been taking antidepressants for over a decade, and the first time since Kurt shot me that I could remember being truly happy was when I was with Rachel.

94

Here is the story with Patrice:

When I first met Patrice, I found her attractive. She *is* attractive, objectively speaking. As you get older, the chances of meeting an attractive, single person who is your age become infinitesimally smaller. And I'm far from picky—believe me.

When Patrice started working at DeWitt—one year after I started—I liked her right away. She was smart and pretty but not so far out of my league that it would have been an impossible dream. So I mustered up all my courage and asked her to go with me for drinks after work. I figured I could always backpedal and say it was platonic if she became flustered.

Patrice said yes to drinks, and I gave myself a little pat on the back. We went to a bar a few blocks from her house, where the conversation flowed easily, and after I had two beers in me, I had nearly worked up the nerve to make a move. Then Patrice glanced at her watch.

"I should probably go;" Patrice said. "I promised my boyfriend I'd make him dinner tonight."

When I later found out that she didn't actually have a boyfriend, I was just grateful that she'd spared me the embarrassment.

That was years ago. Now we're platonic friends, and I've been satisfied with that arrangement, even though, yes, I still find her attractive. But whenever it seemed like she was flirting with me, I reminded myself of that humiliating night and backed off.

When Patrice walked in on Rachel and me, I panicked. I knew Patrice would overreact. She knew Rachel and didn't much care for her, probably because she secretly suspected what was going on. As soon as Rachel left, she laid into me.

"I'm really disappointed in you, Matt," she said in her slow therapist's voice.

I hated when she spoke to me that way, like I was one of her patients.

"It's not a big deal," I mumbled.

"Not a big deal?" Patrice echoed my words. "Matt, you could lose your job. You realize that, right?"

"Yes, of course." I leaned my head against the back of the sofa and stared up at the ceiling so I wouldn't have to look at her.

"Tampering with grades is an incredibly serious offense," Patrice said. "You'd never work again in academics."

"I didn't tamper with her grade," I said.

Patrice appeared deeply skeptical.

"I didn't," I insisted.

"Well, what are you giving her then?" Patrice asked. "The answer key?"

"No," I said. "I'm not giving her anything. We're just… We're in a relationship."

I hated the sympathetic look on her face.

"Oh, Matt. Come on."

It hurt that Patrice wouldn't entertain even the slightest possibility that Rachel could genuinely like me. But it was not entirely unfair. In the three years prior to Rachel coming along, I'd been on exactly one date. It was a woman I met on a dating app, and she dashed out halfway through the meal, citing an emergency that was clearly manufactured. I was so depressed about it that I decided to take a break from dating, which ended up being more permanent than I intended.

"You have to trust me," Patrice said. "This isn't going to end well. For either of you."

I knew she was right, but I couldn't admit it. "It might."

"Trust me, it won't."

I closed my eyes, hating that Patrice was right. But then I felt the couch shift under me, and I realized she was sitting beside me. Inappropriately close, given that last time I got this close to her, she felt a need to invent a fake boyfriend.

"Matt," she said gently. "I've been thinking a lot about us lately. You and me."

I opened my eyes and looked at her in surprise. "You and me?"

Patrice nodded. "All my life, I've been involved with the same types of men. Every boyfriend… my ex-husband... every one of them were these handsome, bad-boy types. I just couldn't resist them."

"Yeah," I muttered, rolling my eyes. "Too bad."

"I don't want that kind of man anymore, though." Patrice scooted closer to me on the couch. She was now uncomfortably close. "I want someone kind and intelligent and responsible."

A blind monkey would have seen where this was going.

"At this point in my life, I don't care about looks anymore," Patrice said. *Gee, thanks.* "It's what's *inside* that matters."

And now, her hand was on my knee. A year ago, I would have killed to have Patrice's hand on my knee, even if she did it while telling me how unattractive I was. Now all I could think about was Rachel. She was the only thing that's made me happy in the last decade and a half. I *loved* her, damn it.

I buried my face in my shaking hands. I felt actually ill, not just fake ill like I'd told Patrice I was when she suggested dinner earlier. I didn't want it to be over with Rachel. But what could I do?

"Matt..." She moved her hand to my back, rubbing circles. "Are you okay?"

"Not really."

"Hey, listen." She stopped rubbing my back and reached into her purse. She rifled around for a few seconds, then as I lifted my face from my hands, she pulled out a little baggie. "I know what will make you feel better."

She was on my right side, and I don't see quite as

well on my right side, so at first, I thought I was imagining things when I realized the baggie had about a dozen little white pills in it. All I could think was, *What the hell is that?*

Patrice shook two of the pills into her palm and held them out to me. "Take these. You'll forget all about Rachel."

I gaped at the pills in her hand. I didn't know what they were, and I didn't bother to ask. There was a lot of whispering among the staff at DeWitt that one of us must be responsible for the drugs making their way to the student body. But I never knew until this minute that it was Patrice.

I always defended Patrice against all the people who didn't like her—and believe me, there were many. A lot of people seemed to take an instant dislike to the woman. And now, I hated her too.

"It's you," I spat at her. "You're the one supplying the drugs."

She blinked a few times, as if surprised by my reaction. As if I would simply be *okay* with what she was doing. "They're going to get it anyway. They're *kids*. I might as well be able to afford a decent house, right?"

I didn't even know what to say. I had never been so angry with anyone in my entire life. Even Kurt—he was just imbalanced, not malicious.

"Take the pills," she urged me. "They'll help—I promise."

"You've got to be kidding me."

She arched an eyebrow. "Are you looking for a cut?"

"A *cut*?" I burst out. "I don't want a *cut*! Definitely

not! And… and tomorrow, I'm going straight to the dean to tell him what's been going on, Patrice."

Her body went rigid, as if it hadn't occurred to her that I might say this. "You're not serious."

"I am dead serious."

"If you tell the dean," Patrice said calmly, "I'll blow the whistle on you and Rachel." I was about to tell her I didn't care, but she saw the look on my face and added, "That would pretty much destroy Rachel's life, wouldn't it? She'd be kicked out of school. No chance of becoming a doctor."

I gave Patrice a seething look, hating her with every fiber of my being. The hate was emanating out of my body with such force that it was hard to believe she couldn't feel it.

"Get out of my house," I said quietly.

"Matt…"

"I won't tell anyone what you've done," I said, "but only for Rachel's sake. And it needs to stop. If it doesn't stop, I'll go to the dean. I mean it."

Patrice shook her head as if she thought I might be joking. Ha ha, really funny. You're a drug dealer—get out of my house.

As soon as Patrice was gone, I called Rachel, and I had every intention, once again, of ending things with her. I'm always full of good intentions, aren't I?

When Rachel returned to my house, I could see the red around the rims of her brown eyes just before she fell into my arms. She'd been crying. It touched me that she'd been crying over the idea that we might be over. That was when I really started loving her.

95

THE NIGHT THAT I FOUND OUT RACHEL BETRAYED ME, I went to the medicine cabinet above my sink, and I contemplated taking every pill in there. I've got plenty, thanks to the array of doctors I've maintained for the medical issues that have haunted me since I got shot in the head. Hell, it wouldn't even have to be all of the pills—just one bottle of painkillers would be sufficient to end it all. If I did it, nobody would have found me until the morning, and by then, it would be too late. After all, people overdose every year at Dead Med—I figured it may as well be me this year.

In the end, I couldn't make myself do it. I was too chicken. Also, I was raised Catholic, and we're not supposed to do things like that.

But as I sat in my office the night before the final exam, rewriting the questions so that the woman I had loved wouldn't be able to cheat, I got to thinking about Rachel. About how I had been so worried about her career, I had gone against my moral code and agreed not to turn in Patrice for what she had done. But I no longer had that concern.

That was when I picked up my phone and called Patrice.

"Matt?" She sounded surprised to hear from me so late. "What's going on?"

"I just want to give you a heads-up." I gripped the phone tighter with my left hand—the only hand capable of grasping anything tightly anymore. "Tomorrow, after the exam, I'm going to the dean about you. I'm telling him that you've been distributing drugs to the students."

There was a long pause on the other end of the line. "If you do that, I'll tell him about you and Rachel."

"So be it."

"You're fine with imploding your entire career and hers?"

"Yes."

I meant it.

"Matt." Her voice had a bit of a hysterical edge to it. "Please think about what you're doing. Can't we talk about this? Please?"

"No, Patrice. My mind is made up."

And then I hung up. I fully expected her to confront me about this in person, but then, the knock at my door turned out to be Rachel. And the things she told me changed everything.

Do I believe Rachel when she says she was blackmailed and that's the only reason she took the exam? Maybe. I suppose I do. Nobody's that great an actress.

It's easier to believe Rachel because I love her. Even when I hated her, I still loved her.

And because I love her so much, I refuse to let her die today.

96

Now, we come full circle, back to that damned gun pointed at my face.

Mason is much more frightening as a shooter than Kurt was. Part of it is how disheveled he looks, his face covered in a half beard, his dark hair greasy and uncombed, his clothes wrinkled and stained. Yet his hand holding the revolver is unwavering and steady, whereas Kurt was shaking like a leaf. Mason looks like a guy who knows how to handle a gun and knows exactly what he's doing. And he seems so *angry*.

He's demanding answers about the cadaver he's been dissecting this year, but I don't know what he expects me to tell him. For privacy reasons, I can't divulge any information about the cadavers. I do know that the man on Table 13 is a former police officer who died at age seventy-three from a pulmonary embolism—a blood clot in his lungs. I could tell Mason this information, but from the look on his face, I doubt he'd believe me.

No matter what I do, he's going to fire that gun.

Most people who get shot in the head don't survive. In that sense, I really am lucky. Surviving two gunshot wounds to the head doesn't seem within the realm of possibility. I am done here. And this time, there's only one thought running through my head:

I can't let him kill Rachel too.

"I'm really sorry," I hear myself say out loud.

I'm not saying it to Mason. I'm saying it to Rachel, partially for having taken advantage of her when she was my student. And partially for getting myself killed when I know she loves me.

Rachel keeps tugging on the leg of my pants, and I can tell she's worried. She wants to come out. That would be an incredibly bad idea, but it's very hard to transmit that sentiment to her without giving away to Mason that someone is hiding under my desk. It's a very delicate situation. I keep pointing to the ground, signaling to her to stay hidden until this maniac is gone.

I've got to save Rachel if it's the last thing I do. And it most likely will be.

Rachel, stay down!

PART VII

ABE

97

THE NIGHT BEFORE THE ANATOMY FINAL EXAM

THE GUN IS IN MY COAT POCKET AS I MARCH INTO THE hospital.

Nobody searches me. Of course they don't. I've got an ID badge, and I come in through the garage from the student parking lot, which requires ID access. Despite my size, I am utterly unsuspicious. There's a guard by the entrance from the parking lot, but he barely glances up at me.

He certainly doesn't know about the gun in the pocket of my coat.

I don't know what my intentions are—I haven't decided yet. But when I think about Patrice, my chest burns with anger. And I feel a little better when I wrap my fingers around that gun.

She said she'd be around Sunday night because we've got our final exam tomorrow. She said she wants to "be there" for us. Which I assume means she's hoping to score some drug sales. Anyway, she said she'd be physically here.

I'm counting on it.

I take the elevator up two stories, and when I get out, my phone buzzes in my pocket. I consider ignoring it, but then I pull it out. There's an unread text that I missed while I was driving, and Heather's name is flashing on the screen. That is a call I'm definitely taking.

"Hey!" I say, trying unsuccessfully to hide my eagerness.

"Hey, Abe."

She doesn't say anything right away, so I prompt her: "What's up?"

I realized I love you, Abe. I don't care why you had blood all over your scrubs. Let's never speak of it again.

"Listen, I'm sorry to bother you." Her voice trembles slightly. "But I didn't know who else to call…"

"Okay…"

"I'm worried about Mason."

That's the last thing I expected her to say. "Mason?"

"I came upstairs to find you," she tells me. "And the door to your dorm room was unlocked. I went inside and… well, your room was a total mess—I'm sure you know that. But especially Mason's desk."

"Uh-huh…"

"And I know it was none of my business," she continues, "but I thought it was *your* desk at first, and you've been acting so strange. And then, by the time I realized it was Mason's desk, I had already started looking through all the papers, and none of it had to do with our classes. It was all these weird articles about dead police officers. And there were random sentences highlighted, notes scribbled in the margins. I didn't know what to make of it. It was really weird."

"It's kind of weird," I agree.

"And then," she says, "I found a bullet on his desk."

A *bullet*?

My heart speeds up as I pull the phone away from my ear. I look down at the text message alert that I had missed while I was driving. I click on it, and sure enough, it's from Mason:

> If I don't return tonight, make sure the police know that Dr. Matthew Conlon killed Frank.

Huh? What the hell does that mean? Frank, meaning *our cadaver*? What is Mason talking about?

It must be some kind of mistake or joke.

"Heather," I say, "I don't know what's going on with Mason, but I'm sure—"

My reassurance gets cut off by a gunshot echoing through the hallway.

"Shit," I say.

"What's wrong?"

"Heather." I struggle to keep my voice steady. "I need you to call 911 now and tell them that someone fired a gun at the hospital."

"*What?*"

And now there's a second gunshot, even louder than the first one. Closer. But I don't mention that to Heather.

"Just do it," I say. "Right now. I have to go."

"Abe!" she cries. "What's going on over there? If someone is shooting, you need to get out of there. Or… or hide."

"Don't worry." My voice is dripping with false confidence. "Come on, I could take down anyone in our class no problem. Right?"

"Abe…"

"Please, Heather. Call the police right now. I… I'll talk to you later."

And then, before she can try to talk me out of what I'm going to do next, I end the call. Almost immediately, the phone starts ringing again. Heather's name is flashing on the screen. I decline the call, put the phone on silent, and shove my phone back in my pocket.

The hallways are very deserted, given it's the middle of the night—my rapid footsteps sound like thunder on the floor. Only half the overhead lights are lit, and several hallways aren't lit at all. But on the plus side, I don't hear any more gunshots.

I round the corner to my first stop, which is Dr. Conlon's office. I figured it was smart to go there first given the content of Mason's message. I hope this is all some weird mistake. That there's a perfectly reasonable explanation for why Heather found a bullet on Mason's desk, and now there are gunshots echoing through the halls.

But when I see the body lying on the floor, any hope vanishes.

It's Dr. Patrice Winters. She's lying on the floor, the

pool of blood beneath her growing wider by the second. Her eyes are open, staring up at the ceiling, unblinking. I don't need to bend down to feel her pulse—she's definitely dead.

I wonder if she made any money tonight, before someone put a bullet through her chest.

I reach into my coat pocket, feeling the gun nestled within. I had been on my way to Patrice's office when I came to the school, and if things had gone differently, would *I* have been the one to pull the trigger? I was mad as hell, that's for sure.

I yank my hand out of my pocket, wishing I hadn't brought the gun. It sickens me to think of what I might have done—I'm not a killer. And the last thing I want is for the police to find it on me.

The door to Dr. Conlon's office is still closed, although light is coming from below the door. I listen for a moment, but I don't hear anything from inside. No voices—nothing. But if Dr. Conlon were here, surely he would have come out of his office at the sound of gunshots in such close proximity. So does that mean…?

I put my hand on the doorknob, not wanting to turn it. Maybe it's better to wait for the police. But what if Dr. Conlon is injured and bleeding? What if I can save him?

I start to turn the knob, but before I can, my attention is jerked away by a sound from around the corner. It sounds like a door slamming shut. It's coming from the direction of the anatomy lab.

Mason must have gone there next.

But there's nobody in the anatomy lab. It's so late. Who would be in the lab with the dead bodies at this hour, even the night before the final? If that's where Mason went, he can't possibly do any harm, can he?

And then the scream cuts through the air.

98

I START RUNNING.

Most people would run in the opposite direction of gunshots, especially after the police have already been called. I always thought I would have. But I'm either an idiot or braver than I thought or a little of both, because here I am.

When I reach the anatomy lab, I can tell from the window in the door that the lights are on in there. My heart is doing cartwheels in my chest as I peer through the window, trying to see what's going on inside without opening the door. Unfortunately, I can't see a thing.

Just as I'm contemplating my next move, I hear a familiar voice from inside the lab: "Do exactly as I say if you don't want to die."

It's Mason. He's in the lab, and there's someone else in there with him.

I crane my neck, scanning the hallways for signs of the police. Heather called them several minutes ago.

How long does it take for the police to arrive? I bet they'll be here soon. Maybe I should wait.

But if I do, it could be too late. Patrice is already dead in the hallway. If someone else dies and I could have stopped it, it will be my fault.

I know what I've got to do.

I take a deep breath and crouch down on the floor. As quietly as possible, I punch in the code that opens the door to the lab and slowly turn the doorknob to enter the room. The second I crack open the door, I can see that Mason has a gun pointed at my classmate, Danielle Stern. The fans in the lab are very loud, and I pray I can sneak in unnoticed and that I don't knock down something on the way inside, giving away my position. I wish I weren't such a clumsy oaf.

I hold my breath as I slide inside the room. I don't look up or even breathe again until I close the door quietly behind me. To my relief, Mason is still pointing the gun at Danielle and has no idea I'm here. I'm not sure if Danielle sees me, but she isn't giving anything away. She's too busy sobbing.

"What do you want?" Danielle whimpers.

I pause, waiting for Mason's answer. "I need you to help me get rid of something… someone…"

My legs quiver and, to my horror, I stumble against one of the tables. Mason whips his head around at the sound. So much for being stealthy.

"Abe?" Mason blinks in confusion. "What are you doing here?"

"Mason, what are you *doing*?" I hiss, taking a step toward them.

Mason is still holding the gun, but it's no longer pointed at Danielle. I consider taking out the gun in my own pocket, but I worry that's just going to escalate things. And when the police arrive, I don't want to be the guy holding the gun. That's a great way to get shot.

"Her," he says. "She heard the gunshots. I have to get rid of the other witness."

His words cause Danielle's sobs to intensify. She buries her face in her hands, swaying as if she might faint.

"Shut up!" Mason screams at her.

Please stop crying, Danielle. You're just making things worse.

"Mason, you need to put down that gun," I say quietly, knowing it's already too late. Patrice is dead, and I'm scared Dr. Conlon is too. "Seriously, put down the gun, and we'll figure this out."

Mason just stares at me. Wow, he looks *really* bad, like he's been sleeping in the gutter. How did this all happen right under my nose?

"You trust me, don't you, Mason?" I say. I very slowly move toward him, careful not to make any sudden moves.

"I… I guess so…"

"You need to put down that gun," I repeat.

Mason's shoulders relax, and his hand lowers as I continue to move closer. Thank God, it's working—Mason is calming down.

At that moment, there's a sound from right outside the anatomy lab, and Mason turns his head in the direction of the noise. Even though I've got the gun in my pocket and I have time to use it, I don't want to hold

Mason at gunpoint. It won't stop him, and the last thing I want to do is kill my roommate. I don't want to kill anyone ever again.

So I take a risk. I lunge forward and tackle Mason, putting all two hundred and fifty pounds of my weight behind the effort. I may be a clumsy oaf, but I can be fast when I want to be, and before Mason can react, he goes down hard, the gun falling from his right hand. I pin him down before he has a chance to try to get away.

"Abe… what the hell?" Mason manages as he stares up at me. "Are… are you in on it too?"

I don't reply, although I'm not sure what I could have said. I keep him restrained until the police arrive and help me to my feet, and Danielle breathlessly tells them everything that happened. Mason is taken away in handcuffs, mumbling to himself the whole time.

He'll never be a doctor.

EPILOGUE

KIERA

Seven Years Later

I'VE BEEN ON MY EMERGENCY MEDICINE ROTATION FOR over two weeks, and I officially hate my life.

It's the third rotation of my third year of medical school. For your third rotation, you're supposed to schedule the specialty you're interested in doing for the rest of your life. That way, you have enough time in the hospital that you don't look like a complete idiot, but you take the rotation early enough that you have plenty of time to get letters of recommendation or change your mind in case you end up hating it. The latter is the case for me.

Actually, I like the pace, the patients, the procedures, and even most of the staff. But what I hate is the senior resident, Dr. Sasha Zaleski. And somehow, that's enough to make me completely miserable.

"Kiera!"

I look up from the computer monitor at the sound of Dr. Zaleski's voice. Most residents allow me to call them by their first name, but Dr. Zaleski does not. I groan inwardly and brace myself.

"What are you *doing*?" Dr. Zaleski demands to know.

"I was just writing up the last patient," I explain. I silently curse the fact that Dr. Zaleski is working during nearly all of my shifts in the ER. I checked the schedule last week, hoping maybe it had changed. It hadn't. Somehow, I have angered the scheduling gods.

"I *told* you to see the woman with suspected appendicitis in Room 3," Dr. Zaleski says accusingly.

Yes, but she also told me that I had to write up patients I'd seen before moving on to the next one. Mixed messages, seriously.

"Sorry," is all I say.

"Well, because you were so slow," Dr. Zaleski says snippily, "I already saw that patient myself. Why don't you make yourself useful and call Surgery to come see her?" She pauses. "And after that, go get me a cup of coffee."

I nod, afraid to say anything to further incur her wrath, even though technically, the residents have been scolded for sending medical students to perform menial tasks like fetching coffee or doing laundry. I don't mind grabbing her some coffee, though. At least it's something I'm less likely to screw up. I know exactly how she likes it after two weeks on this rotation. (Black—like her soul.)

I heard Dr. Zaleski is bad-tempered because she matched for a residency spot at the lowly DeWitt.

Apparently, stellar grades don't make up for mediocre evaluations from attendings on rotations. Dr. Zaleski can't even be nice to the people she's sucking up to.

Not that DeWitt Hospital is so bad. The medical school is one of the best, especially now that it's no longer known as Dead Med. Everyone knows the story about that old nickname, though—it's huge gossip in our school.

So apparently, DeWitt used to have a bad drug problem. Several students overdosed, but they still couldn't manage to crack down on it. Also, the former anatomy professor was this real player, a total Casanova, who frequently used to have affairs with his students. He was having an affair with this girl in the class, and another student found out about it and tried to blackmail him. The whole thing went horribly wrong, and that student ended up murdering the professor and some other staff member. And that anatomy professor was the one distributing the drugs, so after he died, the students got clean.

The student who killed the professor was sentenced to life in prison—first-degree murder charges, I guess. They thought part of the reason he did it was because he'd been abusing drugs, and it was all tracked back to some clinic off campus that was handing them out like candy. It goes without saying that the doctor who worked there lost his license and went to jail too.

Of course, all of these are rumors passed down over seven years. Who knows how much of it is true?

I was always curious what happened to the girl who had the affair with the professor, and that's never been clear, aside from the fact that she transferred to a different school. My friend Meg, who is usually right about this kind of stuff, says she quit med school entirely. I've heard people say she went on to become a yoga instructor, a kindergarten teacher, a ballet dancer, or just that she married rich and doesn't have to work.

Now that I think of it, Dr. Zaleski was probably at DeWitt back then. Maybe she knew that student and could tell me what happened to her. But Dr. Zaleski frowns on personal conversations during work hours.

I call the operator and discover that the surgery resident on call for consults is Dr. Abe Kaufman. It's the only good news I've gotten all night. Of all the surgery residents, Abe is the nicest. Hell, he's the *only* nice one. You call Abe, he comes down right away and doesn't quiz me on a million tests I ordered wrong somehow.

Sure enough, Abe rushes right down after I explain the situation to him. I spot his red hair and his large frame lumbering down the hallway, and I wave. He waves back enthusiastically.

"Appy?" he asks me.

"Uh-huh," I say. "It's a twenty-nine-year-old woman. Right lower quadrant pain, fever, elevated white count."

Abe takes the chart from me and skims the first page. "Huh," he says as his finger lingers on the name Dr. Heather McKinley. "My wife is her primary care doctor."

He strides into the room, a smile stretched across his face. "Ms. Durand!" he greets the young woman, who looks intensely uncomfortable. "How are you doing?"

"Terrible," Elsie Durand groans. "The pain is… It's so bad."

Abe lays his right hand gingerly on her abdomen. It always surprises me that a big guy could be so gentle.

"What did the CT show, Kiera?" he asks me.

"I, um…" I bite my lip, bracing myself. "They haven't done it yet."

"Ultrasound?" he asks.

I shake my head again.

The last time that happened, the surgeon screamed at me for ten straight minutes. But Abe just shrugs.

"Well, it's a clinical diagnosis," he says.

"Can I have something more for the pain?" Elsie Durand pleads with him.

He shakes his head abruptly. "No. No pain meds. You're going straight to the OR."

I nod in agreement, relieved.

"By the way," Abe says with a wink, "how's Sasha treating you?"

I don't even know who he's talking about at first. "Do you mean Dr. Zaleski?"

"Oh, Christ." Abe laughs. "I think that answers my question."

I glance around nervously. "She's, um, fine."

"I'm sure." Abe rolls his eyes. "Well, if you ever need someone to straighten her out, give me a call." He cracks his knuckles and adds, "It would be my pleasure."

He's joking. I'm almost positive.

I find Dr. Zaleski back at her computer station, writing up a patient encounter. The moment she hears my footsteps, she whips her head around to look at me accusingly.

"Well? Are you going to tell me what happened with that patient, or do I have to guess?" she asks.

"Dr. Kaufman is going to take her to surgery."

She raises her eyebrows. "He doesn't want to wait for the CT results?"

"No," I say.

Dr. Zaleski mutters something under her breath that I can't quite make out. "Where's my coffee?" she finally says.

"Oh…" I look down at my hands, like if I wished hard enough, a Styrofoam cup of coffee might magically appear. "I'll get it for you right now."

She nods curtly. "*Now*, please. You'd think I'd only have to tell you once…"

Less than two weeks to go…

I sprint down the hall to the kitchen, where they have a machine filled with hot coffee that is constantly brewing. I grab one of the Styrofoam cups and press the button to dispense coffee. Of course, nothing happens. That's exactly what kind of night I'm having.

"Problem?"

I whirl around, nearly dropping the cup on the floor. A slim woman in her late twenties wearing a pair of scrubs is standing behind me, her dark hair piled on top of her head. The ID badge on her chest reads Rachel Bingham, MD, Psychiatry Resident. It's very late, but her eyes are bright, and she doesn't seem the slightest bit tired.

Unlike me. Even my *bones* are tired. I didn't think

such a thing was possible until my third year of med school.

"The coffee machine won't work," I grumble.

She arches an eyebrow. "Why are you drinking coffee at midnight?"

"It's for Dr. Zaleski."

"Okay, then. Why are you Dr. Zaleski's coffee slave?"

"I don't mind getting it for her." I don't want it getting back to her that I've been bad-mouthing her behind her back. The residents talk amongst themselves, even between departments. "And she's got a lot to do."

"Here," she says in a voice much kinder than my own resident's voice, "let me help you."

Dr. Bingham takes the coffee cup from me and fiddles with the machine. A minute later, the coffee machine starts dispensing piping-hot black liquid. I let out a sigh of relief. Dr. Zaleski definitely would've screamed at me if I came back to her without coffee. If I couldn't get this machine to work, I would have had to hide in a supply closet for the rest of my shift.

Dr. Bingham turns her back to me as she finishes filling up the coffee and places the Styrofoam cup on the counter. "She takes it black, right?"

"How'd you know?"

She hesitates for a moment. "An old friend she used to have coffee with all the time told me."

"Oh…"

"Anyway," she adds, "she's always so hyper when she calls us for consults. It must be the black coffee… or else she's on speed."

I snicker. "Dr. Zaleski on *speed*? No way. She would

never take that kind of chance. They do random drug tests all the time here, and she would wreck her entire career."

She nods. "Yes, you're probably right. It would be very stupid, wouldn't it? Anyway, you better get her this coffee before it gets cold and she screams at you again."

She isn't wrong. I reach out to take the coffee cup from the counter, but that's when I see it. A sprinkling of white particles dissolving into the black liquid. I squint down at the cup, trying to figure out what they are. But before I can, Dr. Bingham retrieves a plastic lid and pops it on top of the cup.

I start to ask her about what I just saw, but then I shake my head. What am I supposed to say? *Hey, why were there little white specks in the black coffee?* I'll sound nuts. It's probably a visual hallucination from lack of sleep.

The psych resident picks up the cup of coffee and holds it out to me. "Good luck tonight," she says.

As I take the coffee from her, our eyes meet. A chill runs down my spine, although I'm not exactly sure why. I can't help but think that I didn't imagine those white specks in the coffee. While she was turned away from me, Dr. Bingham had a chance to do whatever she wanted to that coffee.

But why would she? I *had* to have imagined it. I *must* have.

After all, who would want to drug Dr. Zaleski?

THE END

ACKNOWLEDGMENTS

This book was originally written as *Suicide Med* and published back in 2014. In my original acknowledgments, I thanked my mother (who is devastated that I got rid of the eye #IYKYK), Dr. Orthochick, Laura Waller, Nathan Geissel, Jessica Schuster, Jenica Chung, as well as Roy Arnold, who helped me with his extensive knowledge of firearms.

Now that the book is officially *Dead Med*, I'd like to add on thanks to readers Emily, Nelle, and Val. As well as a thanks to Red Adept Editing for your help getting rid of those pesky typos. And I can't leave out my agent, Christina Hogrebe, who gave me her blessing when I said I wanted to rewrite this book to get rid of the butt eye.

And finally, I want to thank my own Dr. Conlon, my anatomy professor in medical school, who made the class the most grueling, fun, amazing, and important course I've ever taken in my life. And don't worry, nothing funny went on between us… or did it?

(No, it didn't. He was super old.)

ABOUT THE AUTHOR

#1 New York Times, Amazon Charts, *Wall Street Journal*, *USA Today*, and *Publishers Weekly* bestselling author Freida McFadden is a part-time practicing physician specializing in brain injury. Freida's work has been selected as one of Amazon Editor's Best Books of the Year, and she has been a Goodreads Choice Award nominee. Her novels have been translated into more than thirty languages. Freida lives with her family and black cat in a centuries-old three-story home overlooking the ocean.